StarDoc

A NOVEL BY

S. L. Viehl

D1009013

RoC

A ROC BOOK

ROC
Published by New American Library, a division of
Penguin Putnam Inc., 375 Hudson Street,
New York, New York 10014, U.S.A.
Penguin Books Ltd, 80 Strand,
London WC2R 0RL, England
Penguin Books Australia Ltd, Ringwood,
Victoria, Australia
Penguin Books Canada Ltd, 10 Alcorn Avenue,
Toronto, Ontario, Canada M4V 3B2
Penguin Books (N.Z.) Ltd, 182–190 Wairau Road,
Auckland 10, New Zealand

Penguin Books Ltd, Registered Offices:
Harmondsworth, Middlesex, England

First published by Roc, an imprint of New American Library,
a division of Penguin Putnam Inc.

First Printing, January 2000
10 9 8 7

Copyright © S. L. Viehl, 2000
All rights reserved

Cover art by Donato

Printed in the United States of America

CRITICAL CONDITIONS

Charge Nurse T'Nliqinara made a garbled report that rattled through my tympanic insert in staccato fragments: "Dr. Grey Veil . . . crisis . . . possible internal trauma . . . visible signs of seizure . . ." There was a guttural burst of sound, then my nurse made a gurgling noise. Subsequent hysterical screams in the background blocked out most of what she said before I caught the last words. "—hostages . . . terrorist . . . weapon."

Someone was in the waiting room, using weapons?

The last thing I wanted to do was go out there. It was also the only thing I could do. Very slowly, making sure to keep my hands visible, I walked down the short corridor and into view.

My charge nurse's four eyes rolled wildly toward me, and I saw why she had choked out her report— the business end of a pulse rifle was pressed tightly against her larynx. Terror had mottled her smooth vermilion hide with dark splotches.

On the other end of the weapon was a monster. A big, ugly, green monster. . . .

For my daughter, Katherine Rose Viehl.
May you find your place in the universe
more than you ever dreamed,
and for Catherine Coulter,
who made a dream come true.

PART ONE:

Initiation

CHAPTER ONE

Terra

Into whatever houses I enter, I will go into them for
the benefit of the sick.

Hippocrates (460?–377? B.C.)

I bet Hippocrates never stepped one foot into a dump
like this, I thought as I peered through the tavern's narrow entrance. Oath or no oath.

At that moment I was deep in the labyrinth of back
streets in the worst section of New Angeles. I was also
thoroughly disgusted, scared, and ready to give up. Earlier stops at four crowded taverns had produced no results. Oh, I'd gotten plenty of propositions, some even
a sexdrone would find challenging. Credit-jammers still
watched me from the shadows, remote scanners ready,
hoping I'd access a public bank console. Glide snatchers
had tried twice in the last hour to swoop down and grab
the case I was carrying. In *broad daylight*, the vultures.

Now I paused outside the fifth and last sleaze pit on
Tavern Row. Above the entrance the words "SLOW LAZY
SAX" were projected in foot-high, bright blue dimensional lettering. Charming name. The only good thing
about the place was it was nearly deserted. I wouldn't
have to push through another gauntlet of drunks to have
a look around.

I counted two hulking figures at the end of the
counter, arguing in low growls while steadily draining
their drinks. The proprietor ignored them, his attention
fixed on a vidisplay screen overhead. A rusted comdrone

4 S. L. Viehl

unit clutching a saxophone was huddled in one corner, deactivated and badly in need of maintenance. Farther back in the tavern was a third patron, seated alone, wearing what could have been a pilot's flight suit.

That got my attention. I took another step and crossed the threshold. The sour bouquet of unwashed bodies, spilled drinks, and burnt tobacco greeted my nose. A fat roach scuttled past my right foot to join some of his pals creeping around the tables. My skin wanted to shrink from the smoke, filth, and hopelessness.

Time had almost run out, I was desperate. What choice did I have? I walked in.

I started with the stocky man working behind the bar. He was idly rinsing out plas servers beneath a sputtering biodecon unit. His eyes were riveted to the screen as it televised the near-electrocution of two penalized runbacks.

He swore fluently when both shockball players had to be carried off the field by medevac. "Devoids. Miavana Fins wasted that 'un sure." He examined me with mild surprise. "Ay-lo—get ya a swig, Fem?"

I was glad I'd researched the inner city dialect before coming down here. In his crude patois, the guy was trying to be polite and ask what I wanted to drink.

"No, grats. Eyein' to get an offjaunt in a blip. Ya spill a taker?"

"That 'un," the bartender jutted his chin toward the loner. "Ship's the *Bestshot*. Jaunts the trades."

I squinted once more at the pilot. At this distance I easily made out the details of his countenance. He looked like he was ready to go through puberty, not an interstellar flight.

One of the hulks at the bar snorted, catching my attention. A thin rivulet of bitterale foam ran down his stubbly chin as he bared his chipped teeth at me.

"Ay-ay-ay, Fem," he said, and went on to make the usual lewd proposition. At this rate I'd be an expert in pornographic slang before the day was over.

"Grats, redder lip a junker," I replied. *Thank you, but I'd rather kiss a drone.*

I debated whether to approach the man or move on to tavern number six. *Bestshot* wasn't an inspiring name for an interstellar passenger shuttle. Not to mention the painfully juvenile appearance of my potential escort, and the lack of taste he had in patronizing this waste station.

"Gotta gripe, Fem?" The bartender wanted to know what was wrong.

"That 'un eyes raw," I said. *He looks too young.*

"Cap's *Oenrallian*," the man told me. "Those 'uns eye plenty raw 'til mid-doin'." *The pilot was an alien, whose species didn't appear to mature until middle age.* "Jaunt much, Fem?"

I *didn't* jaunt, period, one reason why I hadn't realized the pilot was an offworlder. Embarrassed, I smiled my thanks and started toward the pilot.

Lanky, pallid-skinned, and sporting a thick thatch of orange hair, the Oenrallian still appeared more like a kid who had swiped his dad's glidecar than an experienced starshuttle pilot. The guileless amber eyes he lifted toward me only iced the cake.

"Ya pard, eyein'—"

"I speak standard English," he interrupted in a oddly pitched voice.

"Oh. Good." It was a relief to abandon the local jargon. "May I have a moment of your time?" I decided not to offer my hand, it might be considered offensive. "My name is Cherijo Grey Veil."

"Dhreen, of Oenrall," he said as he lifted his plas server to his thin lips. With his free hand he gestured to the empty chair opposite his own. I saw five digits, but they were splayed at the ends and had no nails. Spoon-fingers, I thought absently. I bet he didn't have to bother much with standard Terran utensils.

I sat down, took a breath. What were those things on top of his head? "How did you know I spoke standard?"

"You're too sanitary to be local." His eyes made a

brief survey. "What's a pretty Fem like you doing in this part of the city?"

"I need transport to the Pmoc Quadrant."

"Why?"

"I've been transferred to Kevarzangia Two." Opening my case, I extracted the data discs for his examination. It was becoming impossible to take my eyes from the two round red nubs that poked up beneath his hair. Horns, maybe?

"Why not get space on one of the Terran transports?"

I was ready for that. "There's no space available, and I need to leave today if I'm going to make my arrival slot." I made a "silly me" face. "There was so much to do before I left. You know how it is. I simply forgot to make a reservation." Sure, and if he checked it out, he'd learn I could lie through my teeth, too. I was counting on his greed to prevent that. "How much to make the trip?"

"Ten thousand, if I decide to take you." His tone was definitely not Terran, despite his familiar use of the language. He sounded like a sterilizer duct beginning to clog. There was an odor coming from him as well, something like pineapple mixed with chocolate. The smell wasn't bad, just weird.

"That's fine," I answered, and quickly put the necessary credit chip next to the transfer data. I thought the sight of all that currency would settle the deal. Dhreen only slouched back in his chair.

"Why transfer to the border, Fem?" His curiosity was casual, dangerous. "Not a spot you Terrans usually pick."

"I've been assigned to the colony as a medical physician." I pulled out two more discs that would verify my identity and contract. The table was getting crowded.

"A doctor?" Dhreen frowned at me from under thick brows. "A neonate like you?"

It was the usual reaction.

I looked older than the Oenrallian, but not by much. I was short for a Terran female, too, just under five feet tall. It had earned me delightful nicknames at Medtech, like "Igor" and "Half-CC." My weight seesawed between slender and skinny, depending on my surgery schedule. I liked to eat, I just didn't always have the time.

I wasn't homely. I had a smaller version of Dad's prominent nose and the same tilted dark blue eyes. The first was slightly beaky, the last vaguely exotic. My long black hair reflected a silver sheen (inherited from a distant Native American ancestor, my father claimed, with the same "grey veil"), and was braided so it stayed out of my face. I wore a shabby, neutral-shaded jumper with no accessories. My physician's tunic was much more dignified, but wearing it here would have put a sign around my neck that said *rob me, immediately*.

"I'm a fully qualified practitioner."

He lifted a shoulder. "If you say so, Fem."

I pushed my ID disc across the table. "Check the data, if you don't believe me."

"Data can be rigged by any kid with half a neural center," he said.

"So can a starshuttle," I retaliated without thinking, then inhaled sharply. Had I insulted him? Dhreen made an odd, hiccuping sound and slapped his spoon-shaped fingers against the table.

He was either laughing, or having a seizure. While I was trying to decide which, the Oenrallian swiveled his head to one side. Whatever he saw made his mirth come to an abrupt halt.

"Look out." He scooped up his flask and server, and I glanced back at the counter. A plas bottle missed my nose by inches as it flew past and hit the wall beyond us. I grabbed my discs and shoved them back in my case.

The two burly Terran patrons who had been arguing before were now trying to beat the brains out of each other's skulls.

"Larian Scum-sucker!" one shouted, knocking over his stool as he staggered back on unsteady legs.

"Eat my waste!" the other responded, just as cleverly.

Plas containers, I soon discovered, were effective projectiles. I ducked behind my chair to avoid a particularly dangerous volley that shattered when it slammed into our table. Dhreen lifted his drink to me in silent salute.

No doubt he considered this idiocy as impromptu entertainment.

The drunken pair began pummeling each other in earnest, knocking over tables, trashing the counter, generally making a mess. Snarled obscenities punctuated the thuds of fists and limbs as they battled. The bartender displayed no inclination toward stopping them.

"Can't someone do something?" I demanded, and cringed as pieces of a broken stool flew overhead. Another one crashed into the comdrone, which abruptly activated and began trying to play "A Love Supreme" through the dented saxophone.

"They're just emitting some condensation," Dhreen said.

Blowing off steam was one thing, but this was getting out of hand. I scrambled to my feet the moment I heard the unmistakable sound of a bone snap over the blaring music. Dhreen reached out and caught my arm.

"You better stay out of it," he said, but I tugged free.

"You!" I pointed to the bartender as I approached. "Get over here and help me, or I'll signal Area Security myself!"

He reluctantly moved from his display to separate the two, which proved simple, given their level of intoxication. I pushed, he pushed, they fell over. The first was groaning miserably as I crouched down next to him.

Up close, he was the most unhygienic specimen of humanity I'd ever encountered. His garments were beyond filthy, and from the thick envelope of body odor, I gathered he hadn't personally deconned in months. No wonder it stank in here. The moment I put a hand on him, he howled and bared his teeth at me again. This time he wasn't leering.

"Mitts off, ya—"

"I'm a physician. A patcher. Turn loose ya arm."

He actually tried to hit me, the ingrate. "Off me! Ya puny back hacker—"

"Clammit," I said, and shoved his flailing fist away from my face. When he kept struggling, I pinned him in a prone position with my knees. A swift, ample dose of sedatives rendered him unconscious in seconds.

My scanner confirmed the break was a transverse fracture of the ulna. I immobilized his arm with a bonesetter from my case and scanned him for internal injuries. Filthy but lucky. Despite the ferocious tussle, he was fine. The comdrone's damaged audio was steadily getting louder, and I scowled.

"Fuse that junker, will ya?" I shouted at the bartender as I went to look at the other man. The discordant version of the Coltrane masterpiece was cut off a moment later.

The second oaf had a number of minor contusions, but otherwise was just as dirty and healthy as his opponent. After a brief examination, I closed my case.

"Done?" I demanded. "Or ya crave a nap-stick, ditto?"

The undamaged brawler muttered something uncomplimentary to the female gender, got to his feet, and returned to his stool. In a moment he was drinking again, as though nothing had happened.

"No one has a shorter conscience than a drunk," Maggie used to tell me. "Except your old man."

After I'd sent the bartender to contact area medevac, I rolled the sedated male to his uninjured side, and tagged him with an MDID for transport. I used a chip I'd filched from a colleague in my building. The last thing I needed was this sort of incident on my records. When that was done, I returned to Dhreen's table.

The pilot watched me sit down as he took a considerable gulp of spicewine. I opened my case and held out the price of my passage again.

"I like you, Fem." He palmed the disc, eyed the credit balance, then pocketed it. "Okay, I'm your jaunt."

"We have to leave today," I reminded him as I

smoothed a loose bit of hair behind my ear, then replaced the stack of transfer discs in front of him. "All
my authorizations are here, and in order. They are *not*
rigged."

"Sure, Fem, no heat." He grimaced at the discs.

"Call me Doc," I said. "May I ask you a personal
question?" He nodded. Good, I simply had to know.
"What are those two things beneath your hair?"

"They're not horns." Dhreen grinned, rubbing his
spatulate fingers over the protuberances I found so fascinating. "They're close tó what you call ears."

I checked with a discreet glance. He didn't have ears.

"Sorry." I decided to risk one more question. "How
much have you had to drink?"

"This stuff?" Dhreen hiccuped again as he raised his
plas. "Syntoxicants don't alter my internals, Doc."

"If they don't, what's the point of coming to a
tavern?"

"Only place to get work," he said after he'd swallowed. "New Angeles doesn't permit non-Terrans to so-
licit on Main Transport premises."

I was mystified. "Why not?"

He shrugged again. "Your world, not mine."

"You must pick up some . . . colorful clients."

"Oh, sure. Last trip I made was for a Terran I met
here. Seems he had to transfer because of these three
girlfriends. Only one was Terran, you see, and when she
found out about the other two being non-Terrans, she
tried to amputate his—" Those golden eyes squinted at
my expression. "Maybe I'll save that one for the jaunt."

"Yes, please." I brushed some fragments of shattered
plas from my jumper. My father would have been horrified to see me here. Correction. My father would have
gone into full arrest, and expired on the spot.

"You've got good reflexes," Dhreen said.

Yeah, I was a real pro at dodging things. Too bad I
couldn't find a way around my present quandary so I
could stay on Terra.

"Never been in a tavern before, have you?"

I thought of Maggie, who had managed the last eighteen years of my home life. She had died a few months ago, of a disease my father and every other physician she'd seen couldn't cure. My "maternal influencer," as Dad called her, had once been a tavern waitress. She had been a great mom, although she'd never gotten rid of her saucy tavern waitress' mouth. My father blamed Maggie for my irreverent humor and irritating speech patterns, among other things.

"No." I gazed around me without bothering to hide my disgust. "Slow Lazy Sax" indeed. The city code enforcers should run a full structure decontamination on this pigsty, I thought. Then again, maybe the filth was the only thing holding the plasteel walls together. "My first, and hopefully last, experience."

"You handled that scrapper like you knew what you were doing," Dhreen said. I acknowledged the compliment with a smile. He continued with a casual air, "So, who are you running from?"

My smile didn't waver—did it? "I'm not *running* from anyone," I lied. "Check out the data. I'm not wanted for questioning or detainment." *Yet.*

Dhreen didn't press the issue.

"Look, Doc, I'm firing the engines in exactly four stanhours. You want space, you got it. Just don't change your mind halfway to K-2. I'm not back-jaunting if you get chilled appendages."

"Cold feet," I corrected him while mentally reviewing what I could accomplish in the short interval before launch. If I drove like a madwoman, and no one tried to stop me, I would just make it. "That's fine." A thought occurred to me. "How many other passengers will be on this flight?"

"Just you and me, Doc."

Just me and him? Great. Just great.

Dhreen's thin lips quirked. "Don't get your scanners in overload. You'll be perfectly safe."

I had good reason to be cautious. Like everyone, I'd heard the horror stories about unsuspecting passengers being abducted and sold off to slavers in distant sectors. Still, even independent shuttle pilots were required to put up guarantee collateral to earn trade routes from Terra. It took hefty credits, too. A lot more than Dhreen could earn by selling a *dozen* young Terran females.

Looking at him, my instincts told me he was harmless. Should Dhreen forget to behave himself, however, I could quickly disable him—another of Maggie's legacies.

I'll only have to find out where his genitalia are located, I thought. If he has any of the external variety, that is.

The Oenrallian broke into my musings when he asked, "What's your cargo look like?"

"It's below the standard weight limits. Some personal belongings, medical gear, and a cat."

"A cat?" Dhreen frowned. "Legal or illegal? Wait"— he held up his hand—"Don't tell me. Just put the thing in a carrier, and make sure it doesn't get loose."

"I will. Thank you, Captain Dhreen."

"Dhreen, Doc. Just Dhreen." He lifted his drink in another mocking salute. "See you at Transport in four hours."

"Where, exactly, will your ship be?"

Dhreen's thick eyebrows rose.

"Launch Position S-17. Can't miss her. She's the ugliest hunk of spaceware in dock."

Days before I had found Dhreen, I'd begun to quietly move my possessions out of my father's house. Now all I had to do was get Jenner and my last case, retrieve and load my hidden cache into my glidecar, and get down to Transport.

Piece of cake.

I trotted back to the hoverlot where I'd left my glidecar. Since it was still there, I paid the attendant the last half of the substantial bribe I'd promised him for watching it.

"Zap back quick, Fem," he said, and grinned. *Come*

back soon. I didn't bother to tell him that I'd never come back here—or anywhere else on Terra.

No, I just smiled back, waved, and hit the accelerator. Hard.

Dad had commissioned a palatial estate just outside the city, after the New Angeles Corps of Engineers had permanently stabilized the San Andreas fault. I'd been born on the grounds and had lived there ever since.

The house itself was four stories and thirty thousand square feet of marble and glass that rivaled the Allied League Headquarters in Paris. Architectural students often came out to study the unique symmetry of the roof gables. Furnishings and decor were changed at least twice a year, and exclusive designers regularly made tour appointments so they could photoscan and copy the interior for their clients.

I hated it.

Once I returned from the tavern, it took only moments to collect my things from the estate. Leaving the mansion was not quite as simple. The drone staff were ever-vigilant, and one intercepted me as I was sneaking Jenner out through the side entrance panel.

"Dr. Cherijo." The automated housekeeper slid to a stop behind me. "Inquiry?"

"Proceed," I said, trying to sound like Dad when he was in a hurry.

"Reason Jenner is being removed?"

"Routine veterinarian treatment," I lied, hiding the case behind my legs.

The housekeeper couldn't sense deception by intonation, as far as I knew, but it didn't withdraw. "Item is not annotated on the daily household schedule."

"An emergency," I said, improvising quickly. "Non-life-threatening," I added for good measure, just in case the drone became too helpful and volunteered to chauffeur me.

"Understood. Expected time of return?"

"A few hours, maybe more."

"Will you require assistance?"

"No." I peered at the drone's display and saw the entry being saved. "You may erase this entry."

"Last command disregarded. Dr. Joseph ordered staff record all of Dr. Cherijo's activities."

Yeah, I bet he had. Dad was nothing if not eternally obsessed with my activities.

"Confirmed. I'm leaving now. Tell my father—" I stopped. Bad move. The drone would question the message, since I was supposed to return before Dad. "Never mind."

"Acknowledged, Dr. Cherijo."

From the house I drove like a madwoman to my office. There I retrieved my cache of cases from the lower-level storage facility. Ducking a few curious glances while I used the hover lifts, I loaded up everything that was important to me.

It wasn't much, I thought, looking at the pathetic little pile, then at Jenner's carrier. I had packed more when I went to Asia for spring break during my Medtech freshman year.

I slammed down the hatch and broke speed records getting to Main New Angeles Transport. No fatalities, but I did put a good dent in my passenger panel when I glanced off the front thruster of a glidetaxi. I even learned a few phrases they never taught in Medtech, courtesy of the extremely irate cabbie.

Less than four hours after I'd entered the tavern, I stood in front of the starshuttle *Bestshot.* I put my cases down and rubbed a hand over my eyes, just to be sure I wasn't hallucinating.

"*That* is a starshuttle?"

Dhreen's ship resembled a refuse heap. Okay, maybe I was being uncharitable. An *organized* refuse heap.

In comparison to the streamlined vessels crowding the shuttle docks, the *Bestshot* was a towering mass of mismatched alloys and energy-scarred panels. The viewports were covered with streaks of reentry carbon. Something was rattling and sparking beneath the booster section. Something that looked *important.* I spotted the bottom half of the Oenrallian hanging out of the discharge vent of what could have been the starboard engine, or a recycled glidebus chassis. Or both.

"Dhreen?" I called out as I marched over.

His bright head popped up, and he waved a greasy arm at me. "Jump in, Doc, I'll join you in a blip."

This is what happens when you dump your entire life and go racing off to the other end of the galaxy, an inner voice intoned with dark glee. You end up on a ship called the *Bestshot*.

I located the entrance ramp, squared my shoulders, and entered the shuttle. The main cabin inside appeared little better than the exterior. The decor was basic junk. A conglomeration of navigation and control equipment crowded the deck, most of it salvage goods. The scent of burnt wiring lingered. I wondered if Dhreen was serious about piloting this heap through fourteen light-years of unforgiving space.

"She won't win any appearance competitions," said a voice behind me, and I glanced back. Dhreen patted an external sensor display. "But she's stable, dependable, and delivers me where I'm routed." A grin appeared as he noted my expression. "In the same basic physical condition I started."

"That's reassuring." No, it wasn't. I indicated my cases and animal carrier. "Where can I secure my stuff?"

"I'll show you to your quarters."

Dhreen led me through an untidy gauntlet of tangled cables and various unidentifiable apparatus to the back of the shuttle. With a grunt and a push, he opened a door to a small, tidier section. My spirits began to elevate an inch or two. There were comfortable-looking rest slings positioned above the lower deck, which provided tables, chairs, and even a small viewport. It even smelled clean.

"Home for the next week, Doc." He pointed to a corner sectioned off by hastily rigged plaspanels with inhibitor webs to keep something small confined. "I fixed up a space for you to put your cat."

Jenner would loathe it. "That was nice of you."

"Just keep it out of the main cabin. You know how to strap in before we take off?"

I nodded. Now was *not* the time to mention I'd only been on one starshuttle in my entire life. "You'd better secure your animal's carrier, too," Dhreen said. "Use the rigging on that wall over there."

At this reminder I put down my cases and peered into the carrier. Huge eyes glared back at me. Uh-oh, now I was in for it. I felt Dhreen hovering behind my shoulder.

"Anything else I need to do?" I asked.

"No, unless you're going to change your mind."

I straightened, and gave him my best imitation of my dad's normal demeanor. A blast-freeze unit on rollers, with lips, nose, eyes, and some hair added. That was Dad.

"Thank you for your concern, Dhreen, but I'm absolutely certain of my decision." Even to my own ears, I sounded authoritative.

"Well said." Was that a smirk of respect, or amusement? "I'll leave you to settle in." With that, Dhreen withdrew.

I waited until the door closed before I sagged into a chair, and ran a hand over my perspiring face. I wasn't certain of anything.

At that moment Jenner made his presence known from the depths of the carrier. It was a single yowl of feline indignation blended with imperious command.

Let me out!

"Sorry, pal." I released the panel latch and offered a comforting hand, which was summarily ignored. My cat stalked from the carrier, tail high and head erect. Sleek and well shaped, His Royal Highness undulated with each step, silvery fur bristling.

Hell hath no fury like a confined feline.

"Come on."

I scooped him up and placed him in the makeshift space Dhreen had prepared. He sniffed at the plas-panels, and eyed the distance an escape attempt would require him to jump. After he tested the web that prevented such a feat with one paw, he regarded me with irate blue eyes.

You've got to be kidding.

"Don't start," I said, and held out a peace offering of dried mackerel bits. He ignored them, and me, and crossed to the farthest corner. Presenting his back to me, he began to sulk.

Jenner and I had been together since I'd found him eight years ago. Maggie and I had gone out for a rare shopping trip, and I'd spied the wet, bedraggled kitten crouched in a gutter. When I had held out a hand to him, he hadn't cringed away, as I'd expected. Instead he'd pulled himself up into a regal pose of absolute disdain.

You may now rescue me, he'd seemed to convey.

"What in God's name is that?" had been Maggie's reaction to the dripping ball of fur cradled against my chest.

"It's a cat."

"I'll signal Area Animal Control." Maggie had wrinkled her nose, then caught my reaction and shook her head. "Oh, no, kiddo, you can't bring that into the old man's house."

At the time I was in my third phase at Medtech, and when I wasn't studying, I was listening to Dad lecture me at length about his cases. Other than that, I ate and slept. That was my life.

"I'm taking him home," I'd said.

"Joey—"

I'd gazed at her once, the way my father did when she got overly verbal. That was all it took.

Later, I was informed by our vet that Jenner was a Tibetan temple cat, a rare breed with royal bloodlines. That was the only thing that impressed my father, who reluctantly allowed me to keep him.

"At least," he'd said with faint distaste, "it is not a *dog*."

At the same time my new kitten had stared back at

the great Joseph Grey Veil without blinking, the hair along his neck rising stiffly. He'd even hissed.

I'd lost my heart to Jenner on the spot. Since Maggie died, he was the only friend I had left.

"Go ahead and pout," I told him. "You'll get hungry, eventually. Then what are you going to do, Your Majesty?"

Jenner shot me a brief look that promised extensive, painful retribution.

"I'm sorry." I sighed, crouching down next to the plas-panels. "I know this wasn't your idea. But I need you, pal."

Jenner pondered this for a moment, and decided not to argue with me. He rose, stretched gracefully, and padded over to me. Planting himself next to the wall, he lifted his chin.

You may now beg forgiveness.

I was careful not to laugh—Jenner had definite ideas about who was the boss, and it wasn't me. It took two handfuls of dehydrated fish treats and much scratching and stroking, but he finally calmed down and settled in for a nap. I wondered what he was thinking as he blinked his lapis eyes closed.

Probably scheming how to acquire a larger portion of treats next time, I decided.

As for me, despite my affirmation to Dhreen, I wondered if I could really go through with this—transferring to an alien world so far from everything I knew. I had no idea how I would be employed by the FreeClinic. The contract I'd signed had no specific duties outlined other than "medical doctor." Those two words covered a lot of territory.

The alternatives? There were none.

"Hey, Doc," Dhreen's voice startled me. I looked over at the wall display and saw his face on the screen. "Strap in—we're preparing to launch." The display went blank, and I heard the engines rumble into life. Jenner woke up as I slipped him back into the carrier, and objected loudly as I secured it to the wall. Then I strapped myself in. My fingers felt numb, and trembled more than I liked.

"I'm going to love this," I said out loud as I tightened my harness. *Sure,* my inner voice agreed. *About as much as finding out what your father's been doing for the last thirty years.*

How had I gotten into this situation? So many decisions to be made, risks to be taken. All by me, whose life had previously been planned out to the minute. And I hadn't even done the planning.

My father had always decided everything: what I did, where I went, and who I saw. As a result, I had studied to be a surgeon. I had gone to Medtech. I'd never had friends.

After I'd completed my training courses, Dad had me intern in the busiest trauma center on the New West Coast. The first months had been a frantic blur. Snarling senior residents. Endless screens of diagnostic theory. Double shifts in assessment, pre-op, and surgery. When I wasn't working, I was nearly comatose.

"Sure, she'll make one hell of a surgeon," I recalled Maggie once snapped at my father, startling me from a doze I'd fallen in over dinner. "If you don't kill her first."

I survived. I didn't dare do anything else. The few doubts I'd had eventually evaporated. True, dedicating my life to medicine had been *Dad's* idea, not mine. In spite of that, each time I held a lascalpel in my fingers, it became more obvious. My colleagues and superiors agreed: I was born to be a surgeon.

I knew exactly what they'd say when they learned of my transfer.

"I never knew Grey Veil was a simpleton."

"An absolute waste of a promising career."

"Has she gone completely insane?"

The lure of the unknown held no attraction for Terrans. Only incompetents or reckless adventurers transferred from the homeworld. What sensible Terran

physician would trade a profitable career for the perils
lurking on all those disgusting alien worlds?

Well, here I was.

I didn't even know why I had been accepted for transfer. I had no alien experience, and I'd never shuttled
past Luna Colony before.

Then again, rumors about the shortage of medical professionals on the border indicated it was a serious problem. The generous transfer incentives were being
completely ignored. There was even some talk going
around about a possible Conscription Act by League
Worlds. I suspected PQSGO was so desperate, they'd
take *anyone* who knew which end of a suture laser to
point at the patient.

Hardly flattering, but I didn't have time to be offended. I had to get off Terra. I accepted the contract.

The data provided about my assignment was minimal.
I would be working in a Trauma FreeClinic physician
slot on K-2. Apparently these FreeClinics were set up
to treat incoming and settled colonists, shuttle crews, and
anyone else who needed emergency medical attention.
I'd be allocated standard housing quarters—whatever
that meant. That was it.

The data about my compensation was equally sparse.
I'd be paid directly from K-2's Treasury. How much and
with what wasn't clearly specified. I'd heard new colonies were usually poor in resources, unless they were
part of mining or other lucrative projects. K-2 was located in a densely populated region of space, and they
were developing botanical exports. That, combined with
a sophisticated barter system, apparently kept the colony
operational. So far.

The topic had come up while I was scrubbing for surgery one day. One of the nurses began speculating about
transfer incentives.

"Hah! That's a good joke," the anesthesiologist beside
me said as he passed his hands under the biodecon unit.
"I heard they can't even meet their existing contract

obligations. Bet they end up paying the med pros in Cfaric poultry."

I was being forced to abandon nearly everything I owned for a job and a place to live on an alien world. Anyone else would have been throwing tantrums.

But getting paid with alien chickens?

There was no choice in the matter. I had to leave. I wouldn't be leaving behind many emotional ties. Orphaned himself, my bachelor father decided to have a child, and engaged a professional surrogate. I was the result. Evidently the experience proved to satisfy Dad's urge for kids, too. I had no brothers or sisters.

My father's work kept him busy, so I was raised by a succession of domestic supervisors, drone monitors, and hired companions. He'd made sure I'd had no time for friends. Maggie was dead. That should have made leaving the planet all very simple. There was only one problem.

I couldn't tell Dad I was leaving.

Shortly after Maggie died, I had made an appalling discovery, something I was never supposed to know about. After the shock wore off, I'd gone to the nearest waste disposal unit, and thrown up what seemed like everything I'd digested for a month. Only one person could possibly be responsible for what I'd learned.

Dr. Joseph Grey Veil. My dad.

If he was capable of what I'd discovered, what would he do when he learned I knew every last detail? I knew my father. I could imagine what he'd resort to. Drone surveillance. Forged psych-evals. Personality electra-rehab. Anything to shut me up.

If that didn't work, well, Medtechs were always looking for fresh cadavers, weren't they? I'd end up a hunk of practice meat for some green cutters. Dad would be hailed for his unselfish act of charity under devastating circumstances.

My life wasn't worth a jammed credit.

I waited until he attended the annual System Medical Association Convention on Jupiter's fourth moon (he was the guest speaker), then began my search for transport.

Dad had influence at so many levels that making the usual arrangements was out of the question. Thus my visit to the tavern district, where I'd met Dhreen and contracted his services.

There was only one problem I had left to face. Kevarzangia Two was inhabited by over two hundred different species. Less than one percent were Terran. Even more alien races inhabited other nearby worlds and traveled regularly through the sector.

Despite seven years as a practicing surgeon, I'd never provided medical treatment for an offworlder. Ever.

CHAPTER TWO

K-2

Fourteen light-years sailed past the *Bestshot* in a blur of color and form. Since the pioneer days of interstellar travel, scientific advances had made the enormous distances between star systems as easily traversed as from one city to another.

"We don't jaunt a straight track through physical space, Doc," Dhreen said after I admitted my ignorance of the basic mechanics involved in light-speed travel. "No way to compensate for tangible time loss."

"Tangible time?"

"Actual duration of physical space—where you, me, the *Bestshot*, and anything with mass, reside." Dhreen made a minor course adjustment and indicated the ship's central chronometer. It appeared frozen at launch point. "The stuff that makes this turn, in short."

"So we don't occupy tangible time?" I tried to reason it out, but it still wasn't making any sense to me. I was better with practical things like bowel resections and kidney transplants.

"No. The ship's molecular structure is modified by the shuttle's flightshield, and the engine drive propels us through—or *between* might be a better word—real physical space. As a result, we don't experience significant tangible time loss."

"The molecular structure modification, does that include us?" I asked, sending a panicked glance down at my body.

Dhreen grinned. "That's right. For the entire flight, you don't occupy real space."

"Hey, I like real space. I like occupying it, too," I said.

"Nothing the ship accommodates can remain unaltered."

I tentatively touched my arm. It didn't feel intangible. It felt like an arm. "Why not?"

"Once the flightshield was initiated, the ship's altered structure would slip around you." His inculpable eyes gleamed. "You'd be left hanging in orbit."

Great. I should have paid more attention during my courses in astrophysics, too.

Despite the ship's altered composition, there was still visual contact with real space. I watched as we passed through one system after another, the planets swelling majestically as we drew near, then dwindling to mere specks. Stars that shimmered burgeoning crimson, placid gold, and fierce cerulean soon faded into anonymous luminary fields.

The universe was God's trinket box, Maggie once told me. We used to slip out of the house at night and sit on the precisely manicured lawn, just watching the stars. He had a great collection, she added, but needed to work on straightening it up.

One day the shuttle skirted the edge of a supernova, and I gazed out at the tattered luminescence, wisps of jeweled brilliancy all that remained from an epic stellar explosion. It reminded me of twilight on Terra. My appreciation dimmed as I realized I could never see that sky again.

No more Maggie, sunsets, or nights looking at Terran star vistas. Never again.

My interest in the exotic panorama around the ship subsided. It was exceptionally pretty, but ultimately there was only one world I was concerned with. Kevarzangia Two.

By the time I'd been on board the *Bestshot* for a few days, self-induced claustrophobia was setting in. After a week, I knew a lot more about the Oenrallian. At first I kept my distance, but the crowded confines of the vessel made it inevitable that we spend more time together. I didn't object. Without his friendly overtures, I would have driven myself crazy. Dhreen was curious about the life of a Terran surgeon, for which he swapped stories of his adventures as a pilot.

"So after two weeks in orbit, I decided to go down and see what the delay was—strictly a humanitarian visit, you understand," Dhreen said on the last day of the trip.

"In other words, you violated Nbrekkian space without official sanction," I said. He hiccuped without remorse and continued.

"Good thing I did, Doc. The whole colony was pulverized. Some witless citizen studying alien cultures decided to ferment a shipment of offworld grain. Seems he sampled it, thought it was tasty, and passed it around." Dhreen shook his head sadly. "It must have been some festival while it lasted."

"Then the Nbrekkians found out they had no means to digest the alcohol," I guessed.

"You can't believe how much gratitude some hemotoxin neutralizer can buy you."

"You are a blatant opportunist, Dhreen," I said, then chuckled when he assumed his usual innocent demeanor.

Dhreen took a large portion of the meal I'd prepared, and tasted it with a grin. "Did I mention this is orifice-salivating, Doc?"

"Mouthwatering," I corrected. To repay Dhreen's undemanding hospitality, I'd coaxed some more sophisticated dishes from his limited food supplies over the past week. The preparation unit he possessed was, like everything else on the *Bestshot*, a conglomeration of salvaged parts. Yet with a little inventive programming, I was able to produce some appetizing fare.

It also helped to keep me occupied. The closer we came to K-2, the larger the mistake I might be making seemed to grow. By the last day, it was nearing the dimensions of Jupiter.

It didn't always help, I thought ruefully, to keep busy. I had no appetite left, and declined to eat my full share of the meal. Dhreen happily polished off the last of the spicy vegetable and synpro stew.

"If you ever decide to give up medicine, you should open a restaurant," he said, sighed, and glanced down at himself. "I've put on at least a couple of kilos with you on board."

"You're welcome," I replied, trying not to sound too ironic as I added, "it's nice to know I have something to fall back on. So tell me, where are you headed after K-2?"

"Plenty of traders around the border looking for cargo space," Dhreen said, rubbing one of his almost-ears. I had learned that gesture was the Oenrallian equivalent of a smirk. "Lots of newlies pay hefty credits for return passage to their homeworlds, too."

"Newlies?"

"Newly established traders . . . newly installed jaunt routers . . . newly transferred physicians . . ."

"Not a chance, friend," I said. "You've gained your last credit from my account."

"Listen, Doc . . ." Dhreen's good-natured features sobered. "I haven't grilled about your plans, like I said, none of my business. But you should know the territories . . . well, they aren't like your homeworld."

I was counting on it. "Don't worry, Dhreen. I'll be fine."

"If you say so." He checked his wristcom, which reflected the helm status. "Looks like we'll be arriving in 2.5 Terran stanhours. Time enough to take a nap, if you'd like."

Sleep. Right. Was he kidding?

I spent the last hour pacing my cabin, checking the viewport every five minutes. At last I forced myself to sit down and try to relax. Sleep, however, was out. Music, I thought, and opened one of my cases.

As I sorted through my collection, I recalled how much it had irritated my father that I didn't share his taste in music. I liked a little of everything, and a lot of jazz. He preferred more conservative compositions by ancients like Wagner and Beethoven.

I frowned at one disc without a label. *What's this?* I was about to load it in my player when Dhreen announced that we were in orbit. I dropped the headset and case, tripping over my own feet in my dash to the viewport.

Below the ship loomed a massive, grayish-green orb surrounded by an asymmetrical ring of some twenty moons.

Kevarzangia Two.

Thin swirls of pale green clouds softened the atmosphere of the enormous globe. Beyond K-2's outer curve, I spotted the distant, twin suns, glowing with amber-orange light. Two blazing giants caught forever in each other's magnetic allure.

"Suns," I murmured softly. Now I understood why that word was used as an expletive out here.

According to the data, Kevarzangia Two was somewhat larger than Terra by a difference of three thousand kilometers. Somewhat larger? Who were they trying to fool? It was enormous. The length of a standard day was almost identical to Terra, due to the increased rotational speed of the planet. There were two distinct continents, immense land masses, and the colony was located in the northwest region of the largest.

I knew I couldn't see it from here. I still tried to see if I could pick it out.

K-2, like Terra, was a water world. The highest order of native life-forms were once aquatic beings who had evolved into an amphibious, intelligent civilization. It had been noted that the natives had no objection to their world being colonized. It would be interesting to find out how the 'Zangian aborigines really felt about offworlders.

Maybe they would be more friendly than Terrans

were. Which meant they wouldn't spit on the ground when I walked by.

"Prepare for final approach, Doc," Dhreen called back through the shuttle's display.

Slight turbulence from entering into the upper atmosphere shuddered through the hull of the *Bestshot*, but I didn't react to it. I wasn't afraid. I was a thoracic surgeon, a trained professional. If working as a physician on K-2 proved to be a disaster, I'd survive. Like Dhreen said, I could always open a restaurant.

I was *not* going to beg the Oenrallian to jaunt me back, no matter how many knots formed in my stomach. I was much more afraid of what waited for me if I returned to Terra.

It took an intolerable amount of time for Dhreen to land, dock, and secure the shuttle. I didn't remember launch taking this long, why all the delay? Once on the ground, requisite procedures dictated full biodecon of the ship, cargo, and both of us before we could step foot on the surface.

I was at the about-to-scream stage by the time Dhreen reported to Colonial Transport. "Scans are negative."

Permission to disembark was given by a transdrone after clearance was confirmed. Thank God for efficient automation. I gathered up my cases, Jenner's carrier, and hurried out to the main cabin.

Dhreen stood next to me as he pressed a panel release and the outer hull doors parted. "Doc, meet Kevarzangia Two."

The recruit station had given me the usual planetary survey vids and statistical facts along with my assignment contract. Dry, dull facts. None of that prepared me for the breathtaking vista that sprawled out like a primitive Eden all around the ship.

"Oh, my." If I looked and sounded like an awed kid, I didn't care. Around me, K-2 flourished with a bewildering profusion of life. Towering groves soared hundreds of feet in the air, making Terran forests look like a bunch of leafy twigs. The planet was an enormous ocean of vegetation upon which the colony's structures floated. My homeworld might have been like this hundreds of centuries before Terrans began manipulating the environment.

I looked up. Above my head lacy swirls of cloud drifted peacefully across the bright emerald sky. The unusual color effect, I understood, was attributed to a harmless biochemical substance in the atmosphere reacting with the strong radiant light coming from the suns. A verdant world, mirrored in the sky, a seamless envelope of life.

I knew the atmosphere was almost identical to that of my homeworld, with a rather heavier content of nitrogen. My first breath was crisp and oddly invigorating.

"Fair place, isn't it?" Dhreen said, noticing my rapt interest. "You'll do well here, Doc."

I turned to him. "I plan on it." My hand, I was glad to see, didn't tremble as I held it out.

The Oenrallian pressed his wedge-shaped palm to mine. "If you ever need this hand again, signal me."

"Thank you, Dhreen." There were a thousand things more I wanted to say, but my throat was suspiciously tight. Acting like an awed kid was fine, crying my eyes out and getting Dhreen's flight suit all damp wasn't. I smiled instead, picked up my cases, and strode down the gently swaying ramp.

It took a moment to register that I had walked straight into chaos.

The *Bestshot* was docked in the center of a noticeably improvised Transport zone. Ships of myriad shapes, sizes, and origins hovered, landed, and took off all around me. I thought of bees, racing back and forth to the hive. There was an incredible amount of beings milling back and forth to the stationary shuttles, and an even greater amount of cargo being off-loaded by huge automated conveyors. Beyond the shuttle docks stretched a chain of structures, more oversized building blocks drifting on green waves.

I spotted Transport Administration and made my path toward that first indicator of civilization. It was housed in a sprawling bunker that had been patched together from an assortment of emergency site shelters.

This was not anything like the beautifully designed edifices of my homeworld. Terrans demanded perfection, and got it. K-2's construction crews were obviously forced to make do with limited materials. Still, even to my Terran-acclimated view, it had a certain unaffected charm.

Transport Admin's designation was posted above the main entrance in several distinct pictographs and languages, and I was surprised to see my own native alphabet as well. Less than one percent of the population, and Terrans still merited a share of the signs? Someone must have complained. Terrans took pride in being the most obstinant race in our Quadrant. They sure didn't leave their attitudes at home when they traveled.

Through unseen audiocoms, I heard automated voices speaking in different tongues, for those species which had no written language. The building itself was the second largest next to Cargo Dispatch/Receiving.

"GfiRidhety juilTopp!" someone barked out behind me, and I turned as a huge, grey-furred creature jostled by.

"Sorry," I said, then had to avoid another colonist who slithered around me from the opposite side. "Excuse me."

Now I focused on the steady stream of colonists and visitors who poured in and out of the structure's threshold around me. There was a bewildering variety of lifeforms. Humanoids of every color and appendage count. Beings in self-contained envirosuits, some with fantastic garments, others pelted or scaled. A small group appeared to be walking jellyfish. Another had prismatic bodies that created iridescent rainbow haloes in the twin suns' light. I forgot about trying not to gawk and simply drank them in with my eyes. So many differences. So

much life. It astounded me. Then the unexpected outrage struck hard, and fast.

My father's prejudices had denied me all of this.

"What were you so afraid of, Dad?" Saying that out
loud earned me a few curious looks. Yeah, watch the
Terran female talk to herself, I thought, ducking my
head in embarrassment. I'd have time to be mad at my
father later. I joined the queue entering the facility.

The interior of the Administration Building was even
more crowded. Over the heads of dozens of marvelous
beings, I searched for the station I needed. It was simple
to find; no one was crowding around that terminal. On
either side, however, I saw an extended line of newly
transferred workers waiting to check in for Habitat Sub-
sistence and Colonial Security.

I knew there was a shortage of med pros, but I
couldn't possibly be the *only* incoming transfer. The others must have arrived sometime before me.

I put down my cases and addressed the blank display
marked "FreeClinic Services." Incredibly, I had to wait
a few moments before it blinked into sluggish operation.

"Welcome to Kevarzangia Two, FreeClinic Services
terminal," the antiquated panel blared. "Please identify
aid required."

It thought I was hurt? "Cherijo Grey Veil, Physician,
transfer arrival." The screen blipped for an instant, and
then I saw a real face staring out at me.

It was dusky vermilion in hue, glistening, and had
three olfactory orifices below a quartet of enormous,
brilliantly faceted eyes. Exactly like a gigantic, four-eyed
preying mantis.

The face moved, and rapid-fire speech rattled over the
audio. "T-tche-tcher juro-etterche—" Belatedly I activated my wristcom, and the chattering became translated
language. "—To K-2, Dr. Grey Veil. I'm T'Nliqinara,
the charge nurse on duty. Dr. Mayer will be there to
meet you directly."

"Thank you." I gazed around, but I was still standing
alone. "Where are the others?"

The nurse assumed a surprised air, if I was reading its facial musculature correctly. "What others, Doctor?"

I *was* the only med pro expected. "Never mind. I'll be here."

After the signal terminated, I spent a few minutes downloading my transfer discs into the terminal. Once the formalities were over, I took a position by the exterior viewers and watched the shuttles land and take off.

I tried not to look for Dhreen.

"Cherijo Grey Veil?"

I started at the sound of a human voice—I hadn't seen one Terran so far—and turned around.

One glance took in the taller, stern-faced man. Craggy features below a thin wreath of white hair. Sharp dark eyes that glinted like the beam of a lascalpel. An immaculate physicians' tunic, meticulously tailored over a spare, disciplined frame. Lean, beautiful hands.

A powerful man, I thought at once. One I do not want to aggravate. "Yes, I'm Dr. Grey Veil."

"Dr. William Mayer," he said. His voice was low-pitched and even, but gave no indication of welcome. The automated terminal had been cordial compared to this guy.

"How do you do?" I said, and offered my hand. Dr. Mayer's grasp was brief and indifferent.

"I'll escort you to your living quarters, Dr. Grey Veil," he said. "After you check in, we'll continue on to the facility."

Be still my heart. "Thank you." I wasn't imagining the tension; he was practically hitting me over the head with it. Since he didn't look the type to volunteer as a porter, I picked up my belongings.

"This way." He abruptly gestured for me to follow him as he turned and strode off. Feeling like a chastised medical student, I followed.

My quarters were located about half a kilometer from Transport. Dr. Mayer's glidecar provided a scenic, if silent ride to Main Housing. Mayer himself said nothing, nor did he respond to my one attempt at conversation.

After that rebuff, I ignored him and concentrated on my surroundings.

According to the data I'd studied before my transfer, many of the indigenous vegetation were biologically similar to that of preindustrial Terra. Yet there was little I could recognize as remotely comparable to the carefully sculptured landscapes of my homeworld.

Green, blue, and gold foliage crowded each other, greedy for the twin suns' abundant light. Flora hemmed a lacy tangle around the large open tracts of cleared land. Everywhere were bursts of color, from dazzling red crystalline flowers to towering growths of something like fern, which cascaded showers of thin, elongated yellow fronds for dozens of meters to the soil.

A green sea, spangled with a rainbow of life.

I was startled to see what seemed to be a trundling mass of thick spiny shrub slowly moving parallel to the glidecar path.

"What is *that*?"

Dr. Mayer didn't answer. I belatedly recalled that several native plants were nomadic in nature, moving from one spot to the next in order to take advantage of nutrients in the soil. He could have told me that. It wouldn't have killed him.

The colony appeared to have had little impact on the natural biosphere. What structures had been erected were already becoming assimilated by the environment; wild green runners embraced the artificial dwellings, incorporating them.

I compared this to the geometric flawlessness I was used to, and found the contrast almost comical. Terra was coldly shaped by human hands. K-2 embraced its colonists with a warm, fragrant hug. Dr. Mayer was living on the wrong planet.

The glidecar drew to a stop outside a structure centrally located within the housing area.

"Your transfer data, Dr. Grey Veil?"

My eyebrows elevated, but I brought out the discs and

handed them over. He stared at them, and then again at me, this time with unconcealed aversion.

The man definitely did *not* like me. But why? "Is something wrong, Dr. Mayer?"

He ignored the question. "I will expect you in one half hour."

There was no justification for his attitude, so I had to hope it was a personality defect. When you worked in the medical field, you ran into a lot of egos. Walking brick walls of egos. Impenetrable, aggressive, often unconsciously offensive. To be honest, there were times I was no diplomat myself.

I collected my cases, Jenner's carrier, and left without another word.

Inside Main Housing, I checked in with the drone custodian and was directed to my quarters. A short walk down a side corridor brought me to the West Wing, and my new home. I keyed open the door and found three large rooms had been allocated to me, with plenty of space for both a physician and a feline. Furnishings were stanissue, dull and boring, but I doubted I would be spending a great deal of time at home.

That was the only assumption about K-2 I had figured right.

I dumped my cases, then fed and watered Jenner as quickly as His Royal Highness would allow me to before putting him back in his carrier. I had to jog to make it back in time to Mayer's glidecar, but I refused to be late. He stood waiting anyway, with the same taciturn set to his face.

"I'm sorry if I kept—" I broke off in amazement as he brusquely turned his back on me and got back in the vehicle. For a moment I stood there with my mouth hanging open, then collected myself and climbed in after him. The door snapped shut too fast under my tight fingers, and that earned me a frown.

Too bad, I thought mutinously. You started it.

The trip to the FreeClinic took us back in the direction of Transport. The facility was close to the shuttle docks, dangerously so, it seemed to me. As I studied the facility, Dr. Mayer stopped the glidecar abruptly and turned to me. His intelligent eyes were blazing.

All this, because I slammed the door? Maybe it was time to exit the vehicle.

"Just a minute, Doctor. I want to talk to you."

Did he know? Had my father already tracked me down?

"Before you enter my FreeClinic, understand this," he said, underlining each word with deliberate threat, "I will not tolerate any excuse for incompetence. I don't care what you did to get this slot. If you cannot perform the duties required of your position, you will be discharged."

"I see." He didn't know! Despite my relief, instant resentment sprang up. Incompetence? I'd be discharged? Who did he think he was? *My FreeClinic,* he said. Like he owned it. "May I ask what *your* position is with this facility, Doctor?"

William Mayer regarded me with open contempt. "Chief of staff." With that, he exited the glidecar and marched off into the facility.

Well, I'd really impressed my new boss.

When I walked into the FreeClinic a few minutes later, I spied the same insect-like charge nurse who had greeted me via display at Transport. The cut of the uniform indicated a senior professional, and that T'Nliqinara was a female. As I approached, she looked up and ceased entering data on the console beneath her single-clawed appendage.

"Dr. Grey Veil." The angular set of her features sharpened. "Welcome to the FreeClinic."

"Thank you." I resisted the urge to cross my fingers behind my back. "It's a pleasure to be here."

She consulted a data pad to one side. "I just received a signal for you. You're expected at HQ Administration in one hour for orientation."

I grimaced. All doctors hated adminwork, and I was

no exception. The last thing I wanted to do on my first day was to sift through and acknowledge a heap of bureaucratic data, then listen to some clerk go on for hours about the rules and regulations. Surely my time could be put to better use. Like showing Dr. Mayer exactly how wrong he was.

"Any chance I can check in with Trauma first?" I knew what Trauma units were like. I'd look in, meet an overworked staff, and be up to my elbows in charts within minutes.

"Of course." The elegant skeletal figure rose ominously from her position behind the reception desk. T'Nliqinara towered over me by at least a meter. I was reminded again of a very large preying mantis as she crooked one of her multi-jointed arms in a sweeping gesture. I wondered if she meant, *come this way,* or, *I'd like to eat you as an afternoon snack.*

"I'll give you the usual tour along the way."

Doctors were not squeamish by nature, especially surgeons. When you'd been up to your elbows in someone's abdomen, cutting and patching together the squishy contents, it tended to give you a certain tolerance level. I could handle T'Nliqinara. I just didn't want to be around when she *did* get hungry.

A few steps down the corridor, and I forgot about the tall nurse altogether.

During my surgical practice on Terra, I could send my patients to a dozen different facilities that provided every possible service a doctor might need. All within a few minutes' travel from my office.

As I walked alongside the lumbering charge nurse, I saw the clinic barely resembled those efficient institutions. Resembled? The tavern where I'd met Dhreen would have been an improvement. The structure housing inpatient wards, clinical services, and the trauma center was originally a series of cargo storage bays. Incredibly old and shabby storage bays at that.

"FreeClinics are always close to wherever the Transport is," T'Nliqinara said as we made our way through the facility. "Convenient both for incoming transfer medevals and the prime zone of accidental injuries in newly established colonies. And if anything crashes, we have first salvage rights."

"Effective," I murmured. Not to mention rather macabre.

"It is," the nurse said. "Staffing creates difficulties, but we've handled patient load so far. Trauma gets the major portion of the available medical equipment."

"*Available* medical equipment?" I echoed.

"We barter for whatever we can to supplement, which isn't much out here. On each shift, three physicians rotate the two medsysbanks we have. Have to roll them on carts in and out of exam rooms."

Diagnostic equipment on carts? What would be next? Fabric bandages? "Wonderful."

T'Nliqinara snorted with what I guessed was contempt. "Half the instruments and non-disposables should have been replaced before I was hatched. The other half invariably break or disappear. Bartermen will acquire anything if it's not secured."

"Bartermen?"

The alien nurse directed another snort at me. "Oh, you'll get to meet them *very* soon, Doctor."

There was no more time for discussion as we entered the Trauma Unit. Like any other emergency center in the universe, it was in a state of near-bedlam. A handful of serious cases were separated from the general waiting area, while three nurses and an orderly scurried around them performing triage evals. The remainder of the patients waited, in states that ran the gamut from silent acceptance to vocal indignation. In one corner a couple of kids with discernible flippers played while two larger parental versions bickered with each other in squeaking tones.

I smiled. For the first time since I'd stepped on K-2 soil, I felt at home.

"Dr. mu Cheft is on leave until tomorrow, and Dr.

Dloh is probably on a rest interval," T'Nliqinara said as she led me past Assessment and into Examination and Treatment. "I'll take you to Dr. Rogan, he's primary for this shift."

Terran? I found myself speculating on the name as I rounded the corner and followed the nurse back into the exam rooms. So far I hadn't met anyone (with the disagreeable exception of Dr. Mayer) from the home-world. I chided myself. Why transfer fourteen light-years from Terra if I wanted to see another human being?

Inside an unoccupied treatment room, an average-sized, rather overweight humanoid male sat with his back toward the door, fiddling with the controls of an aging medsysbank propped on a portable cart. The tunic he wore was white and blue, identical to the one worn by Dr. Mayer. It was not, however, as spotlessly neat. Splattered blood, bile, and other unidentifiable fluids soiled the fabric. The wrinkle pattern suggested he'd worn the same tunic for days without bothering to steril-ize, the slob.

When he turned, I flinched slightly. His head was shaped like mine, but there ended the resemblance. Lid-less, protruding eyes slid to the nurse, then over me with a slick eagerness. Around these two bulging orbs, his face was deeply scored with long, parallel grooves. Each elongated pit was edged with thousands of tiny, undulat-ing grey polyps.

Ugh, I thought. My repugnance tolerance level just dropped a dozen notches.

Rogan's skin was a jaundice-yellow in tone, but a healthy amount of human-looking dark hair grew on the back and top of his skull. He even affected a patchy growth above his four lips. This sparse mustache neatly parted as his mouth flowered open over pegged, yellow-ish teeth.

"T'Nliq!" he said in such an ordinary Terran voice that I recoiled again. "This damn thing is worthless. Can't see what the *suns* is wrong with the sensor ports."

"Dr. Phorap Rogan, Dr. Cherijo Grey Veil." The nurse made another of her sweeping moves.

He nodded toward me. "Hey, Doctor. Who did you spit on to get this slot?"

T'Nliqinara looked more than slightly peeved at Rogan. "Have you notified Facility Maintenance about the medsysbank, Dr. Rogan?"

"Those slackers?" Rogan's teeth snapped together audibly. "They'd take at least a rotation to get here."

"Then, you must make do," the nurse said with another of her snorts. "Excuse me, I have work to complete." She turned and ducked beneath the entrance molding as she left the room. Dr. Rogan turned back to the diagnostic console.

"Know anything about this kind of tech?" he inquired, his halfhearted efforts ineffective after several minutes had passed.

"Probably as much as you do." I had already taken the top chart from the tall stack waiting for his attention and switched it to display. Clearly Dr. Rogan wasn't in a hurry to treat any patients. "Quite a crowd out there in Assessment," I said, deliberately casual.

"They'll wait. They always do," Rogan said. He didn't sound especially concerned. He stood, and suddenly gave the cart a swift kick. A static whine snapped, and the equipment hummed as it came back on line. He danced around it, chortling with glee. "I got it! I got it!"

I ignored his less than graceful frolicking. The initial eval displayed on the next scheduled case had my full attention.

"Good for you." I shrugged off my outer jacket. "See if it will profile diagnostics on an adult Orgemich female with moderate abdominal distress." I gazed around the interior of the room and located the central display. Time to get to work.

"Hey, there's no hurry!" he said. "Don't you want to take a look around first, see the rest of the 'clinic'?"

"Sure. After we clear these cases."

"I said *they'll wait*." Dr. Rogan's voice took on a distinct whine: I don't want to and you can't make me.

Stifling a sigh, I removed a platinum slide from my tunic pocket and secured my braid with a practiced twist.

"I know," I said. "I won't."

CHAPTER THREE

First Shift

Dr. Rogan capitulated to my desire to start working, but not without attitude.

"You're not *scheduled* for duty today," he said as the patient I had called for trudged in. "New arrivals have to report for Orientation—"

Gripe, gripe, gripe. Was that all Rogan could do, besides dancing badly and kicking sensitive medical equipment? No wonder Assessment was packed. "Let's bend the rules, and they might give us a raise," I said.

The Orgemich female with moderate abdominal distress turned out to be an ursine creature with a wide, powerful set of jaws lined with row upon row of equally impressive, serrated teeth. This patient also sported a massive digestive paunch, which she held with her stubby paws in evident discomfort. Tiny, close-set pink eyes glared at me and Rogan.

"Hurts it does!" the Orgemich said. "Dying I am!"

"On the exam pad you get," Rogan growled back at her. The patient reluctantly complied, groaning as she eased her bulk onto the table. "Still now hold!" Using an antiquated scanner, my colleague made a quick sweep of the swollen abdominal expanse.

I prudently stood aside to observe while Dr. Rogan examined the patient. It didn't take him long to com-

plete his scan. By the time I blinked twice, he was done.
He skipped the usual patient interview, and merely
waited for the medsysbank to extrapolate a diagnosis
from his scanner's initial input. I reviewed the chart once
more while I waited.

"Here we are," Phorap Rogan said as he read the
console's displayed recommendation. "Just as I
thought." He withdrew a syrinpress from a supply chest,
and calibrated it for application.

I frowned slightly as I surveyed the treatment schedule
myself, which called for a powerful digestive aid. "Severe gastroenteritis?" I read the diagnosis aloud.

"Orgemichs are gluttons, *suns* only knows what she
ate," Dr. Rogan replied rudely as he administered the
infusion. He shook the patient's upper pectoral area, and
addressed her in harsh tones. "Take care of it this will.
No more than single rations for the next week you must
consume. Understand do you?"

While the patient grumbled out her acknowledgment,
I shifted my gaze again to the medsysbank. Rogan
hadn't bothered to run a single organ scan. True, the
pain was typical of simple gastric distress, but why accept
the obvious?

"Do you want to run an organs sequence?" I asked,
and got a baleful glare in return.

"What for? The medsysbank established the cause."

"Equipment can often be inaccurate." I tried to be
politic. "Another series of scans would rule out—"

"No, Doctor," he said, all offended dignity. "I'm finished here." He signed off the chart and released the
Orgemich.

"Dr. Rogan—"

"In here." He gestured for me to accompany him to
the adjoining room. Playing the cooperative consultant,
I followed.

From the clutter, I guessed it was an improvised
lounge and break area. The untidy space was littered
with old charts, supplies, and the remnants of at least
three or four meals. Was there no regular sanitation

crew? I noticed the outline of a multiple-limbed form huddled under a metallic thermal sheet. The Dr. Dloh mentioned by the charge nurse, no doubt. It was snoring.

"You're new, so I'll overlook your interference," Phorap Rogan said.

I smiled. I could do this. "On Terra, we call it consultation."

"I've got some advice for you, Doctor. You'd better lose that attitude, if you want to stay here long enough to unpack."

A disagreeable odor now seemed to be coming from Rogan. Did his species possess noxious glandular sprays triggered by strong emotions? I wondered. I tried to step back discreetly.

Naturally, Rogan stepped forward to compensate. "My father was Terran," he said, his voice rich with scathing condescension. "He raved about all the endless resources, easy credits, and specialized treatment centers on your planet."

"Really?" I tried not to wonder what the father had ever seen in Rogan's mother. Perhaps it had been a tragic case, involving blindness, or dementia. "How— flattering."

"You know what I think? Terran doctors can't clean their anuses without a consult."

That was fairly direct. It was becoming harder by the moment to deal with this jerk. "I've managed to, so far."

"You aren't on Terra anymore," Rogan said.

"No, I'm not."

"This is frontier territory, Doctor. Do you have any idea of where you *are*? Don't you think you'd better rely on those with *experience*?"

Sure, I agreed silently. As soon as I meet someone who actually *uses* it.

"I'm willing to help you, once you understand the way it is." Rogan leaned forward in emphasis. I held my breath. "Don't come in here, trying to change everything. FreeClinic duty is set up just the way we like it here."

I risked a gulp of air. "Thank you for your recommendations, Doctor. I'll let you know if I need your assistance." Specifying that this would occur only during a frosty day on the surface of the twin suns was unnecessary. My new colleague wasn't *that* thick-headed.

"You do that, Dr. Grey Veil." With that, he stalked out of the lounge.

Okay, I thought, I was *not* going to win a popularity contest with my boss or Rogan. I'd have to tread carefully where Dr. Mayer was concerned, but how much harm could one odious, rather smelly half-Terran colleague do?

Enough, it turned out.

After that confrontation, Phorap Rogan was as good as his word. I was on my own. Back inside the exam room, I spent a few moments familiarizing myself with the location of supplies and equipment. The medsysbank was gone. What instruments I did find were either outmoded or barely functional.

I thought about what I had left behind. Back on Terra, my father had supervised every detail when I opened my private practice, and spared no expense. Only the best for Cherijo. His handpicked assistants welcomed patients into a tastefully decorated reception area. In my treatment rooms, I'd worked with the finest of instrumentation, while my patients reclined on luxurious cradles of antistress foam and listened to old-world masters like Count Basie and Harry Connick, Jr.

As a crowning touch, Dad had personally directed the installation of a massive diagnostic database unit, which took up half of my office. That had provided precise information on every known aspect of the Terran medical field.

Highly skilled assistants, plenty of cases, and top of the line equipment. It had been Physician Paradise. Just the thought of all that efficient, pristine gear I'd left behind made me grumble as I inventoried the equipment. If it could be called that.

"This stuff belongs in a *museum*," I muttered.

There were scanners with components rewired so haphazardly that I was afraid to activate them. Old-fashioned compression injectors to supplement the meager stock of newer syrinpresses and infusers. An emergency kit with tubes and bottles of medicines, and curious metallic devices to measure vital stats.

And yes, even several rolls of real *fabric* bandages. At best, it was a motley assortment. At worst, I might kill someone using this junk. I went to the room console and signaled Assessment.

"Nurse?" I picked up the next chart in sequence. "Send back the cases from p'Kotma VII now."

The chart display reflected scant assessment data on two colonists, recent immigrants from a neighboring system. They were sisters, and complaints listed were pain, unremitting vertigo, and impairment of most of their nine senses. They'd been isolated away from Assessment for some unspecified reason.

I quickly discovered why.

Two hysterical beings burst through the doorway. They appeared exactly like huge, bright red sea anemones. On the pocked surface of their forms, hundreds of small slots were trying very hard to communicate.

They were all screaming.

"You must help us—"

"We are suffering so—"

"Please, Doctor, the pain—"

"Unbearable—"

I was deafened by the swarm of pleas, howls, and cries for help. None of the mouths spoke collectively, which made it impossible for my wristcom to continue to translate. The subsequent feedback from my translation device harmonized with the sisters as their wailing rose to painful octaves.

"Calm down!" I had to yell to be heard, but the p'Kotmans ignored me, and squashed their pulpy bodies against each other as they writhed in agony.

I separated them, and thrust each on either side of the exam pad. By now my ears were ringing. I had to wrench myself away from the clutch of their imploring tendrils to hit the display console with a clenched fist.

"Get a nurse back here, *stat!*"

Within moments, T'Nliqinara hovered just outside the door. I was busy adjusting my wristcom to follow what my patients were trying to tell me.

"T-jher recher attech?" she shouted.

"How can I get them to quiet down?" I demanded to know at the top of my lungs. The sponge-shaped sisters screamed even louder.

The nurse shook her head, unable to understand me or communicate in return.

"Medsysbank!" I pantomimed pushing a cart.

The charge nurse glowered at me with censure. I stepped toward the door, and my wristcom began to work at last.

"Not available!" T'Nliqinara bellowed, then snorted at the patients as their cacophony reached a shrill crescendo. She took a deep breath, and barely managed to relay the next words through the din. "Dr. Rogan said you wouldn't need it!"

Touché, Phorap, I thought furiously.

The nurse leaned down and put her mouth next to my wristcom in order to be heard. "I'll get help!"

I shook my head. T'Nliqinara made an impatient sweep of her elongated limbs, but waited for my next direction.

Mentally blocking out the noise, I tried to connect the symptoms with a viable cause. I was good at this, after years of Dad's lectures.

Vertigo and sensory impairment, obviously related to the excruciating pain. Why? No injury or disease was apparent. It wasn't possible to interview them, the symptoms only worsened when I— Hold on, I thought. They went crazy when I spoke, at the whine from my wristcom, when the nurse yelled. *Sound.* Was it an exposure reaction? Too much input could theoretically do as much damage as an injury. My own ears could attest to that.

I flapped my hands at T'Nliqinara, gesturing for her

to leave us. The nurse was only too happy to escape the commotion. I ignored my vociferous patients completely as I checked over their chart once more. That had to be it, I told myself.

I activated the exam room's quarantine seals, and set the room envirocontrols to discharge all sound waves. It was a tactic usually employed when performing neurorepairs in open cranial surgery. We were all going to be very, very quiet.

Slowly the lack of sound penetrated the p'Kotmans' hysteria. They in turn began to settle down. The voices died, one by one, until the three of us sat in a vacuum of silence.

It worked.

We handled most of the treatment in that manner. I used a chart screen to communicate with them, setting it to translate what I typed into their native written language. They did the same. Incredibly, I learned the sisters already knew they were having an allergic reaction to alien sonics. The problem had been that they couldn't escape the unbearable exposure and become coherent long enough to tell anyone about it.

I provided a solution by offering a temporary acoustic-dampening agent. I had to ask them to specify what chemical compounds would be most compatible with their physiology, but luck was with me again. They knew exactly what they needed. Permanent full-body shields, I was told, were required for long-term alleviation of symptoms.

"We've sent for them," one of the p'Kotmans whispered once the injection had taken effect. She explained these shields were readily obtainable on their homeworld, given the susceptible nature of their physiques. Unfortunately, the original ones they'd packed to bring with them had been somehow lost in transit. "Until they arrive, can you provide more medicine?"

I scheduled them for follow-up visits at the Primary Care Clinic, then—my ears still buzzing—I requested the next patient. I assumed after handling the p'Kotmans, I was prepared for the worst.

I was wrong.

One patient, a humanoid male with multiple lacerations from a tangling with a malfunctioning cargo loader, jerked when I began to repair one of his wounds. I hadn't anticipated the movement, and burned my wrist with the suture laser. I was appalled. I'd never fumbled instruments before, not even in my *student* days.

"You're hurting me!" he said.

"Of course I'm not hurting you. Try to remain still," I said through gritted teeth as I ignored my own minor burn and repositioned the laser.

"I can't help it. I can feel it! It's searing hot!" the patient said.

After a quick neuroscan, I was horrified to discover I *had* been burning him. The anesthetic agent I'd given him had not taken effect, as it was incompatible with his neural system. I had to test three other compounds before finding something that would actually work.

Suffice to say, he didn't thank me when we were done. He did, however, teach me what his species call incompetent Terrans. At length.

Another case involved an adolescent who seemed to be suffering from an acute surface response to some unknown substance. Since the boy had immature vocal organs, and no written form of his language existed, he couldn't tell me what was wrong.

I didn't need him to tell me. His hide was sloughing off in gigantic sheets, literally peeling a thick layer of flesh from his limbs. When I attempted to repair the damaged tissues, he fought me wildly, poor kid. We were wrestling with a dermal regenerator between us when his parents entered the exam room.

"We were concerned because it was taking so long," the mother said, then nervously stepped forward. "Excuse me, Doctor, but why are you trying to stop Sodro's process?"

"What process?" I asked, halting my frantic efforts to keep his outer hide in place.

"He's in seasonal transition," the father informed me blandly. "He reported to get an emollient for the itching. The new derma is very sensitive."

My young patient was *molting*.

After several hours I muddled through another half-dozen cases. I had not seen one Terran patient, I was almost thoroughly unnerved, and despite several requests, the two medsysbanks in the FreeClinic had yet to be made available for my use.

That was when Dr. Dloh decided to stop by and introduce himself. I didn't even flinch at his appearance, which was exactly like that of a gigantic, well-fed spider. One positive aspect of alien medical experience was that *nothing* shocked you after a couple of hours in FreeClinic Trauma.

Dr. Dloh wore a modified physician's tunic over his exoskeleton. His carapace appeared as shiny and hard as obsidian, and was mottled with irregular green markings. A lustrous cluster of bead-sized eyes gleamed at me over a U-shaped orifice that could have been an ear, nose, or mouth.

"Dr. Grey Veil, delighted to meet you." Dr. Dloh uncurled three of his appendages toward me in a sort of wave. I eliminated the U as a mouth—his voice came from the vicinity of his thorax. I was startled by the fact that my colleague spoke in my native language without the assistance of a wristcom. But then, he didn't have wrists. "Zo zorry to have delayed making your acquaintanze."

"It's good to meet you, too, Dr. Dloh," I said, and decided to capitalize on the friendly reception. So far, it was the only one I'd gotten. "Perhaps you can help me. I need regular access to one of the clinic's medsysbanks."

The appendages moved in harmonious agitation. "But Dr. Rogan told me—"

"Dr. Rogan is"—oh, the *words* that came to mind—"mistaken."

Dr. Dloh apologized, and generously promised to provide any assistance I might need. I decided I preferred giant spiders to Terrans and half-Terrans, hands down.

"I'm zurprized you choze K-2 for your tranzfer," Dloh said. He rotated his eye cluster downward. "My natural appearanze requirez my azzignment to a, zhall we zay, highly diverzified, culturally zophizticated population."

I could understand that. On Terra, if he'd ever attempted to work as a medical practitioner, my species would have retaliated with conservative resistance. Which meant reviving public stonings and lynch mobs.

Dr. Dloh continued. "But you are quite the ztandard humanoid, Dr. Grey Veil. You could have chozen more familiar zurroundingz clozer to your home."

He may have looked like a big bug, but he was obviously intelligent and perceptive.

"I liked the idea of treating many different species, Doctor."

"And prove yourzelf to be more than zimply a *Terran* zpezializt? Or provide a meanz of ezcaping other limitationz?"

Uncomfortably perceptive.

"I'm satisfied that I can be of use here, Dr. Dloh. Hard as that may be to believe."

That seemed to placate his curiosity. "Good luck, Doctor. I will offer a word of caution, if I may. Rumor haz it that Dr. Mayer, our ezteemed chief of ztaff, waz, zhall we zay, dizturbed after meeting you."

"Disturbed?"

"Affronted may be a more appropriate term."

"I see." Well, I didn't like him, either.

"Dr. Rogan, our lezz ezteemed colleague, haz acquired an equally negative feeling toward you."

"Dr. Rogan needs to get a job," I said flatly.

"I agree. Unfortunately, hiz main preoccupation iz to avoid the one he haz at all cozt." Dr. Dloh shuffled to the door. "Dr. Grey Veil, az Terranz zay, watch your back." After an elegant, shuffling sort of dip, the arachnid physician departed.

Dloh was pretty nice. The nurses must have told him about my blunders, but he hadn't said a word about them. Maybe I'd found an ally. And I needed one, badly. I was tempted to leave Trauma before I further embarrassed myself, but I forced myself to stay until shift change. I wasn't a coward, and Mayer was wrong.

For the rest of my voluntary shift, Dr. Dloh shared the medsysbank he used. That helped me get through the remaining cases without any more disasters, although I still had problems when the data didn't seem to correlate with my personal diagnosis. A few times I had to rely on instinct and theory, and make an educated guess.

The patients were at times shocking in appearance, but most were humanoid, or close to it. I began to see an anatomical standard among my fellow colonists—a superior cranial-sensory case, main torso, and regular appendages. They also had the usual complaints requiring emergency care. Infants and children generally had infections in every possible orifice (and a few I'd never dreamed of). Older siblings and young adults comprised most of the accidental injury cases. Minor lacerations, sprains, and broken bones were common among the construction workers, transport officers, or those assigned to agricultural projects.

Since the elderly or diseased were uniformly barred from immigration, there weren't any cases of chronic or degenerative disorders. No upwardly mobile colony wants aging dependents on their hands. I noted the universal reluctance to discuss family history, too. Who wanted to have their resident status revoked due to genetic handicaps?

In turn, I seemed to fascinate my patients.

"You have a pretty coat." One furry child tentatively touched my coiled braid as I extracted a spiny burr from her flank. "Why have you removed the rest of it?" I explained the (to her) bizarre fact that Terrans grew most of their hair on their scalps. "Don't you get cold?"

"Terrans have smooth skin," another patient said when I cautiously checked his damaged femoral muscles.

His leg was covered in thick octagonal plates of thorny exocartilage. "Reminds me of some of the hides we use for garments on my world." He eyed me as if sizing me up as a jacket.

"I've never met a Terran female before," a small, ornithic man chirped. His throat was inflamed from his unsuccessful efforts to capture a consort. I prescribed a soothing syrup and less singing to the ladies of his species. He gave a strained warble and tried to put a wing around my shoulders. "I don't suppose you'd be interested in cross-species mating?" Thanks, I replied, but no thanks.

Others weren't exactly enchanted.

"Are you immature?" One towering, heavily bosomed matron with postpartum cramps demanded to know.

"Not that I'm aware of," I said, my lips quirking as I added, "I'm sure I can be patronizing at times."

She peered at me suspiciously. Several of her five chins quaked when she said, "My newest litter's runt is twice your size!"

Two of my potential patients took one look at me, made an abrupt turn, and walked out. I signaled the charge nurse each time, who informed me the patients had requested to see another physician. A *non-Terran* physician, was the implication.

Thanks to men like my father, there were going to be instant prejudices against me. Maybe they were afraid I was going to spit on the exam floor in traditional Terran fashion.

"That takes care of the last chart," I told the charge nurse thirteen hours later. I was bone-tired, itching from a mishap with a dermal applicator, and convinced I'd made the stupidest decision of my life. "Any objections if I take the rest of the day off?"

"You're to report to HQ for orientation tomorrow, then work Beta Shift here," the central display audio snapped back at me. Then, on a somewhat softer note, T'Nliqinara added, "Go get some sleep, Doctor."

Dr. Rogan intercepted me just before I reached the

main entrance. He smiled hatefully, while his skunklike odor reached new levels of offensiveness. I breathed through my mouth to keep from retching on his footgear.

"Shift over? Did you find you need anything *now*?" Sneering spoiled the phony concern.

I shrugged. A list came to mind: an explanation for my father's activities, a hot water bath, three days of sleep, a gallon of hot fudge poured over a vat of vanilla ice cream. I said none of those things. I suspected Phorap Rogan had absolutely no sense of humor.

There was still a lot medical science couldn't cure.

"I can handle it, Doctor."

"Can you?"

I nodded, too tired to continue the useless verbal sparring, and despite my efforts, about to vomit from the stink.

"But thanks for asking," I said as I brushed past him.

Outside the main entrance, I strolled past a long line of unoccupied glidecars and followed a path toward the Housing Transport I'd spied while with Dr. Mayer. Until I requisitioned my own personal conveyance, it was public transport for me.

I climbed on board the glidebus and stood in the crowded aisle as the big vehicle started moving. My new world beckoned to me as it swept past. Come on, Cherijo, it isn't that bad, it said. The green stillness was enticing, and I looked forward to off-duty hours, when I could explore. The horizon began to darken, and stars appeared above the horizon to the east of the colony perimeter. The darkening green parted as an erratic stream of glowing moons caught the last rays of the suns and divided the sky. Wow. My eyes widened at the sheer radiance of the celestial show. Compared to this, Terran night skies were downright barren.

"Maybe I won't miss Terra, after all," I murmured to myself.

I disembarked at housing with a tide of passengers, and watched as they departed, paired off or in larger groups. Everybody knew everybody—except me. A few curious glances came my way, but no one approached. I didn't make any overtures, either. In time, I promised myself, I would get to know them.

Right now I was ready to drop with exhaustion.

Sixteen hours after I'd stepped foot on K-2 soil for the first time, I crawled onto my sleeping platform. I was in no mood to unpack, eat, or even appreciate the comfort of the biomalleable mattress as it adjusted under my weight. Alone at last in the darkness of my new quarters, I pressed the heels of both hands over my burning, swollen eyelids.

"Congratulations, Dr. Grey Veil," I said. "A memorable beginning. You dimwit."

The fiery sting of my eyes wasn't due to tears, or lack of them. The cause was from a ridiculous accident with the last patient I'd treated that day. How I managed to turn a dermal applicator backward and spray myself with topical anesthetic was still a mystery. There was no permanent damage. Just a lingering irritation to remind me of what had been, I had to face it, a depressing ordeal.

I was beginning to enjoy torturing myself. I couldn't have made a worse start if I'd tried. Laying there in the dark, I mentally relived every single miserable incident, highlighted by Mayer's belligerence, Rogan's hostility, and Dloh's warning about both of them.

"Idiot," I muttered. Whether I was referring to myself, or Phorap Rogan at that moment was debatable. No doubt a similar term could be used by the FreeClinic staff to describe *me*.

I accepted my humble status as a new arrival, and I could swallow my badly battered pride until I gained some experience; everyone had to start somewhere. What troubled me the most were the conflicts with my supervisor and colleague. I'd never handled that kind of naked animosity before, except sometimes from—

"Jenner."

I rolled off the bed as soon as I spied his carrier. The latch was uncoupled, the small door flung open. Empty. Damn, damn. I kept swearing under my breath as I searched my quarters.

"Jenner? I'm here now. Come out, pal."

Not a sound in reply, no sign of him at all. Where could he be? As I hunted through my rooms, tears finally stung my reddened eyes at this last confirmation of my inadequacy.

Nice going, Cherijo, I thought. Run away from home, screw up first day on the job, now you lost the cat.

The chime of my door panel rang, interrupting my search, and I reluctantly went to answer it. When the door slid open, I saw the lustrous form of a slim, silvery being holding one equally silvery, disgruntled feline.

"Yours?" I was asked. I was too relieved to do more than nod. I held out my arms, and Jenner leapt gracefully into them. He butted urgently against my fingers while I stroked his head.

"Jenner." I buried my face in his fur. "Oh, thank God. I'm sorry. I'm sorry."

"All the doors are keyed to release domesticates upon any audible signal, unless you modify the setting." The husky voice was pleasant and even. "I found him wandering around the corridors."

"Thank you so much."

"I tried to communicate, but I was unsuccessful. I tracked his scent path to this dwelling."

"Jenner is just a cat. I mean, he's nonverbal."

"He was distressed, I believe, from the sounds he was making."

"*Suns.*" I hugged him closer, feeling even worse. "I just arrived today, and reported immediately to work. I forgot all about him."

"I understand." This acknowledgment was rich with irony, and drew my attention from my precious pet.

Jenner's rescuer was slightly taller than me, but much leaner. I couldn't tell if it was female or male—or androgynous, as some alien races are. The thin torso, limbs, and bullet-shaped skull were all covered with a short, platinum pelt. Delicate, pointed ears flickered whenever I spoke. It wore an intriguing series of folded strips of metallic fabric, attached to a filigree necklace studded with small multicolored gems. Two mild, colorless eyes studied me in turn.

"I'm Alunthri," it said.

"Is that your name, species, or planet of origin?"

"It is my name. You're from Terra?"

"Yes. Dr. Cherijo Grey Veil." Suddenly conscious of my impolite behavior, I stepped back. "Won't you come in, please?"

"Perhaps another time." Alunthri nodded toward Jenner. "Your companion needs your attention at present. Welcome to the colony."

"Thank you. Are we neighbors?" Alunthri's tapered head tilted to one side, while the small ears flared. Something wasn't translating. "Your quarters," I said. "Are they close by?"

"My owner's quarters are located in a parallel wing."

"Your owner?" Now I was confused.

"I, too, am a companion. Like your Jenner."

All at once I realized the necklace Alunthri wore was a collar, bearing standard animal inoculant and license chips.

Alunthri was a *pet*. A giant, talking, alien kitty cat.

"Well, I appreciate you finding him." I was very uncomfortable. It was understandable. I was used to speaking to a cat, not getting answers back from one.

"You are welcome. Please remember to adjust your panel settings." Alunthri stepped back and twitched its nearly invisible whiskers. "Fare you well."

Jenner shuddered in my arms as the door slid shut, and I rubbed my face once more against his soft coat.

"Whew! That was very weird." I felt a renewed sense of guilt. "Pal, you've got to be hungry."

The mention of Jenner's favorite subject made him leap from my arms and prowl restlessly around my feet. Once I'd arranged a feast for him, I reprogrammed the door controls as Alunthri had advised.

Drained of the last of my energy stores, I sank down on the bed and watched my hungry cat devour his food. *I'll only lay my head down for a moment,* was my last thought.

It was a shrill sound from my display panel that finally woke me up. I staggered over to the console. The interval indicator told me I'd slept almost seven hours straight. I tapped the response key.

"Incoming message from HQ Administration."

"This is Dr. Grey Veil," I said after a huge yawn.

The metallic features of a comdrone appeared on the vid. "Please report to the Administration Building in two hours for arrival orientation."

"Confirmed," I replied, reaching for the disconnect key.

But the drone wasn't through yet. "One message remaining."

Uh-oh. "Inquiry—point of origin?"

"Direct interstellar relay. Sol Quadrant."

From my homeworld system. Well, it didn't take a genius to figure out who was sending it.

My father, Joseph Grey Veil, was revered for his pioneering work in Terran transplant technology. One of his numerous contributions to mankind had been to make major organ transplants available to anyone who needed them. *Anyone,* regardless of credit status or social ranking. Dad had devised a method of cloning the patient's own diseased organ, destroying invasive cells during the process, thus creating a custom-designed, healthy replacement. Millions of people owed him their lives.

"My philosophy has always been to restore genetic integrity," Dad said once when addressing a Medtech graduation. He was invited to all of them, every year. "Cleanse the cells of aberrant or mutant DNA, and you can re-create the organ as it was meant to be."

It was unfortunate that Dad felt the same way about *people* as he did mutant DNA. A decade before I was born, he and a large number of his colleagues had instigated the Genetic Exclusivity Act. The legislation, unanimously supported by the World Government, had effectively barred all alien immigrants from settling on our world.

They should have just hung a big sign in orbit above Terra: Aliens, Go Home.

Dad's speech before the Unified National Assembly was considered one of the most powerful ever made. His opening statement had said it all: "The influx of alien species to Terra must be seen as a direct threat to the future genetic integrity of the human race."

Steadfast, compelling, bigoted to the toenails. That was my dad.

Despite the lure of politics, it was the only time Joseph Grey Veil ever bothered to involve himself in Terra's complex system of government. His place in history would be defined by what he accomplished as a scientist and surgeon, not as a public figure.

In the ensuing years, my father changed the way Terran internal medicine was practiced forever. Oncologists, surgeons, and hematologists worshiped him.

I didn't. I never had. Legends made lousy fathers.

Now it was time to deal with the unpleasantries. I tapped the panel and watched as the familiar face coalesced onto my screen.

Dad could have been considered attractive, in a remote sense. Silvered-black hair. Austere features. Short in stature, like me. A mild obsession with exercising, which had built up his physique. Women found him interesting, until he opened his mouth. I stopped wondering why he had to pay someone to be my mother a long time ago. To Dad, you were either a colleague or a potential patient. That's all.

When he was severely agitated, he tended to curl his upper lip a little. At that precise moment, he looked like he was sneering at me.

"Daughter," he said with a trace of outrage and reproach coloring his voice, "I have been attempting to contact you for more than ten Terran stanhours." And he was none too pleased about being put on the equivalent of *interstellar hold,* I saw that right away. "I cannot fathom this reckless decision to transfer without my consent."

"Hi, Dad. I'm fine. How are you?"

"I am currently revising my estimation of your maturity level," he said. The scornful upper lip practically folded over on itself.

"I'm sorry I left without informing you of my plans."

"Your apology is accepted." Uh-huh, I thought. Right. About as much as my escape. "The journey was uneventful?"

"Of course. Interstellar travel is quite safe now."

"Yes, regular transport vessels are." He abandoned the polite line of inquiry at once. "You, however, were not booked on any of them."

"I obtained passage on an independent starshuttle."

"The name of this independent vessel . . . ?"

"If you really want to know, Dad, you'll find out." I wasn't going to help him bar Dhreen from Terra. "Don't take your anger out on an innocent bystander."

"I did not say I was angry, daughter."

"Dad, you look like you're ready to detonate."

My observation seemed to force him to forego whatever tactful entreaties he had left to make. "Cherijo, you will return to Terra immediately."

Here was the fun part. For the first time in my life, I was going to stand up to Joseph Grey Veil: Tyrant. Genius. Demi-god of Terran medicine. It really wasn't that hard. After all, he was fourteen light-years away. "No, Dad."

He didn't like that. At all. "*What* did you say to me?"

"You heard me. I'm staying."

The dark blue eyes became slits. "I will have you brought back."

"I'm over the age for consent to transfer, Dad. You can't." This was beginning to feel pretty good, if I ignored the fact my stomach was turning into a calcified lump.

"You were not trained in the finest medical institution on Terra to waste your talents on some anonymous multispecies border colony."

My father carried around about five thousand years

of nearly undiluted Native American DNA in his cells, one reason for his arrogance. I ought to have known— I was capable of the same behavior, on occasion.

"How I choose to practice medicine is my decision, Dad."

"Your decision?" The Great Man hissed. Actually *hissed.* "Who brought you into existence? Who assured you had the finest education? Who—"

"You chose my career for me. You decided that I would become a surgeon. You decided how I should practice. You *set up* my practice." You, you, you.

"A father does no less for his only child," Dad said, regaining a margin of stoic dignity.

"You did a lot more than that. Take my patients, for example. You might have mentioned that you personally examined every single case before I saw them."

"Are you implying—"

I didn't have to fake the sigh. "Did you think I wouldn't find out?"

"It is true that I prescreened your cases." He conceded that much, taking the "it was for your own good" approach. "Junior practitioners benefit from close guidance."

"Junior practitioners," I echoed. "Hello? Dad? I've been a surgeon for more than seven years now."

"That is no reason to resent my supervision, Cherijo. I have five times your experience."

In his opinion he was Dr. God, and I wasn't worthy to kiss his footgear. Dad was beginning to sound very much like Phorap Rogan.

"Please." I squeezed my eyes shut, shoving back the need to lash out. Not now. "Spare me the excuses."

"When you return, I will allow you—"

"You aren't listening. You aren't in charge of me any more. I'm an adult, and I'll do exactly as I please."

"On an alien world, in a primitive settlement? I cannot begin to imagine the hazards, the possibilities for disease. It cannot compare to Terra in the slightest degree."

"For your information, Kevarzangia Two's colony is

not a collection of scavenged plasbrick huts." Well, mostly, I guessed. "The facility is quite . . . innovative."

"A FreeClinic!" He spat the word out. "I cannot believe you wish to exchange a prestigious surgical position to be a—a colonial alien practitioner!"

"Yeah, well, surprise, surprise."

He practically choked on his next words. *"It is an insult to my name."*

"No, Dad, it's what I want to do," I said. I wouldn't have called my father a snob, or a fanatic; it would have insulted those groups. I was sure someone would eventually invent a worse term. "Don't worry, I'll be fine."

My father considered this for a long moment. Then he attacked. "Consider the patients. You have no experience with nonhuman races." *You don't know what you're doing, and you're going to kill someone in the process.*

"I'll continue my education," I said through clenched teeth.

"Your assignment could be revoked," my father said. Would he try to use his influence to get me back? I wouldn't put it past him. "New colonies cannot devote more than a rudimentary effort to retrain their physicians."

"So I'll get fired." Exasperation was turning into bravado. "Maybe I'll open a restaurant."

I must have rattled him with that, he appeared horrified. "That is absolutely unacceptable, Cherijo!"

Was that *my* Father, shouting? "Dad." I was tired, and getting depressed. "I appreciate your concern. I know how much you—love me." Another lie. I knew exactly how he felt about me, and love wasn't involved.

"You will not listen to reason," my father said as he inspected me one last time.

I couldn't stop myself from saying what I did next. "I'm sorry, Dad." He was already turning away from the screen. "Bye, Dad." The signal terminated.

It hadn't been too terrible. Having open-heart surgery minus anesthetic would have hurt more. Maybe. I stood

under the heated port of the cleanser unit for a long
time before I hauled myself out and got dressed. I
trudged over to my food station.

"Breakfast." My selection of bread, tea, an omelet,
and fruit preserves appeared palatable. The only problem was my appetite, which my conversation with Dad
had killed. He usually had that effect on me. So did the
prospect of my next shift at the FreeClinic.

"What if I'm wrong?" I asked.

It wasn't going to be difficult to adapt to this world,
the job, my colleagues, and the patients. It was going to
be damn near impossible. On Terra I'd been at the top
of my field. Here I'd have to work hard just to avoid
malpractice.

I could resign from my contract. There was always an
open-return clause, in case someone changed their mind.
My father could never be sure I'd discovered his secret,
especially if I destroyed the evidence.

My food cooled, then congealed. Jenner appeared and
sniffed at the rim of my tray, then regarded me patiently.
My cat loves me, I told myself. Even if it's only for my
food.

"By all means." I indicated the plate, even though I
knew he'd gorged himself last night. "Help yourself."
He delicately devoured the meal, then curled in my lap
and allowed me to stroke him absently with my palms.

"Dad called," I told him, and his wide blue eyes
blinked warily. "He wants us to come home." It sounded
almost beguiling as I said it aloud. Home.

My cat yawned, leapt from my lap, and crept under
the sofa for a nap. Obviously the suspense wasn't killing
him. I glanced at the display, then jumped to my feet.

"No! I don't believe it!"

I was about to be late for arrival orientation.

CHAPTER FOUR

Taboos, Duty, Chickens

I reached HQ Administration just in time to make an extremely late entrance into the orientation auditorium. My arrival was observed by every one of the three hundred new transfers, who watched as I walked through the doors.

The wrong doors.

I discovered I was standing behind the presentation platform, directly in front of the audience. I did what anyone would do: pretended I was invisible, and hurried around the podium to find an empty seat.

The speaker of the moment, a willowy Terran woman, paused in mid-sentence, then waited patiently until I dropped into a space in the front row. She smoothly continued her speech while I tried to tell myself my face wasn't as red as it felt.

"The Colonial Militia will take into account your newly arrived status when enforcing minor ordinances, but all inhabitants are required to adhere to the Colonial Charter without exception."

I wondered why the huge room was so quiet. There were additional administrators positioned at satellite points around the speaker, translating her speech in different nonverbal forms. Yet the only sound I heard was the blond woman's voice. Why wasn't anyone using their wristcoms?

"My empathic sense tells me you're all eager to get started with your group orientation." She could read minds? That was a rare ability among Terrans. "Please remember, our origins may be different, but as a community we can achieve success." Her bright gaze swept the room. "The key is not in our diversity, but in our united strength. Thank you for your attention."

As she stepped down from the platform, I watched her. Had to admire the way she had delivered her remarks. Firm but cordial. The lady knew how to talk.

More administrators descended from the sidelines, separating the audience into smaller groups they subsequently escorted from the meeting. The only other Terran I saw present was the blondhaired speaker. She wove a graceful, steady path toward me through the thinning crowd. My interest was met by a direct smile.

"Dr. Grey Veil, welcome to Kevarzangia Two. I'm Administrator Hansen." Up close, I saw she was my senior by perhaps twenty years. Big deal, she looked great. Careful grooming gave her an unshakable sophisticated air. Hair, makeup, fingernails, all perfect. The amber tunic she wore was superbly tailored. My own hastily donned garments, still creased from packing, looked grubby by comparison.

"Sorry I'm late, Administrator," I said as I rose to my feet. "I missed the general transport, and had to walk over from housing." Actually, I'd sprinted most of the way, but she didn't need to read my mind to figure that out.

"Please, call me Ana. Our first priority will be to requisition a glidecar for you, after the orientation." She frowned at my damp brow. "Unless you'd prefer the exercise."

"No, thank you. And it's Cherijo." I enjoyed physical exertion, but not *that* much. "Where do I report from here?"

"I'll be your escort, and review the entire program

with you," Ana said. "I pulled rank on my assistant when I saw you were listed for this session."

"Really? Why?"

"I was originally assigned as liaison for a large group of Rilken construction workers." She smoothed a long-fingered hand over her hair, then her voice dropped to a conspiratorial murmur. "They are half a meter tall, have viscous skins, and invariably try to look up my skirt."

Imagining this refined woman surrounded by a hoard of small, over-inquisitive aliens made me laugh. She chuckled, too. Maybe under all that exquisite poise was someone I could relate to, after all.

One of the other administrators passed us, followed by a queue of gangly creatures draped in heavy sheets of thermal insulation. The new arrivals ogled us with arching, curious eye stems. I could imagine what they were thinking. *Hey, everybody, look—a couple of Terrans! Hideous little things, aren't they? Be careful not to get too close—they have a tendency to spit.*

An odd smile curved Ana's lips before she resumed her formal expression. "Here." She held out her hand. Sitting on her palm was a tiny, flesh-colored lump. "You'll need to wear this tympanic insert at all times outside your personal quarters."

"What's it for?" I asked as I retrieved it. Tympanic meant I had to stick it in my ear. I wasn't overjoyed at the prospect.

"Your TI translates all languages on record with our database, and provides the means to trace you to any location on the planet."

"Quite an improvement over the wristcom." I admired the small device before inserting it. No wonder the auditorium had been so quiet. It fit comfortably, and in a moment I wasn't aware of it at all. "Why don't we have these on Terra?"

"No demand." A moment of mutual silence acknowledged the absurdity of that fact. "So tell me, how was your first day on K-2?"

Awful. Depressing. Exhaustive. "Fine," I told her instead.

Ana's cheeks dimpled. "Your thoughts aren't exactly what I'd call 'fine.' "

I supplied a shrug. "It was . . . difficult."

"It can be. My first day on planet was just short of a disaster, too." Aware we were drawing even more attention, Ana added, "Let's continue this in my office. Follow me, please."

As we walked through the building, I answered her polite inquiries about my trip, refraining from making any unfavorable comments about the previous day. That kept me busy blocking thoughts about, oh, nearly every experience I'd had since walking down the docking ramp from the *Bestshot*. Being around an empath was a pain. In a few minutes we arrived in the central administrative unit.

Ana's office was large and attractively furnished. Antique chairs and side tables were an inviting note, especially the genuine fabric upholstery. The overall feeling was warmth and comfort. She had a small collection of ancient statuettes from our homeworld. The displayed artifacts reminded me of my father's collection of Navajo pottery. He was the official shaman for the Native Nations of North America. One of a zillion honorary positions he held. It got him a lot of pottery for nothing.

"They're from Hopi, Anasazi, and other tribal civilizations," Ana said. "I was born and raised in Colorado, but I traveled all over the old Southwest region to acquire them."

I admired a small sculptured version of Kokopelli, then gestured around me. "You have a gift for design."

"This is my home away from housing." She smiled with satisfied pride. "I contracted shipment of every single item I possessed before I transferred." Her eyes were expressive as she added, "Pmoc Quadrant is not known for its conveniences."

"I wish I'd thought of that," I said, recalling the regulation stanissue furnishing my own quarters. Not that I could have smuggled more of my own stuff out of Dad's house without alerting the drone staff.

"Please, make yourself comfortable." I sank into a cozy, beige armchair as Ana went around her desk. She pressed a button on her central display and requested coffee, glancing at me for my preference.

"Tea, if you have it," I said. I'd never developed a taste for the bitter brew so many Terrans loved. She added that to her order, then sat back. Her survey was calm and unhurried.

"Since you skipped this session yesterday, I gather you've found the FreeClinic and living quarters." Ana waited as a slim humanoid subordinate entered and served a tray of steaming beverages to us. "Thank you, Negilst."

"Herbal?" I asked, and Ana nodded. I savored the flavors of cinnamon and rose hip tea while the administrator sipped her dark brew. How had she managed to get homeworld provisions?

"I bartered for a kilo of real Columbian beans, among other Terran delights," she said answering my unspoken question. "It was worth a month's supply of floral concentrate."

"Perfume for coffee." I considered this absently.

"The Rilkens don't need any more stimuli than I *already* give them," she said, her lips curving slyly. "They aren't among those who consider Terrans hideous, and likely to spit."

Served me right, I thought, and chuckled. *"Touché."* I set down my server and asked the most obvious question. "How did you end up here—"

"—so far from Terra?" Ana finished for me. She reached across her desk and turned around a small photoscan, which showed her in a wedding tunic standing next to her husband. He was smiling and handsome, and not entirely human. "My mate, Elars, was refused permanent resident status."

There was a shade of old pain in her voice as she added, "He was killed ten years ago, during a transport

accident at the colony where we lived, on Trunock."
She smiled sadly. "After Elars died, I couldn't imagine
returning to Terra, and Trunock held too many memories. So here I am."

"I'm sorry for your loss." Damn my father.

"It was a long time ago." With both hands she lifted
a bulging disc holder and passed it over the desk to me.
"On to happier subjects. Here's all the hard data you'll
need to familiarize yourself with as quickly as possible.
Sociopolitical structures, historical overview, community
service criteria, the lot."

"You did say *happier*?"

She grimaced at my gentle quip. "I know, but it's mandatory for new arrivals. Please pay specific attention to
the Charter outline; it's a priority as you can't claim
ignorance of Colonial law after one-fifth revolution. Dull
and boring, I'm told, but in your line of work you're
probably used to that sort of data."

I sighed. "We doctors live for it."

"Splendid. Now, let's address your status." She inserted a disc into her desk terminal. "You're contracted
as a medical physician to the colony, assigned to the
FreeClinic Trauma Center." Ana studied the display for
a few moments. "You have quite an impressive background, Doctor."

"Cherijo. If you call me Doctor, I have to make a
chart notation."

"Of course." She skimmed through my transcripts.
"Test scores and educational records consistently off the
scale. Graduated first in all your classes. A distinguished
practice on the homeworld. Honors and awards in educational and professional areas." Her curious gaze made
me squirm a little. "You're quite the prodigy."

"I was lucky, my father is also a physician." My hands
were clenched, and I forced them to relax as I kept my
thoughts innocuous. "His guidance was responsible for
most of my achievements." If you could call what he'd
done to me guidance.

She frowned. "I see you're the only new transfer

we've been able to procure for the FreeClinic in this position for over two revolutions. I had no idea staffing was so low." She gave me an apologetic glance. "I'm afraid you're the first physician I've ever in-processed. I'll have to follow up on this." She made a note on a data pad.

"Two years?" I said, then muttered, "No wonder there's no line at Arrivals."

"This can't be right." She stared at the screen. "According to my data, Drs. Mayer, Rogan, Dloh, Crhm, and mu Cheft constitute the entire resident physician staff at this time."

"Who's staffing your clinical positions?"

She checked. "Nurse practitioners, interns, and one Omorr healer who takes care of the more . . . superstitious patients."

I shook my head. It couldn't even be called a skeleton crew.

"What's the current population level?" I was afraid to hear the answer.

Ana accessed her data base again. "As of today—74,014."

A silent indicator flashed on her desk console, and she excused herself for a moment. While she spoke to her caller, I worked it out. It was a staggering figure. I put down my tea and waited until she was finished with her call.

"You know what this means if you have any sort of serious emergency. Crisis allotment would be more than twelve thousand per doctor." I didn't know whether to be outraged, terrified, or try to signal Dhreen to get me the hell off this planet. "Ana, if there was an epidemic—"

"We'd be helpless, I know." She deactivated her terminal and proceeded briskly. "I'll make a point of bringing this to the attention of the Council. Until we procure more physicians, we'll manage." She popped the disc out, and inserted another. "I've also given you an annual projection for your schedule. Except for today, you're on Alpha shift this week."

"Days?"

"Yes. Beta is mids, Cappa swings. You'll be given time off in direct relation to patient caseload. Probably four on, one off, but I can't promise you'll always get your off days. Insufficient staffing makes schedules subject to change."

"I understand." I really couldn't demand more. "You said you'll see about personal transport for me. Who do I see if I need anything else?"

"Each housing facility has a resource manager—you'll be meeting yours today, when we stop by your building. All requests are customarily handled by them. There is the Bartermen Association, as well."

"I've heard these Bartermen mentioned. Who are they?"

"Many races prefer barter to monetary systems. A group of beings formed an organization to meet this need." A faint expression of distaste touched her features. "The organization isn't officially sanctioned, but the Militia have enough to do without chasing down unauthorized traders." Ana gazed at her coffee, now wistful. "To think, I'll have to sacrifice another liter of scent for my addiction to this. Ah, well. Now, there are other matters to discuss."

"Why do I get the feeling you've told me all the good news first?" I asked.

"You must be empathic yourself, Cherijo. There are, of course, issues I must address regarding personal conduct, community service, and the much-talked about and ever-popular subject of contractual compensation."

"Taboos, duty, and income," I said.

"Exactly. First item: All colonists' personal conduct is subject to chartered ordinance including specific guidelines against cross-cultural transgressions."

Live and let live, I thought to myself.

"You've transferred to a colony inhabited by beings from many different worlds. As with any community, neighbors and coworkers often find themselves at cross-purposes. An Irdoffa security officer, for example, may want to praise his six thousand spiritual essences at the top of his lungs."

"That's fine with me."

"Not if it happens in the adjacent quarters to yours, say, in the middle of your rest interval. If he refuses to stop, you can't go over and get into a physical altercation with him."

"I just sit there and listen to all six thousand praises?" I was skeptical. Rest intervals were scarce enough in my line of work. I was personally in favor of *Live and Let Sleep*.

"No. You file an immediate grievance with your assigned administrative officer—that's me, by the way. No matter what time of occurrence, day or night. I then personally contact the Irdoffan and charge him to cease and desist."

"If he doesn't?"

"I contact the Militia, and have him removed and charged with a Charter violation."

There's always the accidental collision with a syrin-press full of sedatives, too, I thought. "What if he does agree to stop?"

"I direct that in the future he practice his praising in one of the soundproof rooms at the Cultural Center."

"Good system," I said, "but I bet it doesn't work all the time."

"No, it doesn't. We then go to the Council, and file a formal protest. Should their ruling not be heeded—and this has only occurred twice during my time here—the transgressor's permanent residence status is revoked. Compulsory escort offplanet, etc."

"You deport them?"

"Yes. No exceptions."

"Whew!" I let out a whistle.

Ana took a sip of her coffee before continuing. "It may not seem equitable compared to the legal system on Terra, but the ordinance has virtually eliminated disputes between inhabitants."

"Who is on the Council?"

"Members are chosen at random from the population—and service is mandatory, just to note, in the event you're called to serve. Length of service is set at one cycle, about four months in Terran terms."

"No one can claim prejudice." I saw the wisdom of it.

"None have as of yet. Appeals are allowed, under extreme or extenuating circumstances. However, I have yet to see an appeal granted."

I could understand the value of simplicity with such an eclectic population. At least there was no room for corruption or misinterpretation. You broke the law enough times, you had to go. "What about my obligations as a colonist?"

"Community service provides dedicated, noncontractual stanhours and labor for the improvement and maintenance of the colony. All inhabitants are required to contribute one hundred hours per cycle."

That would roughly be a few hours a week, I calculated. "No exceptions," I said automatically, and Ana smiled.

"I think you'll enjoy this feature of life on K-2. We have a wide range of ongoing projects, from instructor positions at our academy to experimental horticultural ventures. You are allowed to choose when and how you serve your quota hours." Ana glanced at her carefully manicured hands and flexed her fingers. "I break at least two nails per service at the botanical gardens."

Somehow I couldn't envision myself doing the same. Working in gardens, not breaking nails. Doctors were incapable of maintaining a manicure for more than a day. "Sounds interesting."

"It is. Just remember to watch out for a variety of the ambulatory plants called cryscacti. They tend to bump into you without warning, and the needles can leave some nasty wounds."

So can some of the colonists, I thought, remembering

the spiny patient I'd treated the day before. "Duly noted."

"Which leaves the subject of personal compensation."

Good. I still had very little idea of how I was going to be paid. I involuntarily pictured an ever-increasing flock of small, feathered alien birds in my quarters, and Ana burst into laughter.

"Oh, no, my dear Cherijo, we won't compensate you with live animals," she said after regaining control. "I promise you that."

"Now I know I'll sleep well tonight."

Ana wiped her eyes and sighed. "I can't recall when I've enjoyed a session more," she said. "On the matter of compensation, however, I will be frank with you. The colony is still in first-stage settlement. Revenue in offworld export, the sole source of income for the Treasury, is limited, but developing."

"What about taxation?"

"There is none. The originators of this colony were unyielding on that subject. Excise Acts of any kind are prohibited by the Charter." Ana selected a disc and handed it to me. "Here is a copy of your salary schedule." She named an annual sum that wasn't going to make me the richest physician in the Quadrant, but would keep me from having to moonlight. "You will be paid in accordance with the terms of your contract, although I admit we do sometimes issue delay vouchers. The colony will exchange them at any time upon request." Her eyes gleamed merrily. "In standard credits, not poultry."

I tucked the disc in with the rest of them. "Just let me know if the policy changes."

"Absolutely." She got to her feet. "We're nearly at lunch interval, are you hungry?"

Due to the appetite-murdering confrontation with Dad, my breakfast had ended up in Jenner's belly. I nodded. I was starved.

"We'll stop at the Trading Center on the way over to

your housing unit," she said. "You have to try Café Lisette."

"Sounds intriguing."

"A former administrator's concept, teaching people to appreciate a proper croissant."

The Administration Building and adjacent structures were strategically arranged around a cultivated expanse of ground. Inventive landscaping produced a natural maze of gardens and flower beds, which encompassed a wide ring of trade establishments. The various enterprises offered everything from exotic meals to commodities from a dozen different worlds.

"The Trading Center began as an experiment, like most of our projects," Ana said. "Some of the colonists prefer self-employment, others wanted to import nonessentials from their homeworlds." She nodded to a passing group of colonists, who were enjoying what appeared to be chunks of glowing black ice cream.

We halted at an authentic-looking sidewalk café, where a number of Terran customers were dining al fresco.

"Here we are," Ana said. "Lisette Dubois' foster family owned a restaurant in Paris." I smiled at the group from my homeworld, until my attention was drawn to a particular pair of eyes.

The Terran male sat alone. Unlike the others, he didn't wear a professional garment, but instead was attired completely in black. His thick, light hair was long, framing features that were handsome but oddly inanimate. It was weird, the way he was looking at me so intently. What color were his eyes? Blue—no, grey. Or were they green?

I became distracted by a sort of daydreamlike image in my mind. I could picture that man standing beneath a towering, purple-leafed tree. A nimbus of white light surrounded him that seemed almost magnetic. His glacier eyes flared as his hands tightened over someone's wrists. Delicate, feminine wrists he held before his face . . .

I blinked once, twice. The images were gone. What the hell was that?

The man continued to stare at me. I wondered if I had a big dirt smudge on me somewhere and didn't know it. My attention veered away from him as Ana called over the café's service counter.

"Lisette? Come out and meet someone."

An Amazon walked out and planted herself before us. She was at least six feet tall, with a long mane of platinum curls falling around her like a gleaming curtain. Bejeweled gold glittered at her ears, throat, wrists, and fingers. She was big, blond, and beautiful, which gave me every right to hate her at once.

Like other merchants, she wore dark red, and it complimented her fair coloring. Her face was an artist's dream, full of smoldering mystery. Ana's impeccable style may have made me feel untidy, but compared to this woman I resembled a skinny boy.

"This is Dr. Cherijo Grey Veil. Doctor, Lisette Dubois."

"Hello," I greeted her politely.

"A doctor?" Her dark eyes swept over me with skepticism.

I nodded.

"You work at the FreeClinic?" She made it sound like I recycled waste for a living.

"Dr. Grey Veil was a surgeon back on the Terra," Ana said.

"Yes, it's safe to give me a knife." I gathered from Lisette's darkening countenance she wished that I and my sense of humor had *stayed* on the homeworld.

"I was telling Dr. Grey Veil about your incomparable croissant," Ana hurried to compliment her, evidently aware of the simmering animosity the woman projected.

"Has the Council instituted a Health Board?" a masculine voice inquired, and I saw the tall, lean owner of the unsettling eyes had joined us.

"No, Duncan, Dr. Grey Veil is a newly transferred physician. Cherijo Grey Veil, this is Duncan Reever, our chief linguist."

Lisette was not amused at the implication that her culinary skills were suspect. Combined with whatever was going on behind Reever's shuttered countenance and my own growing discomfort, Ana was receiving a bewildering cross fire of emotions. Her reaction reminded me of a homeworld transdrone during downtown rush hour.

"Duncan, go away." Lisette turned to Ana, ignoring me entirely. "Sit down, I will bring you a croissant and café au lait." She didn't spare me another word as she flounced back to her work space.

"Don't mind Lisette," Reever said. His voice, like his eyes, was as flat as a sheet of ice. "She dislikes competition."

"Competition?" Ana said, still confused.

I studied the arrangement of flora surrounding the café. I had no interest in personal dramas or obscure agendas. The flowers were pretty, though.

"Lisette considers any woman under thirty and breathing competition, Ana," he replied. "Doctor, when do you estimate you'll return to Terra?"

The man was beginning to seriously annoy me. "I don't. Shall we sit down, Ana?"

He followed and joined us at the table without invitation. Since Ana still appeared to be in a muddle, I decided to deal with him myself.

"Chief Linguist Reever, a pleasure to meet you." I smiled. Thin civility frosted each word. "Please excuse us."

"Call me Duncan." He was unperturbed and definitely not in a hurry to go. "You're not Asian, are you?"

"My patriarchal genealogy is endemic to North America," I said. "Apache, some Navajo, as well. My matriarchal lineage is listed as Caucasian."

He jumped right on that. "Listed as?"

"My father contracted a professional surrogate." It was an accepted practice on Terra; I had no reservations about revealing it. It was the direction of his questioning that made me uneasy. Just what was he getting at?

"A pity your matriarchal line is undefined."

Now I was completely lost. "My maternal ancestry— and my lack of knowledge about it—has no effect on my life," I said. "It doesn't matter."

"On this world," he said.

"I don't understand what you mean." Which was better than telling him it was none of his damn business, and to stop bothering me.

"Duncan, we do have a limited interval here . . ." Ana said. I was puzzled by her subtle deference to him. Was Reever's position so superior to her own?

The chief linguist kept staring at me. "On the fifth planet of a system two light-years away, you'd be ritually sacrificed for having those eyes."

"Really?" I faked a dry tone. "How . . . interesting."

"Yes." His countenance reflected a flicker of what might have been humor. Whatever it was, it faded quickly as he stood. "Excuse my intrusion, Ana. Doctor Grey Veil."

Lisette intersected his path as he departed, and said something inaudible. He lifted a slim, badly scarred hand and pressed it to her cheek briefly. It was a tender gesture, completely at odds with the stone-faced man. After a moment Lisette returned to her counter, and Reever gazed back at me.

What was his problem? I wondered. And why was he looking at me like that? The professional side of my brain was intrigued, as well. What had caused such severe wounds to his hands? Why hadn't the injuries been treated properly? Such scarring was virtually unknown in Terrans, due to the advances in dermal regeneration.

I barely noticed as a plate heaped with flaky pastry and a steaming server were thumped down before me. I was too busy watching the tall, silent form of the chief linguist as he turned abruptly and walked away.

"What an amazingly obnoxious man," I said once Lisette had departed. Discretion required that I not make the same observation about the owner of the café.

"I've never seen him so . . . confrontational," Ana

murmured, then seemed to remember I was new here.
"I'm sorry. Duncan is an eccentric, and usually makes a
terrible first impression. Especially on other humans."

"That charmer?" I smirked. "You're kidding."

Her eyes reproached me. "It isn't his fault. He doesn't
spend much time around his own species. He wasn't
even born on Terra."

"Oh?" That was peculiar, given my estimation of his
age. At the time of his birth, Terrans were not yet transferring to alien worlds. I took a sip from my server, and
made a face. I'd forgotten that café au lait was coffee.
"That's pretty unusual."

"His parents were two of the first Terran intergalactic
anthropologists," Ana said. "Duncan was born on a non-
League world in some distant system."

That justified his odd interest in my ethnic ancestry.
Maybe.

"According to his personnel data, he traveled exten-
sively during his childhood, until his parents discovered
his linguistic talent, and sent him back to be educated
on the homeworld. He was still in school when they were
killed during some intersystem hostilities."

I had to admit, it was a tragic tale. I thought of my
own father's manipulation, recent revelations, and spoke
without thinking. "He must have been lonely."

"Perhaps." Ana's awkward tone made me realize the
rather personal slant to my observation. "None of us
know him very well. The colony was very fortunate to
contract someone with his expertise."

"Why have a chief linguist at all?" It didn't make
much sense to me. "You already have all the native languages of the inhabitants loaded into your data base,
don't you?"

"He's a telepathic linguist. Some traders and a few
new arrivals do use languages that aren't in the system.
Duncan is invaluable in those situations. After he estab-
lishes a mental link, he can easily absorb the language,
then interpret until he programs the system translators."

"He *programs* your system?" I said, incredulous. That type of work required some serious training in itself.

"Of course. He created the linguistic data core himself."

Conceited, too, I bet, I thought before I could stop myself, then grimaced at Ana.

"He can be rather imperious," she said.

"Is he able to read thoughts, like you?" After meeting him, mine hadn't been very friendly. Maybe that was why he'd acted like that.

"Not according to his records, but I suspect he has more talent than he admits to. I can't read minds most of the time, you know. Merely thought fragments, and intense emotions." She picked up her croissant and bit into it. "This is delicious, try yours!"

Eager to change the subject, Ana went on to describe some of Lisette's other specialties. She even ordered me a server of tea when she realized I wasn't drinking the café.

The light repast was enjoyable, and the administrator refused to let me pay for the meal. At the counter Lisette stubbornly declined Ana's credits, too.

"It isn't worth my time to debit," she said, then her scowl softened. "You are good for my business." She eyed me belligerently as I offered my thanks. All I got in return was a regal nod.

"Lisette should meet my cat," I said to Ana as we walked from the café. "They'd love each other."

"You have a cat?" the other woman asked. "From Terra?"

I chuckled. "I'll have to introduce you to His Royal Highness."

Ana escorted me to the glidecar she had requisitioned for me, and we rode over to my housing unit. On the way she pointed out several aspects of the colony's outlay, conveniences, and projects.

Once inside my building, she reviewed the use of the central managerial unit, available for general purposes like nonemergency repair requests and individual climate control. Good to know where to input complaints if something broke. She then introduced me to the unit resource manager, a cheerful, corpulent alien named Lor-Etselock.

"Goodtomeetyou." He raced through his words almost faster than my TI could follow. "LetmeknowifIcanhelpyou."

Ana then stopped by my quarters so I could check on Jenner, and admired my pet so much that he deigned to allow her to stroke him a few times.

"He's gorgeous," she said. Jenner closed his eyes in silent ecstasy as Ana's long nails trailed through his fur. Kitty cat Heaven. "You know, we've discussed using the image of a pet as the colony mascot—a symbol to represent K-2. He's just what we've been looking for."

"No, please." I groaned. "He's egotistical enough already. If you start posting his image everywhere, I'll never be able to live with him."

Ana laughed, while Jenner treated me to a disdainful glare.

"You'll have to take him over to the enclosed habitat area we've set up for pet owners to use. Since he can't be allowed to run wild, it would give him a chance for some exercise. Maybe he'll make friends with some of the other colonists' pets."

"I met someone's pet last night," I said later as we left the building. "It called itself Alunthri. I wonder if Jenner would be that polite, if he could talk."

Ana slipped into the passenger's side of my glidecar. "You met one of the Chakacats. They are very congenial." She stared out at the road, and her lips thinned.

There was more she wanted to say, I guessed, and decided to probe a little farther. "How is it that such an obvious sentient is someone's *pet*?"

"They're feral on Chakara, the owners' homeworld. Once captured and trained, they are sold as domesticates. They're exported to other worlds, too."

I was shocked. "That's slavery!"

"There is some controversy about their classification,"

Ana said, her features taut. "Efforts by Council petition to have them recognized as sentient life-forms have been consistently denied."

"How many times have you petitioned the Council, Administrator?" I asked.

Ana smiled with self-mockery. "Twenty-four at last count." I stopped the glidecar at HQ Administration to let her off. "We've reviewed all items on the orientation agenda. Do you have any questions?"

"Not at the moment. I'm sure I will."

"Then, I can count on seeing you soon." Ana held out her hand, and I grasped it firmly. "Good luck, Cherijo. Please let me know if I can provide any further assistance." She winked. "And anytime you need a good listener, give me a call."

"I appreciate it, Ana."

After I returned to the FreeClinic and secured my glidecar, I walked up to the main entrance. Orientation hadn't been so bad. I had a feeling Ana and I were going to be good friends.

Now all I had to do was learn to be a FreeClinic Trauma physician. From scratch.

CHAPTER FIVE

Hsktskts Squared

During my first week on K-2, I spent my off-duty hours learning my way around the colony, and introducing myself to some of the other occupants of my housing unit. Took the tour, saw the sights, met the neighbors.

I also went through the requisite orientation data. It was lackluster reading—not that it mattered. I had yet to find a hematology abstract, for example, that didn't make me yawn. There was no such thing as the fascinating world of circulatory fluids.

As for work, I never experienced a repeat of that horrendous first shift. There were times, admittedly, that ran a close second. In the weeks that followed, I devoted my spare time to reeducating myself as a physician. Between cases I often haunted Assessment with a scanner. After my shift ended, I downloaded the readings I'd taken into the terminal in my quarters. My nights were spent studying case profiles and medical abstracts from the FreeClinic database. It was time-consuming, but it would be stupid to rely exclusively on the medsysbanks. Especially with the way Rogan kept kicking them.

I had help, too. Unlike their counterparts on Terra, the nursing staff (all non-humans) turned out to be a friendly group, and kept me out of trouble. Like the time I discovered some colonists couldn't wear TIs.

During a stroll through Assessment, I almost stepped on what looked like a Terran snail. I picked it up and went to drop it in the nearest waste receptacle. One of the nurses who was walking by at that moment grabbed my arm just in time.

"You don't want to do that, Doctor," she said, and gently removed the tiny thing from the palm of my hand.

"Why not? It's just a snail, right?"

"This 'snail' is reporting for follow-up treatment of antennae fungus," she said, then gave me a rueful grin. "And happens to be a senior supervisor in the Saprophytic Administration Group."

It could have been worse, I told myself after I'd apologized through a specially adapted wristcom to the justifiably indignant creature—*he/she/it* could have been a *medical* administration supervisor.

Rogan, having appointed himself as my arch-enemy, was as inconvenient as an incurable rash. A fragrant one at that. I spent a lot of time avoiding him. As for Dr. Mayer, I hadn't spoken with him since my first day on planet. Whenever he worked my shift, he avoided *me*.

"The chief practically built this FreeClinic with his own hands," K-Cipok, one of the charge nurses, said during a break. She was a placid, thick-framed being who would have been comfortable in a cow pasture back on Terra. "We wouldn't have half of what we use without his influence over PQSGO."

The staff saw Dr. Mayer as a sort of founding father/ superhero. Able to build FreeClinics out of salvage scrap with his bare hands. Intimidating bureaucrats with one single steely-eyed glare. Curing patients without breaking a sweat, even in surgery.

Oh, brother.

Despite Mayer's celebrated efforts, adequate treatment was continually thwarted by malfunctioning equipment, low supplies, or lack of data. I learned to like the constant challenge to my resourcefulness. It was a good thing, too. Several weeks after I began working at the

FreeClinic, I had my first experience providing treatment at *gunpoint*.

When it happened, I was the only physician on duty. Dr. mu Cheft was busy with a complicated rehydration procedure on the other side of the FreeClinic. He had been working all day on one of the less-evolved aborigines, an aquatic who had inadvertently beached herself. Dr. Dloh had already gone off duty, and Dr. Mayer had yet to arrive.

I was left covering all incoming emergencies. I had finished with my last case and was waiting for the next when the display began to chatter, audio only.

Charge nurse T'Nliqinara made a garbled report that rattled through my tympanic insert in staccato fragments: "Dr. Grey Veil . . . crisis . . . possible internal trauma . . . visible signs of seizure . . ." There was a guttural burst of sound, then my nurse made a gurgling noise. Subsequent hysterical screams in the background blocked out most of what she said before I caught the last words. "—hostages . . . terrorist . . . weapon."

Someone was out there, using weapons?

There was no way for me to apprise the Militia of the situation without routing my signal through T'Nliqinara's main Assessment console. That could provoke whoever might be holding the charge nurse and the patients hostage to resort to more violence.

The last thing I wanted to do was go out there. It was also the only thing I could do. Very slowly, making sure to keep my hands visible, I walked down the short corridor and into view. See the nice, peaceful, unarmed doctor.

Most of those awaiting treatment, along with the duty nurses and orderlies, were clustered in a panicked mass against one wall. A remote energy emitter projected a tight control field around them.

My charge nurse's four eyes rolled wildly toward me, and I saw why she had choked out her report—the business end of a pulse rifle was pressed tightly against her larynx. Terror had mottled her smooth vermilion hide with dark splotches.

On the other end of the weapon was a monster. A big, ugly green monster.

It was a sextupedal, reptilian being with a number of minor contusions on its head and upper limbs. Close to ten feet tall and weighing over four hundred kilos, it towered over T'Nliqinara. An unfamiliar metallic uniform covered a brutal frame thick with broad ropes of muscle.

Whatever it was, it meant business. One limb gripped the pulse rifle pressed to my nurse's reed-thin throat. Another held a second, smaller weapon trained on the terrified staff and patients. A third limb supported the writhing form of a smaller compatriot, who seemed to be in a state of frenzied convulsions.

I could manage this situation, I thought. Just not by fainting.

Viewport-sized, glaring yellow eyes revolved to focus on me. A toothy jaw dropped, and a serpentine black tongue lashed out. It said something that definitely wasn't, "Hi, how are you?" The language it spoke was nothing but a series of clicks, hisses, and grunts. My TI was not translating.

Somehow I had to get them away from the other patients. I suspected my looking all Terran, haughty, and intimidating wasn't going to work. Large caliber weapons and a squad of Militia probably wouldn't work.

I carefully approached the pair. Sweat began to trickle down between my shoulder blades, and my knees felt fairly rickety. Passing out was not an option, I reminded myself, and concentrated on visual assessment of their injuries. The smaller one was in trouble.

"Come with me," I said to the larger one, then used my arm to support the other side of its companion's twisting torso. I pointed back toward the Examination and Treatment area with my free hand. "This way."

Big, green, and hostile evidently understood but didn't like my suggestion. Fetid breath blasted in my face during its consequent tirade. It had a lot to say, too. I had to resort to mouth-breathing to keep my nausea under control (experience dealing with Rogan proved beneficial in this instance). Meanwhile, the smaller one kept knocking its wildly undulating limbs into me at random moments.

"Come with me," I said, holding on with one hand, emphasizing each word with the other. I suspected it had some kind of translation device, or it wouldn't have risked landing on an alien world to get help. "I can help you and your friend." I began tugging the injured one forward, and at last the other moved in tandem.

The intruder still held the weapon trained on my nurse, who was forced to scuttle backward before us. Despite its mammoth proportions, the less-injured terrorist moved with both precision and agility. Good thing, since we had to struggle together to drag the thrashing, hissing form between us back to the Severe Trauma room.

Once within the treatment room, the smaller one broke free, and started smashing our equipment with a powerful prehensile tail appendage.

Visible signs of seizure, indeed. I had to get this one strapped down before it further injured itself or started on me and the nurse. Its gun-wielding companion stepped between us and blocked my path. It made an ugly sound and jabbed the rifle into my chest. Pain blossomed instantly. I ignored it and drew myself up to every inch of my nearly five feet.

It might have a weapon, but this was *my* exam room.

"Get out of my way," I said, and controlled an urge to yelp when the rifle prodded me again. "*Suns, move!*" I pushed the rifle aside. I barely got hold of the now-sagging patient just before it collapsed. I swiveled my head to glare at the charge nurse, who was just standing there, gaping. "Get over here and help me!"

It took every muscle T'Nliqinara and I had to maneuver the patient onto the exam pad, and into restraint clasps. I turned and found the barrel of the lethal weapon inches from my nose, while the intruder spat another incomprehensible string of orders. Aware of the danger but tired of the gibberish, I held up my hand.

"If you want me to help, get this thing out of my face." Just in case I was wrong about it understanding me, I used simple hand gestures to punctuate my statement. The rifle held steady, but so did I. With great reluctance, it backed against one wall out of the way. The weapon never lowered.

"They're going to kill us," T'Nliqinara muttered next to my ear. "They're Hsktskt."

It was amazing how fast things could go from bad to awful.

I'd never seen a photoscan or composite image of a Hsktskt. However, I'd heard the stories about them. Everyone had.

The Allied League considered the Hsktskt Faction as nothing more than a bunch of sadistic, merciless killers. Their sporadic raids on distant League outposts had destroyed whole populations. Survivors were usually captured and sold as slaves. If they lived long enough to make it to the Faction's slave depots. Hsktskts, some whispered, got hungry during the long jaunts back to their home system. Very hungry.

My eyes narrowed as I reinspected the two intruders. If they were here to attack and invade K-2, they'd picked an odd way to go about it. Come to think of it, where were the rest of them?

"Hsktskt raiders," I said as I carefully worked the metallic uniform off the patient's torso. From the arrangement and type of external genitalia, this one, I saw, was a female. "I thought no assault force could penetrate the colony defense grid. Someone in Security is about to have a very bad day."

"If they're part of an assault team—" T'Nliqinara's voice broke on the words, and I gazed up at her. Her eyes were wet. "My hatchlings," she said.

We both knew what a successful invasion would entail. Children had little value on the market. Most of the adult inhabitants would probably be killed, as well. I had the cold comfort of recalling that medical personnel were almost never slain during these raids. We're *very* valuable.

"Don't think about it," I said. "Let's begin our scan, and try to get her stabilized."

I punched in diagnostics, and saw with disbelief that the Hsktskt species was not recognized by the medsysbank.

No accessible data.

That meant I had *no* medical history of the species, *no* data to use for diagnosis, and *no* idea of a course of successful treatment. No wonder verbal communication with the patient was impossible—no language base for the TIs to work from.

"This *can't* be happening to me."

T'Nliq looked over my shoulder. "Hsktskt data hasn't been made available to us," the nurse murmured bitterly. "PQSGO delayed the upload on the medical database until next cycle."

"Why did they do that?" I asked through clenched teeth.

"Nonessential data. They won't send the uploads because they don't want to send what's needed to upgrade our database and hardware. They use the same excuse every cycle."

I wondered what excuse they'd come up with to explain how a large chunk of our colonists got slaughtered because they were too cheap to send us a few computer components. "Remind me to complain to someone important when this is over."

"It wouldn't have helped anyway. No one knows much about them, except that the Hsktskts butcher anything that moves," T'Nliqinara said.

"It might have its *own* sort of TI," I murmured. The nurse hissed in a fearful breath. "Steady, T'Nliq. Read me its stats."

The patient's vital signs were fluctuating wildly, but body temperature was barely 18 degrees Celsius. Far too cold for a life-form dependent on outside stimulus for temperature regulation.

"Apply thermal packs," I said, then turned to the intruder, locking gazes once more. "I need to signal my associate."

The Hsktskt waved the weapon in my face, and hissed furiously.

"Look," I said, all smiling congeniality. "If you want to shoot me, be my guest. If you want me to help your friend, however, I need to communicate with my colleague."

It did have a translator device—as I said the words, I noticed its gaze went to the patient, then over to the central display panel. I almost knew what it was thinking—would I risk our lives just to set off some kind of trap, rather than help them?

It made a curt gesture with the weapon.

Quickly I sent a brief signal to Dr. mu Cheft. He wasn't pleased by the interruption: the rehydration process was always tricky. I quickly related the details of the patient's symptoms.

"No idea, Dr. Grey Veil," mu Cheft said. "Do whatever the *suns* you can."

I was on my own, as usual. Or maybe not. By now someone should have released the staff from that control field, I thought, and rerouted my signal to Assessment. I was in luck, a nurse answered. Quietly I requested a linguist who spoke Hsktskt be sent back.

"You want a what?" the nurse said incredulously. "Doctor, we've got a whole platoon of Militia out here!"

"*Space* the damn Militia," I told her in a whisper. "Get me a translator *now,* please, nurse, before this extremely upset Hsktskt decides to get a second opinion."

I had to keep busy until I could effectively communicate with the patient. I played doctor. Checked the useless display once more. Frowned slightly. Made a chart notation about nothing. Nodded wisely. Calibrated an empty syrinpress. Looked thoughtful. I went through the motions, hoping the armed Hsktskt wouldn't realize I was stalling. I rather liked my chest without a big hole in it.

When I ran out of faked tasks, I attempted to treat the larger Hsktskt's lacerations, but it shoved me back and wouldn't let me touch it. Fine, I thought. Be that way.

I drew and analyzed a sample of circulatory fluid from the smaller alien. The scanner readings meant nothing to me. With a great deal of impatient key tapping, I was able to force the medsysbank's program to extrapolate a broad-based diagnosis from available readings.

Toxic response to hypothermia, the readout belatedly offered.

"This piece of junk"—I nodded toward the console—"says the patient is too cold, T'Nliq."

My nurse gave a snort through her three nostrils that distinctly expressed her opinion.

Somehow I had to get the patient stabilized. I mentally ran through cases I'd studied. There was that case of a cold-blooded being who had been treated for hypothermia after a shuttle accident, I recalled. The physiologies were similar. The one with the rifle was starting to make those curt motions again. I was out of time.

I filled a syrinpress with the adrenadaptive that had been used to treat the other patient. Hopefully, I thought as I administered the drug, it wouldn't *kill* the patient at once.

My theory worked. Within a few minutes the patient's vital signs began to level out, and the thermal packs brought her temperature up quickly. It was then I noticed an odd, undulating distention in her lower abdominal cavity. Something I'd read about the evolutionary aspects of highly evolved reptilian life-forms from an old medical journal came back to me. A comparative study revealed some were capable of mammalian proliferation—

"Sterile field, *stat*!"

At once the containment generators isolated me with the patient in an impenetrable bubble. Unfortunately, this locked out T'Nliqinara and the other Hsktskt in the process. The intruder charged at the glowing wall around us, and bounced off as a painful bioelectric charge repelled him.

I ignored him. I barely felt the vacuum from the air replacement unit as I sprayed a skin seal over the Hsktskt's lower limbs. After I masked and gloved, I searched for the aperture I had to find.

Gingerly, I inserted the tips of two fingers into a natural breach in the octagonal green scales just above the patient's lower appendages, and promptly received a nice, sharp *bite*. I snatched back my fingers, and swore lightly. I had, nonetheless, reached a unshakable diagnosis.

My patient was about to *deliver* whatever bit me.

The translator from MedAdmin chose that moment to show up. The small, harried-looking humanoid was in such a rush that he didn't notice the warrior leveling the pulse rifle at his skull.

"Language used by patient is Hsktskt," I was told.

"We know. What's she saying?" I asked with thin patience.

As he began interpreting the hisses, he finally noticed the other Hsktskt and the weapon he held. Terrans weren't the only beings who turn pale with fear, I saw. The quaking translator's stutter filtered through the low static of the containment barrier. "T-This f-f-female must b-bear her y-young at this t-t-time."

I nodded, and tried to reign in my ever-growing irritation. "I gathered that much. Why was she so cold?"

The small humanoid relayed this, and my expectant mother groaned something miserably.

"The female promises that this male, referencing to him with explicit profanity, will meet his demise at her hands in a particularly cruel and protracted manner." The translator risked a nervous glance at the expectant father.

"I won't stop her," I said. "But that doesn't answer my question."

The larger Hsktskt shifted his weapon from one claw-clutch to another, then hissed at the terrified interpreter.

"This male indicates he tried to force this ungrateful female into cryogenic suspension to prevent premature emergence of the young."

"That would explain his contusions," I said. "He tried to put her in the freezer, and she thought it was a really bad idea."

The male Hsktskt glowered at me as this was relayed. I turned my attention to the female, and tried to look sympathetic. It was rather difficult to do that when my patient was looking at me as though deciding which end to start gnawing on first.

"New fathers always seem to panic at the worst possible moment," I said prudently. I had no wish to meet *my* demise. As it was, things couldn't get much worse. "Does she know how close she is to delivering?"

The patient rattled off an impatient succession of hisses.

"Only minutes remain. Anticipate at least four newborn young, and isolate each upon emergence." The small humanoid coughed, then turned slightly green. "If the young are not immediately separated from all other life-forms, the result will be . . . carnage."

Things just went from awful to horrible.

"T'Nliq, I'll need a half-dozen quarantine cribs, reinforced with plasteel panels and inhibitor webbing." I checked the birth aperture gingerly; the first of the young was almost crowned. My patient began to make a high, keening sound. "In about a minute." I deactivated the containment field.

The pulse rifle was back in my face.

"This male wants to know why the female is crying out," the translator said.

"It hurts," I replied. I wasn't going to admit I had no idea if pain was a natural occurrence during Hsktskt childbirth.

The Hsktskt male responded furiously.

"This male believes you are causing the female's distress." The humanoid's voice was strained. "He thinks—"

"It's okay." I saw what the big, mean bastard thought as he fingered the firing mechanism of his rifle. Leaning close to the Hsktskt male, I smiled nastily. "Tell him if he kills me, he'll have to deliver the young by *himself*."

He was told. The weapon was retracted. Slowly.

T'Nliqinara had in the meantime quietly ordered the equipment I needed. It arrived with two orderlies who wisely stayed outside the threshold. I nodded my appreciation toward the nurse, then turned back to my patient. She was screeching in real agony now. The gap in her scales widened, then peeled back as the crown of the newborn bulged out.

"Here we go." I slid my fingertips just inside the aperture, cradling the small skull. "T'Nliq, run a continuous scan on her vitals." The rest was up to the female, and her instincts. "Tell her to bear down—now!"

The first of her young made an abrupt and rather messy entrance into the world. Like most scaled lifeforms, it was a miniature version of its parent. It also had a mouthful of very well-developed, keen-edged teeth, which it bared at me as it took its first inhalation.

"Hello, little one." I smiled down at the small Hsktskt in my arms as I severed its umbilical connection to the mother. It was a male. He hissed furiously and struggled as T'Nliqinara suctioned the excess mucous from his mouth. "Just as cheerful as your dad, I see."

I quickly placed the newborn into one of the isolation cribs. My wrist received a sharp bite in the process, but I had no time to do more than swivel and assist with the next emerging sibling.

The delivery continued in this rapid, dangerous manner. The newborn were vicious, poised to kill from the moment of consciousness. I knew it was a survival instinct, but it didn't make my job any easier. I wrestled three more young from the birth aperture before my patient paused as if to gather the final dregs of strength.

This struggle culminated in a horrible scream and the expulsion of the last infant.

She was nearly twice the size of the others. Her calm, buttercup-colored eyes regarded me solemnly before the tiny head lunged. My aching arms protested as I fought to keep her from tearing out my throat. The little darling was strong, too. T'Nliqinara wrenched her away just in time, and thrust the squirming bundle into a crib. After I took a deep, bracing gulp of air, I turned back to the dazed female.

"Congratulations." I tried to smile and began to clean up the mess of body fluids and birth sac remnants. "It's three boys and two girls."

That was when I felt the cold rim of the rifle barrel nudge the side of my head. At the same time, Dr. mu Cheft walked in.

He was short for a native, only seven and a half feet tall, and his turquoise hide was constantly flaking from spending so much time out of the water. His recessed eyes rotated toward the cribs. Dr. mu Cheft, like the translator, didn't at first register the fact that the proud parents were savage killers or that Daddy had a rifle pressed to my skull.

"Dr. Grey Veil," he greeted me cheerfully as he beamed down at the infants. His rehydration must have gone well, I guessed. "Ah, a delivery. How enchanting. We don't often see such happy events in Trauma, do we?"

"Not like this," I said.

Mu Cheft started to reach in one of the cribs and pat one of the quints. Luckily, Nurse T'Nliqinara grabbed his flipper and yanked it back before he lost some flesh. He sobered at the sight of all those small, effective teeth, and the further realization that the proud father was holding a weapon on me.

"Perhaps not quite as *enchanting* as I thought," the native 'Zangian said.

"Daranthura." I waved my hands over the mother to distract the father, who seemed to be ignoring mu Cheft anyway. "Get the hell out of here." My colleague slowly backed out of the exam room.

Daddy hissed at me again.

"This male wants to know if the brood is healthy," the translator said.

"Yes, they appear to be." I eyed the Hsktskt down the length of the weapon. "Tell him to get this stupid thing away from my head."

The translator made a diplomatic interpretation, and relayed the Hsktskt's terse reply as the rifle was lowered. "This male commands you to complete treatment swiftly."

"I plan to, rifle or no rifle." New fathers were so predictable, I thought. Once all the excitement was over, they went right back to strutting.

The female Hsktskt spoke up.

The translator smiled. "This female asks to know about her young."

Through the translator I reported the condition of the infants once more, and received a rough smack on the shoulder from her. A gesture of Hsktskt gratitude. It hurt, but I smiled anyway.

"The female wishes to express her recognition of your assistance," the interpreter told me. "Your name will be used to designate the dominary, or last-born, as honor to you."

The male made what I personally interpreted as a thoroughly disgusted sound.

"Thank you." I observed a shadow moving across the opposite wall of the corridor outside. "I think we have a more important issue to discuss now." I addressed the male Hsktskt. "You know the Militia has arrived."

The translator stifled a groan before he interpreted the furious reply. "This male indicates that defense forces for this colony are less than worthy of his attention."

"Worthy or not, we'd better negotiate safe passage for Daddy here to get off this planet." The Hsktskt's huge eyes narrowed to slits. "Surprised?" I asked as I completed my postpartum scans. "I'm only interested in preventing any further violence. From anyone."

"This male agrees," the translator told me. "The female and the young will accompany him."

"I don't know." I eyed the exhausted mother and five cribs uneasily. "She's been through a lot, and the newborns need individual examinations."

My advice was ignored, of course.

I really couldn't blame the Hsktskt for taking his family with him. Security was outraged that their defense grid had been so easily compromised. Not to mention how all the other patients felt, being terrorized and held hostage. No, it was better that the entire family got off-planet in a hurry.

Thanks for visiting K-2, please don't come again.

The Militia swiftly agreed to the terms I negotiated on behalf of the Hsktskt. Everyone was eager to see the intruders depart as quickly as possible, afraid that detaining them might provoke a direct invasion by the Faction.

T'Nliqinara, the translator and I escorted the Hsktskt group to the exterior of the facility. We had put the quints in a cargo unit with individual shielded compartments, to prevent them from eating each other. The weary female walked alongside the young, a curious sort of contentment illuminating her harsh features.

The small, heavily armed shuttle the Hsktskt had used to penetrate the security grid lay just beyond the back entrance of the FreeClinic. The male Hsktskt kept his weapon trained on us as he backed up to the shuttle, shielding his family with his huge body.

"Are they alone? Are there more of them?" one of the Militia asked me, and I shrugged as I watched them board the vessel.

"I have no idea. Do *you* want to ask him?" I pointed at the male, who had paused on the boarding ramp and turned to look back at me. He stared at me for several long moments, then disappeared inside the vessel.

"You're welcome," I said.

Dr. Mayer appeared at my side as I watched the shuttle fire its engines and rise rapidly to disappear into the emerald sky.

"Dr. Grey Veil." His shrewd eyes reflected the usual intense dislike and a new glimmer of outrage. He wasn't going to slap me on the back and thank me for a job well-done, I could see that. "Come with me."

I would have preferred to deliver another batch of Hsktskt killer-babies.

The chief had a small, sterile office in the MedAdmin section of the facility. I sat down in front of his desk and resisted the urge to defend myself before he said anything. I wouldn't have to wait long.

"I want to know precisely what happened."

I gave him the particulars of the incident in the same terms I would have made a chart entry. When I was finished, it only took ten seconds for him to start in on me.

"What did you think you were doing?"

"Treating a patient," I said. "Under dangerous conditions."

"You recognized both as Hsktskt assassins, didn't you?"

"I recognized a female in the final stages of labor. The male threatened us only to insure she would get proper treatment."

He made a disgusted sound. "I want a complete report on this incident before your next shift, Doctor." I nodded. "According to Militia reports, no one was injured during this attack."

I wasn't going to show him *my* bruises. "It wasn't an attack."

"You may thank whatever God you worship for that, Doctor."

"I'm delighted no one got hurt," I said. "Everything I did was an effort to make sure no one would, Dr. Mayer."

"Is that what you think?" His eyebrows lifted. "Your

reckless actions today *endangered* the lives of the FreeClinic staff, the patients, and every other inhabitant of this colony." He placed his hands on the edge of the empty desk, and I noted the whiteness around his knuckles. Gee, he was upset. "Colonial Security will conduct a full investigation of your role in these events, subject to established statutes under the Charter." The Chief didn't have to say it was at his request. He wasn't finished, either. "You gambled with too many lives today, Doctor."

"What else could I do?"

"There were any number of means at your disposal to disable both of those terrorists. Even a medtech student knows a syrinpress can be used as a weapon."

I thought about the number of times I could have been killed that day, and what Dr. William the Almighty Mayer would have done in my place. I looked away from my boss, and spotted a small, old-fashioned holographic document hung on the wall beside me.

" 'I will follow that method of treatment which, according to my ability and judgment, I consider for the benefit of my patients, and abstain from whatever is deleterious and mischievous, I will give no deadly medicine to anyone if asked, nor suggest any such counsel,' " I read out loud.

The chief's eyes darted over to his copy of the Hippocratic Oath, the pledge that all Terran physicians swore to uphold. His lips were getting white now.

"Excuse me, Dr. Mayer." I got to my feet and strode out of his office. And walked promptly into Duncan Reever.

It was, well, *unnerving.* I let out a yelp and jumped back. He registered my response by arching a light eyebrow.

"Dr. Grey Veil," he greeted me, no inflection coloring his voice. I shoved my way past him and marched down the corridor. "Doctor?"

I didn't expect him to trail after me as I strode out the main entrance. K-2's twilight was deepening from olive to emerald, while the moon ring glowed like a broken necklace of pearls. I paused, glanced over my shoulder and made an exasperated sound. For a telepath, Reever was incredibly dense.

"What do you want, Chief Linguist Reever?"

"I'll walk with you," he said. Like he was conferring some kind of significant honor.

"I'm not *going* anywhere," I said, then walked off. He kept pace with me until I lost the last of my patience. I halted and turned on that fathomless gaze. Managed to avoid shouting. Barely. "Reever, go away!"

"You're walking in circles around the FreeClinic," he felt he had to point out.

"I *know*."

"You're upset."

"There's a *keen* observation." I pushed a handful of dark hair from my eyes. "Anything else?"

"One of my subordinates was present during your treatment of the Hsktskt raiders," he said.

"Yes, of course." I had forgotten about the translator, and now felt a little ashamed of my outburst. "He was wonderful."

"I'm pleased to hear that."

"More than wonderful. To be honest, our success was due in large part to his excellent skills and performance under adverse conditions. You should give him a raise in compensation." There, I'd made the appropriate comments. He would have to be satisfied with that.

He wasn't. "It was reported that the female Hsktskt named you as designate to the dominary infant."

"So?"

"You invited a significant honor on yourself."

"Invited?" I was incredulous. "Believe me, Chief Linguist, I didn't ask her to name her kid after me."

"In Terran terms, such a distinction would rank with that of a *godmother,* Doctor."

My foot began tapping the ground. "I'm still missing a point here. If there is one."

"Being that infant's designate virtually guarantees you'll never be taken as a Hsktskt slave."

What was he trying to insinuate? That I—"For God's sake, Reever, I wasn't given a choice at the time!"

"Weren't you?" he asked. "You brought five more Hsktskt killers into existence."

First Mayer, now this. "I treated a *female giving birth,*" I told him. "Under extreme duress, I might add, but that doesn't matter."

"It doesn't?"

"No, Reever. It doesn't." I moved in. "I would have treated her no matter what happened. Threat or no threat. While the colony was under attack. Even if her mate began executing the others." I made sure I had his full attention, our eyes locked, my face a mere inch from his. "With my last breath, Reever, *I would have delivered those five Hsktskt killers.*"

The chief linguist nodded as though satisfied. He lifted his hand, and trailed the tips of his fingers over my rumpled hair. The gesture baffled me. "You would be unyielding to the end."

"Leave me alone, Reever."

I stalked off, and was relieved to see he didn't follow me. It took a few moments to collect myself before a nagging inconsistency emerged from my muddled thoughts. Something the charge nurse had said during the delivery of the Hsktskt quints.

"No one knows much about them," T'Nliqinara had stated. So how did Duncan Reever know all this stuff about their "godmothers"?

PART TWO:

Application

CHAPTER SIX

Bartermen

Colonial Security did investigate the incident involving the two Hsktskt intruders. Thoroughly. For an entire day it seemed like anyone with a security clearance took a shot at grilling me. After all that, it was officially concluded that no Charter violation could be cited against me.

My clearance didn't sway the popular opinion held by enforcement and defense officials. Namely, that my actions during the treatment of the Hsktskt female had been reckless.

"Doctor, you medical people aren't trained to operate under hostage situations," one of higher-ranking Militia felt obligated to point out. "You should have left the decisions to the on-site negotiator."

"I'm trained to deal with crisis," I said, a distinct edge to my voice.

"Let me give you some advice that saves lives," the man had the audacity to say. "The next time you're faced with a terrorist threat, make Militia notification your first priority. Then do *exactly* as you're told."

Ana Hansen, who had come along as my personal adviser, chose that moment to pull me to my feet. She was strong, and fast, too. Before I could reply, I found myself unceremoniously pushed toward the door.

"Thank you, and please excuse us," Ana said as she

practically dragged me out of the office. Once we'd left the Security building, she released me and exhaled with audible relief.

"I wasn't going to hit him," I told her, rubbing the spot she had gripped so tightly. "Not very hard, anyway."

"You know, Cherijo, for a doctor, you have an impressive temper."

"Under ordinary conditions, *I don't*," I said. "It only comes out during certain situations—like when I'm being accused of criminal negligence. Who did that jerk think he was? I was just doing my job!"

"I believe you did the best you could in a very dangerous situation," Ana said. "That's all anyone can be expected to do."

"Not according to that thick-skulled cretin—"

"—who would not have appreciated you casting doubts on the legitimacy of his birth. Or learning of your painfully low estimation of his intelligence. Or knowing the exact anatomical location on his body you thought would best accommodate his advice," Ana said.

"I thought you only picked up thought *fragments*," I said, and she gave into her laughter at last.

"My dear, an inorganic rock formation could have read what you were thinking while he was lecturing you."

Our path intersected with one of the Terran engineers in my housing unit, Paul Dalton. By this time I had become acquainted with several of my neighbors, but conflicting work schedules kept me from forming genuine friendships. Paul, I noticed, was with someone I hadn't seen before.

"Friends of yours?" Ana asked, following my gaze.

"The Terran lives down the corridor from me. I don't recognize the tall blue one."

The unfamiliar humanoid wore a pilot's flight suit. He was a massive, well-muscled male with the most startling sapphire-colored flesh. Straight sable hair fell around strong features in lustrous wings. His eyes were completely white, no iris or pupil discernible beneath the pearly corneas. Yet from the way he was looking at me, I knew he wasn't blind. I tried not to stare back.

Paul hailed me. "Hey, Doc!" With unremarkable coloring and an average build, the Terran engineer appeared ordinary at first glance. Until he opened his mouth. Paul had a great sense of humor, and was so popular with our neighbors I sometimes wondered if he really *was* Terran.

"I think you're about to find out who he is."

I glanced at Ana, who was beaming with evident satisfaction. She'd been nagging me lately to spend some off-duty time "enjoying myself." Before I could stop her, she patted my shoulder and started off.

"Must go, have some work to catch up on back at the office."

"Ana—"

She turned and made one of those graceful little waves of hers that I could never imitate, even if I practiced for years. "We can get together later this week."

"Forget what you're thinking," I told her as I tugged the edge of my tunic straight. "Right this minute."

"Who said I'm thinking anything at all?"

She didn't fool me. "I'm too busy."

"My dear, no one could ever be *too busy* for a male who looks like that!" She smiled at the approaching men before skipping off to her glidecar. Some friend she was, abandoning me like this.

I told myself I'd only stop long enough to exchange greetings, and satisfy my curiosity about the blue-skinned pilot's identity.

"Long day patching up the sick?" Paul asked.

"Not today." I grimaced, then teased him. "There was an interesting case I had a few days ago, though. A Terran with a strained larynx. Reminded me of you."

"I love it when you talk anatomy to me," Paul said with a mock leer. "You'll have to teach me all the good words."

"I've been too busy studying structural engineering," I said, deadpan. "I want *your* job."

That made Paul's companion chuckle softly. I looked up at him, kinking several neck muscles in the process.

"Hello, I'm Cherijo Grey Veil," I held out my hand, palm-up, as I'd learned was the least offensive gesture of friendship on K-2 to all species. It was swallowed in a large, six-fingered grasp. His handshake was firm but careful.

"Kao Torin," he said, his voice deep and resonate. He made a formal gesture with the other hand that must have been some type of accompanying greeting. The big pilot had noticed my surreptitious curiosity, for he added, "From Joren, in the Varallan Quadrant."

"Watch out for this one, Kao," Paul said. "She'll demand your medevals, if you let her."

"I'm still reading up on the aberrations in yours, Paul," I said, and smiled up at the big pilot. "It's a pleasure to meet you."

"You're off duty now?" Kao inquired, and I nodded. "Would you join us for a meal interval?"

Paul groaned, rolling his eyes to the upper atmosphere. "I can't take him anywhere," he said. At my arched brow he laughed, and Kao Torin assumed a long-suffering demeanor. "This fly boy," my neighbor said, "is responsible for breaking more hearts in the Pmoc Quadrant than I am."

"You're in luck, then," I said, giving Kao a grin. "I'm a surgeon, I can repair them."

Both men laughed, and we agreed to continue on together to the Trading Center, and dine at Café Lisette. Over the past weeks I had made slow but steady progress with Lisette herself by my repeated patronage. When we arrived, she greeted me with a sort of distant benevolence.

Like Jenner, she wasn't a pushover. You may not have liked it, but you had to respect it.

Over fragrant servers of real wine (produced from K-2's extensive vineyards) and deep bowls of Lisette's delectable version of coq au vin, we chatted easily. The discussion revolved around a prevalent topic among colonists: What do you miss the most from the homeworld?

"A real beef steak," Paul said. "With barbecue sauce and smoked legumes on the side."

"I'd trade everything I own for a tub of vanilla ice cream, a barrel of hot fudge, and a spoon," I said, and added a wistful sigh. "What about you, Kao Torin?"

"There is something I do yearn for," he said as he contemplated his goblet of amber wine. "My ClanMother's morning breads. I never properly appreciated her light touch with baking as a youth."

After I prompted him, he went on to elaborate about his homeworld. Joren was situated thousands of light-years away, in the distant Varallan Quadrant. I'd never heard of the system or quadrant, much less his planet. Kao's people had evolved from what he described as nomadic warrior clans into a technically advanced race of insatiable explorers.

"My race enjoys exploration. Jorenians are scattered throughout this sector and many others." He made another of his curious hand gestures, and I wondered if his language was part corporeal. Not even Ana could do something that fluidly harmonious. "My HouseClan travels the fringe systems, where there is more unknown to us."

"You must like the challenges," I said. "Are most of your people explorers, or pilots?"

"Pilots, course plotters—any helm position is favored. We have a natural sense for navigation, which is useful when instrumentation fails."

"Do Jorenians customarily contract their services?"

"No, we have our own vessels. We contract our services as part of—" He searched for a term, then asked, "Introduction to other species?" I smiled and nodded. "It can be as stimulating as exploration." Kao looked thoughtfully at my tunic.

I glanced down, too. "Did I dribble something on myself?"

"The colors you wear are that of my HouseClan." He

briefly touched on the complex use of colors by Jorenians to differentiate kindred, rank, and occupation.
"Your HouseClan—people—are born healers?"

I frowned for a moment as I thought of my father.
"A few are, but it takes years of education before we
qualify as physicians on Terra. The same way Paul studied to become an engineer."

Kao shot a sardonic look at Paul. "Paul claims he
never had to study." He went on to describe some amusing anecdotes about Paul when he first transferred to
K-2, then Paul retaliated with some rather outrageous
accounts of Kao's own reputation.

"Truce!" I threw up my hands, and laughed. "Are you
sure you two are *friends*?"

Kao nodded solemnly, while Paul laughed.

"Doc, I wouldn't *think* of getting on his bad side,"
the engineer said. "Jorenian warriors are notorious for
pursuing their enemies. To the end of the galaxy, if need
be. I won't tell you what they do when they *catch* them."

I didn't like hearing that. "Your people still practice
offensive warfare, Pilot Torin?"

"No, Healer. Most of my people are trained as warriors, but only in defense of the HouseClan. We are a
very peaceful species."

"Don't let him fool you, Doc," Paul said. "The reason
they're so peaceful is no one in their right mind would
ever cross a Jorenian."

"That is the right of—" Kao began in serious tones,
then realized he was being needled. "My friend reminds
me I must improve my knowledge of verbal banter."

"Stick around, fly boy," Paul said. "I'm an authority."

We finished our meal shortly after that, and it was
with real regret that I said it was time for me to go.
Again, I received the friendly clasp of that large blue
hand on mine, while the dark head dipped down so that
Kao's words were for my ears alone.

"Thank you for saving me from hearing all of Paul's
EngTech tales for the fifteenth time," the pilot said. His

grasp subtly changed to a near-caress. "I would like to see you again, Healer Grey Veil."

When you've spent most of your life with your nose buried in medical books, or involved with patients, you forget how other people see you. Apparently, he saw me as an attractive female.

"Perhaps we might share another meal—alone?" Kao asked. I could see how he got his reputation. By breathing.

"If you can find me off duty," I said with a quick grin. I didn't add "good luck" to that; it wouldn't have been polite. I didn't want to get my hopes up, either. "Until then, Kao Torin."

The white eyes crinkled with his slow smile. "Walk within beauty," he said.

I certainly walked within a daze as I headed for home.

Lor-Etselock was standing just outside my quarters as I strode down my corridor. He was perspiring despite the excellent climate control, and his chubby face appeared almost haggard with anxiety. The moment he saw me, he began trudging toward me.

"DoctorIregretIcouldnotrefusethementrance," he said, and I frowned as I tried to follow his incomprehensible babbling.

"Regret you could not—what?" I held up one hand as he opened his mouth. "Slowly, please, Lor. My TI will blow out my eardrum."

"Forgiveme." He took a deep breath. "Bartermen arehere toappraise. In yourquarters."

The infamous Bartermen? In my quarters? To appraise what?

The door to my quarters was partially ajar, and I walked past the fearful resource manager and nudged the panel aside. Within the room was a small group of aliens who were methodically searching through my personal belongings. I heard a muffled yowl of outrage and stepped inside.

"What the—"

My appearance made no effect on the culprits, who were all dressed in identical charcoal garments that cloaked their forms. Short abbreviated hoods covered what seemed to be square-shaped, elongated skulls. Jenner shot past me and scrambled under my sleeping platform.

"How did you get in here?"

One of the group turned at the sound of my voice.

"Appraisal is nearly completed."

"Hey!" I followed him as he moved away, and prodded his shoulder. I was almost sorry when he turned around. From the shadows of the hood, gaunt features stretched under ashen skin into a parody of a smile. I'd seen more attractive cadavers. A musty, damp odor rose from the rustling robes. Smelled better corpses, too.

All he said was, "Ready yourself."

"What are you people doing here? Why are you handling my belongings?" Once more I prodded the being, who was ignoring me. "You—explain this!"

"DoctorIcanexplaintoyou—" Lor had followed me in, and put a damp hand on my arm. I shook it off.

"No, Lor, this one is going to explain it to me, aren't you?" I leaned forward, and snatched away the article of my clothing he was fingering. In shock, he recoiled away from me. Like *I* was the problem here.

The others—I counted five—assembled quickly around us in a circle.

"Appraisal has been completed." The appointed spokesman sounded smug. "Barter?"

"Barter what?"

"They wantto tradewith youDoctor," Lor said. "Forwhat youbrought tothecolony."

"You want to *barter* with me?" I asked, incredulous. I scanned the six faces. "Don't you wait until you're invited?"

"Bartermen do not wait."

"How about making an appointment?"

"Bartermen do not make appointment."

It was time to see if Bartermen knew how to get out,

I decided. I pointed to the door. "I don't want to barter with you. Please leave."

"Appraisal is minimal," the Bartermen's spokesman said. "Assortment of clothing, medical articles, live domesticated animal. Barter only for entirety."

I think I was being insulted. "Leave, now."

"Dr. Cherijo Grey Veil, *minimal appraisal*."

Like I should care. "Okay, I want names. Right now!"

"Bartermen."

"Your *names* are Bartermen?"

Lor decided to intervene again. His plump hand trembled against my arm. "Namesare notused Doctor. Against theirdoctrine."

"Lor, stay out of this." I surveyed the group once more, speaking slowly and clearly so they couldn't claim later that there had been some terrible misunderstanding. "I'm telling you for the last time to exit these premises immediately."

"Bartermen remain, complete barter."

I didn't have to surrender my privacy to a bunch of grubby little opportunists looking to turn a credit through intimidation. No, sir. I whirled around and went to my display panel. "HQ Administrative Office, Ana Hansen."

Ana's face appeared instantaneously.

"Cherijo? What—"

"Ana, there is a group of six individuals in my quarters calling themselves Bartermen. They have evidently entered illegally and sorted through my possessions. They now demand I barter or trade what I own."

"Oh, no."

I wasn't through. "I've asked them repeatedly to leave. They refuse. Send some Militia over here, will you? File a Charter violation complaint against them for me while you're at it."

Lor nearly fainted.

The Bartermen conferred among themselves as Ana advised me to stay put and say as little as possible. Within minutes two of the Militia stood inside the doorway. The spokesman for the grey-cloaked aliens looked at me again.

"Barter is *not* violation of Charter," he said.

"Violation of my personal space without my specific invitation or consent is. Try reading section seven, paragraph fourteen, lines three through eight." I nodded to the Militia officers. "Remove them, please."

The Bartermen stepped forward collectively as their speaker said, "Appraisal may have been under-estimated."

"*Appraisal* was not requested," I said. The Militia looked at each other uneasily. "Do you officers have a problem with my grievance?"

"No, Doctor."

"Then, clear them out of here. Now."

The Bartermen speaker decided to try to persuade me one last time. "Considerable appraisal for one item, live animal domesticated. We will barter equal exchange."

"Get out!" I shouted.

They filed out silently, while Lor gibbered something and scurried after them. The Militia officers gazed at me with something like horror mixed with admiration.

"Well?" I demanded.

"Well, Doctor," one of them said. "They *are* Bartermen."

"What is *that* supposed to mean?" I threw up my hands. "They have free license to go through my personal possessions? They can just walk in here and—" Ana chose that moment to appear in the doorway.

"Oh, dear," she said as she surveyed the mess. "There has been a huge misunderstanding."

"You've got that right," I said. "Who do these Bartermen think they are? They forced their way in—"

She shook her head. "Lor let them in."

"What?"

"They were acting on a filed trade summons. I was notified almost immediately after your signal by the Association about the situation."

"A trade what? What are you talking about?"

Ana's shoulders shook suspiciously as she cleared her throat, then gave me a careful look. "A trade summons. Bartermen have an extensive and rather complicated communication system set up within the colony."

"In words of two syllables or less, Ana."

She pressed her lips together, then went on. "I believe you stated that you would trade everything you own for some ice cream, fudge sauce, and a spoon?"

I related the bizarre incident to K-Cipok, who was my charge nurse on duty the next day, and she substantiated what Ana Hansen had told me about the aggravating practices of the Bartermen.

"And they just barge in on people like that?" I asked.

"I'm surprised they didn't file a complaint with the Council," K-Cipok told me. "They don't like to be turned down, especially on a first bid."

"They're definitely fanatics," I said, recalling their single-minded behavior.

She made a noncommittal sound. "In your view. Some cultures consider procurement of trade items as important as, say, you Terrans view daily cleansing rituals."

"But to base all that on what I said"—trying to explain my side of it had me frustrated. "It was just an expression. You know, wishful thinking."

K-Cipok made a low thrumming sound so much like a bovine moo I had to swallow a giggle. "I wouldn't think out loud anymore, Doctor."

The next case was rushed in from Assessment, and my humor dissipated at once. "Chart?"

"Can't account for it," the harassed orderly manning the gurney said.

The patient displayed evidence of severe internal trauma. Her abdomen was taut and hot to the touch, her vital signs thready. Shock was going to kill her unless we moved quickly.

"Let's shift her."

K-Cipok's spindly limbs, which appeared incapable of keeping her heavy torso erect, hefted the patient from the gurney to the exam pad without effort. The orderly made a hasty exit, and when I looked at the contorted face, I went still.

"It can't be."

She was the same Orgemich female Phorap Rogan had diagnosed with gastroenteritis during my first shift at the FreeClinic. I scanned her once. That was all it took.

She didn't have an upset stomach anymore.

"Prep her for surgery, stat," I said to the nurse, then signaled Dr. Dloh, who was working that shift with me. "I've got an emergency here; I have to operate."

"I'll notify Azzezzment and cover," he replied. "The Orgemich they juzt brought in?"

"Yes. It looks like an unrelieved blockage in the ileum caused the bowel to turn gangrenous." I thrust aside thoughts of what I'd like to do to Rogan. "I'll use K-Cipok to assist. Advise MedAmin and Dr. Mayer for me, if you would."

K-Cipok, like all the nurses, doubled as an anesthesiologist. She had the patient prepped and under sedation as soon as I laid out my instruments. We scrubbed, masked, and gloved, then initiated a sterile field around the three of us.

I positioned the lascalpel to make the initial incision. A bubble of putrid gas bulged beneath the outer abdominal wall.

"Suction," I said after I swiftly made a tiny slit for K-Cipok to insert the extractor's tip. Whew. The smell was horrific, but the effluvium was soon evacuated. I breached the tough outer tissues. "Clamp. Aqueous suction, yes, right there." I peeled back the heavy layer of fatty tissues, secured the clamp, and stared. "My God, what a mess."

K-Cipok gasped. "How did she manage to walk around like this?"

The entire colon was strangulated by a massive obstruction, which had caused severe tissue degradation. The gangrene was so wide-spread, I didn't know if anything I could do would save her.

This was a direct result of Rogan's incompetence.

"Orgemich species," I said under my breath, concentrating. "Redundant organs include heart, spleen, liver, colon . . ." I probed beneath a portion of the necrotic colon and confirmed that. "She's got two sets of large and small intestines, and only one has been compromised." I gazed at my nurse. "We're going to perform a complete ileostomy and colectomy, K-Cipok." I straightened and adjusted the clamp. "Start thinking of a fancy clinical term. We may get credit with inventing this procedure."

"She's going into cardiac arrest, both hearts!" the nurse said. "No pulse!"

"Damn, damn, not now," I muttered. The ventilator K-Cipok activated took over for the Orgemich's lungs as I began compressions over the twin hearts. Sweat beaded on my brow, trickling into my eyes as I looked up at the nurse. "Stats."

"No pressure, no pulse." K-Cipok said, intent on the indicators.

"Fifty cc's Epinephrinyl." I snatched the syrinpress once it was calibrated and injected it directly into the primary heart. I checked for a pulse, but felt nothing. "Come on, lady," I said. "Don't give up on me!"

"Got something." K-Cipok squinted at her console screen. "Bradycardiac rate primary heart, 48. Secondary heart showing ventricular fibrillation. I've got thready BP, 47 over 30."

"You can do better than that," I said, waited as long as I dared, then looked at K-Cipok.

The nurse shook her head. "She's not coming out of it."

"Twenty cc's of synmeperedine." The next syrinpress was slapped hard against my palm, and I glanced up before I administered it. The charge nurse was not happy. "Problem?"

"She's not a Terran," K-Cipok said.

I administered the drug. "No kidding."

"Doctor, she's an Orgemich, and you don't have a chart. Are you sure—"

"Let's chat later, after we keep her from dying on us, okay?" I squelched the outrage I felt at being questioned. "Stats."

"Still fluctuating," K-Cipok monitored the readout with a frown. "Wait, she's starting to stabilize. Both heart rates rising, BP looks better—" She raised her large, placid eyes and smiled. "Better than when we got her. 90 over 60."

"Close enough. Let's get moving." I ducked my head so the nurse could blot the sweat from my face, then held out my gloved hand. "Clamp."

It took nearly four hours, but I was able to complete the surgery successfully. The Orgemich female was in critical but stable condition as she was transferred to post-op in the surgical intensive care unit. K-Cipok stayed for a few minutes after the patient was removed.

"Dr. Grey Veil, that was—well, incredible."

"Thanks." I smiled to remove the sting from my next words. "Just don't start arguing with me in the middle of surgery next time, or I'll make you do the next one."

"I apologize. I was worried—I wanted—how did you know so much about her physiology? I mean, I know you aren't—" She made an uncomfortable gesture.

It was understandable. "I've been studying."

"You must have. I've never seen anyone operate like that."

We were joined by Dr. Dloh, Mayer, and the relief charge nurse, Ecla. I reviewed the procedure briefly and ordered full scan analysis on the diseased organs I'd removed. Despite the temptation, I made no mention of the role Phorap Rogan played in this patient's near-tragic case. My boss nodded and withdrew without a word.

So much for appreciation, I thought with a certain caustic pleasure. I turned to Dloh. "I know I'm scheduled for three more hours on duty, but would you cover the rest of the shift for me?" My adrenaline surge was subsiding fast. "I'm exhausted."

"Of courze, Dr. Grey Veil." Dloh gazed around him.

"Will you excuze uz for a moment, pleaze?" The nurses departed, still talking about the operation. I noticed a certain agitated movement to my colleague's normally languid limbs.

"Something wrong, Dr. Dloh?"

"I wanted to tell you the orderly had zomehow mixed that patient'z chart in with one I rezeived. By the time I notized, you had activated the zterile field." His brittle voice fell to a whisper. "I regret it did not come to my attention zooner."

"I didn't need the data," I told him. "Forget about it."

"You know zo much about Orgemich phyziology that you did not require chart referenze?"

"I observed Dr. Rogan's treatment of this Orgemich on my first day at the FreeClinic, and reviewed her chart." I should have insisted on those internal scans, I brooded. If she had died . . . "I remembered the particulars."

"How fortunate. Still, pleaze aczept my apology for the miztake. It won't happen again."

I shrugged. "No harm done."

"Doctor, may I azk you another queztion?"

"Sure." I was a bit impatient with Dloh's insistence. I liked success, but I didn't want to dissect it.

"Where did you pozition the poztzurgical ztoma?"

"On the left upper quadrant, beneath the secumous junction, of course." I mentally pictured the incision I'd made in the mesentery. Nothing wrong with that.

"Not where you would locate it on a Terran," Dloh said.

"Of course not. The anatomical differences require—"

"I know what they require. What I did not know iz that you knew." Dloh paused significantly. "And you dizcerned thiz from reviewing the chart of thiz Orgemich patient zeveral weekz ago."

I could see his point. "I have an excellent memory."

"You have a phenomenal memory, Doctor."

"Thank you, Dr. Dloh." It was time to get some fresh air. "If you don't mind, I'm tired. I'll see you tomorrow."

"Not at all," he said as he stepped from my path.

"Do one more favor for me, Dr. Dloh." I smiled grimly. "Keep Phorap Rogan away from my patient."

The sound of an incoming console signal greeted me when I returned to my quarters. My Orgemich patient? No, I had a gut feeling she was going to make it. Maybe it was Kao Torin, I thought. I answered it and was disappointed to see a comdrone instead of the handsome blue face of Paul's friend.

"Good afternoon, Dr. Grey Veil. One message, direct interstellar relay."

That told me who it was, but I asked anyway. "Inquiry—point of origin is Sol Quadrant?"

"Confirmed."

Well, why not? It would make my rotten day complete. I accepted the transmission.

"Cherijo," my father greeted me.

"Dad."

"I have been in contact with the Pmoc Quadrant Surgeon General's Office. Preliminary reports indicate you have performed adequately in your capacity on Kevarzangia Two."

"Haven't killed anyone yet. Why are you wasting credits calling me?"

"I thought you might wish to further discuss your impulsive actions."

"I don't." I thought of what this man had done. "Good-bye, Dad."

"This disrespect is unacceptable, daughter."

"What are you going to do about it?" My temper exploded. "I'm fourteen light-years away! You can't exactly suspend my entertainment privileges, can you?"

"I have spoken to Dr. Mayer."

"Speaking of entertainment, that must have been fun. You two have a lot in common. Maybe he's your long-lost brother."

Dad wasn't amused. "He feels you may be on the verge of an emotional collapse."

"He couldn't feel a dermal probe if he sat on one."

"Cherijo—"

First the Bartermen, then Rogan's mess, now this. My patience was in the red-range. "Get to the point!" I shouted.

He drew back from his console, appalled at my lack of control. How uncivilized of me. It felt pretty good, too. "It is in your best interests to resign and return at once to Terra. We will discuss this again, daughter."

He ended the transmission, and I was left feeling like a mouthy kid with bad manners. Jenner peeked out from under the sofa.

"I won't let him talk me into going back, Jenner. I won't."

After the signal from Dad, I spent a number of my off-duty intervals escaping my studies and my quarters, taking Ana Hansen's advice to relax more. At the time, it didn't seem like rationalization to me.

One evening I wandered into the Sports Complex, intending to explore what type of workout equipment was available. I might find something that would take the edge off my three main frustrations. Namely Mayer, that fool Rogan, and my father.

The favorite sport of my homeworld, shockball, was not practiced on K-2, much to my relief. I'd never understood the thrill of watching eighteen athletes juggle a computer-enhanced sphere between twin goals. A sphere that jolted them with electrocardial shocks if the referees caught them committing penalties.

Milder pastimes were preferred by the colonists. Individual competitions against dimensional simulators, table games, the like. I could handle something basic, I thought.

Right. I ended up feeling like the biggest greenhorn to set foot on extee-soil since *Challenger IX* landed on Mars and Terrans found out the rusty sand made them break out in hives. It was my own fault. I should have known better than to accept a challenge from a

FreeClinic orderly. Especially one as innocent-looking as Akamm.

"Hey, Dr. Grey Veil!" He gestured for me to join him and a group of staffers at the whump-ball tables. "I'm trying to figure out how to play this game, can you give me a hand?"

I heard a snicker as I approached. Maybe someone suspected I'd never worn a whump-glove in my life. True, I'd never played the game, but it didn't look *that* difficult. How hard could it be to direct the small, colorful globes into a series of pockets?

Well, Akamm swindled me out of five navvaroot beers and a plate of Ontabbaren grain-chips before I finally caught on. Most of the medical support staff frequented the Sports Complex. By the time we reached our fifth game, a large group of them stood around, watching my humiliation. What finally penetrated my thick skull was their muffled laughter each time Akamm registered yet another point.

I was being hustled

I did extract a small amount of revenge. Maggie had taught me some tricks she'd learned during her tavern years. Akamm had set up for game six, and turned away to retrieve his glove from the dry-rack. When he turned back around, he didn't notice that I'd successfully exchanged his ball for a pressurized chalk-sack. I was careful to step back from the table as he approached. He took aim with confidence and hit the sack, which imploded.

After the air cleared, the orderly stood blanketed with a thick white layer of chalk.

"*Suns*—what the—"

"Good try," I said with a straight face. "Wrong target. You'd better forfeit and hit the cleanser units before one of those Whelikkan albino females over there thinks she's found a soul mate."

The staff didn't try to subdue their laughter any longer. I even got a round of applause. After bowing my acceptance, I got the feeling someone was still staring at me. A quick scan of the games room brought my gaze to meet an intense pair of white eyes. Kao Torin rose from his vantage position (he'd obviously watched the entire fiasco), and crossed the space to join me at the service terminal.

"Healer Grey Veil." He greeted me with one of his fluid gestures. "May I never face you as a games opponent."

"I'll take that as a compliment." I peered up at him. "I think."

"I find myself, as Paul puts it, at loose ends this night." His smile was doing strange things to my pulse. "Would you join me for a walk outside? The moons are aligning in a particularly interesting pattern."

I wondered briefly if this was the alien equivalent to being propositioned. I wouldn't mind taking a stroll with him, if that's all he had in mind. Anything more . . . well, I'd have to think about it. "Sure."

Kevarzangia Two's evenings were always spectacular in some form or another. Outside the Complex, I looked up and saw the satellite ring was positioned in a staggered diagonal stream across the night sky. This created another dazzling effect, throwing off curved bands of light that shimmered like a hundred wide moonbows.

"I always forget to look up," I said with regret. "I'll have to make a point of it. This is fabulous."

I felt his fingers brush briefly against the sleeve of my tunic as he guided me around a cluster of colonists exiting the Complex. Smooth move. I was startled by the response I felt to the momentary contact.

"I agree," he said, looking at me, not the moons.

We walked for a long time without speaking. It didn't bother me. The longer I was with Kao Torin, the more at ease I felt. He pointed out a distant, tiny light just above the horizon and called it home.

"I will have to return soon," he said. "I am obliged to Choose a bondmate."

I had done some research (purely educational, of course) on the culture of his homeworld. According to the database's scanty outline, Jorenians apparently had complete freedom. They could go anywhere, do anything, have lots of fun. Until they attained emotional and physical maturity, that is. This was measured not by age, but by some unspecified internal biological clock.

From what I surmised, when this clock's alarm went off, all Jorenians were required to return to their homeworld to take a bondmate during some unspecified ceremony. The HouseClans of his world did not let anyone hit the snooze switch, either.

"Do you have someone waiting for you?" I asked, my throat tight. It seemed very important that he tell me now.

"No." He stopped, and his hand curled around my arm. His hand was so large that his thumb overlapped his knuckles. "I have not Chosen."

I stared up at him. Surely he wasn't thinking—"I hardly know you, Kao Torin."

"And I you, Healer Grey Veil." He didn't sound too worried about that. "I have wanted to know you, from the first moment when I saw you wearing my HouseClan's colors."

I grimaced as I looked down at my tunic. "That was just a coincidence. Every doctor wears these colors."

He inclined his head. "A happy one for me, all the same."

"Kao." It was hard to resist so much charm. "I'm Terran."

"Yes." He waited.

"A physician." I was beginning to sound like a complete imbecile. "Contracted to this FreeClinic for a standard revolution."

"I know."

There was so much more I couldn't say.

"Cherijo?" His eyes gleamed like the moons above us, and then his hand touched my face. "Come with me."

CHAPTER SEVEN

Falls and Links

A week after my first whump-ball game, I met my first Trytinorn at the FreeClinic.

I'd seen a few of them at a distance, of course. They were impossible to miss. The Trytinorns lived on the colonial perimeter, and only rarely strayed from their specially reinforced housing. It wasn't because they were shy. Trytinorns were the largest of all species allowed to immigrate under K-2 transfer standards. The mammoth beings made the Hsktskt look downright *scrawny*.

An exterior structural panel had to be removed just to get the injured male Trytinorn into the facility. Since we couldn't fit the Trytinorn in one of the regular exam rooms, we set up a makeshift version of the same in a storage bay.

Now I knew how that snail-sized colonist felt, I thought. The top of my head came to just below the patient's knee. I had to resort to using a grav-ramp just to do the abdominal scan series. I completed my examination, lowered the ramp, and set my scanner aside to make a chart notation.

Charge Nurse Ecla fluttered around the hastily rigged exam table, her lithe form transforming simple movement into ballet. The Psyoran's lacy physique reminded me of a bouquet of animated flowers.

"Doc?" our far less dainty patient groaned from above. "What is it?"

"Costal chondritis."

I stepped back on the ramp, raised it, and showed him the affected area on his chart display. I went on to explain that the thick band of cartilage between his ribs and the lower breastbone was badly inflamed. The result made breathing exceedingly uncomfortable.

"Why is this happening to me?" he asked.

I checked his chart for a moment. He was a dockworker in Cargo Dispatch/Receiving down at Transport. Most of the Trytinorns were. "Probably because you haven't been using a lift rig to protect yourself at work," I said.

Belligerent eyes glared down at me from beneath a thick brow plate. Yep. I was right on the money.

"That's for low-weights," the Trytinorn said, then grimaced at a fresh wave of pain. His colossal form relaxed once I injected him with an analgesic to relieve the symptoms.

"While you're on medical leave for a week," I told him, ignoring the subsequent bluster of outrage, "you'll have plenty of time to study all the safety rig data I'm going to give you."

Ecla changed places with me, and wrapped his torso with yards of support braces while I finished making the chart entries. Trytinorn curses were particularly expressive and colorful. In spite of that, I hummed cheerfully. The indignant dockworker was still swearing when the orderlies assisted him to his feet and he stomped out the way he came in.

As we walked back to Trauma, I noticed the Psyoran was giving me a lot of odd looks. Okay, my humming wasn't going to win any prizes. I never said I was perfect.

"You're in a good mood," Ecla said back in the exam room while she sterilized the pad for the next case. The ruffled ridges on every visible part of her rainbow-pigmented body stirred at my grin.

"You'd rather I stomp around like that?" I nodded

after the Trytinorn, whose footsteps were still echoing through the facility. My nurse made one of her species' infamous nonverbal gestures. "I won't ask what that means."

"It means you should sing more often." Ecla's exquisite features were quite earnest, a sign she was joking.

"My only failing," I said. It was funny that I did one thing so miserably, and still enjoyed doing it. "My maternal influencer claimed I had a tin ear."

"You're humming to yourself all the time these days."

"I never let the lack of appreciation for my musical ability intimidate me." I finished making the chart entry and gave her my undivided attention. "Okay, Ecla, stop dancing around and tell me what's on your mind."

"Word has it that you and a certain pilot have been seen together," the Psyoran said. "At least three nights this week."

Kao Torin and I were the latest sensation. His elusive reputation, combined with the fact I was being very closemouthed, stirred the facility's staff to torrid speculation. One nurse had asked me if it was true Kao was pregnant with my child.

"I never knew my personal life was so riveting," I said, purposely bland. "I won't ruin the suspense by telling you all the details."

"Thanks a lot!" Ecla's sarcasm was softened by a delicate laugh. She signaled Assessment. "Next patient, please."

Dr. Rogan chose that moment to enter the room, carrying an armful of assessment charts. He was ranting at top whine before either of us could say a word.

"Give me the medsysbank," he demanded. "I've got three crisis cases"—he thrust the charts in my face—"so you can handle these. Where the *suns* is Dr. Mayer?"

I stepped back and indicated the portable unit wordlessly, while Ecla retrieved the stack of charts. From the quantity, Rogan's contribution to my caseload would probably double the length of my shift. Since one of the medsysbanks was now permanently disabled (Rogan had kicked it once too often and fused the memory hardware a week ago), his emergencies were largely invented.

He wheeled the diagnostic unit out, no word of thanks offered. Not that I expected any.

Nurse Ecla sighed as she sorted out the charts by priority. "Dr. Rogan unloads half his patients on you," she said. I shrugged. "This bunch will keep you here until moons' rise."

"Not a problem."

I was lying. I did resent Rogan dumping his unwanted cases on me whenever we pulled the same shift. There was simply nothing I could do about it.

If I went to Dr. Mayer, I was convinced he would view any grievance as argumentative and uncooperative. If I refused to take the cases, Assessment backed up and the disgruntled patients were dumped on Dr. Dloh and mu Cheft. Since they had both treated me fairly, I was reluctant to pass the problem along to them. Not to mention that Rogan would relish the chance to tell Mayer if I did.

"He'll be hiding in the lounge for the rest of the day," Ecla said, her ruffles bristling. "When was the last time you sat down?"

"I'll sit later," I told her as the next patient came in.

The afternoon dwindled down to twilight. My last case was a comical sight: the patient's densely furred pelt was saturated with some kind of viscous resin that acted as a glue for thousands of tiny purplish leaves. An acrid odor surrounded him, probably from the organic material.

Alun Karas, according to his chart, was a field botanist.

"Good evening, Mr. Karas," I said as I circled around him to inspect the mess. No surface trauma that I could see. Not that there was a whole lot of surface showing. "Trying to bring work home with you?"

"I was taking root and bark samples," the patient told me. "One of the resin tappers clogged at the intake, and the reservoir burst while I was working to clear it." He pawed ineffectually at the sticky mess. "Then I tripped and fell into a pile of gnorra leaves."

"You certainly did," I said.

"I've got a fresh batch of depilatory spray ready," Ecla said, and the botanist sneezed before moaning miserably.

"I don't think that's necessary," I said to Karas. "Start an immersion tank, Ecla, with diluted, *hair-friendly* solvents, please." The Psyoran still snickered as she left to make the necessary preparations. "Here, climb up on the exam pad for a moment."

I discovered the smelly, gummy coating of leaves and sap had permeated the outer fur layer. Just like the proverbial Terran tar and feathers, I thought. My smile faded as the scanner began to register. The sap was so dense that it was affecting both body temperature and fluid levels.

"Can you get this stuff off me?" Karas sounded weak. "I can't breathe."

Although suffocation was a possibility, due to his pores being sealed, my scanner was telling a different story. He was beginning to pant, and I heard the thickening rattle of congestion behind each breath.

"Did you have an infection before this happened?" I asked, and scanned his lungs.

"Infection?"

"A cough? Cold?"

"No."

Something was rapidly attacking his pulmonary system, from my readings. No sign of a pathogen, however. "You're sure? Not even a sniffle?"

The patient began to cough before he could work up a reply. "No."

"Tell me the name of your species."

"Chakaran," was his strangled answer.

I was now reading a rapid buildup of sputum and pleural effusion. To make matters worse, body temperature was starting to spike. I put him on oxygen and cursed under my breath as I rescanned. Still no trace of contagion. All that registered was the organic matter plastered to the outer fur layer.

"The tank is ready, Doctor—" Ecla had returned and halted as she took in the change of situation.

"Seal the room. Now."

"Quarantine protocols?" she asked.

"No." I scanned a third time. A fourth. "There's no bacterial or viral presence. Nothing." I blew out my breath, then addressed the patient again. "Did you breath in any of this sap?"

"It w-was spraying everywhere—" the Chakaran said. "I might have . . ."

I adjusted the oxygen flow, then deep-scanned his lungs again.

"Aspiration pneumonia?" Ecla asked, echoing my thoughts.

"Possibly." I bit my lip, unwilling to commit myself. No trace of anaerobic pathogens registered. "Let's get him into the tank, then we'll run a complete biodecon on the three of us. Did you come in contact with anyone out there?"

"Dr. Rogan brushed past me, coming out of the lounge. His odor . . ." She curled a brow ridge in disgust. "It made me sneeze. I didn't touch him otherwise, but . . ." The nurse knew it didn't matter.

I dashed to the display. Rogan's treatment room was empty, the lounge was deserted. I signaled the front. Assessment took a moment to report back.

"Dr. Rogan has gone for the day," the triage nurse said. "Shall I signal him for you, Dr. Grey Veil?"

"Yes. I need to talk to him, immediately." I turned back to Ecla. "Let's get Mr. Karas into the tank."

It took almost an hour to clean the organic matter from the Chakaran's beautiful golden fur. By the time we were done, he was delirious from fever. Massive infection had set in so fast I was forced to treat his case as potentially life-threatening.

Rogan finally signaled after we had finished the last of our decontamination procedures.

"Doctor, we may have had contact with an unknown contagion here," I told him, and briefly profiled Karas's condition. "Ecla was exposed, by casual contact so were you. Where are you?"

"In my quarters, if you must know." Rogan didn't sound worried. "What came up on the scanner?"

"Nothing. But the patient developed severe pneumonic symptoms within minutes after reporting to the clinic."

"If there's nothing on your scanner, there's no contagion!" Rogan said.

"I'm not so sure about that." I resisted the temptation to shout. "Run a full biodecon scan on yourself. Contact anyone you've encountered since leaving the FreeClinic and tell them to do the same."

"I haven't come in contact with anyone. There's no reason to run a full bio."

"Dr. Rogan—"

"You can't declare a quarantine, there's no contagion." Before I could respond, he went on with pompous superiority. "If you're done playing games, I have better things to do." The signal terminated, and I stared at the blank screen.

Much as I loathed to admit it, Rogan was right. I couldn't justify quarantine protocols.

"Ecla," I said, willing my frayed temper to a faraway place, "I need to make a full report to Dr. Mayer. Check with Assessment, make sure no one came within a hundred feet of Dr. Rogan when he left." There was little more that I could do. I had the patient removed to an isolation room, and went to see my boss.

"Despite no evidence of bacterial or viral pathogens, you still performed the decontamination procedures? Then you admitted Karas to isolation?" Mayer asked once I'd finished making my verbal report in his office.

"Doctor, your emergency appears to be nothing more than the product of an overactive imagination."

"I've followed standard medical procedure," I replied. "By informing you of this situation, I've satisfied proper protocol." I rose to my feet, but he held up one of his hands. Clever hands, stupid man.

"Sit down, Dr. Grey Veil." I thumped back into the chair. "Your eagerness to return to duty is commendable." He made it sound like the exact opposite. "However, I suggest the strain of your duties is taking a serious toll."

"Are you saying I can't handle my job?"

"I'm suggesting that is indicated, yes."

"Tell me something, Dr. Mayer." It was high time to confront him, or tell him what I thought of him. I opted for the first choice. Less bad words involved. "Why are you doing this?"

"I don't know what you mean."

"No?" I sat forward, locking my gaze on his. "I'm not a complete idiot, you know. You've had it in for me from day one. Remember when you threatened me with dismissal for incompetence? Since then, you've done nothing but berate my abilities, criticize my work, and condemn my decisions. You told my father you think I'm teetering on the edge of a breakdown. Now you're implying I'm crazy for taking steps to contain a potential contagion. What's next? Are you going to have me arrested because you don't like the way I make chart entries?"

"You're exaggerating."

"Am I?" His hands clenched, and his skin tone darkened, but I'd gone this far, I thought to myself. Might as well jump all the way into the hole I was digging. "Why would you approve my transfer application—" His eyebrows beetled, and I nodded. "Yes, I found out you had the final endorsement. Why approve it if you thought I was incompetent? What's the real reason I'm here?"

Mayer sat back, pleased. "Now a persecution complex." He smiled with a trace of gloating satisfaction. "If these tirades continue, I will recommend PQSGO instigate a complete reevaluation of your contract."

I didn't blink. Neither did the chief. "I've got the message." If I hadn't been sure where I stood with the man before, I was crystal clear now.

"Dr. Grey Veil?" His voice stopped me at the threshold of his office. "Report back to me on the Chakaran patient before your shift ends."

He was only covering himself in the event I proved to be right, I told myself bitterly. Good boss tactics. "Yes, sir."

Once the door closed behind me, I had the urge to kick in the plaspanel wall section before me. Mayer knew exactly what buttons to push, and I was reacting like a damned drone.

Duncan Reever chose that moment to show up.

"Do you have some kind of monitor set up out here?" I asked. He shook his head. "No, of course not. Your timing, as always, is perfect."

"I take that to mean you don't want me here."

"Take it anyway you like, Chief Linguist."

I stalked down the corridor, not surprised when he caught up and joined me. Terran pitt-shepherds were less tenacious. I thought of the stack of charts waiting for me in Trauma, the formal report I still had to compose and file. All to be completed before I could crawl back to my quarters and try to remember why I wanted this dumb job. Reever was just a top note on the whole sour situation.

"Another altercation with Dr. Mayer?" Reever inquired.

"You could call it that." A thought occurred to me. "Were you listening at the door?"

"It wasn't necessary. Both of your voices carry quite well."

I considered this, and kicking *him* hard, for a moment. By now we had reached Trauma, and I stopped to check in with the charge nurse. Ecla had gone off duty, and

T'Nliqinara was waiting for me. So were a dozen patients, two emergency cases, and the latest stack of lab data discs. Dr. mu Cheft had called in; he was going to be late for his shift. Reever hovered until I noticed him again.

"Okay, Chief Linguist, I can give you exactly one minute," I said as I retrieved my charts. "What do you want?"

"We must confirm tomorrow's agenda."

I drew a complete blank. "Tomorrow's agenda for what?"

"Your community service quota," he replied. "You are scheduled to work in the Botanical Fields."

"What has that got to do with you?" As I said this, the specifics of the service data came back to me. I closed my eyes briefly. Just my luck. "Let me guess. *You're* scheduled to supervise me."

"That is correct."

All new colonists were assigned senior project managers during their first service. The veterans supervised the rookies and insured they didn't make a mess. I knew I should have picked that construction project. I would have been scheduled with someone more affable, like that Trytinorn patient I'd seen earlier.

"Okay, Chief Linguist." It was a day for the inevitable. "What do you need to confirm?"

"A time and place to meet in the morning."

"I'm pulling an extra shift, and I need five hours of sleep to be human." I doubted five years would do the same for Reever. "Meet me at my quarters, Main Housing Building, West Wing, at Alpha shift commencement." I turned and headed for my exam room.

"I can request another supervisor for you," Reever called after me.

"Don't bother," I called back. "Someone obviously thinks I deserve this."

An hour later, I was notified by the inpatient nurse that Alun Karas had descended into a coma. I left Trauma for the ward at a flat run. Time blurred from there as I tried everything I could think of, but the progression of his pneumonic infection, as well as the coma, proved irreversible.

Six hours after my initial treatment, I found myself reporting Alun Karas's death to Dr. Mayer. I recited the stark facts, and terminated the signal after the chief issued orders for a full autopsy. Once I'd notified Dr. Crhm in Pathology and requested MedAdmin inform the next of kin, I left the FreeClinic and drove my glidecar home.

I sat behind the controls outside housing for some time before I summoned the energy to drag myself to my quarters. There, for the first time since I'd arrived on planet, I wept.

Unemotional, irritating Duncan Reever quickly added another item to my list of his shortcomings.

He was *punctual*.

The following morning, my door chime rang precisely at the time I'd specified.

"Wait a minute."

Grumbling, I dragged myself out of bed and pulled on a faded tunic and trousers. On the way to the door panel, I dialed up my morning tea.

"Be charming," I told Jenner as I opened the door. He yawned back at me. "Come in, Reever. I'm almost ready."

The chief linguist walked in. He was similarly clothed in shabby, comfortable garb. As I drank my tea, he examined Jenner with remote interest.

"A domesticated animal?" he asked, but made no effort to touch my cat.

"Uh-huh." I drained my server.

His Majesty, on the other hand, took an incongruous, instant liking to Reever. He padded over and curled around one of the chief linguist's ankles. Plaintive yowls for attention began to increase in volume.

"What does it want?"

"His name is Jenner," I said. "He wants you to pet him."

"Why?"

"Didn't you ever—" I recalled his unusual upbringing. "That's why they're called pets, Reever. You *pet* them." I quickly wound a band around the end of my braid. "Most alien cultures have domesticated animals, don't they?"

"No. However, there are several species who consume such small mammals as their primary dietary—"

I shuddered. "Never mind. Forget I asked." I reached down and gave Jenner an affectionate stroking. My cat glared at me—*I don't want you*—and continued to implore Reever for attention. The chief linguist just stood there, imitating a tree. I gave up and straightened with a sigh. "Come on. Let's go."

Reever's glidecar waited outside my building. I noted it was a sleek, handsome model much newer than any other I'd seen on K-2.

"Who did you bribe to get this?" I asked as I slid into the luxurious interior.

"No one. It was a gift."

"I see."

"I doubt it." His lips didn't curve, but for the first time since I'd met him, he seemed almost human.

"Okay, who gave it to you?"

"A grateful Furinac who had been unable to communicate with Colonial Militia during an unauthorized transport."

"He must have been really grateful," I said as I caressed the soft seat covering. "What exactly did you do for him?"

"That requires a rather lengthy explanation." Reever abruptly changed the subject. "Have you toured the Botanical Project Area yet?"

"Some of it." Kao Torin had taken me to the hybrid gardens. At the time, my interest hadn't been focused on the scenery. Today I wasn't interested in much of anything.

"You're disturbed. What is it?"

I closed my eyes and leaned back against the seat cushions. "I lost a patient last night."

To his credit, the chief linguist didn't offer any false sympathy or pursue the subject. Good thing, too. I was feeling pretty raw, and not in the mood to treat Reever for any injuries I inflicted.

"We'll be working in the hybrid cultivation area today. There are a number of offworld specimens being crossbred with native plants in production."

I yawned. "Excuse me."

"You did not get your five hours' sleep."

"No." It had been less than four since I'd left the FreeClinic. Two since I'd fallen asleep against a decidedly damp pillow.

"Charge Nurse T'Nliqinara told me you've worked four extra shifts this week."

"Uh-huh." I gazed out the passenger viewer. The last thing I wanted to do was grub around a bunch of plants. Not while the thought that I could have done more to save Alun Karas haunted me.

There *was* something more I could do, I thought, mentally smacking my palm against my forehead. After completing my service quota, I could visit the accident site. See if it held any clues as to what had killed him.

"Is Dr. Mayer aware of your extended work hours?"

Reever's persistent intrusion on my thoughts was becoming like the jab of a dermal probe in the same bruised spot. "Dr. Mayer probably spits whenever he hears my name," I said. "Drop it, all right?"

"What would you care to talk about?"

I was beginning to suspect Reever enjoyed provoking me. He certainly did it often enough. "Nothing, Chief Linguist." I didn't have enough energy to parry with him. "You can be the conversational navigator."

"Very well." We drew up to a cluster of clear-walled structures, and Reever halted the glidecar. "Tell me what you know about agricultural cultivation."

"Absolutely nothing outside of a few required Botany

courses during secondary school. All of which I paid little or no attention to." My sarcasm, as usual, failed to provoke him.

"We'll begin with something basic," he said. "Perhaps planting some seedlings."

Two hours later, as I watched Reever patiently dig up and replant the last of my seedlings, I scuffed one foot over the loose, dark soil.

"How was I supposed to know the white things are the roots, and the brown part is supposed to be above ground?" I muttered to myself.

He heard me. "If you had listened when I explained the procedure to you, you would have known."

I got indignant. "Reever, you never once said the roots were the *white* things."

His shoulders tensed as he paused for a moment. "I was not aware I had to specify that fact."

"Well, I didn't kill any of them," I said, then peeped over his shoulder. "Did I?"

"They'll survive."

"Great. Tell me, what did that raving maniac mean when he said I had a black thumb?" I referred to the botanical scientist who had thrown a tantrum when he discovered I'd planted every single one of his precious weeds upside down.

"He meant you need to be assigned to another project."

"Even better." I had taken an instant dislike to the deliberate cultivation process anyway. As a physician, I had too great a prejudice against dirt and its microorganic contaminants. "What would you recommend I try next, Chief Linguist?"

"Working with something inanimate."

"Very funny."

Duncan dusted off his hands and consulted his wristcom. "We're finished," he said.

"But I—"

He raised one hand. "You've done enough."

"Not yet," I said. "Hear me out."

While we washed the clinging soil from our hands, I explained the circumstances around Alun Karas's case. Reever agreed with me that it might help to visit the site where the botanist had been collecting samples.

"I am familiar with his work assignment. He was over in a section adjoining the south range. We can reach it from here on foot."

Walking through the gardens with Reever, I recalled a recent interlude with Kao Torin. Anything to keep me from beating myself up over the Chakaran's death.

"Thinking of pleasant memories?"

"You're certainly interested in what I'm thinking all the time," I said.

"Occupational hazard."

It was a reasonable attempt by Reever at humor. I shrugged, but my mood lightened considerably. By now we had left the main fields and were walking through some dense growth into the uncultivated areas. Reever's hand caught my arm as I stumbled over a hidden tangle of roots, and he stopped while I regained my balance.

That was when it happened.

Reever loomed over me, blocking out the brilliant glow of both suns as his free hand bracketed my other arm. I brought up my hands in pure reflex, and he slid his grip to my wrists.

Wrists in front of his face. I'd seen that before. I felt very hot, yet frozen at the same time, drained of will. A strange sensation invaded my limbs.

"What are you doing?" I whispered, sure he was responsible. I could feel him—God, I thought I could feel him inside my head.

"He was here with you," the chief linguist said.

"What?"

"The pilot. Torin. He was here with you, wasn't he?"

"How do you know—" Horror overcame the paralysis, and I wrenched away from his hands. The bizarre encroachment on my senses ceased at once. It *was* coming from him. "What was that? What did you do to me?"

"I linked with you."

"Linked?" I stepped back. "What the hell does that mean?"

"I established a mental link with you, when I touched you. I have tried before, but you did not realize—"

His audacity stunned me. "You did this *before*?"

"The first time we met, at the Trading Center." He grabbed my wrists once more and raised them. "This image was one I shared with you."

"Reever—you—" I was so angry I was sputtering. "I never said you could touch me or—or—"

"I don't have to touch you."

He dropped my wrists. I whirled around, prepared to stomp off in high rage. A heartbeat later my body stopped cooperating. A choked cry burst from my throat as I halted, the sound dying away. I couldn't move.

I could still feel the breeze on my skin, hear the stirring of the purple leaves, smell the rich, dark soil. But I couldn't move. Not an inch. From the corner of my eye I saw him come around me, his eyes intent on my face. My throat worked to produce a sound, any sound. Nothing happened.

My brain was still working. *He's doing this to me,* I thought. Telepathy was not a skill necessary to become a surgeon, so I knew very little about it. Not that psychic ability was a predominant trait among Terrans, anyway. *No, it's not possible.*

Yes, it is. I heard him say. But his lips didn't move, and I was hearing it in the wrong place. His voice was behind my eyes.

I tested it. *Reever? Can you hear me?*

Yes. I hear you. He stepped closer, his face only a few inches from mine. There was a peculiar fascination in his cold eyes.

You are really doing this. It was inconceivable, yet I could hear his thoughts, and he could hear mine. *Why? Why are you doing this to me?*

You're the only one I've never had to touch.

He was *experimenting* on me with this thing? Not for

long. After I got him out of my head, he'd never try a stunt like this again. He'd be too busy recuperating. *Enough, Reever. Get out of my head!*

Wait. His hand touched me. I felt cool fingers thread through mine. *There's more.*

More what? I demanded.

Images began popping into my thoughts. Disjointed fragments of color and sound and emotion, one after the other, there and gone before I could grasp all the details clearly.

A little boy . . . frightened . . . alone . . .

Contempt . . . vague faces . . . a Terran man and woman . . .

A blade slashing over a small child's hand . . .

Gnawing hunger . . . pain . . .

There was soon too much to comprehend. I began seeing images of incredible alien worlds, strange creatures, cultures. Heard thousands of languages, voices that whispered, sang, screamed. Tasted bizarre flavors and textures, smelled flowers, chemicals, death. At last I understood.

I was inside Reever. In *his* mind. Experiencing *his* memories.

The images paled. I felt someone's fear. Suffering. Fury. This was what had changed . . . shaped . . . something else . . . what did it mean? Then it struck me. If I could read his thoughts, see his memories, then Reever could do the same with me.

I had to stop him. Now. *Let—me—go.*

For one terrifying moment nothing happened. Then the telepathic link that held me suspended vanished. I regained control of my body, but the sensory backlash made me sag to the ground. I heard my trousers rip, felt the rough soil against my knees.

I saw Reever's hands reaching for me, and in a panic awkwardly crawled backward. "Don't touch me!"

"Cherijo." Reever made an impatient sound as I cringed. "I won't hurt you." With an impersonal grasp he pulled me to my feet. I tried to make my legs support me, but they weren't ready. That forced me to hold on to him. "Are you injured?"

"Injured?"

He looked down. "You've grazed your knees—"

"You just took control of my mind and body, against my will, and you want to know if my knees hurt?" Frantically, I shoved his hands away and staggered back. "Get away from me!"

"I apologize."

He had to be joking. Had to. I stared at him. Nope, he wasn't.

"Take your apology and stuff it." Steadier now, I swiped at the dirt and leaves clinging to my trousers.

"I meant no harm."

"Right." I managed a shaky laugh. Sure, no harm done, Cherijo, what are you getting upset about? "Do you do this a lot?"

Those remote blue eyes narrowed. "No. Never with another human."

Oh, I was his first, was I? That did it. I stepped forward until we were only a few inches apart. He looked puzzled, but not for long. I swung, and put my back into it. He landed on his backside a few feet away, eyes wide, holding one scarred hand to his face. My knuckles throbbed painfully. It felt wonderful.

"Don't ever, ever touch me again!" Then I did stomp off, with great pleasure.

"Cherijo, wait."

"Go to hell!" I shouted back at him.

"You're going in the wrong direction."

"Damn!" I stopped, closed my eyes, spun around, glared. Reever was back on his feet, gingerly rubbing his jaw. "Where is it?"

He pointed to a spot a few yards away. "There. Where the gnorra trees are."

The small clearing still contained the ruined equipment and hardened sap sprays that covered a three-yard radius. I examined the container and gazed around at the benign-looking plant life. The acrid odor of the resin made me sneeze several times.

"Karas must have aspirated some of this gunk," I muttered to myself as I took some samples of the dried resinous substance. "Got to get this over to the lab; maybe they have a test to prove it caused the pneumonic symptoms."

"I had no intention of harming you," Reever said from behind me.

I didn't bother to look at him. "Collect some of these leaves, will you?"

"I apologize for frightening you."

My teeth clenched. "I saw some empty containers over there. Use one of those."

"I didn't expect the link to be so complete."

"Reever." I stopped ignoring him, turned on him. "There's no excuse for what you did." Was that dismay in his eyes genuine? Probably not. I let out a long breath, then said, "Next time, *ask* first, okay?"

"I understand. Will you link with me now, Joey?"

The man was as dense as plasteel. "No!"

"Why not?"

"I don't want to talk about it, Chief Linguist." I enunciated each word slowly, carefully. Never let it be said I'd broken a man's nose because he hadn't comprehended my meaning.

Reever nodded, and sneezed himself.

"We've got to get out of here, this sap may cause an allergic response." There was another possibility—could Karas have died from an anaphylactic reaction to this gunk? "Now, help me get these sample tubes filled." I handed him some vials. "One more thing."

"What is it?"

"Don't call me Joey."

CHAPTER EIGHT

Dangerous Games

After I got rid of Reever, I dropped off the samples at the FreeClinic for bioanalysis. They weren't happy to see me. The lab, like all the other clinical services, was backed up and understaffed. I finally got the attention of one of the technicians when I dumped the samples of resin and leaves on his console.

After I explained what I was looking for, he frowned.

"We can do a full spectrum bioanalysis, but if you've already run it through the scanners . . ." I got a doubtful shrug.

"Look, there may be a chemical component my scanner didn't pick up. I want these samples scrutinized down to the molecular structure, if necessary. Got it?"

"Doc, it's not like someone's going to die if we don't find—"

I glowered. "Someone already has. Do it."

I had the rest of the day off—a rare enough occurrence—and headed back to my quarters. I was too agitated to sleep, and in no mood to study, so I played grab-the-fiber-ball with Jenner. He eventually got tired of beating me and disappeared under the sofa for a nap.

It was too quiet. I didn't want to think about Reever and the incident at Karas's accident site. That would have made me mad enough to disassemble my furniture.

Time to relax, Cherijo. I took one of my cases out and thumbed through my disc holder for some music. In the middle of the holder, I came across the same anonymous disc I'd spotted during my journey on the *Bestshot*. Odd, I had always labeled them. I popped it into my player to hear what I had recorded.

Maggie's voice poured into the silence.

"Hey, kiddo," she said, shocking me so much that I dropped the player. Her rich laughter filled the room. My knees gave out and I sank down on a chair. "Yeah, it's me. I'm sorry I couldn't hang around longer. This blood rotting—whatever it is I've got—is a real bitch."

"Maggie?" I whispered. "How . . . ?"

"Sit down and don't start bawling. I know I'm dead, that's why you're listening to this. I've programmed one of the old man's housedrones to put it in with that crap you like to listen to. Once my death notice has been logged by the metal moron, that is."

"God." I couldn't take a deep breath, much less cry. It felt like I had been punched squarely in the solar plexus.

"Now, listen up, Joey." I straightened at the commanding tone. "The old man thinks he has it all planned. I don't need a Medtech degree to know he's wrong about you. You're too smart not to find out about all this crap he's been up to."

Maggie knew about it, too?

"He's setting you up. He'll have you thinking you have to protect his good name, safeguard the family integrity, blah, blah, blah. That's how he'll make you do what he wanted in the first place. Joseph has a thing for control. You know what I'm talking about."

"Understatement of the decade," I mumbled.

"No matter what that son of a bitch tries to do to you, you are in charge of you. Not him. Got it?" I nodded. "You're probably wondering how I know about this whole mess."

A kind of stupor settled over me, from the shock, I supposed. When my thoughts cleared, Maggie's voice seemed weaker.

"—made sure of that. What he doesn't know is he talks in his sleep, and I'm a great listener."

What was she talking about?

"He'll try to stop you. He may even tell you about us. And yeah, I know you're not going to be thrilled to find out I was sleeping with your dad."

I wasn't thrilled. I was aghast.

"I usually have much better taste, but it was necessary. It kept him quiet, and it kept me with you. That's why I did it, kiddo. Not because he was God's gift in bed."

Maggie and Dad? Having sex?

"Pay attention, Joey. You've got to get the hell off this planet. Get away from the old man, and find a place where you don't have to be his personal drone. Do it, baby. You'll know what to do when it's time." There was a faint thickness to her voice, as if she was choking back tears. "Joey, I love you like you were my own daughter. Don't grieve for me. I had a great life, and you were a great kid."

"Maggie." A single tear slipped down my face.

"Now pop this disc out, destroy it, and start packing. Pronto." She chuckled, and then the sound faded away.

I didn't destroy the disc. I sat and stared at it for a long time. Maggie had known the truth, apparently about everything, and never said a word. Why? Had she been trying to protect herself, or me? Or both of us? Why make sure I wouldn't know until *after* her death?

I had to do something; the walls were beginning to close in on me. I put Maggie's message away and went to my console.

Kao Torin answered my signal with a slow smile. "Healer Grey Veil. I was just thinking about you."

Too bad I couldn't have said the same thing. "Hello, Kao. Are you busy?"

"I am preparing to report for my shift." His grin faded. "Cherijo, what has happened?"

"Nothing," I lied. "Have a good rotation."

"I will, if you tell me why you have been crying."

Damn. "Me? Crying?" I forced a chuckle. "Not at all. I'm fine. Just got something in my eye."

He wasn't convinced, but didn't press the issue. "I will be off duty tonight. Will you share a late meal with me?"

"Sure. Call me when you get back."

After I terminated the signal, I changed my tunic and headed out to my glidecar. If I couldn't spend time with Kao, I could check in with Trauma, see if they needed an extra pair of hands. That would keep me from brooding over Maggie's message.

When I arrived at the facility, there were a number of priority cases on hold. The remaining patients in Assessment were audibly irate.

Nurse Ecla greeted me with an air of great serenity— if that's what two clusters of frills along her cranial ridge meant. She told me Drs. Mayer and Dloh were involved with two critical cases from a glidecar collision. Dr. Rogan, it seemed, had not bothered to show up for his shift, and could not be located.

"Have you tried tracking him through his TI?"

"Yes, but since he never wears it off duty, it was a useless exercise." The Psyoran turned to deal with one of the more contentious patients and quickly soothed him. Ecla wasn't the type to let dire circumstances rattle her. I suspected very little ever did. She escorted the patient back to the waiting area, then returned to the Assessment desk.

"Any sign of the contagion involved with Karas?" I asked, and she shook her head.

"No other cases reported. I even ran two scans over myself, to be sure. Both were negative. What are you doing here?"

"I'm just restless." I looked around Assessment once more, and sighed. "Tell you what, Ecla, I'll take Rogan's shift until he shows. Who's next in line for treatment?"

"Springfield, Kyle," she said as she handed me the chart.

"Terran?"

"Uh-huh. Just brought in, and spitting mad, too—GravBoard injuries."

I winced. We treated a lot of children with injuries, but an increasing number of them were lately due to GravBoard accidents. An impromptu track had been erected behind the Sports Complex, and the kids were crazy about it.

"Serious?" I said, and Ecla made an affirmative gesture.

Our young GravBoard enthusiasts generally sustained multiple lacerations, bad sprains, and even some broken bones. The track was elevated, and it was a long way to fall. Last week I'd treated two cases of serious compound fractures. I had promised mu Cheft I'd make a formal report to HQ Administration on the next case.

"This is going to make me popular," I said to Ecla. "You'd better notify Mr. Springfield's parents and tell them to get over here."

Kyle Springfield was thirteen years old, according to his chart, and displayed the normal amount of Terran adolescent attitude as I walked in.

"Hey, can you fix me up so I can get out of here?"

"Hey, *Dr. Grey Veil,* can you *please* fix me up," I said as I made a visual survey of his wounds. "Be polite, and it will open every door, Mr. Springfield."

"Whatever. Can you do something about this?"

He had the usual assortment of scratches and gashes, but I didn't like the way his right leg was turned. He propped himself up on the exam pad. I noticed it took considerable exertion.

"Sure." I picked up a scanner, and gestured for him to lay back. "With your cooperation, and some luck." He reclined, muffling a whimper as he shifted his weight. I frowned at the resulting data. Evidently his right hip had taken the brunt of his fall. "Looks like you took quite a spill."

"I'm—I'm okay. Stupid board's stabilizer blew. Marv ride, 'til then."

"I bet." I dealt with the hip first. He flinched under

the gentlest touch. "Your landing must have been fantastic."

"Yeah, I just—" One traitorous tear slid from his lashes, and he swore as he knuckled it away savagely.

I knew just how he felt. "Watch the language, pal." I took the sting from the reproach by adding, "You'll give Terrans a bad rep."

"We already—hey!" He pushed my hand away from the injury, and tried to sit up again. "I don't believe this. If Dad finds out—"

"I'm afraid he'll have to. Your hip is dislocated." Sympathy softened my tone as the boy's face reflected his dismay. "The cuts and bruises you can hide, Kyle, but you're not walking out of here."

"Marv. Just marv." He sagged back down, and I touched his shoulder briefly.

"It will work out. Trust me."

"You don't know my dad."

"I think I have a pretty good idea of what he's like." I thought of my father as I injected the boy with a mild combination of analgesic and muscle relaxant. After a few minutes, I swiftly manipulated the hip into place. He shuddered with relief.

"There," I said, and ran a scanner over him once more. "That's got to feel better."

"Dad's gonna space me." The boy's fierce expression relaxed as the painkiller took effect. "He doesn't know I swapped my glideskates for a GravBoard." He grimaced once more. "He's got this Terran thing about alien tech."

"You won't be GravBoarding for a while, kiddo," I told him.

"But everyone—"

"Dr. Grey Veil, Harold Springfield is here," Ecla said via display, interrupting us.

I patted the boy's tense shoulder. "Relax, Kyle. I'll go talk to your dad."

I left one of the nurses to clean up his lacerations and suture the gashes that needed it, while I went to speak with the father. I spotted a Terran male pacing restlessly in front of the Assessment desk and approached him.

"Mr. Springfield?"

The man was obviously a pilot, from the flight suit he wore. Springfield repeatedly thrust his fingers through his thinning hair as I related the particulars of Kyle's condition. When I mentioned the GravBoard, he froze.

Terrans tended to flush when they lost their temper. Springfield's face went right past flush into purple rage.

"Damn contraptions," the Terran said. "I've had enough of this! No transfer bonus is going to make me change my mind!"

"Transfer bonus?" I was confused.

He sneered at me. "Why else would I be here, rubbing elbows with all these filthy offworlders, if not for the credits? Well, that's it. I'm shipping my family back to the homeworld as soon as I can invalidate my contract."

No one had offered me a transfer bonus. Not that it mattered. "Mr. Springfield." I was aware of the many sets of alien eyes watching us. Time to get him calmed down before one of the filthy offworlders decided to shut him up. "Kids fall and get hurt all the time. It could have happened back on the homeworld, with our own tech."

"I'm sick of this place! All these—these—freaks!"

"That's enough," I said. "I know you're angry, but lower your voice. You're upsetting the other patients."

He laughed at me. "Yeah, well, it figures you'd care what they think. You're that big Jorenian's plaything, aren't you?"

"Mr. Springfield," I said, "you are out of line!"

"Doing it with an offworlder!" He looked at me, then spat on the floor. "That's what I think of you!"

"I'll have Kyle transported to your quarters when he's ready." I gestured toward a couple of sizable orderlies. "You, Mr. Springfield, can take your filthy mouth out of my clinic. At once."

"Why, you slut, I—"

I shut out the rest of what he shrieked as he was hauled out of the facility. Once Springfield was gone, I saw I had the full attention of the patients waiting to be seen. Dr. Mayer watched me from the Assessment desk.

"He *belongs* on Terra," I said. I didn't wait to hear the response as I brushed past the chief to enter the treatment area. I thought I heard him say something under his breath, but I'd had enough insults for one day. I got back to work.

"One of Bind 02376," Ecla said as she fluttered up to me and handed over the chart. "Separation anxiety, I believe, since it arrived alone. It wouldn't let anyone touch it or examine it."

A group of Binders (colony slang for them, I hadn't a clue how to pronounce their species name) were visiting K-2 while applying for transfer. Just another group of tourists.

Problem was, some bizarre error occurred with the transport schedules, and several of the interdependent pairs had been separated. Their vessels were a light-year out of orbit before K-2's perplexed translators figured out what the Binders who had been left behind were telling them.

Binders were born in sets of twos, psychically joined from birth. They were emotionally as inseparable as Terran Siamese twins before the development of in utero segregation. An advisory had come out warning that special interpreters were needed if any of the stranded Binders required medical treatment.

"Request a Binder translator from Admin," I told Ecla. "I'll check on Springfield one more time." I found the boy resting comfortably and didn't bother to tell him I agreed with his opinion of his father. Once I had checked the nurse's work, I went to take a look at the Binder.

The special translator was already waiting in the exam room with the patient. "Dr. Grey Veil." It was none other than the chief linguist, Duncan Reever.

"Every time I turn a corner," I muttered, averting my gaze toward the exam pad.

I'd never seen a Binder before, but the frail creature enchanted me at once. Like something from an old Terran fable, the being had a fey, elfin countenance. It couldn't have weighed more than twenty kilos. The torso and limbs vaguely resembled a humanoid's, but there were several orifices, like extra mouths, arranged on its iridescent derma. A shimmering fleece of transparent tendrils covered its ethereal frame.

"Just like a fairy." I smiled.

"Excuse me?" Reever broke into my reverie.

"A fairy, Chief Linguist." At his blank look, I demanded, "Didn't anyone ever tuck you in and tell you a bedtime story?"

"No."

"Your loss." The patient was curled into a tight fetal position, shuddering with each shallow inhalation. I caught the faintest scent of a chemical odor. "What is that smell?"

Reever breathed in, and frowned. "Binders do not exude that odor naturally."

Curiously I checked the room controls and dialed an analysis of the room's air content. What I read on the console made me freeze with dread down to my toenails. Swiftly I relayed the readings to the front desk and hoped my charge nurse wasn't occupied. Ecla was going to have to be very busy for the next several minutes.

"Cherijo, what—" Reever said, before I interrupted.

"Do you know anything about KleeFourteen?"

"I know what it is."

"That's good, because you're standing in a room with twenty times the safe limit dispersed in the air," I said as I secured the entrance to the exam room. Not that quarantine seals would help us directly, but they would keep people *out* and the toxin *in*. "Try not to breathe deeply, and don't make any unnecessary movements," I told Reever. Slowly I moved over to the exam pad and passed my scanner over the Binder. "Our friend here has ingested it."

"Skin seals—"

I shook my head. "It's already saturated and begun the transdermal process." Disaster was only minutes away. "Ask it exactly how much it swallowed." My scan revealed the potent toxin, but I had to know the exact amount in order to prepare an antidote.

Reever turned to my patient and said something in a guttural language, simultaneously pressing a careful hand to an orifice on the upper torso. The patient's tendrils undulated while it whispered a reply.

"Half a stanliter," I was told.

I met his dispassionate gaze with a steadiness I didn't feel. "That's enough to do the job."

I prepared the correct countermeasure as fast as I could. My hands didn't exhibit any sign of the internal trembling I was trying to ignore. A brief display signal from Ecla confirmed she was evacuating the entire facility.

"Why did you order an evacuation?" Reever asked.

"Given the amount in the Binder's system, the blast radius will be close to one kilometer. If I don't do this right, that is."

"Do you have sufficient time to stop the process?"

"I don't know." Not that it mattered. I might blow us into orbit simply by resorting to the only course of treatment—forcing the Binder to exude the rest of the toxin.

KleeFourteen, once used as a soil enhancement agent, had been a serious problem in the Pmoc Quadrant. Tons of it were once kept in agricultural storage facilities, considered an inert, harmless substance.

However, once the rather tasty fertilizer was ingested by a living organism, the digestive process altered the chemical composition of KleeFourteen. Unfortunately, not to the benefit of whatever ate it. A scientist had figured all this out when some little rodents on another planet began exploding inside the storage facilities.

Most colonies had destroyed their stock, but K-2 had held on to their supply for bartering purposes. A system-wide notification had warned of the danger, but it had been ignored as none of the mishaps had occurred on our planet.

Until today.

The syrinpress was ready. "If you pray, Reever"—I lifted my eyes to the cool gaze watching me—"do it now."

He didn't comment on the grim advice. "How long to complete the exudation?"

"Two minutes. Can you hold your breath that long?"

He nodded as he watched me glove. "KleeFourteen is very efficient."

"You don't say."

The only chance we had was to introduce the antidote as close as possible to the arterial system through an intramuscular injection. I gently slid restraint clasps over each of the Binder's limbs and tightened them to immobilize it.

The Binder murmured something, which Reever explained was sincere regrets for its actions. I finished setting the room controls to full discharge.

"You must not have wanted to die too badly, if you came for help." I smiled down at the patient's timid face. The back of my tunic was growing damp.

The Binder imitated my smile, and replied with visible weariness.

"It had second thoughts after the act," Reever said. "Two of Bind 02376 will not survive without it."

"Love triumphs over despair," I said as I gently touched one trembling limb. "Hold the arm still for me, Reever. Like this. I'm going to inject at the bicepular joint. I have to get this next to the plasma stream, or we are all going to be vaporized." I carefully positioned the syrinpress, and administered the counteragent. "Now, take a deep breath, Chief Linguist, and shut up."

After that, it was just a matter of waiting. Ten seconds, twenty. We stayed in position, holding our breath, unable to move. Once the antidote took hold, the Klee-Fourteen ingested by the Binder was directly exuded into the air. It would take the environmental units at least two minutes to evacuate the deadly toxic gas and neutralize it. If we breathed it in, it would kill us. If we moved, it would ignite. The catalyst effect could be triggered simply by disturbing the air.

I watched the first minute pass on the console readout. I admit, I was scared. Dad's secret seemed meaningless now—and wouldn't *he* be delighted to hear his only child had been turned into a small pile of ash.

Reever was staring at me. I decided his eyes were blue, but they seemed to change color every time I looked at him. Some Terrans did that with cosmetic lenses. Reever probably used some weird mental trick.

Finally, the evacuation units switched off. Reever and I both exhaled in relief. I wiped my eyes with the back of my hand. Sweat and what might have been tears made wet tracks on my skin. I offered the chief linguist a wobbly smile.

"Do you need anything else, Doctor?"

"I can handle it from here."

"Good." Reever exited the exam room without further ceremony. It was understandable. I felt like collapsing into a quivering, sobbing heap myself. I gazed down at the remorseful Binder.

"*Next* time," I said, "try crying on someone's shoulder, okay?"

I expected to be summoned by Dr. Mayer at the end of my voluntary shift, but oddly enough there were no orders waiting for me. Ecla was effusively grateful as we discussed the last of the cases and the incident with the Binder.

"You saved a lot of lives today, Doctor," she said with a fluid undulation of her ruffles.

"Thanks, Ecla." Why did I still feel so restless? "I'm out of here."

All I had to do was wait for Kao to finish his shift. I went back to my quarters, got cleaned up, and played chase-the-yarn-ball with Jenner for a few minutes. His Highness quickly got tired of entertaining me and stalked off.

Before I realized it I was out the door panel and walking, so wrapped up in my thoughts that I didn't notice where my feet were taking me. That had happened a lot to me since Karas had died. Absently I followed one of the pathways leading to the Cultural Center. A few minutes later I found myself in some type of gallery.

It was the flickering light that finally drew my complete attention. I had wandered into the Hall of Art and Expression, which was filled with works by some of the most talented painters, sculptors, and light manipulators in the colony. I'd never found the time to properly tour it. It was beautiful.

I stopped before a particularly fascinating illumination sequence of deep-space microorganisms. The tiny critters were found in asteroid belts, hosting even smaller parasites. The purity of the blues and greens intermingled with the most astonishing bursts of bioluminescent light.

"Beautiful," a deep voice said next to my ear. I yelped and nearly jumped out of my skin. Jorenian males had this pesky ability to be absolutely soundless whenever they wanted.

"Don't do that!" I said. Kao smiled at me, and my irritation shrank a few degrees. "Sorry, I didn't hear you."

"I know," he said. "I have been following you since you entered the gallery, and twice called your name."

Had I been *that* lost in thought? "I thought you were going to signal me when you got off work," I said.

"I attempted to. You were not in your quarters." He studied my face. "You are distressed."

"Are Jorenians capable of telepathy?"

"Empathy is not uncommon among those who Choose," Kao said. He gave me this significant look, then folded my hand in his. "Walk with me."

We made our way down the long hall, and Kao quietly commented on the artworks we passed. I didn't concentrate on the compositions or even what he said. It was soothing just to be with him, to hear the deep music of his voice. At last we stopped at an observation dome, where the entire night sky of K-2 sparkled above us in a glittering display of moons and stars.

Kao turned me to face him, and cupped my shoulder with one large hand. "Tell me about what has happened."

I didn't want to talk about Maggie, or the tense moments with the Binder. Instead I found myself describing the unpleasant encounter with Harold Springfield.

"Cherijo, did he harm you?"

Something in Kao's voice made me look up. My eyes widened. His expression was ominously still.

"Of course not." Why was he acting like this? I knew Jorenians didn't appreciate someone hurting their relatives, but I wasn't part of the family. "He never laid a hand on me, Kao. Even if he had, I could have handled him."

He ignored that. "Did he threaten you?"

Evidently I *did* qualify for the same ferocious protection. "No." As much as I disliked Kyle's father, I didn't want to see him in a lot of small pieces all over the colony. "He didn't do anything to me. Stop it."

"I know this man," Kao said, still looking every inch the warrior bent on a rampage. "He has a careless mouth."

"He was just being Terran." Which was becoming a universal synonym for *bigoted idiot*, I thought sadly.

The Jorenian's tense frame relaxed. "There are many differences between our people," he said, smoothing his palm over my cheek. "Do you regret being associated with me?"

"No." Until that moment I hadn't given a lot of thought to certain aspects of our relationship. Still, I wasn't ashamed of being involved with him. "I don't care what anyone says about us."

"I can never be Terran, Healer."

We belonged to two different species. So what? "I'll

never be Jorenian." I shrugged. "Springfield is a jerk,
Terra is welcome to him."

"Tell me what is in your heart."

I looked up into his strong, beautiful face. How could
I even describe how I felt? When I was with Kao, everything else in my life seemed to fade away. I was deeply
involved with a blue-skinned alien man, and I didn't
even know how that had happened. It just occurred to
me that it had.

There were problems, I reminded myself. "Tell me,
how many times have we been together in the past
two weeks?"

"Let me think," he said, pretending not to know. Jorenians had incredible recall. "Four?"

"Five times, and you know it. Twice I had to leave
you because of an emergency at the facility."

"I do not expect you to sacrifice healing for me," he
said. "As I recall, once *I* had to leave your company for
an unexpected change in the flight schedule."

"There will be more emergencies," I said.

"We both of us have occupations which demand much
of our time."

His open, confident manner had me blurting out,
"You want more than just my time, Kao Torin."

One blue finger traced the line between my brows.
"Yes. I do."

"Okay." I took a gulp of air. "So do I."

"Are you certain?"

"Not exactly." His keen eyes made me grimace.
"What if we can't fulfill—if I can't—" I made a frustrated gesture. "I don't know what the term is in your
culture. In mine, it is a relationship. What if we can't
make this work? What if my job demands more of my
time than you'd like? What if—"

"*What if* seems to preface most of your worries," Kao
said. "I can present similar concerns. What if I am permanently consigned to an inter-sector flight run? What
if I am injured in a shuttle crash? What if I am exposed

to HydroTyrannial Radiation and turn a disagreeable shade of yellow-green?"

I made a disgusted sound, and turned away to stare at the jewel-rich darkness above me.

"Forgive me." Kao gently pressed me back against his large frame. Even in my aggravation, my body responded to the proximity of his. He was big, warm, and alive. His palms began a gentle stroking motion over my shoulders. It gave me a sense of being sheltered, cherished.

It also made sweat bead along my hairline.

"On my world, there is a philosophy we learn as children: *The path may change swiftly. Live in the now.*" Kao's hand moved down the untidy cable of my braid. "There are no guarantees in existence, Cherijo. Not even if you had Chosen—if you had a relationship with another *Terran*."

Another Terran. Who? Duncan Reever? Now, there was a distinct impossibility. "So we take a chance on the future?"

"We take the now. Tomorrow—that will come."

"I know how serious it is for a Jorenian to Choose," I told him. "It means forever."

His hands stilled. "You have been educating yourself on my culture."

"Your HouseClans were founded on the ritual of Choice." I turned to face him, feeling panicky now. "If you Choose me, you're stuck with me, for life. That's a long time, Kao. Then there's the other minor problem with getting bonded. Like packing up everything and moving to Joren."

"We are not bonded," Kao said.

I yanked my braid from his grasp. "You're thinking about Choosing me." I threw down the statement like a dare.

"Yes."

"If you do that, you can't change your mind. You'll have to bond with me."

"Of course," Kao said. "Someday."

"Someday?" I said. That wasn't in the data I'd read about my boyfriend's culture. There was a definite, *short* time frame involved in the progression from Choosing to bonding on Joren.

"Cherijo, I respect HouseClan traditions. Indeed, I hold them close to my heart. Yet I have journeyed through the stars for many revolutions. Were you a Jorenian female"—Kao made a small gesture I'd learned meant mild exasperation—"my ClanParents would be constructing a ceremonial chamber and sending a bond proclamation to every Torin within signal range."

"But I'm not a Jorenian female," I said. "Does that mean your parents will hate me?"

Kao chuckled. "No, my heart. The fact that you are Terran will not alter their happiness for us."

"Then, I don't see what difference it makes."

"Terran culture has its share of customs regarding these matters. Do you think I would demand you follow the practices of my world and ignore your own?"

I was slow, but it finally dawned on me. "You mean, if you Choose me, you don't expect me to bond with you right away?"

"Not unless you are willing, and the time is correct for you." Kao released a sigh at my obvious disbelief. "Cherijo, how could you think me so uncompromising?"

I still wasn't entirely convinced. "You're sure you'd be willing to wait?"

"Yes," Kao said. "I could not honor you without honoring your beliefs, your work. Even when at times it seems there are a thousand and one demands upon you."

Two thousand and one, I thought wryly. "That won't change."

"It is part of what you are. A strong, dedicated, compassionate healer." Kao pressed his lips upon my forehead, and his arms came up around me. God, it felt wonderful when he held me like that. "Believe in what I say."

"I'm sorry. I do." I nuzzled the lower vault of his chest. "I want to be with you, Kao."

"I want to be a part of you, Cherijo. I want to wake with you upon each star rising, I want to sleep with you, like this. I will wait for all those things. For both of us." His eyes gleamed. "I would wait an eternity for you."

"I don't think it will take *that* long," I said as I cuddled against him. "As long as Dr. Mayer doesn't personally plan my schedule for the next thirty years, that is."

"There is another matter I would discuss with you," Kao said as he worked my hair from the long braid, and spread it free. His fingers were magic. He breathed in the fragrance of the cleanser I used, and a deep sound rumbled under my cheek. "Terrans do not require a bonding ceremony to know one another intimately. Do they?"

"Oh." I tried not to sound like an idiot. I failed. "Terrans generally—I mean, it's accepted that—" I cringed. I was babbling. I never babble. "Uh—no. Why?"

"In this matter, Cherijo," he said as he lifted my chin, "I do *not* wish to wait an eternity."

Kao kissed me. How can I describe it? It was stimulating, exciting . . . no. It demolished me. I stopped breathing, stopped thinking, and just held on.

I never knew kissing could be such a fierce, prolonged, arousing activity. It was sort of like being caught in a cardiac stimulator set on continuous biofeed. My nerves sizzled as his mouth and tongue moved over mine. He tasted exotic, dark, and delicious.

When he lifted his head and our lips parted, I was much more experienced on the subject. I was also breathless, clutching him with tight, numb hands, my limbs trembling, my blood roaring through my veins.

"Okay," I managed to gasp out. "How about now?"

"Not yet. You are not ready." My pained expression made him chuckle. "Soon, I promise. When we are both decided."

I began to ask him exactly what I was supposed to decide. A group of students chose that moment to enter the observation dome, and we were forced to leave. Kao escorted me to my living quarters, where he embraced me once more.

If women back on Terra ever learned how well Jorenian males kiss, the Genetic Exclusivity Act, along with the World Government, would be overthrown in a week. I would have drawn him into my rooms, but he stepped back.

"Soon," he said, before making that elegant farewell gesture and turning away. The way he looked back at me over his shoulder made me swallow, hard. "Think of me."

From the way my nerves were humming, I didn't have much choice.

CHAPTER NINE

Confrontations

The next rotation's shift was busy enough to keep me from brooding about Maggie, my father, and even Kao. I treated the usual routine cases of infection, injury, and other complaints. Hectic, but soothing in its own way.

When I came off my shift, Jenner was waiting for me, and plaintively indicated he'd had enough of our quarters for one day. At the same time, my display panel flashed.

"Let me get this first, pal," I said. When Joseph Grey Veil's face appeared, I felt an eerie sense of fatalism.

This was going to get ugly.

"Hello, Dad." I looked at him and tried to imagine him with Maggie. Couldn't do it.

My father never wasted time when he had a specific purpose. "There are matters I must discuss with you, Cherijo."

There was only one thing that mattered to him. "I'm not returning to Terra."

Joseph Grey Veil's dignity never wavered. "It is time I gave you certain information, Cherijo. Information that will alter your decision."

I sat down and pulled Jenner into my lap. He glared at the image of his nemesis while I stroked his pelt. "Nothing you say is going to—"

"More than thirty years ago, I made a discovery," my father said. "During my work with cellular replication processes."

I didn't need this again. "I've listened to all the stories, Dad. Believe me, I have them memorized."

"Please have the courtesy to listen without interruption." I reigned in a sigh. "It was during the initial trials with cloned organs that I found a successful method to identify and modify DNA strands in human beings."

I stiffened, and Jenner jumped from my lap. My cat made a sound that indicated he, for one, had heard enough.

"A method that would have been declared unethical, had I made it known to the medical profession at large."

My God, I thought. He was going to *tell* me. About everything. Here and now.

"It was necessary to forgo the usual manner in which I conducted my experiments, and explore this new method in secrecy. I set up my laboratory in a concealed location. A few dedicated subordinates volunteered to assist with my work."

I rose from my chair. "This is all very fascinating, but I just remembered I have to—"

"Sit down!" he said. Out of lifelong habit, I obeyed. "I am your parent. You *will* hear what I have to say."

"Fine." I could be dignified, too. "Go on."

"Given my reputation and body of work in the past, what I must tell you may seem at first reprehensible."

Reprehensible? I thought. No, Dad, not you. Say it isn't so.

"I could not, however, turn from what stood to be the next step in the evolution of mankind."

Naturally. Dad wouldn't have worked on the next step in something like, say, hangnail control.

"I spent the subsequent years redesigning Terran physiology. I won't detail the specifics, but in the end I was successful."

"You redesigned a human being."

"Yes, I did."

"Why?"

"Because I could, Cherijo." He permitted himself a haughty smile. "I implanted my own DNA in a fertilized ovum, then performed the genetic augmentations. It was a resounding success. The subject developed without flaw in an artificial embryonic chamber."

All this time, I realized, I'd been hoping it was just someone's idea of a sick joke. It wasn't. "How . . . ingenious of you."

"The enhancements I made on the subject's DNA sequence translated my theories into fact."

I felt nauseous. "Why are you telling me this now?"

"*You* are that subject, Cherijo."

I wasn't clever enough to manufacture a reaction for his benefit. Over fourteen light-years, we stared at each other. Father and daughter. Scientist and experiment.

"You knew *before* you left Terra," he said. I nodded. "I was made aware, of course, that certain materials had been removed from the lab. It was only logical to assume you had taken them." I didn't bother to correct him.

"I have been monitoring your progress since your conception. You have fulfilled every expectation and in most categories exceeded them."

My hands curled into fists. "Glad I made you happy."

"You can understand now why you must return to Terra."

No, but I had a whole new understanding of patricide. "I beg your pardon?"

"My research cannot continue until you return," he said. "You have an undeniable responsibility."

His lack of emotion still managed to amaze me. Me, the daughter who was nothing more than a glorified culture dish to him. "Is that it?"

"That is all I have to say."

"Good. Now it's my turn." He nodded regally. "How *could* you? How could you do this?" He opened his mouth to reply, but I held up a hand. "Never mind, you already answered that one. You even named me after the experiment. Comprehensive Human Enhancement Research, ID: 'J' Organism. C.H.E.R.I.J.O."

"An acronym seemed appropriate."

"And here all this time I'd thought you'd searched through the old family tree for a sentimental name to give your daughter."

"You may change your name, if you like."

"I think there's been quite enough changing of things in regard to me, thank you," I said. "You broke some serious statutes to do it, too. Still, why let a silly thing like world law mess up your tests?"

"Legislation can be changed," was his smug rebuttal.

"Yes, well, you and your gang of Genetic Exclusivists were very effective once. Why not again?"

"Once the specific applications are presented—"

"Ironic, isn't it?" I said. "The same legislation you orchestrated denied you the scientific freedom to openly pursue your experiment." I paused as something occurred to me. "Wait a minute. I get it. You were making sure no one else could experiment on human DNA. It was illegal. The field would be clear for you!" I laughed, appalled. "God, Dad, you make Machiavelli look scrupulous!"

"That is irrelevant," he said. "If I must continue to conceal the project in order to protect my work, I will. It will not prevent the research from proceeding."

"How moral of you," I said. "But we won't debate that now. I can't deny I exist because of your work, how can I? It's a shame you didn't program me with blind obedience along with the rest of the tinkering you did."

"Your consent and active participation was never integral to the experiment. I considered it counterproductive, in fact."

God, he had an ego the size of a League Troop Freighter. "Do you even *know* what you've done?" I expelled a choppy breath. "I never demanded you love me. Not once. But you *acted* the part of my father, for research purposes. For my entire life!"

"It was necessary—"

"It was monstrous!"

"You do not understand."

"No." Thank God, I didn't. I hoped I never would.

"Cherijo, the fate of our species rests in your hands. Once the advances I've made are known, there is no limit to what we can do for human beings."

It all came down to that. My father might unlock the secrets of life itself, but only Terrans would benefit. If I had ever entertained the idea of going back, it was gone forever now.

"I won't be your lab specimen."

"You can't refuse me—"

I wanted to scream. "Can't I? I still have all the evidence, don't I? If you try to force me to come back, I'll expose you. How do you think the World Nations would react to *my* speech?"

"You would only guarantee your execution."

"If that's what it takes," I said. "My life. My choice."

"You are in shock. These delusional—"

I'd never call this man my father again. "Good-bye, Dr. Grey Veil." I deactivated the display and pressed my hands to my face.

There were no tears. He didn't deserve any.

A summons from MedAdmin was waiting for me when I reported to the FreeClinic the next rotation.

K-Cipok frowned at me as I made to enter the exam area, and put out a tentative hoofed appendage to stall me. "Doctor, the order came from Dr. Mayer."

"Notice, K-Cipok, I don't instantly drop to my knees when you say his name." I hadn't slept, and the edge of my temper was tattered. Ignoring her pleading looks, I made to brush past her.

"Please, Dr. Grey Veil." She made a low, beseeching moo. "You know how he is about—"

"Me?" I uttered a short, dry laugh. "I'm an expert on that subject. What the hell—I'm in the mood for a good fight."

Dr. Mayer was not. When I entered his office, he rose to his feet and directed that I accompany him to HQ Administration. As in "Now, Dr. Grey Veil." I followed in his wake, fixing my gaze on his rigid shoulders. He drove me over in his personal glidecar, and this time *I* wasn't interested in being friendly.

Joseph Grey Veil worked fast.

A gathering of strange faces awaited us as we walked into one of the larger conference rooms. Everyone was wearing the formal robes donned only for occasions of strict protocol. They looked pretty silly, I thought. You'd never get me to walk around in one of those mini-tents. Ana Hansen approached me the moment she saw us enter. Her smile was as artificial as the lighting.

That was the first confirmation—I was in trouble.

One being rose from the center of a long table. He was vaguely humanoid, bright emerald-furred with innumerable short, whiplike arms that slashed the air as he addressed me directly.

"Grey Veil, Cherijo, Doctor?" I nodded. "The defendant has appeared. I now convene this hearing."

The defendant? What, was Dad suing me?

Ana steered me away from Dr. Mayer to a smaller table where we sat down. She spoke low and fast. "I'm your appointed representative. Don't do anything but answer their questions."

Which meant, don't volunteer anything, I surmised. Not a problem. I had no desire to confess that I was the result of an illegal experiment.

The members of the Council rose and individually identified themselves for the record drone. A Lankhi humanoid called Dsoo, an Ataderician who made a series of tonal belches instead of vocalizing, and two others who used nonverbal gestures. The one with the tendrils was called Z-cdew-nyhy, and seemed to be in charge.

"The Council will now hear the charges."

I listened as the record drone sonorously listed four separate violations of the Colonial Charter: Aiding and

Abetting Known Malefactors. Breach of Verbal Contract. Malpractice. Endangering the Lives of Fellow Colonists.

I was in *serious* trouble, and it had absolutely nothing to do with Joseph Grey Veil.

Ana got to her feet and started in the moment the drone finished. The absurd robes somehow looked stately on her as she paced before the assembled Council. Her smooth voice hovered somewhere between grave and outraged.

"Council members, this attack on Dr. Grey Veil is a deliberate orchestration of the lowest order. These charges have been brought solely to defame a distinguished new member of our community."

"Defense counsel's opening statement is so noted." A tendril snapped in the air. "Dr. Grey Veil, how do you respond to these charges?"

I glanced at Ana. "Do I get some *explanation* of these charges before I respond?"

Z-cdew-nyhy fixed all of his eyes on me. "As to count one, you treated and aided two Hsktskt intruders—"

"Dr. Grey Veil was cleared of all charges in conjunction with that incident," Ana said.

"Criminal, yes. These are civil charges. As to count two, Dr. Grey Veil defaulted on a verbal agreement made with the Bartermen Association."

"Assumption of agreement," the administrator said. Ana resumed her seat next to me, picked up a data pad, and waved it at the Council. "Check the incident records. Dr. Grey Veil never contracted formal barter with the Association."

Z-cdew-nyhy's fur bristled into stiff green spikes, but he maintained a bureaucratic monotone. "So advised. Count three regards the disposition and treatment of colonist Alun Karas, deceased."

I assumed Dr. Mayer had personally filed that particular charge, the heartless bastard.

"Count Four refers to a recent procedure during

which a dangerous amount of explosive toxin was deliberately released inside the FreeClinic facility."

"The Binder," I muttered to Ana.

"What Binder?" she whispered back.

A tendril cracked as the Council chief demanded attention.

"Ignorance of the Charter cannot be claimed. These are serious charges that individually represent grave concerns to Colonial Security. Collectively they portray an individual who poses a serious threat to the welfare of this settlement."

Thoroughly disgusted by this point, I leaned toward Ana. "Do I have to sit here and listen, or do they deport me now?"

Ana compressed her lips. "Give me a chance," she said.

Dr. Mayer was the first witness summoned to answer questions from the Council members. This was the perfect opportunity for the chief to get rid of me, I thought. He'd probably add a few more charges to the list to clinch it.

"Dr. Mayer, do the defendant's actions constitute a threat to the general welfare of the FreeClinic Medical Facility?"

"No."

"What is your opinion of her performance as a physician?"

"Dr. Grey Veil has performed her duties to the best of her ability and my complete satisfaction," Dr. Mayer said.

My jaw almost hit the floor.

The Lankhi Dsoo scratched his lateral fin with a two-fingered hand as he said, "You seem distressed by this hearing, Dr. Mayer."

My boss's imposing figure was practically vibrating with unspoken contempt as he turned and addressed the humanoid. "Distressed? No, Council member. I find it insulting."

Dsoo seemed perplexed by this. "But was it not a

member of your own staff who brought forth most of these charges?"

"Which staff member would that be?" the chief demanded.

"Dr. Phorap Rogan. You were aware of his petition, were you not?"

Rogan? That sneaking, odious little—

"No." Mayer's voice had an edge that sliced through the air. "I was not informed."

"Would you care to make a statement at this time regarding these charges?"

"I would. It is an insult that Dr. Grey Veil has been summoned before the Council without regard for protocol, to answer charges which constitute nothing more than pure slander."

I rubbed my eyes to make sure I wasn't hallucinating. No, it was definitely *Dr. William Mayer* who had made that statement.

"What did you do?" I asked Ana in a whisper. "Drug him?"

She smiled at Dsoo and said between clenched teeth, "Shut up."

The Ataderician Council member belched out an observation, which was translated to: "The Council has been advised that Dr. Grey Veil is vastly underqualified in her present position."

"Indeed?" One of Mayer's platinum eyebrows arched. "Who has provided such . . . advice?"

"Dr. Phorap Rogan."

Mayer uttered something inaudible that was not, I gathered, complimentary to Rogan. Dsoo leaned forward. "You wish to dispute, Doctor?"

"I do." Mayer's eyes were glacial with contempt. "Dr. Rogan has used Dr. Grey Veil's skills to cover his own ineptitude. His unprofessional behavior while on duty has subjected Dr. Grey Veil to countless indignities."

"I'm going to kiss that man's feet," I murmured to Ana. "For several hours." She camouflaged a chuckle with a cough.

The chief went on. "It is apparent that Dr. Rogan has personal issues which should be examined." He swept the room with a glance. "Where is Dr. Rogan? Is he not required to be present and substantiate his accusations?"

"What about this charge of malpractice?" Z-cdew-nyhy asked. "Gross negligence resulting in the death of a colonist is a serious accusation."

Mayer frowned. "Who charged Dr. Grey Veil with responsibility for Alun Karas's death?"

Dsoo consulted his file display and rolled his eyes. "Dr. Rogan."

"And the rest of this nonsense?"

The Council members exchanged silent looks before Dsoo answered once more. "All were filed by Dr. Rogan, with the exception of count two, which was filed on behalf of the Barterman Association."

"I challenge Dr. Rogan's charges."

"Understood." Z-cdew-nyhy's fur smoothed out. "These charges will be suspended until such time that Dr. Rogan and Dr. Mayer appear before the Council."

Ana leaned close to explain, "That means we don't have to defend you on those counts until an investigation has been conducted."

"Or I find Rogan," I muttered back.

The Council chief continued. "As for the charge of Breach of Verbal Contract, Dr. Grey Veil, do you wish to speak in your defense?"

Ana nodded at my glance. I rose to my feet and addressed the Council.

"Yes, I do. While at a meal interval with two friends, who will testify on my behalf, I made a 'wish' during a nostalgic discussion. It was not a trade summons. No Bartermen were present. I have never contacted the Association to request such a contract. I admit I was ignorant of the methods used by the Bartermen to secure agreements, but I don't believe it is their right to monitor personal conversations between others."

"We are familiar with the zealous nature of the Association." Dsoo seemed sympathetic. "Your case is not the first of this nature to occur."

"The Council can be assured that Dr. Grey Veil will not venture to make another such unguarded verbalization—" Ana said, but I shook my head.

"No, Administrator, I can't say that I won't. Respect for personal privacy must exist in any society. In this case the Bartermen have violated *my* rights."

"An interesting point, Dr. Grey Veil. The Council will take it under consideration." All five members rose to their feet after a short interval of deliberation. "We find the defendant innocent of charge two, Breach of Verbal Contract. All other counts are suspended until further notice."

The Council adjourned, and Dr. Mayer left the conference room before I could speak to him. Ana stayed behind to help me complete the requisite adminwork the Council needed.

"I'm not surprised that Rogan is behind all this," I told Ana when we were finished. "What I can't believe is that Dr. Mayer spoke on my behalf. He hates me more than Rogan does."

"You're wrong," Ana said as she handed me my disc copies of the hearing records. "He contacted me and insisted I act as your representative after he received the summons order."

I shook my head. "It was the perfect chance to get rid of me. Why did he do it?"

Ana smiled. "Ask him, Joey."

A half hour later I found myself standing outside Mayer's office, one hand extended to knock. Did I really want to know what motives the chief of staff had? The door opened unexpectedly, and Dr. Mayer eyed me with a distinct lack of enthusiasm.

"Come in," he said, and held the door open wider. I walked in, sat down, and waited as he took his chair. "You're here to find out why I defended you."

I spread my hands out. "Can you blame me?"

Dr. Mayer sat back in his chair. "Your father contacted me. He requested that I discharge you and have you deported back to Terra. When he couldn't persuade me to do as he asked, he began to make threats."

Curiouser and curiouser. "When did this happen?"

"Yesterday. He claimed you left home without his consent and against his expressed orders."

I made my response flat and matter-of-fact. "Dr. Joseph Grey Veil is no longer in a position of authority over me, Dr. Mayer." The white-haired head inclined in agreement. "To be blunt—why am I still here?"

"You expected me to comply with your parent's demands?"

"Dr. Mayer, you've been looking for any excuse to dismiss me."

"Prior to my conversation with your father, I would have agreed with you. My position, however, has subsequently changed." He adjusted his tunic as he straightened. "I don't respond to intimidation tactics. Even when they come from the great Joe Grey Veil."

My mouth unhinged. I'd never heard anyone refer to my father as "Joe." Ever.

"When I received your transfer application, I originally rejected it. We are in desperate need of qualified physicians, but I believed your inexperience made you of little value to this facility. I was subsequently ordered by the Quadrant surgeon general to approve your transfer." His expression told me plainly what he'd thought of that. "I took it for granted that your father had used his influence to secure this position for you."

"He didn't." What the chief had said explained a lot, but not everything. "Dr. Mayer, what *exactly* did my father say to you yesterday?"

Mayer made a rusty sound that might have been a laugh. "He demanded a dismissal based on incompetence. He claimed you are delusional and in need of long-term psych evaluation and rehabilitation."

"I recall you saying something along those lines when I reported the initial findings on Karas," I said.

For the first time since I had met him, William Mayer appeared uncomfortable. "I have made several erroneous assumptions about you." His lips compressed. "I do not habitually agree with your methods, Dr. Grey Veil, but I cannot deny your competency. You are an excellent physician."

Praise from Mayer. What would come next? A marriage proposal from Rogan? "Thank you."

"Don't fool yourself into believing this issue has been resolved. Your parent is a powerful man. However, in the future, I will do what I can to support your tenure here."

"I don't know what to say."

"Joe and I were students together at Medtech. He was a pompous ass, even in those days." Mayer's glance dared me to make the same observation about him. I didn't twitch a muscle. "It was his work on the Exclusivity Act that made me decide to transfer from the homeworld."

"You didn't agree with it?"

"No. I don't believe our species should isolate itself from the rest of the universe." He rose to his feet. "I've been informed Trauma is in dire need of our services."

"Let's go." I was more than willing to get back to work.

Mayer held up one hand. "If you see Dr. Rogan, don't confront him about these trumped-up charges he filed against you."

Given my temper and Rogan's penchant for gloating, that would be virtually impossible. "Why not?"

Mayer actually smiled this time. It was an awful thing to see. "I'd like that particular pleasure for myself."

Dr. mu Cheft stopped in during my shift to congratulate me. The facility grapevine had spread the tale of my skirmish with the Council, and Dr. Mayer's support.

"Phorap must be spaced to try something like this," mu Cheft's fishy features were drawn in dour displeasure. "Still, Dr. Mayer can't dismiss him."

"Believe me, Daranthura, we'd be better off if Rogan left," I said as I made a chart entry.

"There's only five of us now."

"Rogan's not much use without a medsysbank, you know that," I said. "I could train an orderly to do what he does."

"There's a thought."

I recalled Mayer's former attitude about me, and decided even Rogan deserved another chance. "On the other hand, maybe we can train him to do his own work."

"Compassion, Dr. Grey Veil?" Mu Cheft grinned.

"I wouldn't go that far," I said with a glare. "Still, everyone is entitled to make a mistake. Even Phorap."

"You're right, I suppose. It's not as if we're in a position to be choosey until we get better staffing."

"Have you seen Rogan today?" I was curious to know if Mayer had confronted him yet. I was hoping I could watch.

"No, and he's missed another shift. That's four in a row." Mu Cheft made an irritated sound. "Doubling up the rest of us. Dr. Dloh has mentioned spinning a cocoon for himself in the lounge."

"He hates the cots." I chuckled in sympathy. "They aren't very comfortable for him."

"I may demand my own immersion tank," mu Cheft said before he left. I consulted the next chart and found Paul Dalton was waiting for follow-up treatment for lower-back strain. According to the notes, Dr. Rogan had done the initial exam several days ago, and the Terran reported no improvement.

I signaled Assessment. "K-Cipok, send back Mr. Dalton, if you would."

Paul's appearance shocked me. He had lost a substantial amount of weight and was limping badly. His cheerful grin was now a hard white line he managed to bend up at the edges when he saw me.

"Hey, Doc," he greeted me, and then coughed and

groaned. "Wouldn't you know it, I threw out my back and now I'm getting a cold?"

"Trying to keep me busy, Paul?" I tried to tease, but I couldn't keep the concern from my voice. I lowered a foam cradle, harnessed it, and suspended his body for examination. The muscles were tightly knotted in the lumbar spinal region, but that didn't shake me as much as the scanner's data when I completed the sweep.

Paul Dalton's lungs showed signs of inflammation and multiloculated infiltrations.

I consulted his chart. "Did the muscle relaxant Dr. Rogan administer before have any effect?"

My neighbor shook his head, and coughed again. A fine spray of saliva and mucous landed on my tunic, but I ignored it as I repeated the scans.

"Paul, your back muscles are severely strained, and you have some fluid in your lungs. I'm going to admit you to the inpatient ward for treatment and observation."

"Am I contagious?"

"Not according to my scans," I said.

"Great." Dalton closed his eyes, then chuckled. "Do me a favor, will you, Doc? Call my supervisor and tell him I'm not the one who spread the infection around in my department. Must have been someone else."

"Your department?" I said, and my intuition kicked me. Hard. "Paul, how many people have this infection?"

"Almost everyone, but it's not—" He began to cough again, and I scanned his lungs once more. I didn't like what I saw.

It was the same type of pneumonia that had killed Alun Karas.

"Look, Doctor," Paul's supervisor was sympathetic but not concerned after I contacted him about the infection Paul described. "People get sick all the time here on K-2. Reaction to the new environment, a bug that comes in on a shuttle, you know how it is. No big deal."

"I need to check it out, just the same, Mr. Skrople."

"I can't have my entire staff report to the FreeClinic," the supervisor said. "We have nearly fifty people working per shift on this project."

"Then, I will come to you," I said, my own shift nearly complete. I had hoped to see Kao after work, but this would have to come first. "Is that acceptable?"

"Sure, I guess so."

The Engineering Department was working on a structural augmentation project on the fringe of the Colony. Clusters of gnorra trees and other native plants had been landscaped around the old storage building.

Low-rising beams were being set into place next to the existing structure, and I watched for several moments as grav-cranes positioned support posts for a new wall. The laughs and shouts the busy workers exchanged made me smile. Some kids never outgrew their building toys.

A small, wiry alien with dusky skin and an extra pair of lower limbs shambled over to me and handed me a head protector.

"Geef Skrople." Paul's supervisor introduced himself. "Sure you want to do this, Doctor?"

I eyed the crew. Now that I had been noticed, the good-natured jesting had stopped completely. "It will be the high point of my day," I lied. "If anyone objects, they will have to report to the FreeClinic for formal evaluation. At once."

"Uh, Doc—" The engineer looked sheepish. "If anyone objects, just let me handle it. It's safer."

Skrople stayed at my side. He had to intervene several times, joking with the surly workers to defuse what might have escalated into something really unpleasant. I wondered how someone with such a noticeable lack of bulk had gained such respect in this field.

I got my answer when one of the support beams began to work loose from a grappling hook. Skrople left me at once to handle it. My eyes rounded as the small alien wedged the heavy beam back into place using only his hands and a shoulder.

One of the crew standing by me saw my face and said, "He can hoist ten times that."

Paul's supervisor returned, and we continued our rounds. Once I'd finished the last scan, I tallied the data. The readings were disturbing.

I gazed directly at Skrople. "Eighty-two percent of your people display symptoms of viral infection in some form or another," I said. "Except no virus is registering on my scanner."

"Are you telling me they're sick but they're not sick?"

"I don't know what to tell you." I surveyed the busy site. "I have to report back to the FreeClinic with this information. The best thing to do is send everyone home, tell them to stay in their quarters, and take it easy."

"What about the next shift? They'll be reporting in four hours."

They would have to be checked, too. "I'll contact you before that and let you know what has to be done."

Skrople touched my arm. "Are you talking quarantine here, Doctor?"

"No." If this contagion was spreading, I had to keep panic from doing the same. "Don't worry. I'll be in touch."

CHAPTER TEN

Hazard Clause

By this time I had finally figured out *why* they put that Liability/Hazardous Duty clause in my contract. Being held hostage by an expectant father and nearly blown into the upper stratosphere by a suicidal fairy hadn't been enough. Now I was facing an unidentified, contagious pathogen on a planet that had only six physicians to cope with it.

No, PQSGO was definitely not giving me enough compensation. I'd have to see someone about a raise.

I left the engineering site more unsettled than I cared to admit. My instincts were screaming at me to declare level one quarantine conditions. I couldn't do it. Without hard evidence, that would be seen as premature, and almost assuredly would create panic throughout the colony.

The people in charge tended to frown on untidy things like mass hysteria and uncontrollable rioting.

I left my glidecar a short distance from the FreeClinic. The brief walk would give me a chance to sort out my thoughts before facing Dr. Mayer with my suspicions.

The night sky was filled with moons and stars that dimmed beside my growing sense of dread. It was no wonder I didn't see Phorap Rogan until he was almost on top of me.

"You!" It was screamed like a curse, accompanied by a spray of mucous that spattered over my face. My head snapped back.

Rogan was staggering, unable to remain in one position. His arms and legs shook badly as bursts of coughing racked his frame. Not good. His facial polyps were barely moving, slick with green, oozing rivulets of infection.

"Dr. Rogan? What—"

"Terran bitch!" He took a wild swing at me, and I ducked under his arm and spun away. Rogan lost his balance, then somehow pulled himself upright and shrieked, "Come here!"

I danced out of reach, at the same time trying to examine him. "Rogan, what happened to you?"

"You did this—" He broke off into tearing coughs, and spat a mouthful of phlegm on the ground between us. Not good at all. His breathing became labored as he ran his fingers over his facial grooves. "You did this to me . . . infected me . . . what is it?" He lunged and grabbed at me again.

I made a quick sweep with my leg the way Maggie had taught me, and hooked him behind the knee. In his wild attempt to compensate, he threw himself forward. I leapt out of the way. Rogan fell—hard. A hideous squelching sound accompanied the impact of his face on the walkway. He made a feeble attempt to rise, then collapsed again.

"Damn it!" I rolled him on his side. He was half conscious, but fever-induced delirium now converted his speech to incoherent babbling. Within seconds we were surrounded by other colonists, seeking to provide aid.

"Get back!" I yelled at the ring of faces. The thick stench rising from Rogan's body made some draw back abruptly.

"Let us help you—"

"No!" I refused the colonist's compassionate suggestion. "Move back, ten meters, now! He's contagious!"

That effectively dispersed the crowd. I shouted for one

of them to call for medevac as I loosened the neck of Rogan's filthy tunic and checked his pulse. His lungs were obviously filled with fluid; he was turning cyanotic around the open membranes. If I didn't get him to the FreeClinic fast, he'd suffocate.

I spotted two Militia approaching and shouted a warning to them. They took up positions to keep everyone at bay until the medevac team arrived. The mobile unit appeared moments later.

"Quarantine condition one," I yelled, and the team went into action.

Barriers were erected, colonists removed from the scene. Someone tossed a field aid case to me, another threw a heavy, insulated bundle. I released the ties and pulled on the thick biocontainment suit. Once I activated its seals, I rolled Rogan onto the gurney the team pushed over to me.

"Hold your position," one of the Militia said as he activated a remote biodecon unit. My suit and Rogan's gurney shroud were quickly sterilized.

"Clear a corridor to the back of the FreeClinic for us," I told one of the Militia team. I punched a touchpad on the evac unit's outer hull, and Dr. Mayer's face appeared on the display screen.

"What's your status, Dr. Grey Veil?"

"Dr. Rogan tried to attack me. He is infected with a pneumonic contagion. I've had direct physical contact."

"ID?"

"I can't tag it. It doesn't show up on my scanner."

"Method of transmission?"

"Unknown. Probable airborne or contact contamination."

The chief glowered. "Recommendations?"

"Institute level one containment at my location. Get air samples taken right away once we've cleared. Dr. Rogan's personal quarters should be sealed as well." I didn't ask that everyone who had been in contact with Rogan be checked for the contagion. That could be half the damn colony.

"What's Rogan's condition?"

"He's critical. We're coming in now."

I couldn't remove the bulky biocontainment suit until we were transported to the back of the facility and isolated in the special unit reserved for such cases. Once there, Mayer appeared outside the barrier as I hauled Rogan's heavy body onto an exam pad.

"Give me an update, Dr. Grey Veil."

"In a minute," I said. There would be no nurse to assist me now. No one else could risk being exposed. I stripped off the awkward suit and began my scans.

Rogan was dying from oxygen deprivation. His lungs were almost completely filled now, and his vitals were off the grid. Higher brain function was beginning to fail.

"All four lobes are severely inflamed. Massive pleural effusion, heavily multiloculated empyema, and abscesses forming as I speak. I need to get his lungs clear, or he's going to suffocate."

"Counter with antibiotics first."

I glared. "Meds won't do it fast enough. His physiology is only half-Terran. I have to ventilate him now."

"He isn't stable enough—"

"There's no more time!" I yelled at the barrier. "No more options!"

Mayer nodded curtly, and I went to work.

Rogan's eyes opened when I tried to insert the endotracheal tube through his mouth. Despite his condition, he got an arm up and shoved me away.

"No. I don't have time to anesthetize you," I said, and he twisted his head as I reintroduced the tube. "Stop it—don't fight me!"

His mouth sagged open, and he struggled to draw in enough air to enable his larynx to function.

"Noooooo . . ."

I had an idea of what would work. "Listen to me, you have to help me, Phorap," I said. "I can't do this by myself. Please!"

Appealing to his vanity worked. He allowed me to insert the tube and ventilate him. It was only a temporary measure, but might keep him alive long enough for me to find a treatment. I'd have to operate later and insert a tube to drain off the fluid from his lungs.

"Status," Mayer's voice was thin with impatience.

"We're all right for the moment. I've intubated Dr. Rogan." I turned to address the chief directly. "He exhibits the same symptoms as Alun Karas. Aspiration pneumonia."

"Does Rogan show signs of vomitus aspiration?"

"No," I said. "But *something* got into his lungs. My scanner can't identify whatever it is. Could it be an exotic mycoplasma?"

"An intermediate between bacterial and viral pathogens would still show up on our scanners, Doctor."

"I know that."

"Then, you know it cannot be a mycoplasma."

"Look." I took a deep breath. "I have evidence of transmission of this virus to at least fifty other colonists. I'll transfer my data scans to you. Review them and contact Engineer Skrople. The infected workers were sent home, but we'll have to institute a quarantine. Paul Dalton was admitted a few hours ago, he's infected as well."

"You have no evidence to justify a quarantine."

I stared at Mayer. "Please, just do it. I'll get the proof." He nodded. "I need microscans from the lab work-ups on Karas and Dalton." A thought occurred to me, and I closed my eyes for a moment. "Nurse Ecla was exposed at the same time Rogan was. The last time I saw her, she showed no signs of infection. Neither do I." Ecla, the dancing bouquet of beauty.

Mayer's crisp voice interrupted my thoughts. "I will have the affected workers and Nurse Ecla brought in and examined. But until a pathogen is identified, there will be no open declaration of a quarantine. Do you understand me? Not a word until we know what we're dealing with."

My turn to compromise. The chief was only doing his job. "Yes. All right."

"Keep me informed," he said, and walked out.

*   *   *

Twelve hours later Phorap Rogan began the inevitable slide into a coma. His progression was identical to Karas's; it was just taking a little longer for him to die. I remained at his side throughout the night, pausing only long enough to send a signal to Kao Torin and cancel our date.

There was no way I could tell the Jorenian I was quarantined with a dying patient. It was hard enough to fake a calm expression and invent an excuse about a routine emergency case. "Sorry I have to stand you up again, but I can't leave him right now." At least the last part of that was true.

"I am sorry, too. I am scheduled to leave for the Gra'-capa system tomorrow. The assignment will last several rotations." Kao's steady gaze made me feel guilty, but Mayer's orders had been implicit. "I will see you when I return, Healer?"

If only I could tell him. "I'm counting on it."

Hours later, Dr. Mayer released the barrier seals and walked in. My bleary eyes moved from the data readings on my scanner to the chief's face. I couldn't even work up a good whimper of outrage. "Are you nuts?"

"Bioscans have revealed nothing."

"They're wrong," I said.

"Dr. Grey Veil, I conducted the fifth and sixth repeated scan myself," he told me. "There were no contagions present in any of the samples."

"No *known* contagions."

"Unidentified contaminants would still leave a chemical signature, Doctor. The scans were clean." Mayer surveyed Rogan and consulted his chart. "How long do you estimate he has left?"

"Twelve hours, maybe a little more. His physiology is more resilient than Karas's was, and I've surgically installed an open drain in his chest."

"Fortunate. It will give us time."

"Not much." A yawn tugged at my jaw, and I had to fight the urge to close my eyes. "What about Dalton?"

"No dramatic change in symptoms. No response to full spectrum Terran antibiotics."

"The workers from the project site? Ecla?" I asked.

"No symptoms other than what you originally observed, and no progression. Nurse Ecla's scans were clear."

"So in other words, I'm starting to look like a paranoid moron." Mayer didn't respond, and I began to rub my eyes. "I need to get some sleep."

"Go home."

"Don't you think we should at least continue the quarantine protocols until I can figure out how to identify this contagion?" I asked.

The chief put down Rogan's chart. "I will continue *most* of the protocols for another cycle. We will then review the cases and decide on a course of action."

"We?" The yawn finally won.

Dr. Mayer appeared somewhat affronted. "You and I, Dr. Grey Veil."

Drowsiness fled, replaced by utter astonishment, but the chief dismissed me without elaborating.

Somehow I got to my quarters without losing consciousness, although I was fuzzy on the means I used to get there. I recalled someone helping me into public transport and pushing me out at the front of my unit. I staggered to my door and came to an unsteady halt when I saw the graceful, grey-haired Chakacat waiting patiently beside it.

"Dr. Grey Veil?"

I looked around but didn't see Jenner. "Hello, Alunthri."

"May I speak with you?"

"Sure. Come in." I opened the door panel and found Jenner pacing nervously inside. He made a sound of pleasure and dashed up into Alunthri's open arms.

"Some guard cat you are," I tried to joke, but I was really too tired to do more than shuffle to a chair and drop.

"He is very intelligent for his kind. Affectionate, as well."

"You haven't been around when I get home late."
Jenner glared at me, and I nodded. "You're entitled,
too, pal. My hours stink." I looked at the Chakacat.
"What can I do for you, Alunthri?"

"I am seeking assistance, Doctor. My owner recently
expired, and I find I am without deed."

"I'm sorry to hear that." I tried to sound compassionate, but I was beat. "Uh, what does that last part mean—
without deed?"

"I am under no ownership."

I saw the license chip was gone from its collar. "Isn't
that a good thing?"

"Not under the terms of the current Colonial Charter."

Paragraphs flashed through my mind until I focused
on the exact application to domesticated life-forms. Oh,
no. "They're going to ship you back to your homeworld."

"Unless I can establish deed with another colonist,
yes, I will be sent back to Chakara and resold."

"That's unfair."

"I agree. Can you assist me, Dr. Grey Veil?"

It wasn't hard to guess what form of help Alunthri
wanted. "Are you asking me to take over your deed?"

"Yes."

"Alunthri, I couldn't treat you like a domesticated
companion," I said. "In my eyes, you are sentient."

"Thank you." Alunthri put Jenner down and pros-
trated itself before me. "Yet until such status is granted,
I must find ownership here on K-2, or be sold. Please,
Doctor, help me."

"Why me?" I asked. "I'm a terrible owner. My work
hours really are outrageous. I don't give Jenner the attention he needs. Why would you want someone like me
to own you?"

"Because you would *not* own me, Doctor."

The big cat definitely had a point. "What would you
do?"

Alunthri rose. "Continue my studies. My former
owner was indulgent and allowed me full use of his per-

sonal terminal. I am currently studying primitive art and sculpture among aquatic species in this quadrant."

A giant alien cat who studied art. "Sounds wonderful. What do I have to do to transfer ownership?"

"Simply make a record of acceptance with Colonial Administration." The colorless eyes watched me closely.

"I'll file it as soon as I get a few hours' sleep. Is that okay with you?"

"Yes." Invisible lines of tension relaxed throughout the Chakacat's form, and it smiled. "How can I express my thanks?"

"Let me sleep. As much as possible."

"Of course."

I looked around through bleary eyes. "We'll have to work out our living space."

Alunthri's whiskers twitched above a feline grin. "At your convenience."

"That would be in, oh, say eight hours. I'm going to bed now, before I fall on my face. Do you mind sleeping on the sofa tonight?"

"Not at all."

I didn't want to think about what it was going to be like to have two cats, one that could talk back to me. I stumbled over to my sleeping platform and collapsed atop the mattress. An absent thought crossed my mind, and I called out, "Alunthri? Who was your owner?"

"His name was Alun Karas."

Oh, terrific. "I'm sorry. He was my . . . patient." I was mumbling. "I tried . . . couldn't save . . . him . . ."

Exhaustion pushed me into the dark, and I stayed there. Menacing dreams of an epidemic caused by my own negligence refused to grant me peace. I had missed something. Something important. I was failing everyone.

You saved me, someone murmured next to my ear. You will save others.

The nightmares dwindled away.

Alunthri woke me some nine hours later when a message came in from the FreeClinic. The elegant cat immediately went about serving me breakfast while I listened

to a tired Ecla relay updates on all my possible contagion cases.

"The colonists who came in contact with Dalton have
all shown improvement during the night." The Psyoran's
ruffles looked decidedly wilted. "Dalton himself has no
more pneumonic symptoms, and is only complaining
about his strained back."

"What about Rogan?"

"Dr. Mayer attended him a few hours ago. He came
out of the coma, and his lung condition seems to be
responding to the latest antibiotic regime."

I'd left him dying, and now he was awake and probably giving the inpatient ward as much trouble as he could
get away with.

"Ecla, whatever you did while I was sleeping," I began
in a surly tone, then grinned and said, "keep doing it."

She looked down at her drooping frills and stained
tunic. "No, thanks. All I did was clean up patients. You
wouldn't believe how much mucous a Trytinorn can
cough up on you. I think some of them did it on purpose." She tugged at her collar. "I'll have to spend an
hour under the cleanser."

"Spend a whole day," I said. "You deserve it."

"Oh, I almost forgot—Dr. Mayer would like to see
you in his office as soon as you report for shift change."
Ecla added a gentle, rippling gesture of relief. "I'm
going home."

"See me on your next shift. I want to review your
chart notes with you."

"That will be in two days. I've got to report to the
Botanical projects for another allotment, then I'm off
duty."

"Planting seedlings?" I made a face, recalling my
own fiasco.

"Pruning gnorra trees. It's not bad for an allotment."

"Better you than me. Thanks, Ecla." I watched
Alunthri's graceful movements as it began to clean up
the remains of my meal, and I touched one paw. "You
don't have to do that, Alunthri."

"I would like to."

"Then, you will make me as lazy as His Majesty over there," I nodded toward my smaller, napping companion. "Make me a promise, Alunthri. Promise that we'll treat each other as equals."

"Equals?" The word stunned the Chakacat.

"Sure. That's what freedom is. Being treated like everyone else is. Since I can't give it to you out there"—I swept my hand toward the exterior corridor—"I'll make sure you have it in here."

"I don't know how to respond," Alunthri said.

I grinned and pushed it into a chair. "Why don't you start by telling me what *you'd* like to have for breakfast?"

I made a mental note as I left for work an hour later to contact Ana Hansen and update her on the change of situation in regard to the Chakacat. I had already filed for a new license chip for my new roommate.

The satisfaction this new arrangement brought renewed my spirit. By the time I reached the FreeClinic, I was ready for whatever trouble I was in. I went to MedAdmin and found Dr. Mayer waiting for me in his office.

"Rogan's lungs are nearly clear now. I removed the chest drain." Mayer tossed the chart down. "He's demanding to be discharged and intends to file charges against you for malpractice—again."

"Good. I'll file assault charges."

After the rest of the case histories were reviewed, Mayer paused. We gazed at each other.

"Ever seen anything like this?" I asked.

"No." The chief's eyes bored into mine. "Nothing."

Even though the patients were now recovering, there was no reason they should have gotten sick in the first place. *Something* had infected them.

If it had been caused by an unknown viral pathogen, it could be in the process of mutation. A virus's sole purpose was to invade and parasitize host cells for replication purposes. Sometimes the nasty little bugs went into hiding while they adjusted their attack strategy. Viruses borrowed enzymes from the host, even incorporated themselves into a cell's chromosomes before they began replicating. Such changes in antigenic character could make the virus even more lethal.

I made a last grab at another possibility. "What is the likelihood that we're looking at some kind of drug-induced condition that mimics contagion? One that progresses depending on the amount introduced to the subject's system?"

"Analysis indicates no foreign substances, chemical or otherwise." Mayer held up a stack of data discs. "The complete report from the lab runs. Toxicology, decon, and bio, all ran clear. Nothing."

The facts were irrefutable. "There's no doubt, then. I was wrong."

"No." Mayer tossed the discs back on his desk. "Rogan should have died last night. Karas did. Dalton and the rest displayed beginning stages. You have something here, Doctor."

I wanted to shriek with frustration. "But what is it?"

"You're going to find out. Effective immediately, you are relieved from Trauma duty and assigned to research this outbreak exclusively."

I shot to my feet. "What?"

"Sit down, Doctor."

"You can't reassign me now!"

"I can, and I have." Mayer was unyielding. "Sit down."

I sat. "Why research? For God's sake, use Crhm, or lab services—"

"Dr. Crhm doesn't have your talent for diagnosis. He's a good physician." The chief's jawline hardened. "For this kind of research, I need a genius."

I scoffed. "I'm not a genius."

"You're the daughter of one." That shut me up. The chief went on to briefly outline what he wanted me to do. Under different conditions, I might have been complimented by Dr. Mayer's faith in me. Circumstances that didn't involve my father's legacy, or the lives of the colonists of K-2.

"I hope you know what you're doing," I said. "If I can't identify a contagion—"

"Then I suspect you will be working on this for a very long time," Mayer said. "Or not long at all." We were both thinking of the same possibility.

Epidemic.

MedAdmin had cleared a large space for my new lab between Clinical Services and Outpatient Testing. It was set up with a self-contained environment, complete with new room seals and the best equipment Dr. Mayer could put his hands on.

"Very nice," I said. "All I need is a sleeping platform, and I can move in."

I spent several hours trying not to grumble while the maintenance crew moved equipment to my specifications. If I failed to find this bug, it wouldn't be due to lack of resources. That thought made me unusually testy.

"I can do this," I told myself as I fiddled with an electroniscopic scanner. I propped my forehead on one palm and sighed. "No, I can't."

That was when the movers diplomatically decided to take a break. After a moment I followed their lead, left word with MedAdmin, and took a long walk.

I ended up at the Trading Center. Lisette was currently serving what she called an "English Tea." I decided to try some of the baked items along with a server of fragrant golden Oolong tea.

I was sitting by myself, falling in love with something called cherry scones, when the statuesque beauty pulled up a chair next to me. I eyed her warily. "Lisette."

"I heard of the excitement with Dr. Rogan," she said, tossing back her curly mane as she sat down. "He is better?"

"His condition has improved."

"Can you make him sick again?"

There was a tempting idea. "Sure. Any particular reason?"

She treated me to a lofty sneer. "He owes me more credits than half the colony."

It figured. "File a Charter violation."

"I would, but he claims my cuisine was substandard."

"He's a dead man," I said, and she smiled. "Okay, perhaps a bit extreme. I know, I could inject him with an enzyme to make his mustache fall out."

"Oh, no, not the mustache." Lisette pretended to be horrified. "It is the only part of his face I can bear to look at."

I laughed. "Lisette, remind me never to fall behind on my tab."

"Unlike Dr. Rogan, you would never do so." With all the regal dignity she possessed, she leaned closer and placed one long, elegant hand on my arm. "I did not like you at first," she said. "Now I know you, I respect you, Doctor."

"Thank you," I said and decided to return the compliment, just for insurance purposes. I really liked these cherry things. "And I have never tasted more heavenly cuisine in my life than what you create."

"Humph." She gave me a baleful frown. "You do not eat enough to keep a Rilken alive." Her gaze softened as she noted the shadows I knew were still under my eyes. "Have you seen Reever lately?"

As a matter of fact, I hadn't, not since the Binder incident. I still had no idea if he and Lisette were involved, although her interest indicated some kind of relationship existed. There was also that moment when I'd first met both of them, the way he had touched her cheek so tenderly. I shook my head, and waited.

"Duncan and I were on Terra together, many years ago," Lisette said. "I was troubled. My family was gone. Duncan was—Duncan."

"You were . . . childhood friends?" was my guess.

Lisette smoothed a wrinkle from the sleeve of her scarlet tunic. "More than that. At school he was my protector. When I was sad, he knew. He gave me comfort.''

"You're talking about Duncan *Reever*?"

She frowned at me. "He is a very private man. Very wary of others. Beneath that, he is everything generous." Just as I began to wonder what form of comfort Reever had provided, she shook her head. "No, no, not like that. He was like a big brother. The others at the school, they were cruel. I was too tall, too thin, too emotional. Duncan wasn't like anyone."

No, he wasn't. I pictured Reever, then tried to imagine him as a generous, protective young man. Nope, couldn't do it. I'd have to see photoscans.

"You don't see how he looks at you."

"Lisette, Reever looks at me the same way he would a rather dull botanical specimen," I said. "What possible reason would he have . . ." I faltered as I recalled the incident in the grove. "Why are you telling me this?"

"Precisely because you don't see him, know him as I do, Doctor," Lisette said. "Duncan has feelings for you."

"Feelings for—" I shook my head, chuckling. "No, I don't think so, Lisette."

The tall woman stood. "Pay attention to his eyes, *chérie*," she said. "They are the gateway of the soul." She sauntered away to wait on a new group of customers.

Whatever Lisette had meant to do by our little "chat," the result kept me preoccupied until I returned to the lab. I finished with the maintenance crew, and was left to begin calibrating the analysis equipment.

I completed the last in time to receive a signal hours later via incoming transport. It was a direct relay from Kao Torin's starshuttle.

"Kao!" I grinned as the screen projected his features beneath a flight helmet. "Where are you?"

"I am on the return route from Gra'capa Minor." The Jorenian had been escorting some League dignitaries around the quadrant. After he'd described some of the amusing details of his mission, he surveyed me gravely. "You have been working too many hours, Cherijo."

"I didn't have a reason to leave the facility, except to sleep or eat." I wasn't going to describe the harrowing events of the last two days. "You were gone."

"May I suggest a reason?" I nodded. "Docking Station Sixteen," he said. "I will be landing in two hours."

"I'll be there."

I had just enough time before Kao's arrival to make a stop at my quarters and get cleaned up, if I left the lab immediately. As I drove my glidecar toward housing, I wondered why I felt so muddled.

The unidentifiable pathogen nagged at me, of course. My new responsibilities could theoretically determine the fate of seventy-four thousand lives. What if I failed, and this thing got out of control? I thought back to my orientation with Ana Hansen, when I had warned her of just that sort of scenario. We'd be helpless, and then we'd all be dead.

On the other hand, this could be just the newest version of the K-2 common cold, and I was simply being paranoid.

I arrived at my quarters, and greeted the cats. While I was in my cleansing unit, I forced aside thoughts of my professional dilemma and considered the more personal ones.

Lisette's revelations about Duncan Reever replayed in my head. That little talk had also left me feeling very uncomfortable. *You don't see how he looks at you,* she'd said. Just how *was* the chief linguist looking at me, anyway? *Duncan has feelings for you.* Well, if he did, I had never encouraged him. I'd argued with him, yelled at him, and even decked him once, but I'd never encouraged him. No, I decided, Lisette was simply imagining the whole business.

I fed Jenner and chatted briefly with Alunthri before leaving for Transport to meet Kao. I should have been happy about seeing him again, I chided myself on the way to the shuttle docks. Yet even the Jorenian man in my life had me worried.

I'd virtually agreed to become his Chosen, but had yet to tell Kao exactly *who* he was getting himself engaged to. It was bad enough that I was Terran. How would Kao feel when he found out his bondmate-to-be was a genetically engineered clone? Would it destroy the feelings he had for me? Disgust him? How would I find the words—not to mention the courage—to tell him the truth?

By the way, Kao, my mother was really an embryonic chamber?

Would it bother you to know that my father is actually my twin brother, too?

How does your HouseClan feel about complex deoxyribonucleic acid mutations diluting the family bloodlines?

What frightened me more than telling him was the thought of losing him. I'd never planned to fall in love, but here I was. Unable to imagine a future without Kao Torin in it.

When his starshuttle landed, I was pacing back and forth at ramp sixteen. Kao cleared the last of the biodecon scans and walked down the shuttle ramp behind his passengers. His gaze swept over the crowd until our eyes met.

I expected him to smile, to call a greeting as usual, but instead he went still. An expression of something like pain etched his features as he gazed at me.

No, not pain. Longing. Hunger. Loneliness. How did I know? I felt the same things.

Suddenly I was pushing through the crowd to get to him. One moment I was reaching out my hands to take his, the next I was being lifted into the air. Kao's powerful arms swept me completely off my feet.

"Cherijo," he said. My hands touched his face. For once I couldn't think of a single thing to say. He strode down the ramp and carried me off in front of everyone. I hid my face against his flight suit, embarrassed by the very public exhibition we were making.

Okay, it was sort of romantic, too.

His glidecar was waiting outside Transport, and he placed me in the passenger's seat with great care. He took his position behind the controls, and then my hand with his. I was still at a loss for conversation. We drove away, sharing the silence, our fingers entwined. At his housing unit, he helped me from the vehicle and lifted me once more into his arms.

I liked romance, but this was getting a little ridiculous. "I can walk," I said with a nervous laugh.

His smile was reassuring. "Let me hold you."

I had been in Kao's quarters once before, so I didn't feel uneasy when he finally set me on my feet. What kept me speechless was the way he was staring down at me.

There was no need for a discussion. I wanted to be with him. I knew he wanted the same. I could feel the tension between us growing, flaring when he touched my cheek with his hand.

"I must tell you—" he said, but I pressed my fingers to his lips. Men. They never knew when to shut up.

"Shhhh." I put my hand over his, and rubbed my face against the broad palm. My eyes never left his. "I've missed you."

"You are decided?"

Of course I was decided. I knew what to expect as a Terran, and had researched the database for the specifics involved with his species. There weren't many details, but I had learned that Jorenians and Terrans were completely sexually compatible. I'd even taken the precaution of getting a contraceptive booster.

"I'm sure." Saying that didn't make me feel any more confident. It was my first time, and my hands shook as I fumbled with my tunic.

Kao's hands covered mine. "Allow me," he murmured against my lips.

My body, a disciplined, often-abused tool I always used without thought, slowly became a stranger to me. Kao's hands gently freed me of my garments, and guided me as I helped to remove his. I was astonished to see several scars marring the perfection of his body. Deep ridges of old injuries marked his shoulder, side, and upper thigh.

I touched the one above his heart. "What happened here?"

"Warrior training," he said, pulling me closer.

That first touch of skin on skin was shocking. Before I could catch my breath, Kao began finding sensitive spots I never knew I had. The glide of his fingers over my shoulder left a trail of tingling warmth. Under his stroking palm, my breast swelled and flushed. My thighs trembled as he brushed his lips over my hair.

This wasn't so bad, after all.

He lifted my chin. "You honor me, Cherijo," he said. There was no equivalent for the word "love" in Jorenian, "honor" being the closest to it.

"Yes. I love you, Kao." Okay, so it didn't translate. He understood me.

His skin was damp beneath my fingers. I curved a hand around his neck, and discovered an odd, textured tattoo hidden beneath his hair, just below his left ear.

"More warrior stuff?" It was dark, and shaped like the upswept wings of a bird. When I traced it with a fingertip, he groaned with pleasure and dropped to his knees. That put him exactly at my eye level.

"My HouseClan symbol," he muttered against the curve of my arm. I gasped as his face turned, and his mouth opened over my tightly beaded nipple.

He ran over me like soft, warm rain, until there was no inch of skin he had not touched and stroked into awareness. This was what all the fuss was about, I thought. I could get used to it. My shivering euphoria quickly burst when I heard Kao say, "I would Choose you now, Cherijo Grey Veil."

What? I thought blankly, and went very still. *"Now?"*

Kao frowned. "You said you were decided."

"Oh. I didn't know you were talking about *that*."

What had happened to waiting for an eternity for me? "Um . . . can't we talk about this later?"

His brow touched mine. "I must. We cannot be intimate without Choice. It is forbidden."

Pre-Choice intimacy was *forbidden*? Great. Why wasn't *that* in the database files, under *Before you have sex with a Jorenian, read this?* His timing was less than perfect, too. It would have been nice to know little details like this *before* he'd gotten me naked and half-crazed with desire. The only comfort I had now was knowing I wasn't the only virgin in the room.

I dimly heard him speak in his own language. "Etarra nek t'nili. M'adeunal," he said. Then my TI kicked in when he repeated the ritual words. "Come with me to the eternity we share. Be my Chosen."

This was it. Like it or not, Kao wanted to Choose me. There would be no going back. I closed my eyes, steadied myself against him. Whatever I decided to do now would determine the course of our future forever. There was so much he didn't know. I had to tell him, I thought, and opened my eyes.

"I will not hurt you," he whispered as his big hands moved over me, soothing my tense form. "But I will not let you go."

Maybe he would. "There are things you don't know about me," I said. "I have to tell you about—"

Now his fingers touched my mouth. "It does not matter."

"It will," I said as I pushed his hand away. "I'm not what you think I am."

"You are Cherijo Grey Veil. That is all that matters to me."

"Kao, I'm not—I am a—I'm—" I groped for the right way to tell him the happy news.

"Cherijo, you could be a disguised Hsktskt, and my decision would not change. I will Choose no other."

What he meant was it was me or no one. Period. Forever. From what I knew of his people, he meant it, too. Like it or not, Jorenians mated for life.

"All right," I said at last. On the Jorenian bondmate desirability scale, a clone *had* to be better than a Hsktskt. Even a disguised one. "I'll be your Chosen."

Kao rose to his feet. One arm encircled my hips, a muscle flexed, then suddenly I was at *his* eye level. My feet dangled two feet above the floor. Instinctively I wrapped my legs around him.

In an unexpectedly fierce tone he said, "I claim my Choice."

He certainly did that. There was the sensation of being stretched, filled, pleasure edged by momentary pain. I was so absorbed in watching Kao's reaction that I didn't care. A moment later I was immersed in my own body's response.

The room began to whirl. We were entwined, moving together, until I felt breathless and dizzy. I needed something . . . wanted to . . . the pleasure changed, became torment, driving us together again and again, until the sensations nearly destroyed me.

"Kao!"

When I could breathe again, I floated down like a feather—drifting, untroubled, complete. I opened my eyes. We were still in the center of his quarters, clothing scattered around us. My hair and limbs were wrapped around him. He disengaged our bodies and gently placed me back on my feet. I smiled up at him.

"Wow." Someone needed to update the database. "That was incredible." He brushed his lips over mine, but when he drew back I saw the bleakness in his eyes, felt the tension in his limbs. "Kao?"

"I could not stop myself," he said, his hand stroking the hair away from my brow. "I frightened you, hurt you."

"No." I shook my head, swaying a little. "Not at all." Now I understood why most patients got so upset whenever I had to temporarily restrict certain activities. I'd be mad, too.

He lifted me up, carried me over, and placed me on

his wide sleeping platform. Carefully he pulled the bed linens over me, and made as if to stand.

I pulled him back down. "Don't go."

"You are so small," he said, and touched his forehead to mine. "I hurt you."

"It always hurts Terran females the first time," I said, and smiled. "It wasn't bad. I hardly noticed."

"Cherijo." He sat next to me, held my hand between his. "You honor me, but I—"

Hadn't I said men never knew when to shut up? Exasperated now, I tugged his arm. "If you don't get in bed with me this minute, I'll do a lot more than honor you. You won't like it, either."

His lips curved with relief. "I will never leave you again," he said as he stretched out next to me. He placed one palm over my heart. "I dwell here forever."

Hours passed unnoticed as we lay together, holding each other. I slept for a long time, and when I opened my eyes his hands were caressing me. It was a great way to wake up. Each time we made love, the unique meld of our bodies thrilled me.

"If we were on Joren, would we be bonded now?" I asked him once, my cheek pressed against his chest.

"Almost," was his reply.

I lifted my head warily. "There's more?"

He rumbled a soft laugh at my disbelief. "Wait and see."

While we were together, Kao filled in some of the gaps about Jorenian sexuality. I learned a complete bond could only take place on Joren, where Kao's entire HouseClan would acknowledge the match during a mysterious ceremony, and that Jorenian males control conception, through deliberate glandular repression (so much for my contraceptive booster).

Leaving him after that night was the hardest thing I'd ever done. When I drew away from his last embrace, he turned me to a mirror and lifted my hair away from my throat. There, beneath my left ear, was the faintest shadow of a mark. A mark like the upswept wings of a dark bird.

"E'amyorn keleah es, m'adeunam," he said, and met my eyes in the glass. "You bear the mark of my honor, my Chosen. To remember, Cherijo."

I knew without asking, the mark would slowly grow darker, until it matched his. In the weeks to come, the only thing that kept me going at certain points was to lift my hand and touch the mark he'd left on me.

To remember we would always be together.

PART THREE:

Complication

CHAPTER ELEVEN

Offplanet

A week after Kao left his mark on my throat and my heart, I arrived at the FreeClinic and found my lab had been sealed off.

Despite the apparent full recovery of the latest cases (including Rogan, who had promptly filed another malpractice charge against me), I was sure there was more at work here than a simple infectious bug. I'd spent the last seven rotations scanning, comparing, and dissecting every detail from the case profiles involved. I'd made no significant progress.

Now I couldn't get the damn door to open.

I stabbed an impatient finger at the touchpad, which had been keyed to disregard my pass code. "I know I wasn't that nasty to the sanitation crew yesterday."

"Dr. Grey Veil." Dr. Mayer joined me, flanked by Administrator Hansen.

"Hi, Ana. Dr. Mayer, I can't get into my lab," I said. "Whose toes have I stepped on now?"

The chief turned to Ana. "How many off days did you tell me Dr. Grey Veil has been allocated since her initial transfer, Administrator Hansen?"

"Thirty-two, sir."

I was startled. "That many?"

"Of those, how many has she actually spent off duty?"

Wait a minute, I thought. What exactly was going on here?

"Fifteen." Ana plucked an invisible piece of lint from her sleeve to avoid my glare. "A recent study of work-related stress syndromes illustrated the negative effects of blatant disregard for adhering to duty schedules."

"Negative effects?" I was indignant. "Blatant disregard?"

"Indeed?" Mayer appeared thoughtful. "I would appreciate the chance to review the data myself."

Although they preferred to chat as though I was invisible, I'd had enough. I waved my hand to get their attention.

"Excuse me? This is all very fascinating, but it won't help me get this door panel open. Why has my lab been sealed?"

"That," Mayer said, "should be obvious. You are not scheduled for a shift today, Doctor." Was that *humor* gleaming in the chief's steely eyes? No. I must have been hallucinating.

"Open the lab. Please," I said.

"Not today."

"I'll take tomorrow off. I just want to finish a scan series that I—"

"Not today," Mayer said again. "I have scheduled transport for you that will leave K-2 within the hour."

"Transport?" My voice squeaked. "Offplanet?"

"Think of it as a furlough."

"But I don't want to go offplanet."

"You don't have a *choice*, Doctor," Mayer said. "You will either take a furlough, or report to psych services for a competency evaluation." Nodding to Ana, the chief turned and strode away.

Ana held up her open palms as I turned on her. She looked a little guilty. "Not my decision. Ready to go?"

I closed my eyes. "Where?"

"On a shuttle, into orbit, out of the—"

"I get the general idea," I said. "What's to stop me

from just going home and sleeping?" Or seeing Kao, my guilty conscience added, who had been very understanding lately about my obsession with finding the bug.

"I get to escort you to the shuttle," Ana said, putting her arm through mine and patting it like the good mother hen she was. "Chief's orders."

"I liked it better when he hated me."

We stopped at my housing unit to check on Alunthri and Jenner and pack a few items. Alunthri was delighted by the news of my kidnapping and promised to look after Jenner. Ana admired the new living arrangements, which gave the Chakacat its own room and a private terminal. From what I'd learned, Alun Karas had relegated the big cat to a rug on the floor. I had refused to follow suit.

While Ana was talking to Alunthri, I signaled Kao. There was no answer, so he must have been on duty. I left a message promising to signal him later.

On the trip to the shuttle docks, we discussed my new roommate. Ana proposed that our unique living arrangement could help her fight to gain sentient status for the Chakacat. When we pulled up to Transport, the sight of a familiar, hulking silhouette made my jaw drop.

"The Bestshot!" I said. "Why didn't anyone tell me Dhreen was on planet!"

"He just got here," Ana said, and gave me a big, satisfied grin. "Go on, he's waiting for you!"

I paused long enough to give her a hug, which creased her perfectly pressed tunic and made her laugh.

"Thanks, Ana."

Inside the shuttle, the Oenrallian was replacing some frayed cables with something somewhat less worn. Dhreen cheerfully hailed me as I made my way up the less-than-stable ramp. "Doc!"

"Dhreen, I should have known you'd be in on this." I gave him a half hug. "Still patching the old girl together?"

"I don't repair what isn't fractured," he said. "Come

206 S. L. Viehl

on inside and stow your stuff, we're due for a launch slot. I'm waiting for one more passenger."

"Another passenger?"

"One of the impossible-to-kills like you."

"Die-hards," I said, then chuckled. Maybe I would enjoy this vacation, after all. "Where are they sending us?"

"Caszaria's Moon. A nice little retreat with all the amenities."

The other unnamed passenger strode up the ramp to enter the cabin. With a sinking sensation, I saw it was Chief Linguist Reever.

"Oh, lovely," I muttered.

"Dr. Grey Veil," Reever seemed even more disgruntled than I felt. "Pilot Dhreen." He added something in the Oenrallian's native tongue in too low a tone for my TI to pick up.

"Whatever perfects your shield," Dhreen replied. "Let's get the gear tethered, I don't want to miss this slot."

We took up positions on far sides of the passenger cabin and strapped in while Dhreen initiated launch. I examined the condition of my fingernails carefully. Reever seemed engrossed in a study of his footgear.

The rumors going around the FreeClinic about me and Kao had obviously never made it to Ana's ears. I'd never said much to her, either. I'd been a little *too* discreet about my love life, I decided. If Ana had known about Kao Choosing me, she would have never sent Reever along on this trip. And what was Kao going to say when he found out?

"You can signal Pilot Torin when we reach Caszaria's Moon," Reever said, startling me. He was staring at the mark on my throat.

I covered it with my fingers. "Don't do that."

"Do what?"

"Read my thoughts!"

"They were apparent without need of a telepathic link," he said.

I didn't believe him. "Did Ana Hansen have something to do with you being on this shuttle?"

"Her exact words were, 'Duncan, you either spend a few days offplanet or I have you undergo a psych-eval.' "

"I'll get even with her," I said with dark pleasure. "There must be a Rilken convention I can steer her way in the near future."

Reever didn't laugh, but then, I didn't expect him to. I sighed. It was going to be a long two days and nights.

"Have you ever been to Caszaria's Moon?" I asked. Being polite seemed the best way to handle enforced close proximity. Seeing as I didn't have a syrinpress of sedatives handy.

"Yes."

"What's it like?"

"The asteroid is one thousand, four hundred Terran standard kilometers in diameter, artificial dome-contained atmosphere, five visitor centers which offer—"

I held up my hand to stem the flow. "Okay, okay. Did you have fun?" No reaction. "Did you like it at all?"

"I found it to be a suitable location for the particulars of the assignment."

I swallowed a groan. "You went there as a linguist, then."

"That is correct."

"Reever, have you ever lived on Terra for any length of time?"

His eyes grew even more distant. "Four point two revolutions."

"Did you decide you hated Terrans so much that you would do everything within your power *not* to be like them?"

Reever's face went rigid, while the *Bestshot* rose through the layers of the lower atmosphere and slipped in between space. The moment passed, and his expression was as bland as ever.

"I am biologically human," was his response to my challenge. That was it. I even waited to make sure.

208   S. L. Viehl

"Having the hardware, so to speak, has very little to do with how it operates."

"Perhaps you'd care to show me," he said.

"What?"

"Show me how to be human."

I simply sat back and closed my eyes. Well, I'd really asked for it.

Caszaria's Moon was only a few hours' distance from K-2, in a neighboring system with twelve planets. Half of the sphere was desolate, lifeless terrain pocked by inky craters. The other half was encased by a pressure dome, beneath which the clever Caszarians cultivated verdant fields and forests, dotted with hostels. It was a beautiful place, offering all the nonessentials a tourist could want.

I would have taken a nap on the way, but Dhreen returned to the passenger cabin to regale me and a decidedly silent Reever with his latest exploits.

"I believe the part about the nebular cloud cities, but did you really brush flightshields with *real* space pirates?" I asked.

"Did I mention the shipment of biosamples that began to migrate and grow all over the cargo bay walls?" Dhreen changed the subject, then winked at me. "Plenty of excitement jaunting the routes, Doc."

"I think I'll be content with the FreeClinic, thanks," was my dry response. "It may be dull, but I'll live longer."

"You think so? I heard you had a near-cry with some Hsktskt raiders."

"A close call—and it turned out to be seven of them." I described the delivery of the quints.

Dhreen hiccuped for at least two minutes before he asked me, "Is there anyone you won't treat, Doc?"

"Overly verbal Oenrallians," I said, then chuckled.

"Chief Linguist, what do you think?" Dhreen turned to Reever. "Word has it the desk jaunters were pretty spaced about the deal."

Reever folded his hands behind his neck, and regarded me with the usual indifference. "Dr. Grey Veil believes in her oath."

"Sometimes there is only what we believe in," I said.

Reever's eyes closed. "Beliefs," he replied, "are fragile at best."

Dhreen poured another round of spicewine and offered us a meal, but I shook my head.

"Enough for me," I said as I stood. "I think I'll go take in the view."

"E.T.A. thirty minutes," Dhreen told me.

A half hour later I turned from the viewer to find Reever right behind me. It was so much like the moment when Kao Torin had surprised me at the Hall of Art and Expression that I recoiled in shock.

"Don't sneak up on me like that!" Our bodies brushed as I moved past him, and for a moment I was convinced he meant to try that link business again. "No, Reever! Absolutely not!"

"I could learn more about what it means to be human." Reever's tone was logical, almost insinuating.

"Yeah, well, you'll have to do it without *taking over* another human," I said as I strapped in once more. "Try accessing the database instead."

Landing, biodecon, and admittance to the Visitor Center only took a short interval. Dhreen promised to meet us later that day and left us at the entrance to our lodging.

"Wow." I stood with my mouth open, while the chief linguist waited beside me.

The building was implausible, fantastic, and not a little disarming. The exterior had been constructed to appear like a cascading waterfall of large, semitransparent bubbles, sprinkled with small oases of plants and smooth-rounded stones.

I took a deep breath, and the floral-scented air seemed to permeate my blood, making me rather dizzy.

"If you're finished admiring the exterior?" Reever said at last, and indicated I proceed him.

"Oh, I forgot." I glared as I stalked past. "You've been here before, and spent the whole time measuring the place."

I was relieved to see the interior had a more traditional design. Those bubble things were pretty, but impossible for a Terran to navigate. At the reception portal we were greeted by the resident Caszarian innkeeper, who jumped from a small opening up to the desk.

"Welcome, esteemed guests," the toy-sized, black-spotted feline creature said. Jenner would have gone crazy over her. "I'm Mherrr, your hostess. Please let me know at any time how I may enhance your stay with us."

I had to fight the urge to request a room as far away from Reever as she could put me.

We were directed to our individual quarters, which of course were next to each other on an upper floor.

"I'm surprised Ana didn't make us share," I muttered outside my room.

Reever heard me and looked over. "If you prefer—"

I sighed. "It was a joke, Chief Linguist."

My room was all cool blue and cream shades. The soft, free-formed furnishings possessed no corners or geometric shape to them. A place to be soothed and relaxed.

Luxury had some merits, I decided. I sat down on the edge of my bed. A moan of pleasure escaped me as I sank back on the feathery mattress. I could use two days of sleep. My door panel chimed just as my eyes closed.

I forgot to be polite. "What?"

"Delivery for you, Dr. Grey Veil."

I opened the door and found yet another Caszarian conveying a stack of carriers on an anti-grav pallet. The small feline left them in the room and refused my offer of gratuity credits.

"No need, Doctor." He bowed with a smile and withdrew.

The bewildering number of cartons made me surrender to impulse to be a kid and rip them all open. A few minutes later I stood ankle-deep in wrapping. Scattered around me were beautiful garments, elegant footwear, even small jeweled accessories for my hair, ears, wrists, and throat. There was a disc, too.

When I played it, Ana's face appeared on the screen.

"Surprise!" she laughed. "I thought you might try to sleep through the whole vacation, so I'm sending you some outfits to wear. No one will see them if you stay in your room," she said. "Enjoy yourself, Joey."

"I'd enjoy the sleep more," I told the screen.

"You're probably mad about Duncan being there," Ana's message continued. "I confess, I decided to arrange for you both to spend time together away from the colony. I've sensed something between you two since the day you met."

"Right idea, *wrong* man."

"There's another reason I sent him with you, Cherijo. I know you've been seeing that handsome Jorenian pilot, but you probably don't know that his people bond for life."

"Wrong again."

"There's nothing wrong with exploring other options," she said, as if she'd heard me. "You should know Duncan has some powerful feelings toward you."

"Sure he does," I said. "He wants my brain." Too bad for Reever the rest of me was attached to it.

"Forgive a friend for interfering," Ana said. "Wear the scarlet dress tonight. Let yourself be a woman instead of a physician." She winked. "See you in two rotations."

I'd seen the red outfit, what there was of it. I had no intention of putting it on and parading myself in front of Reever. It would be ludicrous.

I kept repeating that even after I got out of the cleansing unit, dried off, and pulled the silky material over my head. The soft, bloodred triangles and folds swirled around me as I walked to the mirror.

Was that me?

After careful study of my image, I decided the garment didn't show *too* much skin. Maybe I would wear it. No doubt the meal intervals would be thick with other females wearing their best. A physician's tunic here would make me look awkward.

"Be a woman instead of a physician," I told my reflection. The physician in the scarlet dress peered back at me dubiously. "Okay, *try* to be a woman."

I sorted through the glittering accessories, trying to guess what would complement the dress. Medtech had never offered a course in fashion, much to my present regret. I stuck with red sparkling things. It seemed safest.

I started to braid my hair again, then looked in the mirror. Most Terran females left their tresses loose when they socialized. I brushed it out, then checked my image again. Long, straight grey-sheened black spilled over my shoulders and back. Not very inventive, but it would have to do.

Dhreen and Reever were waiting for me by the fountain outside the lodging. The elevated heels on my feet required a slow pace. Even my posture seemed to change as I walked toward them. I held myself differently, the way a woman did when she knew she looked appealing. Or when she suspected her footgear was going to make her trip and fall flat on her face.

Dhreen let out a low, lecherous whistle. "Doc, is that you?" he said, and I smacked him lightly on the arm.

"Behave," I said, then turned to Reever. A small part of me was gratified to see the chief linguist's eyes were riveted to a spot just below my collarbone. It wasn't an area that usually got me much attention. "Reever," I greeted him regally.

"You have a great deal of your body displayed," he said.

I wasn't going to let him aggravate me. "That's the point of wearing a dress like this, Chief Linguist."

"And what a dress!" Dhreen said, looping his arm through mine. "Let's go. You'll really blind the tourists, Doc."

"Dazzle, Dhreen. Dazzle."

The three of us made a short tour of the many dining establishments, and chose one. After the smiling Caszarian proprietor led us to a table, Reever pulled out my chair for me.

He leaned close as I sat down. "I've never seen your hair released before. Is it all yours?"

"I didn't purchase any of it," I said. "Of course it's my hair." I thought I felt his hand brush over the thick mass covering my neck. "Knock it off."

The menu listed so many delicious entrees that I couldn't make a choice. In the end I ordered an Oenrallian entree that Dhreen recommended.

"Follow that with chocolate mousse," I added for dessert.

Dhreen looked intrigued. "What's chocolate mousse?"

"Something wonderfully delectable and terribly bad for you."

"Make that two," Dhreen said.

We were served a vintage Terran spicewine, but I only took a few sips before resorting to a nonalcoholic tea. With Reever only inches from my side, I needed all brain cells fully operational.

Throughout the meal I was aware that our trio drew a great deal of attention from the other patrons. Noted, too, that the chief linguist and I were the only Terrans present. Nothing like standing out in the crowd. Some of the species present I recognized from patients I'd treated back at the facility. Others were new to me, and more than once I caught myself staring. I had to stop doing that.

Dhreen served as a buffer between me and Reever as he kept up a running account of his last jaunt. "So I told the passenger, we go now or you pay me to make a return jaunt," Dhreen ended the story, "and he said, I'll pay you three times your rate to take my mate and tell her you lost me!"

I laughed.

Reever, whose attention had wandered from our conversation, was staring across the room. Something was wrong, I thought as I glanced at him. He wasn't moving, and his pupils were dilated.

"Are you feeling all right?" I touched his arm and discovered the muscles under my fingers tensed to plas-teel-hardness. "Reever?"

Wintry blue eyes bored into me while his hand lifted and closed over mine. At the same time I felt the full blast of his thoughts as Reever linked with me.

Don't fight me. We're in danger.

What are you talking about? Danger from what?

The male by the entrance door. He's been watching you. Reever projected the image into my thoughts. It was a grey-fleeced, nondescript creature studying a menu.

He looks pretty harmless.

He is a Terran disguised as a Dervling. Here for you from the homeworld.

Here for me?

Reever stood and pulled me up with him. I wasn't in charge of my body anymore.

Dhreen, who was oblivious to our silent mental bond, dropped his knife in surprise. "Hey, the food isn't that bad—"

"Dhreen, excuse us," Reever said. "We have a private matter to attend to."

The chief linguist hauled me out of the entrance and into the open walkways. I managed to glance back and saw the sheep-like Dervling following behind us. The link between Duncan Reever and my mind grew stronger with every step.

What does he want?

You. He plans to kill me and take you.

How can we stop him?

Come with me, quickly.

He led me through a series of labyrinthine passages between the lodgings while the alien behind us raced to keep up. After one sharp turn Reever whirled me around and pressed me into a doorway, shielding me with his body.

I won't let him touch you, but I need your help.

I knew what kind of help he was talking about. *This is a bad idea, Reever—*

Yield to me. Yield to me, and I can protect you.

I can't—

Cherijo! Now!

Sullenly I let down the last of the barriers and felt the silent torrent of Reever's mind flood into me. The Dervling rushed by us, only to turn back and peer at the doorway.

Through our link I sensed Reever drawing something from me, then projecting an alien thought pattern. Our link split as he entered the mind of our pursuer. Like a front-row spectator, I watched as Reever implanted some kind of illusion. An image of the two of us, rushing down the corridor ahead of the intruder.

The Dervling shook his head as if to clear it before pivoting and hurrying off after the phantom pair. When he was gone, I regained control of my limbs and sagged in relief against Reever.

That was close.

Yes. Did you actually collide with a glidecab so you could leave Terra on schedule?

How did you— I threw up the barriers again, even though it was too late. *Out.* He was everywhere inside me. *Right now.*

He turned me in his arms, still inside my head, and I saw down into an infinite space occupied by a thousand alien worlds. In every scene was Reever, reflected over and over. It meant something important. At once I was engulfed by a deep, torturous sensation of need. It was as if Reever wanted to—

The link ended.

"We will return to our rooms," he said. I was too shaken to argue. He took my arm and led me into the lodging.

I didn't pull away until he keyed my door panel and pushed me into the room. He followed and secured the door behind him.

"Thanks for helping me," I said, "but I don't think—"

Reever sat down and folded his arms. "Tell me exactly *what* you are."

"I don't know what you're talking about, Chief Linguist." I prepared a stimulating hot drink. Maybe he wouldn't notice my hands were shaking. I gulped it down and promptly burned my mouth. He refused when I offered him the same. He had that "I'm going to wait until the end of time" look on his face. "I don't," I said.

"Tell me about the experiment, Cherijo."

"What experiment would that be? I've been doing all sorts—"

"Your father's experiment. I saw the memories during our link," he said.

Turning my back on him, I shoved the server into the cleansing unit. "The only experiments I know about are the ones I've been performing on K-2."

"You can't lie to me."

I walked over to the wide viewer panel and stared at nothing. I hadn't been thinking about it. He couldn't know. "I can't tell you."

"Tell me."

I turned. "Reever—" I couldn't lie to him. He had been in the deepest recesses of my mind. He'd seen plenty. "You wouldn't believe me if I did."

"I will."

I turned my head and tried to find some comfort in the starry vista beyond me. To say it was in a sense being forced to accept it. Now and for all time.

"I'm not human."

I told Reever about the contents of the package I had received shortly before I left the homeworld. Someone had sent me dozens of data discs, vidlogs, and biosample tubes of blood, tissue, and unfamiliar chemical compounds. "Every detail of the experiment had been meticulously observed, examined, and recorded. For nearly three decades."

"What was this experiment?" Reever asked.

"My father called it *Comprehensive Human Enhancement Research*. He used his own DNA to encode a fertilized ovum once the natural genetic material was removed. During the zygote and embryonic stages, he used a battery of chemical and organic manipulatives to further enhance the DNA. All genetic codes were identified, then most of them were dissected, enhanced, recombined, or replaced entirely."

"He cloned himself, then refined the clone."

"Yes." I was pacing back and forth. "His goals weren't restricted to mere refinement, however. He planned to eliminate susceptibility to all disease and infection. Undesirable physical characteristics were discarded, but the main goal was intelligence modification. Theoretically, higher brain function would exceed normal human capacity by at least fifty percent."

"What happened?"

"After several failures, it worked. Long-term analysis of the tenth trial specimen confirmed his success. The 'J' series prototype was highly intelligent, intuitive, capable of advanced comprehension and memory retention, immune to infection and disease. In essence, the ultimate physician."

"You are the prototype."

"Yes." My pacing picked up speed. "Dad's single greatest achievement in genetic engineering."

He frowned. "You indicated your parent used his own cells for the experiment."

"You mean, why wasn't I born Joseph Junior?" I smiled acidly. "The first nine male clones didn't develop properly in his embryonic chamber. It was easy to genetically alter my gender from male to female. He also planned to use me as an incubator for future . . . siblings, giving a whole new spin on the Terran concept of incest."

"Why?"

I stopped and spread out my hands. "The same reason he had for doing all of it. To see if he could."

Reever considered this. "Why would he experiment

on human DNA in an era when genetic conservation on Terra was at *fanatical* levels?"

I laughed outright. "He deliberately introduced the legislation so he would have a clear field, even if it meant he had to break his own law. He gives new meaning to the term *egomaniac*."

"Legislation still prohibits all human fetal genetic improvements and modifications," Reever said.

I began pacing again. "Somehow I don't think he's worried about getting arrested, Reever."

The chief linguist asked a few pertinent questions but remained mostly silent during my recounting of the events that led to my transfer and subsequent contacts with my father.

In the end I gazed steadily at him. "That's all I know."

"Your father demanded you return to Terra. Perhaps he is the one who sent the imposter tonight."

"You're probably right." I rubbed tired hands against tired eyes. "No one else has a better motive."

"What will you do?"

"What can I do?" I said, impatient now. "Do you know what will happen if I go back to Terra?"

"Your father will force you to take part in his research," Reever said, tilting his head while he watched me tread back and forth. "Or you will be arrested, detained, and probably executed for being the result of an illegal genetic experiment."

"Either way my freedom—and possibly my life—is over."

"Why haven't you told anyone, Cherijo?"

"Who could help me?" I threw out my arms. "Who could I trust?"

He nodded, and rose to his feet. "I have detained you long enough. Sleep well."

"Wait a minute," I said, astounded. "That's it?"

"Yes."

"Reever, I just confessed to being the freak result of an illegal, inhuman experiment conducted by my own father!" At his blank look I nearly shouted, "Are you going to tell anyone?"

"Of course not."

"You expect me to believe that?"

He had crossed the room and was standing before me. As I looked up, he put his scarred hands on my hair.

"Yes." He brushed his lips against mine. "Get some sleep."

Okay, so he kissed me, I thought as he left. It wasn't like we were going to get married or anything. Besides, I was already engaged to Kao. Maybe I should have told Reever that. I tugged the red dress off, shrugged on a robe, then fell into the cloudlike depths of my sleeping platform.

It took a long time to fall asleep. When I did, I dreamed of my father chasing me through chains of bubbles. He was waving a handful of lab slips at me, yelling that it had all been a mistake, that I wasn't a clone . . .

The sound of persistent chimes woke me up. I raised my head, dropped it, and groaned. "Who is it?"

A cheery voice answered. "Your meal, Dr. Grey Veil. Ordered by Linguist Reever."

Duncan Reever's continued existence was in immediate jeopardy, I thought as I got up and trudged over to the door. I had just keyed the panel to open when a blur of movement and brute force spun me around and slammed me to the floor. I felt the cold round mouth of a weapon press on the nape of my neck.

"Time to go home, Doctor," the happy voice said. I jerked as a syrinpress was administered directly to my jugular vein. God, what was he shooting in me? The drugs entered my system at once. My muscles began to grow thick and weak.

"Why?" I said, turning over to see the Dervling from the night before straddling me. He pulled the lifelike mask off to reveal cold Terran eyes and a cruel smile.

"For enough credits, I don't have to know," I was told.

When all else fails, Maggie had taught me, fake a

faint. Gives the jerk a false sense of security. Then nail him.

I pretended to go limp and slump into total stupor, and felt him lift his weight from me. That was when I jerked my numbed leg up and slammed my thigh hard against his testicles.

"Ooomph!"

The weapon fell from his nerveless fingers as white-faced, he toppled over. Through blurred eyes I saw him curl into a fetal position, clutching his wounded genitals.

Had to get to the door. Had to. The distance I crawled seemed endless. My head struck the wall as I groped for the panel release. Almost there . . . almost—

An arm clamped around my waist and jerked me back.

"Oh, no, you don't," my assailant said, dragging me away. "You're gonna pay for that, you—"

The door chimed, and I screamed. "Help me! Help m—"

I was thrown aside, and my head struck the floor. The effects of the drug settled over me, and my vision dimmed. I heard angry shouting, the thuds of fists, groans of pain. Hands reached for me, but I was too far gone to fight them off.

The last thing I saw was Dhreen above me, his thin lips tight as they shaped my name.

CHAPTER TWELVE

Clash of Wills

I woke to find myself back on board the *Bestshot*, and Duncan Reever standing over me. He was taking my vitals with my own scanner. I swiped at him, trying to take the instrument out of his hand.

"What . . . happened?" I said, then groaned as the headache behind my eyes made itself known. With a vengeance.

He handed me the scanner. "The Terran pretending to be a Dervling drugged you and attempted an abduction. Dhreen heard you scream, and fought off your assailant, but the Terran escaped."

"I got him, too." I remembered, and smiled grimly. "He'll be limping for a while." I just managed to run the scanner over myself before my arm went slack. "*Suns*, what did he inject me with?"

Reever removed the scanner from my limp hand and checked it. "Readings are negative for injury. I just ran a blood scan. He used something identified as Coraresine."

"Neuroparalyzer. Damn it." I pushed at the covers over me and tried to sit up. Reever pressed me back to the sling cradle and held me there. I was too sluggish to fight him. "Going back to K-2?" He nodded as my eyelids started to fall. "Don't tell them . . . about me . . . Duncan . . ."

It took the rest of my allotted "furlough" for my body to rid itself of the powerful drug. The next face I saw was Ecla's. She was pointing an optic light in my eyes. I squinted and swatted at the painfully bright beam. Her ruffles danced with relief.

"Turn that off," I said. "Are you trying to blind me?"

She straightened and made a gesture of something less polite. "Well, you're obviously feeling better."

My stomach rolled while my head buzzed. "Better has nothing to do with it, Flower Face."

"I meant the counteragent is working. You had a system full of chill juice."

"So I heard. How long have I been out?"

"Your shuttle landed last night. It is now mid-shift, next rotation."

I sat up without too much difficulty. My head even began to clear. "Where are Reever and Dhreen?"

"Both are still over at Security, being interviewed. Which is where you are scheduled to go, as soon as you can get back on your feet. Maybe tomorrow?"

"Get me some clothes." I got to my feet and was pleased to see I didn't sway or shake at all. Well, maybe a little at the mid-leg point, but Ecla couldn't see that.

"Why do doctors make the worst patients?" the Psyoran mused aloud as she brought my tunic and trousers to me. I dressed as rapidly as I dared. My stomach was still rolling, threatening to make everything even more unpleasant.

I gave her a surly look. "Because we can get away with it."

It took a few minutes to convince the charge nurse to release me without notice to Dr. Mayer or Administrator Hansen. After that, I left the facility to find my glidecar, which had been moved from my usual slot to a space behind the side entrance. I sat in the driver's seat and activated the ignition sequence. The control panel's small vid screen snapped on, and Joseph Grey Veil's face appeared.

"Well, well, look who's in my car." I glanced at the panel. "Direct relay, no less. Keep this up, and you'll have to pawn the pottery collection."

"Cherijo. The incident on Caszaria's Moon was made known to me. I was concerned—"

"—that your plan to get me back didn't work?" I finished for him.

"I assure you—"

"Save it, Doctor." I pointed the glidecar's nose toward Security and began to drive. "I disabled the idiot you hired."

"Will you allow me to finish one sentence?" my father asked.

I glanced at the screen. "Feel free."

"When a scientist cannot maintain control over an experiment, the entire procedure has to be repeated. Original findings must be discarded."

Unbelievable. "Are you threatening me?"

"Merely offering a warning."

"I see." I put a mental clamp on my temper. "Let me get this straight: Since the drugs and the abduction didn't work, if I don't come back, you're going to have me murdered? Then you'll do this all over again to another unsuspecting kid?"

"You have always had a firm grasp of subtlety," my father said.

I pulled up to the Security building, then gave him my complete attention. "All right, Doctor. You'll want to grasp this now. If there is even the slightest attempt to 'wipe clean' your 'original findings,' I will arrange to have a complete report on your activities filed with the League."

"You cannot—"

"I'll throw in the genetic material from your lab as evidence. Understand?"

"They will find you and take you into custody. It will result in your execution."

"Fine." As if I'd ever let him or the League get their hands on me. "The way I feel this morning, it would be a nice change."

"I cannot allow you to do that."

"I know. I'm counting on it." I stared at the screen. "Good-bye, Dr. Grey Veil. Don't contact me again."

"I will get you back—"

"Not if I can help it." My clamped temper gave way, and I saw my fist smash the screen into webbed ruins. Everyone had their limits. He'd just exceeded mine. I patiently wrapped my bleeding hand with a strip of fabric I tore from my tunic's edge, then climbed out of the glidecar.

This was only the second time I'd ever been inside Main Security. From here the colony's defense grid, support operations and transport were all closely monitored. Sort of like intensive care, with no patients. I was surprised to see a few friendly nods after I checked in with the reception drone. A pleasant change from the naked hostility I'd gotten last time I was there

Today's antagonism came in the form of the commander of Colonial Security, Norash. I hadn't met him the last time. He looked down and glared at me when I was escorted into the heart of the command center. No wonder all the corridors around here were so wide, I thought.

"So you're the one," he said after we were introduced by an assistant. He seemed bemused by my appearance.

"Commander." The fact he was Trytinorn surprised *me*.

It must have showed, for he grunted. "We're not all weight haulers, Colonist Grey Veil." He finished instructing a subordinate regarding some console glitch and indicated I should follow him. "This way."

We went to his office, a modest little place about the same size as the entire Trauma unit.

"Very roomy," I said. Well, I had to say something. I hoisted myself up into a Trytinorn-sized chair in front of his desk. My feet dangled a good meter above the

floor. How was I going to climb back out of this thing?
I gave the commander a sweet smile. He'd just have
to help.

Norash's small, sharp eyes were fixed on my self-in-
flicted injury. "What happened to your hand?"

My smile widened. "A display annoyed me."

"Try the termination switch next time." With surpris-
ing dexterity, he punched up a data file on one of his
terminals.

"How are Norgal's ribs?"

He gave me a suspicious glare. "How did you know
we were acquainted?"

"I'd say you were related, from your dermal pigmen-
tation."

Another grunt. "My cousin, as it happens. He's recovered."

"Good. Meeting him was quite an experience."

"Indeed. Colonist, your—experiences—are notorious
topics here at Central," he said, and turned the display
for me to view. There were several data files listed. "As-
sisting Hsktskt terrorists. Brought before the Council on
four counts of Charter violations. Now this attempted
abduction."

"I've been a busy girl."

He tapped the touchpad, and the screen blanked out.
"Tell me, Colonist, do you see a pattern here?"

"A pattern?"

The gigantic frame seemed to fill up the room as the
commander got to his feet and ambled back and forth.

"New transfers commonly violate the Charter, Security anticipates that." I got another stern glare as he
came to a halt before me. Cherijo, you bad girl. "Then
there is *you*."

There was that pesky problem of limits again. My
smile faded. "There's a point here we're going to arrive
at soon, I hope."

"Reckless behavior is a continual lure to such—"

"Wait a minute," I said. "Are you saying that I *asked*
for it?" At his nod an incredulous laugh left my lips.

"Commander, I didn't invite the Hsktskts to use the FreeClinic as a maternity ward. Phorap Rogan is an incompetent idiot who filed some trumped-up nonsense. As for the abduction attempt, all I'm guilty of is being on vacation!"

"You can't deny you attract trouble, Doctor."

"Oh, yeah? Watch my lips."

"I will not tolerate your antics when they jeopardize Colonial Security!" he said in impressive decibels.

"Petition the Council," I said. "Be prepared to stand in line."

The commander eyed me with cantankerous dislike before reclaiming his seat. "You'd better hope your luck improves, Doctor. Soon," he told me before he activated a recording drone. "Conducting routine interview with Colonist Grey Veil, Cherijo."

I gave my account of what had happened, leaving out only Reever's link with me, and my later revelations. When the record was complete, I was dismissed. I managed to jump down without Norash's help. On my way out, the Trytinorn muttered something about not hearing my name mentioned for at least a revolution.

Ana Hansen was waiting for me in the reception area. Reever and Dhreen were nowhere to be seen, but I thought I caught a glimpse of Dr. Mayer walking out the main entrance.

"Trying to avoid me?" the blond administrator asked, smiling.

"Trying to forgive you." She chuckled, then stopped and frowned when she saw the bloody strip binding my hand. "Don't ask. That was some vacation you sent me on. Remind me to hijack the shuttle back to K-2 next time."

"I don't dare send you to one of the more populated League worlds," Ana said. "Norash believes you may set off an intersystem conflict."

"It would be a lot easier if Norash had been there . . . to . . ." I trailed off as something occurred to me. Ana walked me back to my glidecar, noticed the damage to the display unit but said nothing.

"When am I scheduled for my next shift? Swings," I answered myself. I looked blankly at Ana, then shook myself out of my trance. "Sorry. I need to check on something. I'll be in touch with you tomorrow."

"Joey"—she made a helpless gesture—"let me know if I can help. I'm sorry about all this. It wasn't your fault."

"Not according to Norash," I said as I climbed in my glidecar. In minutes I was back at the Botanical Project area and making my way to the original site of Alun Karas's accident.

The gnorra trees were in full bloom, but I noted a slight brownish tinge to the leaves that had not been present before. Some seasonal transition, I guessed, and then walked around the entire area. Phew, I thought, and sneezed. The acrid smell from the resin spill was still strong. My nostrils flared, and I sneezed again. I took more samples. The smelly sap had darkened considerably, and the carpet of leaves was badly decayed.

What exactly had happened to Karas here?

I was taking root and bark samples, he'd told me. A resin tapper had clogged, and when he tried to clear it, the reservoir blew . . . *Then I tripped and fell into a pile of gnorra leaves.*

I tried to reenact his movements before the accident. I pretended to take samples from the trees. Walked from the outer fringe back to the damaged equipment. Touched the tapper's intake, examined the tools still lying beside the equipment. Measured the distance to the shattered reservoir. Threw up my arms, imagined the shower of sticky resin. Dropped down, probed the soil. Noted the number of gnarled roots where he could have tripped. Inspected the thick brown layer of leaves beneath me.

What could have infected him? The collection equipment, the resin, leaves, and K-2 dirt. That was all he'd come in contact with. There were no other botanical specimens in proximity—the gnorra trees appeared to be very territorial—and no other substances within reach he could have fallen on or breathed in.

Which told me absolutely nothing.

I was almost glad to see the signal from the FreeClinic when I returned to my glidecar. Audio only, due to my temper tantrum. It was one of the techs from Lab Services.

"Pathologist Crhm would like to speak with you when you report for shift, Doctor," I was told, and remembered I'd requested some tissue samples from Karas's lungs. I decided to report early and see what the medical examiner had come up with.

Pathology occupied a small section of its own, and was not kept busy as a general rule. Karas's death was the first in more than half a revolution.

Crhm was a hermaphroditic, crustacean-like being with eyestalks. The first time we'd met, I had thought of the Terran lobsters Joseph Grey Veil had regularly flown in for his personal consumption. I was glad I'd never developed a taste for them.

The pathologist saw me and hurried out of its office, exuding an air of excitement as it ushered me in.

"Come, come," its voice buzzed through my TI. "You must see this, Dr. Grey Veil."

I was taken back into the storage area, where remains were kept until final disposition. Apparently Karas had requested to be transported to Chakara in the event of his death. Cargo space to that system was limited, so his remains had not yet been shipped home.

Dr. Crhm and I scrubbed, masked, and gloved before the examination. At the wall of storage containers, the pathologist keyed the compartment reserved for organs removed during autopsy. Internal envirocontrols preserved the tissue perfectly. Crhm extracted the container that held Chakaran's lungs and took it to the exam table.

"I was following up on your request for tissue samples from the lungs when I found the abnormality," Crhm told me as it removed the organs and placed them on a biopsy pad.

The lungs should have been a pale lilac in color, the normal condition for Chakarans. Karas's were necrotized to a dark purple and badly distorted by loss of volume and cellular cohesion.

Dr. Crhm used a light probe to indicate the posterior segments. "Here—do you see this substance?"

I pulled down the overhead magnifier and through it saw a yellowish substance coating the exterior of both lower lobes. My voice was slightly muffled by the mask I wore. "What is that?"

"My first reaction was the same," Crhm said. "What do you think it is?"

"Empyema, perhaps, but that doesn't explain the tissue damage." I lifted the magnifier up and leaned closer. That was strange. Outer tissue appeared damaged, as if several sections of the organ had been eaten away. No, not eaten. Removed. "I've never seen pneumonic abscesses occur *outside* the lungs." There was a remote possibility that it had come from Karas's stomach, but I'd have caught that. I asked anyway. "Any indications of a gastropleural fistula?"

"None. The stomach was intact, and scans were negative for gastric leakage."

"Wait a minute," I said, staring at the tissues. "This would have shown up on my scanner. His lungs were largely intact when he died. No postmortem atrophic response could possibly account for the missing sections!" I peered closer. "Could a colony of anaerobes have migrated and set up house in the cells?"

Most anaerobes required a reduced oxygen tension and solid media for growth; some needed a complete absence of molecular oxygen in order to survive. Maybe they had needed to get *out* of Karas's lungs, and in the process, had killed him.

"Anaerobes usually produce tissue necrosis, and some are aggressively fulminant," Crhm said, following my theory.

"Whatever did this certainly fits the profile."

"I have another bit of evidence." Crhm's eyestalks were nearly bouncing with delight. "I measured the amounts of both the unidentified substance and the missing tissue. They appear to be equal in volume."

"Replaced," I said. "Like a cancer."

Crhm nodded, rather reluctantly this time. "I can't prove that yet, Dr. Grey Veil, as the substance does not register as an anaerobe or any other pathogen on our equipment."

"It could have migrated via the alveoli or the pulmonary capillaries through the visceral pleura into the chest cavity." That didn't explain what it was, or why the missing host cells had not shown up on my scanner while Karas was still alive, but I put those inconsistencies aside for the moment. One problem at a time.

"There are no signs of migration or saturation."

I checked the organ once more. "That isn't conclusive. Anaerobes have been known to migrate and leave no trace evidence." I pushed the magnifier aside and turned to the pathologist with a grin. "Dr. Crhm, you've given me an entirely new direction to pursue. Thank you." I reached out and clasped the shiny clawed appendage it extended to me. "You know this means I'm going to have to name my first child after you."

"I doubt the little one would be grateful." It made a chuckling hiss. "A mention of my findings on your report when completed, however, would be appreciated."

"A mention?" I laughed with delight. "Dr. Crhm, I may just sign your name to the whole thing!"

Pathology arranged to have the organs sent over to my lab, while I stopped by Trauma to see if any new cases of the contagion had been reported.

Rogan had been waiting for me, it seemed. When he heard my voice, he emerged from his exam room and voiced a bellowing tirade against my supposed incompetence.

T'Nliqinara tried to calm him down, but he shoved

her out of his way and stepped right up to my face. His polyps appeared much healthier, I decided, but the stink was still the same. "Who the *suns* do you think you are—"

I'd had enough. "Did you get my postsurgical report on the Orgemich female you treated for gastroenteritis?"

"I don't see—"

"She nearly died because you couldn't be bothered to run a full series scan."

Rogan's odor envelope expanded. "If anyone is to blame, it's—"

"That'z enough, Dr. Rogan," Dr. Dloh said as he stepped between us, pinchers open, front appendages arched.

"She shouldn't even be here! She's been removed from Trauma assignment!" Rogan shrieked. "I've filed charges against her for reckless incompetence and misconduct under the Charter!"

"If you don't zhut up," the big arachnid lowered his voice to a menacing buzz, "I will remove you from Trauma myzelf."

Rogan weighed this for half a second before he whirled and stomped off. I exchanged a rueful glance with the charge nurse before I thanked my colleague for his intervention.

"Zunz knowz, we could uze you here," Dloh sighed, shaking his gleaming head as he gazed after Rogan. "He'z uzelezz."

"Hang in there," I told him. "I may be back sooner than you think."

I retreated to my lab, and immediately examined the tissue from Karas's lungs. Perimeter tissue showed no signs of cellular degradation. An infection didn't eat whole cells and leave the others untouched. Crhm was right, it was almost as if the missing cells had been replaced.

I spent the rest of my shift examining and testing the yellow substance. For a possible pathogen, it was remarkably inert. No discernible cell structures, no DNA. Nothing that would indicate it was anything more than a viscous fluid similar to that of plasma, except this particular plasma was emptied of all nutrients, salts, proteins, and chemical signatures.

A biological broth with nothing in it.

Despite the depressing lack of evidence, I wrote up my initial report and transmitted it to Dr. Mayer. With it I added my recommendation that any future cases be quarantined immediately. I had a feeling we needed to find this bug in *living* tissue. It took only a few moments to transmit a copy of my report over to Dr. Crhm, since the pathologist was responsible for its inception.

I remembered my cat and my roommate some ten hours later, and closed the lab for that day. Before I left, I sealed the organ container and placed a lock on it to assure no one would inadvertently tamper with it. I wouldn't put it past Rogan to try.

At home, I found Alunthri and Jenner playing a simple game of chase-the-toy-mouse, and was welcomed with enthusiasm by the first and disdainful disapproval by the latter.

"He seeks to curry your attention." Alunthri smiled, baring sharp, gleaming teeth at the small cat. "Administrator Hansen stopped by to check on us several times during your absence. How was your vacation?"

"Eventful." I dialed a hot meal and herbal tea for myself, and served it along with the evening meal Alunthri had already programmed for itself and Jenner. "I'll tell you all about it during dinner."

I liked sitting down to a meal interval, now that I had someone to talk to. I related most of what happened on Caszaria's Moon to the Chakacat, and listened as it told me of the latest art studies. It certainly was enthusiastic about something called tonal sculpture, whatever that was. After we finished, Jenner finally forgave me enough to allow me to hold him for a short time.

"You must have been frightened," Alunthri said, referring to my misadventure.

"I was." I had been too angry with my father today to think about my own fear. "The scariest part is just the idea of someone taking me"—I looked at the big cat, and closed my eyes—"against my will. Sorry."

Here I was babbling about the fact I'd been nearly abducted, when the Chakacat had endured so much more. It was something we had never discussed before. Sometimes I was so tactless.

Alunthri curled up on the sofa and fingered a strip of the metallic girdle it wore. With its permission, I had thrown away Karas's collared harness and enabled it to choose and wear garments it liked instead. "No being should suffer such violence."

Maybe it was something we needed to talk about. "Would you tell me what happened when you were captured, Alunthri?"

It nodded. "I was the youngest of eight in my litter. That is why I am so small. Runts fetch a good price on the open market. Even more after we're trained for household companionship.

"A commercial hunter captured my pride. My litter siblings were killed outright for their pelts. My parent was kept alive long enough to accompany me to the market center in the city." At my drawn brows, Alunthri explained, "Newly weaned Chakacats often die of starvation. They will not eat unless their parent is kept with them."

"It's all so horrible . . ."

Alunthri nodded again. "I was sold to a trainer, and taught to speak and serve. The Karas family purchased me as a gift to Alun upon his transfer."

"I can't believe this is permitted." I was filled with sorrow and fury. "Don't the Chakarans understand your kind are intelligent? That you have the same emotions and desires as they do?"

The big cat made a helpless gesture. "We are as we have always been."

"Surely the fact you can talk makes it impossible to think of your kind as primitives!"

"It was not always possible for my kind to speak. Selective breeding altered the physiology of feral Chakacats, who were released back into the wild to repopulate our kind a century ago."

"Making you all the more valuable."

Alunthri contemplated me for a moment. "You have done the same in your society. Trained simpler species to perform complicated tasks. Enhanced their desirable qualities by hybridization."

I was aghast. "But not to be slaves!"

"Domesticated companion, agricultural worker, food producer—all forced against their nature to perform a task for a dominant species. Slaves."

"Just like Jenner," I said, feeling ashamed.

Alunthri sprang off the sofa and hurried to kneel at my feet. "You cannot personally assume responsibility for what has been and will always be," the Chakacat said. "Forgive me for—"

"Don't do that, Alunthri." I raised the big cat up and took its paws. "We're equals here, remember? And you are right." I gazed at Jenner and saw him in an entirely different way. I hunched down and stared into his big blue eyes. "Would you have chosen to come here, I wonder? Even chosen to stay with me when I found you, after I fed you?"

Jenner gracefully inclined his head, then padded away. Okay, I'd take that to be a "yes."

"You should rest now," Alunthri said. "I regret that I upset you."

"The truth may be ugly," I told the Chakacat with a shaky smile, "but don't apologize for making me see it."

The three of us settled down for the night. I had almost drifted off when my door panel gave off a single chime. Another emergency, I thought sluggishly. No, they'd signal me via display. Who was it? I rose in the darkness, hoping it had not disturbed the cats, and keyed the door to open halfway.

"Kao?" Guilt washed over me. I'd completely forgotten to signal him since I'd returned to K-2. Some Chosen I was. "What have you—"

He was swaying unsteadily on his feet, his skin a pale, powdery color. "Cherijo."

"What is it?" I shoved the door panel aside and put my arms around him. "What's happened to you?"

His big frame shook as he began to cough. "I need—" His eyes rolled back into his head, and he slumped against me. His breathing was slow and labored. He was burning up with fever.

The contagion.

"Dear God." From the corner of my eye, I saw Alunthri coming to help. "Stay back!" The Chakacat froze, and I hit the outer door controls with my palm. With a considerable effort, I eased Kao down to the floor. "Alunthri, signal the FreeClinic!" I shouted through the closed panel between us. "Tell them I need a medevac containment team here. Now!"

I insisted on full biodecon before we entered the FreeClinic. Once the scanners were clear, the team took Kao's gurney straight to the isolation unit. Dr. Mayer appeared and listened as I quickly related Kao's symptoms.

"Did you review my report on what Crhm had found in Karas's lung tissue?" I demanded.

"Yes," the chief said. "Report to Isolation. I'll discuss this with you later."

That was fine with me. I turned and ran.

By the time I got there, Kao had been stabilized, but the pneumonic symptoms were growing worse. Dr. mu Cheft was put in charge of the case, and stood towering in his containment suit as he reviewed the chart data with me.

"He's in excellent health, Cherijo; that's why it took so long for the symptoms to appear. From the infiltrates I'm seeing, he's been walking around with this for some time."

Had Paul infected him? "We need to culture a specimen of transtracheal aspirate. And check for a gas-tropleural fistula."

One recessed eye swiveled to stare at me through the plasplate over his face. "You suspect bacteremia? Even though the scans are negative?"

"I'll suspect anything and everything at this point, Daranthura." I lifted my hand to tug a biocontainment suit from the storage rack, but his suit-covered flipper gently touched my hand.

"Low-level containment protocols, Cherijo. Only one physician to be exposed at one time."

"I may be infected myself!"

"You just came up clear on the biodecon scans."

He had me there. "Did you scan the pleural cavity?" I described the biological fluid Crhm had found.

"The chief ordered that scan be done first," mu Cheft said, "and no, I did not find it." The 'Zangian checked his readings once more. "Multiloculated empyema, and negligible lobar tissue damage, although that may change in relation to progression of tumefaction. No pathogenic cause detected." He copied the chart contents to a data pad, which he handed to me. "You'd better study this over, see if you can make some sense of it."

"Damn." I gnawed my lower lip as I looked through the barrier to where the man I loved lay unconscious. "Has the chief initiated a full quarantine yet?"

"No. Dr. Mayer feels that will cause unnecessary panic." Mu Cheft flapped a flipper at my exasperation. "You know he has the final word. Go, do some work, it will take your mind off this."

"He's wrong," I said as I stalked off to my lab with the chart. Once there, I put in a signal to the chief at once.

"Dr. Grey Veil," my boss said from his office.

"We need to institute a level one quarantine," I said without bothering to keep the edge from my tone. "Now."

"That would assuredly invoke colony-wide hysteria over a contagion that we can't prove exists. Dr. Grey

Veil, until you can provide clinical evidence to support your hypothesis, there will be no further escalation in quarantine protocols."

"What about Karas's missing lung tissue?"

"That is inconclusive."

"I disagree."

"That is your prerogative." Mayer signaled off before I could respond.

I could fume, or I could work. So I worked.

I'd gone without sleep for days, back in Medtech. Now I was determined to nail this bug down, even if I never closed my eyes again.

First I reviewed the entire autopsy on Karas, and initiated a database search to locate any other fatalities in the Quadrant who displayed the same cause of death. *No correlation.* I ran a comparison between individual case notes from Rogan and Dalton's charts, including data on their individual physiologies, since Rogan was half-Terran. *No correlation.* I tried the same thing with different combinations: Karas and Kao. Rogan and Kao. Dalton and Karas. *No correlation.*

Teeth gritted, I spent hours programming an analysis program that took all pertinent data from all the potential contagion cases and ran a comparative study, citing such minor details as where the patients' quarters were located in relation to each other. Sixteen hours later, I got my answer.

No correlation.

As I was staring at the screen, unable to believe there was no relation between any of the cases at all, I was signaled from Isolation. It was a very weary-looking mu Cheft.

"Doctor. Pilot Torin has entered a coma."

CHAPTER THIRTEEN

Seductions of Failing

While the man I loved lay dying in an isolation ward, I found myself sipping café au lait and studying an uneaten brioche. Shock combined with exhaustion, I thought. That was the only way I could be drinking coffee. I didn't care, either.

No one approached me. Even Lisette sensed I was in no mood for her usual borderline contempt, and kept her distance. Good thing, too. I might have knocked her on her elegant posterior.

Kao Torin was going to die. I watched the café grow cold. Because of me. My fingers tightened around the server until my joints bulged. My fault. He would die because I was incapable of identifying the pathogen.

"Dr. Grey Veil."

In that hellish vacuum, I lifted my eyes to see Chief Linguist Duncan Reever standing next to my table.

"Reever." I sipped the lukewarm café that I could no longer taste. "It would be you."

He took the chair opposite mine. Reever was either a brave man, or bent on suicide, I couldn't figure out which.

"I understand your friend, the Jorenian, is in critical care."

Something in me flared back to life. "He's not dead yet, Reever."

He looked at me. Saw I hated him just for being there, healthy, breathing, alive. It didn't seem to bother him.

"Dr. Mayer tells me you are conducting research directly related to treating Torin's condition."

"For what it's worth." I put down the server with great care, suspecting I might smash it otherwise.

"The contagion has not been identified."

"No." I did smile now. A baring of teeth often proceeded a howl of fury. "I have not identified the contagion."

Lisette appeared to replace my tepid café and remove the unwanted brioche. She handed a server to the chief linguist, then placed her palms on her hips.

"You are bad for business," she told me. "Drink your café. You." She turned to Reever. "There is no one who needs you to talk for them?"

"Not at the moment."

"Then, shut up, or go away." Lisette stomped back into her stand.

I watched her through dull eyes. "I never thought I would like that woman, but I do."

Reever sat back. "Lisette seldom fails to state her opinion. You are remarkably alike."

"Don't tell her that."

"She doesn't sulk."

That penetrated my desensitized emotions. I gulped more of the café, scalding my tongue in the process. The pain, however, barely registered. "Implying that I do."

Reever's hand reached out and covered mine. "You won't find a cure here, will you?"

I turned my fingers, gripping his hand. Surgeons have very strong hands, and know exactly where to apply pressure for maximum effect. His scars shifted over the bones as I tightened my grip.

"Take Lisette's advice, Reever," I whispered, knowing I was hurting him. "Go." I flung his hand away.

He left. Lisette kept me supplied with café until I

couldn't bear sitting there for another moment. Maybe it was the suns' warm light, or all those unsuspecting colonists strolling by me. I tossed too many credits on her counter, and she slammed them back in my hand with a snarled obscenity.

"You insult me," Lisette said, and somewhere in those smoldering eyes I saw compassion, and friendship. "Go home. Sleep."

It was good advice. I nodded. Drifted in the general direction of the housing area. Somehow I found my quarters. Collapsed on my sleeping platform. Alunthri covered my cold, shivering body with something soft and warm. Jenner's rough tongue abraded the tips of my fingers. I burrowed down, hiding my head under my arms. I wanted to sleep forever, convinced Kao would be dead when I woke up.

In my dreams my father came to me.

He was conducting a class in my old Medtech in the auditorium. A full-length image was hung for all to see, an anatomical vid of some bizarre species.

"Prototype design for future generations."

The students were busy taking notes, glancing up every so often to check the position of the pointer my father used. The image was a dimensional projection of my brain.

"Enhanced intelligence. Yet she could not save her lover."

Shattering pain burst in my chest, and I tried to cry out. I had no voice.

"Immunity to virtually any disease. Yet she infected an entire population."

Was it possible? I thought wildly. Could I be a carrier?

"Limitless memory and comprehensive capacity. Yet she will not access it. She will not access it. She will not—"

I was falling into a darkness that welled up from the bowels of Hell itself. The world became black, feature-less emptiness, while my lungs flattened, my pulse screamed. I fell into a dry, crackling pile of leaves. They smothered me.

I am with you, Kao said. I twisted, clawing at the leaves, trying to see his face. White eyes stared blindly down at me. A sickening yellow light revealed him, hanging upside down from the branches of a tree, his mouth gaping in the frozen yawn of death.

No, no, no . . .

Someone else was there. Stronger and larger than I was. The sense of being possessed rushed over me.

Reever? Reev—

I woke to find myself alone, my quarters silent and dark. I sat up, scrubbed my palms over my face. Just a nightmare, I told myself.

Yet I could still feel a sense of something inside me.

Reever, can't you leave me alone?

The thought that answered was distant, weak. *You needed help.*

I've failed. I can't identify the contagion, and Kao will die. The other colonists, if they become infected, they'll die, too.

Not all. Not all.

I completed the thought. *Not all of them have died, have they?* Rogan was still alive. So was Dalton, and the construction crew. Ecla and I were unaffected. Why? The presence within me expanded, became stronger. *How close are you?* I thought.

Here. Here in you.

It wasn't Reever.

I scrambled out of bed, only to trip and sprawl on the floor in my hurry. What was it? Was it here, in my quarters? I pushed myself up and frantically searched the rooms. Nothing. The cats were both asleep. I was alone.

No, I wasn't.

I keyed the door panel and stepped outside.

The corridor was empty.

How is this possible?

In that instant I was smashed down by an incredible wave of thoughts. I fell, huddled, clutching at myself with my arms. An enormous cascade of energy came from inside my mind, blinding me with a series of rapid, disjointed images.

The sight of Karas's face in spasm as he coughed. The site where Reever first linked with me. Dalton on my exam table. The Engineering site. Ecla's calm face behind the Assessment console. Reever as he made the second link with me.

An image of my homeworld. *Where you belong.*

No, I fought the image. *I belong here, on K-2. Here, with the people I care for. Here, with the man I love.*

Return, return, return—

The thoughts stopped, cut off as if by some merciful internal switch. A horrible fullness rose in my throat, and I made it back inside before I began to vomit. When the spasms had passed, I slid down and rested on the floor until I could trust my legs. The basin of my disposal unit was filled with what appeared to be a regurgitated quart of Lisette's finest.

I disposed of it, more disgusted with myself than my physical reaction. I had wallowed in self-pity long enough.

"He won't die," I said, and stripped off my stained clothing before stepping into the cleanser. "I won't let him."

I returned to the Isolation unit within the hour. Dr. mu Cheft was now closely monitoring Kao's condition, and relayed his status.

"Coma has proven resistant to all the usual methods of treatment," he said. Lines of strain had appeared upon his badly flaking hide, especially around his deep-set eyes. "I won't lie to you, Doctor. It doesn't look good. The effusion is growing worse."

"Any sign of the fluid I described?"

"None."

"I'll be in my lab. Please contact me . . . contact me if—" I couldn't put my worst fears into words, but mu Cheft understood and nodded. "Thank you, Daranthura."

Back at the lab, I reviewed the previous days' notes and tossed the data pad aside in disgust. I had to approach the contagion differently. I reorganized the charts and looked for similarities between case profiles. Similarities the database wouldn't recognize, but I might.

"Come on, come on," I muttered as I rapidly skimmed display after display. "There has to be something!"

Males, females, and alternate sexual genders had been affected. Symptoms differentiated from species to species, though from the dispersal of transmission, it *had* to be an airborne contagion.

"It can't be." I shook my head at my own theory. "The whole colony would be showing symptoms by now."

What did all these cases have in common? All of them may have breathed it in. None of them except Karas died.

I tried an alternative hypothesis by establishing the sequence of infections. The first case had been Alun Karas. Through contact with him, Ecla and I had been exposed. Through Ecla, Rogan. Here was where the first break in the sequence occurred. Rogan had been infected, Ecla and I had not. Rogan in turn had exposed Paul Dalton, who had exposed the Engineering group. Kao Torin may have contracted it from one of them—

My sequence theory was full of inconsistencies. Rogan, for example, had treated dozens of patients as well as Dalton—why hadn't the others been infected? I'd checked the shift schedules, Dalton had not gone back to work after Rogan treated him. That indicated he was infected *before* reporting for the back problem. I had no idea of Kao Torin's movements over the preceding week. Who had infected him? Me? Had my enhanced immune system made me a carrier?

Before I could fill in the gaps in my theory, I had to know if I was infectious. If I had been isolated with a healthy colonist . . . wait, I already had been. For an entire day on Caszaria's Moon, with two of them. I'd had physical contact with both Reever and Dhreen.

"If I'm a carrier, they should already be exhibiting signs of the contagion."

I sent orders to Assessment to schedule routine exams for both men immediately. If I had couched it as an emergency, I was sure to incur Dr. Mayer's wrath.

Assessment signaled back to me. Both Reever and Dhreen had been given a routine medeval when we'd return from Caszaria's Moon. No sign of infection had been found.

Impatiently I refiled my request to repeat the exams at once, and went back to sequencing the charts. Dr. Mayer signaled me a short time later.

"Dr. Grey Veil, Pilot Dhreen is scheduled to launch within hours."

"All the more reason to insure he has no sign of infection."

"He has indicated a definite aversion to repeating the physical exam."

"He would." I forgot how tired I was and chuckled. "I'll contact him directly." I signaled Dhreen's ship and waited for an acknowledgment.

When it came, it was audio-only. "Hey, Doc."

"Dhreen? Isn't your vid functioning?"

"You could say that." He sounded tired.

"Did I wake you up?"

"Yeah, good thing you did, or I would have missed my slot. Thanks for all the fun." He made an odd sound. "See you on my next jaunt by."

"Could you come over to the facility? I just want to check—"

"Sorry, Doc, but I've had enough things poked at me. I'm ready for some nice, quiet space."

"Dhreen, it's important."

"So's my route. *Bestshot* out."

It took a minute for it to register. I was sorting through charts when my hands stilled. That rough burst of sound he'd tried to muffle. Not a hiccuping laugh, or an Oenrallian version of a sigh.

It had been a cough.

I punched a signal through to Main Transport, my fingertips rapping nervously on the console.

"Launch controller's office," I demanded as the automated system responded.

In a moment a gelatinous being stared back at me. "Launch Control."

"Medical priority," I said. "I want the *Bestshot* grounded. Cancel the launch slot immediately."

The controller was a slow-spoken alien who displayed little surprise at my order. In fact, it practically yawned between sentences.

"Sorry, Doctor, he just took a voided slot. *Bestshot* is at escape velocity, and flightshielding has been initiated."

That meant he was offplanet and I was out of luck. I pressed my hands against my burning eyes and terminated the signal. Dhreen had been grumbling, I tried to tell myself. Or choking an obscenity back. Maybe it was a belch from eating too much, as usual.

But please, God, not a cough.

I was notified by Assessment that the chief linguist had agreed to report for a second exam. I was trying to think of how to phrase my concerns to Dr. Mayer when an emergency signal came in.

The lazy controller from Transport looked very alert now. I shot to my feet. "Dr. Grey Veil, Launch Control. We've got the *Bestshot* on tracking. She's going down, fast."

I thought of what a terrific liar my friend Dhreen was. "Where?"

"Botanical Project, North field. Section sixteen."

"I'll send medevac. Transport must use quarantine protocols, first level." Mayer would kill me, but I didn't care anymore. "Keep everyone else away from the shuttle." Seeing his confusion, I demanded, "Are you listening? We've got to contain this!"

The controller was already shaking his head. "If there's anything left to contain."

I ran out of the lab, and directly into a small dark-skinned body. Geef Skrople's powerful limbs steadied me at once.

"Hey, Doc, I just saw—"

"Later." I grabbed one of his limbs and hauled him after me. "I need your help." I explained about Dhreen along the way to the evac unit.

"Why do you need me?" the engineer was still unclear.

"Once the *Bestshot* comes down, Dhreen may be trapped in the wreckage. I can't wait for heavy equipment if we have to get him out quickly." I patted one of his limbs. "You're better than having a grav-crane."

Skrople and I accompanied the medevac team to the outer rim of the Botanical Project, when a huge explosion rocked the mobile unit. A ball of flame and smoke billowed from beyond the tree line—a tremendous, up-thrust fist.

"If that's the shuttle," Geef peered dubiously through the viewer, "we may not be able to get close enough to rescue your friend."

"We'll find him." I leaned forward to shout at the driver. "Move it!"

Moments later we jumped from the unit and ran toward the crash site. Trees had been flattened from the impact blast, huge mounds of soil flung around, and in the center was a mangled heap that once had been a starshuttle. Smoldering chunks of metal were spread out over a half-kilometer radius. Fires flared everywhere. My eyes squinted against the smoke, searching for some sign of Dhreen.

One of the evac team yelled, "Over here!"

An enormous bubble of pitted plasteel lay half-embedded in the surface, still intact. An escape craft! I skirted a tangle of half-melted thrust emitters, followed by the team as we raced toward it. Someone produced a pry bar from the site kit and tried to lever it against the sealed door.

"It's fused!"

"Geef!" I shouted, and saw the engineer was already moving.

Skrople scuttled over the pod to an exposed seam at the very top and shouted for everyone to move back. His limbs strained as he grasped the edge and began to work it loose.

There was an instant when something hissed, then another explosion rocked the ground. I felt a stinging sensation above my right eye, while an orderly standing beside me fell, clutching his side. The rest of the team was on the ground, covering their heads with their arms.

Internal pressure had reacted violently to the engineer's breech and nearly split the bubble in half. I spotted Skrople, who had been thrown to the ground when the shrapnel pelted the rest of us. Apparently uninjured by the fall, the wiry alien clambered back up and peered into the exposed cavity of the cracked hull. I hurried over.

"Doc, he's alive!"

I reached so that Geef could hoist me up beside him, and looked down. Inside, I saw Dhreen smile up at me through a mask of blood. Oenrallian blood, as bright orange as his hair.

"Doc . . ." he hiccuped, then coughed. The smell of not quite pineapple and chocolate stung my nose. "Thought I . . . could get . . . offplanet before . . . it got me." He moaned as we carefully worked him from the tangle and passed him to the orderlies on the ground. I jumped down beside Dhreen. His eyes fluttered, and he saw me again, focused on me. "Sorry . . . was scared."

"Dhreen, when you're better, I'm going to strangle you." I moved my hands down his length, and called out, "Get the triage case over here, stat!"

One of the team appeared next to me with the supply kit and opened it, while I assessed the extent of Dhreen's injuries.

"Multiple compound fractures in both legs. I've got a bleeder on the right thigh. Twenty ccs of adrenalisine." A syrinpress was slapped in my palm, and I administered the stabilizing agent to prevent shock. I tore the flight suit material from his thigh and used the heel of my hand to slow the blood pumping from the wound. "Put pressure pads on that head wound, and get me an artery plug!"

I worked frantically, all the while talking to Dhreen to help keep him conscious for as long as possible.

"Why did you try to run, Dhreen? I'm not that bad a doctor, you know. Most of my patients survive." I stopped flow from the severed artery in the thigh and got the bonesetters aligned. My own wound was seeping, and I wiped at the blood pooling on my eyelid.

"Couldn't—" He broke off into a spasm of coughing. "Couldn't . . . take the . . . chance."

"Hold on to me now." I took his hand, and felt his fingers grip mine. "This is really going to hurt." I reached down and activated the clamps that would immobilize his shattered legs. He arched, groaning as they contracted. "That was the worst part, I promise."

"I . . . was right . . ." He tried to smile. "You . . . will . . . kill me."

"I should kill you. You lied to me—worse, you scared the wits out of me!" I blinked and smoothed the orange tufts around his almost-ears. "Stubborn, foolish boy."

". . . Twice your . . . age," I heard him mumble before he slipped into unconsciousness.

"That's it," I stood up and motioned for the litter. "Let's transfer him now." After wiping blood from my eye with my sleeve, I went to see to the wounded orderly. I had to pull a chunk of metal out of his flesh before bandaging the gash. Skrople took my arm once I was finished.

"Doc—here, let me—" He pressed a pad to my head. "Bad cut you got there."

"Thanks." Now I had to tell him. "Engineer Skrople—Geef—you may have been exposed to an unidentified contagion. You'll have to be isolated until we can check you out." I took the pad from his hand and held it to the wound myself. "Sorry."

He nodded, unconcerned. "Why don't I stay here until Security arrives for site containment? They'll suit me up, and I can warn off curiosity seekers until then."

"Do that. And, Geef"—I smiled wanly while I wrapped a pressure pad around my head. "We couldn't have done it without you. Thanks."

As the Oenrallian was carried from the crash site, the rest of the team rapidly surveyed the area for any other victims.

"We're clear," I was told. "No one was on the ground when he crashed."

One of the orderlies walking back by the tree line sneezed several times in rapid procession. Another standing close to me coughed heavily. I stared at them in dread. Was the contagion mutating? A decrease in the incubation period could mean onset in minutes versus hours.

We took Dhreen back to the mobile unit. While in route to the FreeClinic, my team and I donned biocontainment gear. I was beginning to hate those suits. Security was updated and ordered to isolate Skrople and anyone else having contact with Dhreen or the crash site. People were not happy. Dr. Dloh had already set up a full Isolation ward for Dhreen, the team members, and myself.

Thank God for large, smart spiders, I thought, as we hurried through the facility and sealed ourselves in the containment area.

"Pilot Dhreen makes the third case of unidentified contagion within specified limits according to the Charter," I told Dloh via display as I stripped down. "I'm calling this one. Inform Dr. Mayer and the staff. I want Colonial Administration notified now."

"It will be done," Dloh said.

I began to set up the surgical tray, and was half fin-

ished when I found Ecla's capable appendages removing
the instruments from my hands.

"Sterilize," she told me as she continued the outlay.
At my dazed stare, she undulated modestly. "I volunteered."

"You're risking your life!" I said, knowing it was futile anyway.

She gave me a stern look. "I've already been exposed.
You know it, I know it."

Ecla prepped Dhreen as I scrubbed. His legs were
badly broken, the jagged edges of bone piercing through
the flesh. I counted a dozen deep gashes and twice as
many abrasions. I'd never operated on a friend before.
I gloved and pulled my mask up, blinking back the tears.

"Please help me," I said. No, that wasn't right. Dhreen
would have laughed at me, begging some omnipotent
power to intervene. I got angry, thinking about it. God
owed me. "If you let him die on my table," I told the
ceiling in a clear voice, "I'll get even."

Ecla laughed out loud. "You would, too."

"Okay. Now that I've taken care of that," I said, and
checked the calibration of the lascalpel, "where are we
at, Flower Face?"

"He's ready, Doctor. Vitals are stable as can be
expected."

"I want to intubate him first. Set up the ventilation
system."

Once we had him on the respirator, I performed a
comprehensive scan series. His internal organs were intact, but there were definite signs of advanced pneumonia in what passed for his lungs.

"Remove the artery plug." Ecla extracted the site
dressing, while I rapidly repaired the torn vessel and
closed the thigh. It took an hour to deal with the compound fractures, one by one. All that was left after that
was to stitch up the thankfully minor head wound.

On my last scan, I found his primary cardiac organ
(what performed some of the lung and all the circulatory

functions in his species) displayed the now-familiar inflammation.

"Dilated cardiopulmomyopathy." I yanked off my mask and gloves in disgust. "It's already migrating."

His vitals remained stable, if weak, and a syntransfusion replaced the blood lost in the accident. If his condition degraded much further, none of that would help. I watched as Ecla dealt with the last of the minor gashes.

"Good work. Bring him out of it slowly."

My nurse weaned Dhreen off the anesthetic. I leaned over him and called his name, and watched those guileless eyes flutter open. They were dulled from drugs, pain, and the shock of the accident, but he recognized me and tried to grin.

"Dhreen. I have a tube in your throat that is helping you breathe. Don't fight it, let the machine do the work." He blinked and gave a weak nod. "Good. Now, rest. You're going to be fine."

I wondered if he would forgive me for lying to him.

Dr. Dloh worked fast to carry out my orders. Too fast, Ecla told me later. He bypassed the chief of staff and went right to Colonial Administration, who in turn went to the Council. People weren't just unhappy, they were getting seriously disturbed. I responded to a brief series of inquiries from Colonial Security and HQ Administration via display. I didn't bother to mince words, either. A short time later I saw my boss enter the Isolation ward.

"The moment of truth," I said to mu Cheft, who like me was isolated with the infected patients. "Keep an eye on Dhreen for me, will you?" I went to the display panel and waited for Mayer to chew me out.

"You're injured," he said at once.

I remembered my hasty bandage, still wrapped around my head, and touched it. "Nothing serious, just a bad scratch." I squared my shoulders. "I understand Dr. Dloh didn't make your office his first stop."

"He did not."

We exchanged a long, measuring look.

"I know your position on this situation, and I'm sorry you weren't informed first. The fact remains, I'd be guilty of gross negligence if I hadn't taken immediate action."

"Dr. Dloh can make his apologies later." The chief didn't look too concerned. "How is the pilot?"

"Dhreen's stable, for now. It doesn't look good in his case. What he has for a heart is involved."

"The others?"

"Three of my evac team members show initial signs of pneumonic infection. Pilot Torin is in deep coma. Dr. mu Cheft has him on close monitor." Behind me, I heard the physician smother a cough. My gaze was steady. "Daranthura also appears to be infected."

"You and Ecla?"

"Still no symptoms."

"Yet the incubation rate has evidently decreased," he said. I nodded. "We must determine if you and Ecla are immune, or carriers."

"By deliberate exposure?" I swept my arm back toward the occupied beds behind me. "There are too many cases to deal with now. Besides, who'd be crazy enough to—" Behind Dr. Mayer, I saw the silent, black-garbed form of the chief linguist appear. "No. *No.*"

"He volunteered," Mayer said.

"He isn't a viable test subject. He may already be infected. Or immune."

"He shows no evidence of contagion. The first cases displayed signs of infection within twenty-four hours of exposure."

"Isolate him and give it more time."

"If you and Ecla prove to be immune, we'll need that time to determine why and develop an inoculant."

I shook my head. "This is crazy. We don't even know *how* it's being transmitted!" Dr. Mayer's expression didn't change. "Fine. Go ahead and quarantine the idiot with Ecla. I won't be responsible for—"

"Ecla is Psyoran, her physiology is completely different," the chief said. "Logically, the ideal choice is to isolate the chief linguist with you." Before I could tell him my opinion of his stupid idea, Mayer stepped aside and allowed Reever access to the panel.

His face was as blank as ever. "Doctor."

"Chief Linguist." If I argued with Reever, I'd get less response than I had from Mayer. I turned around and walked from the panel. "Let's get it over with."

In order to expose Reever without placing the rest of the facility at risk, we were to be secluded together. It was not my idea of the perfect date. I suited up and was taken to the isolation room, where Reever waited for me. Orderlies then activated the quarantine seals outside the chamber.

"How long did Mayer say we had to stay in here?" I asked as I removed the suit.

"Twelve hours."

Wonderful, I thought. Half a rotation stuck in an airtight, soundproof room with Mr. Personality. Maybe I could take a nap. I stowed the containment gear and turned back to him. "So, why did you—" Reever was staring at me so intensely that I stopped in mid-sentence and gazed down at myself. My tunic was still damp and stained with Dhreen's blood, but that was all. "What?"

He nodded toward my head. "You have injured yourself."

"Oh. That." I touched the stiff bandage. "A parting gift from the *Bestshot*." Adrenaline and preoccupation had kept the brunt of the pain at bay. Now I felt it begin to throb in earnest.

"I was informed of the incident," Reever said. His voice sounded odd, deeper and slower than usual. Maybe he was already getting sick. "What is Dhreen's condition?"

"Not good. Worse than mine." I tugged at the dressing and winced as the dried blood made it cling to my wound. "Ouch, maybe not."

"I'll assist you." He indicated the exam pad. Dr.

Reever? I didn't think so. At my obvious reluctance, he
added, "Please."

While I climbed up on the table, Reever located a
container of sterile saline. He used it to saturate the
bandage, then eased the soaked dressing from my head.
As he cleaned the gash with a fresh pad, I tried to sit
still. I didn't like him touching me, but there was no way
to avoid it.

"Tell me the truth," I said. "Will I live?"

He studied the wound for a moment. "It may need
sutures."

My humor abruptly disappeared. "You're not pointing
a laser at my head, Reever."

"Perhaps a clean pressure dressing will suffice until
we are finished."

I didn't like the way he said *finished,* or the way he
was still staring at my head. Something was very wrong
with him today. I glanced around to see if there was a
scanner handy. That was when Reever grabbed me.

"Let—" I gasped as he pressed his open mouth to the
wound, laving his tongue over it. Repelled, I jerked my
head back. "Reever! What the hell are you doing?"

His hands tightened on my shoulders, trying to force
me back. "Do not fight me."

I knocked his hands away and squirmed off the exam
pad, putting it between us. "No, Reever." What the hell
was going on here? He looked like he was ready to tear
me to pieces. I retreated a few steps. "Stay back."

"You must yield."

He reached across the platform, and I dodged to one
side. I couldn't keep this up for long. The communications console was my only hope. I had to get to it and
signal for help.

"Don't you touch me."

"Touch is not required," Reever said, and lunged.

I barely avoided his hands. "*I* don't want you to. Got
it?" I was unnerved but sure he wouldn't assault me.
Sure until I saw his face change. Muscles twitched and
bulged. His eyes grew darker, filled with something like

rage or pain. His teeth clicked together as he went still. An instant later his face cleared, and he started after me again.

"Stay away," I said, retreating backward as he advanced. We danced around the room like that for several minutes. He never let me get within a foot of the console. I made a last, frantic attempt to get around him. Strong hands grabbed me and flung me back against a wall. Now I was panting, frantic, struggling beneath him without success. "No!"

My breath was pushed out of my lungs as he pressed his body over mine. I couldn't free myself, and knowing that terrified me. His scarred hands encircled my upper arms, while his body weight kept me immobilized.

I wasn't going to let him see how scared I was. "Back off."

"No." I whipped my head sideways to avoid his mouth touching mine, and felt him slide it across my cheek. The edge of his teeth scraped my skin as he said, "You want this. We know."

I fought to hurt the bastard then. Reever countered every move and relocated his grip to my wrists. Slowly he worked my arms up, holding them above my head out of the way. One hard knee thrust between my thighs as he leaned in, crushing me into the unyielding surface of the wall. I could feel his heartbeat hammering against my breast.

Inexplicably he said, "Humans require rituals of touch before they mate."

Humans? What did he think *he* was? "How fascinating," I choked before a short cry of rage tore from my throat. The top of his thigh was sliding back and forth between mine, deliberate and slow. "Stop it!"

"Your needs can be assuaged."

He was really going to do it, I thought. He was going to rape me. I twisted under him. "You can't—"

"Yield."

"I'd rather die." I couldn't allow this to happen. "Why, Reever? Why me? Why this way?"

His voice was low and rough. "Necessary."

"So is consent!"

"No choice," he said as he put his mouth against my ear. The tip of his tongue thrust in, sending a spasm of unwelcome sensation through me. "Link now."

The violence repelled me, but everything else was having quite an opposite effect, and it showed. My breathing was shallow and rapid. Chaotic nerves were creating acute sensitivity all over my skin. A heavy flush burned my cheeks and throat. I was beginning to feel an aching emptiness between my thighs, where he was still rubbing against me. I'd never been more disgusted with myself, but there was nothing I could do. We were both young, healthy specimens. I had to try something else, quickly, before he used my physical response against me.

"Is this the only way you can get a woman, Reever?" I said. "Psychic rape?"

"No rape," he said. The manner in which his speech had altered and the taut agony in his face frightened me more than any of his actions.

"Then, what in God's name do you think you're doing?"

"Seducing you."

We were linked before I could take a breath, and Reever was inside and outside of me then. I was physically paralyzed again. I felt him enter my mind with undiluted fury, exploding through the barriers I couldn't keep up.

I was waiting for him. *Come on, Reever. Come and get me.*

Reality sifted into the link, and I felt his physical hands stripping me with precise efficiency, hauling me off my feet, placing me on the exam pad. At the same time we circled each other inside my head, linked but unblended.

Within I saw the white light again, the dazzling nimbus containing a newer, darker nucleus. That was more menacing than the hands divesting me of my clothes. I'd never sensed that virulent aspect before. Whatever it was, it made my skin crawl.

Must do this. Cherijo. Must.

Why?

Inside, must get inside you.

On the other side he was removing his own garments. He had an athlete's physique, streamlined, with wide shoulders and compact musculature. I didn't want to know how he looked naked.

You can't, Reever. Don't do this.

He slid over me, and the sensation of our bare skins clashing penetrated the link like a slap. Nerves began to shriek, pulses raced, and I felt my body spiral out of control.

Cherijo. Surrender.

I drew on every shred of will I had left. *Get out of my head!*

As you wish.

He was gone, and I was suddenly alone under an aroused, naked male. Although I'd regained control of my body, his strong hands held me down easily. Whoever he was. It wasn't Duncan Reever. I don't know how I knew that, but I was sure of it.

"Who are you?" I said. He was cradled between my thighs, his erect penis rubbing and nudging against me. "Don't do this."

"You want this," Reever said as he stared down at me. The words were thick and slurred, forced from his throat. His hips stroked with a maddening rhythm. "Admit it, Cherijo."

I couldn't stop him.

My first time with Kao Torin had been beautiful. Everything I had hoped and more. A memory I would carry with me for the rest of my life.

This was nothing like that. This was purely physical. Sex.

I closed my eyes, ashamed to feel my hands clutching at him now, my senses feeding the frenzied need his body drew from mine.

"Give you more than Torin did," he said, and drew my knees up with his palms. "Anatomical advantage." His fingers slid down my belly, over the folds keeping him from penetrating me. One fingertip slowly parted them, stroking and spreading my own slick fluids over me.

"You can stimulate me," I said, and hissed in a breath as his finger slid into my vagina. "You can have sex with me. But you can't have what Kao Torin and I shared."

He removed his hand. "Was is this?" The hard, brutal thrust of his penis into my body forced the air from my lungs.

"Reever!"

"It wasn't, was it?" I felt him withdraw, push in again with slightly less force. "This is what you wanted." Against my own will, my pelvis rose, meeting him. "Yes," he said as he began to move with harsh, heavy thrusts. "Take it. Take it."

I stopped thinking. I took him.

For that interval in time I was no better than he was, an animal seeking pleasure. We were human, made to fit together like this. Small sounds of shock and involuntary pleasure spilled from my lips. My wide eyes never left Reever's strained features.

"Reever—wait—you have to—please—" My head snapped back as release exploded through me. I fell into Reever, into that dark, still place inside him. I heard him make a guttural sound, felt the eruption of his own climax fill me.

Panting, silent, we lay together. Our limbs were tangled, our flesh wet with mingled sweat. Before I felt the shame of what I had done, he linked with me again.

This time there were no thoughts, only images. The flashes of memory were so rapid and powerful they made me writhe. Spiraling black cliffs. Seething red oceans. Reever's face, contorted in agony. A single thought screamed through my head. Reever's voice was filled with fear and urgency.

Danger Cherijo the co-

Reality yanked me back with brutal succinctness.

"No!"

I hadn't spoken, or tried to end the link. It was Reever who had thrust me away. In the next moment I was too busy to think about it. I had to get the chief linguist on his side as he went into a gran mal seizure.

"Damn you, Reever," I said as I kept him pinned down with the weight of my own body.

"No! No!" He kept shouting that one word, over and over. I groped and found a syrinpress by touch, then I flipped the selector and jammed the infuser against his neck.

"Joey!"

Whatever was causing the seizure wasn't stopping. The anticonvulsant I'd administered had no effect. I had no choice but to sedate him. Within moments, Reever's body stopped jerking and twitching, and he began to breathe normally again.

I slid down from the exam pad and sat on the floor for a few minutes, cradling my temples with my palms. I felt Reever's semen seeping from my body, and with a disgusted sound I got up and cleansed myself. I couldn't bare to look at the physical evidence of what had happened, and disposed of the pads I used quickly. I remembered to pull on my clothes and Reever's before I put the containment suits over them.

No matter how much I wanted to forget what had happened, I had to report this. Wearily I walked over to the console, switching it to audio-only.

"This is Doctor Grey Veil. I need some help."

I sat down beside Reever and monitored his vitals while I waited. I went through every curse I could think of, and made up a few before the orderlies arrived and released the room seals.

"Get him to the Isolation ward," I said, rising from the chair. "He's had a seizure, among other things."

The conspicuous scent of sex and my disheveled hair had the orderlies staring at me with considerable interest. I signaled Dr. Mayer as I walked out with the gurney, and heard him respond directly on the audiocom in my suit.

"Mayer."

"It's Chief Linguist Reever. He's had an abnormal gran mal seizure. You'll need to run a full cranial series."

"The contagion?"

"No." I drew a deep breath. "No sign of it."

"Then, what happened?"

"He attacked me." I looked down at the man on the gurney. "The seizure occurred later. After he forced me to have sex with him."

CHAPTER FOURTEEN

K2V1

"I wasn't raped. At least, not by Reever."

Outside the Isolation ward, Ana Hansen listened as I recounted what had occurred in the Isolation chamber. Behind me, mu Cheft and the conscious patients politely pretended not to be listening.

"You said it was as if something was controlling him."

"He was different. I don't know. Driven. Even the way he talked was wrong." I loathed the way I sounded, as though trying to make excuses for him. "He used force at first, but—"

"You did what you had to?" Ana said in a brittle, shocked voice. "Submitted to avoid further injury?"

"No." Aware this was an official report, I had to be completely truthful. No matter how bad it made me look. "In the end I cooperated."

Ana was skeptical. "Rape isn't something Duncan seems, well, capable of."

"That isn't Reever." I turned my head to look at the unconscious form of the chief linguist. "Not the Reever I know."

"Have you learned anything about this seizure he had?"

"It was what we call a gran mal, or serious, episode. Almost fifteen minutes in duration. He has no history of epilepsy or related disorders. There was no apparent neurological damage. No sign of contagion or pneumonic infection. He's perfectly normal."

"Why is he still unconscious?"

Dr. mu Cheft joined me at the communications panel as I explained. "We brought him out of it an hour ago, and he began seizing at once. Because of the risk of brain damage, we have to keep him sedated until we know what's causing the convulsions. Or find a way to stop them."

The native 'Zangian coughed heavily as he lifted a flipper to get my attention. "Sorry to interrupt, but you'd better start a chart on me now."

I left Ana long enough to get mu Cheft on an exam pad and start Ecla scanning his vitals. When I got back to the panel, I could see the underlying dread beneath her calm exterior.

"One more thing. I formally request that PQSGO be notified we have an uncontrolled contagion present on K-2." I hated to put her in that position, but it was her responsibility as well as mine to take the appropriate actions.

"The Council hasn't decided events warrant—"

"*Space* the Council, Ana. We have to quarantine."

"But you haven't identified a contagion yet." Ana tried to reason with me. "Joey, we can't simply shut down the colony and tell everyone they are going to die."

"No, you don't have to do that." I glanced back at the row of occupied beds. "Why should you? Why try to keep it confined to this planet? Let it spread to another world. Another system. Another Quadrant!"

Ana shook her head. "It won't happen." She had never faced the reality of an uncontrolled epidemic. Neither had the Council.

"It will, and I'll tell you exactly how it will," I said. "After a population is exposed, a number of infected individuals will panic and leave the planet. They'll scatter and go to other worlds. There are fifteen in this system alone they can reach in a few hours. It only takes one person to infect an entire population. Let's say only ten are able to escape here, and make it to ten different planets. And ten from each of those worlds leave, and infect ten more planets, and so on." I did the calculation in my head. "Given the incubation period of this contagion, one-quarter of the inhabited worlds in the Pmoc Quadrant will be contaminated within a month. If the mortality rate is only fifty percent, then at least 728 billion lives will be lost." I leaned forward, pressing my hands against the containment barrier between us. "Do you really believe 728 billion people should die because the Council wants to play God?"

"That many?" Her voice cracked as she blanched. Her lovely eyes were wide. "My God, Cherijo. I didn't know. I really didn't know."

"Go. Make them listen."

Later, after I had made Dr. mu Cheft comfortable and finished rounds, Ecla nudged me toward an empty cot.

"You have to sleep."

"Not now." I went back to Kao Torin's bed. His bright blue flesh had gradually lightened over the past days. Only his closed eyes were bracketed by deep shadows. I hated to see the tubes entering his body, life-supporting connections that soon would serve no purpose.

"You'll be useless unless you rest." Ecla guessed my thoughts. "I'll wake you if he shows any signs of system failure. I promise."

She took his chart out of my hands and guided me to the cot. Every muscle I possessed protested as I dropped and flung an arm over my eyes. How could I sleep? I had to come up with a treatment, a symptom suppressor, *something*. There had to be a way. I simply had to review it in my head until I discovered the key.

"Karas." Walking into the exam room, a comical sight, covered in purple leaves. Worried we were going to strip him of his pelt. Dying less than twelve hours later. He was the beginning of the chain. "First stage."

Ecla and I had gone through decontamination procedures. Rogan had not, and he was the only one who
contracted the symptoms.

"Rogan, second stage."

I knew biodecon scanners had no effect on the contagion. Dhreen had scanned himself when we had returned
from Caszaria's Moon. I'd checked his docking logs
personally.

"Me. Ecla. No infection." Why? What did we have
in common?

We were both female, both exposed at the same time.
There seemed to be no other similarities. Was there a
hidden link between us? Something we physically shared
that protected us? I dismissed the latter thought. Psyor-
ans and Terrans had distinct, very different physiologies.

I lifted my arm and watched as three more Transport
workers were brought in. All displayed signs of the contagion. With a groan I rolled off the cot and took their
charts, while Ecla hurried to make beds ready.

If I didn't discover the common denominator soon, it
wasn't going to matter anyway.

"ID the contagion as K2V1," I was told as Dr. Mayer
reviewed my shift report via display.

"Catchy tag," I said as I made note. "As in Kevarzangia Two Virus One?"

"You have a better suggestion?"

I shook my head. "No, all I can think of is pneumonic
plague of unknown origin, and that isn't exactly
reassuring."

Mayer's lip curled. "I'm having the contents of your
lab moved to the isolation wing." He gazed at my nurse.
"Give me an update on the number of new cases."

"We've admitted fifteen new cases in the last hour,"
Ecla read from her patient roster. She stretched and
made a haunting movement that rippled through her me-
dian ridges. We were both far past exhaustion and running on nerves. "Current bed count is thirty-seven."

"Transport has shut down operation. I've ordered

their people to undergo screening in one of the storage facilities," I said. "We'll be forced to move the ward itself to one soon. We can't allot space for more than twenty additional cases."

Mayer nodded. "The Council has contacted PQSGO and put the colony on quarantine status."

Ana had made them listen, after all.

"Any chance some volunteer professionals will shuttle in?" my fatigued nurse asked. "We could use some help."

I was the only attending physician. Mu Cheft was growing worse, and Ecla was practically wilting before my eyes. That left me and the two orderlies who were still ambulatory to deal with thirty-seven cases. Twenty of whom were critical.

"No," I said, despite that. "I don't want anyone else exposed."

Mayer shook his head. "Even if they wanted to, the surgeon general has prohibited any transport to or from the surface. No exceptions. Quadrant cruisers are being dispatched to enforce the quarantine."

That meant Quadrant officials were beginning to panic. "How far will they take enforcement measures?" I asked.

Mayer was grim. "The cruisers have orders to destroy any unauthorized transport."

"Suns."

"Be prepared. Rumors are spreading. Security can't cope with too many hysterical colonists."

I knew what that could mean. "Do you think we need to move the patients now?"

He indicated a troop of Security officers had been dispatched to protect the FreeClinic. "Stay alert."

"Right." No problem. The threat of an epidemic and mob riots would do just fine as a stimulate.

"Some of the nurses have volunteered to work with you, and assist with the incoming cases."

"Excellent," Ecla said with a weak ripple. "Send them over."

"No," I said. "All I need is Ecla. I'm not *that* tired."

"Dr. Grey Veil," Mayer said, the same way he'd say *Stupid Woman*, "your nurse is ready to collapse."

"I'll put her to bed and tuck her in."

His lips thinned. "You cannot oversee this ward alone."

So did mine. "Watch me."

The chief wasn't impressed by my tough act. "When the bed count reaches fifty, I will send in one volunteer nurse per hour." He stepped away from the panel and stalked off.

I felt my teeth grind, and then I heard voices and looked up through one of the view panels. A Security team darted back and forth, taking up defensive positions. A dense crowd had formed just beyond the facility. They didn't look like anxious family members, either.

Rumors spread faster than contagion—so did hysteria.

Dr. mu Cheft and seven others had to be intubated within hours. I ordered more ventilators and threatened Ecla with sedation to get her to rest.

It was quiet. Most of the patients were too weak to create much trouble. Medical staffers, with their experience, stayed grimly silent. The transport workers were less cooperative. I had to restrain and sedate one dock hauler who decided he'd had enough and started yanking tubes from his body.

Dhreen was still in a coma. The synplasma and surgical repairs helped, but not enough to slow the effects of the contagion. He wouldn't have to worry about learning to walk again. He was dying.

I left examining Kao Torin and the chief linguist until the end of my rounds. Reever first.

Duncan lay there, sedated, harmless. I scanned him quickly. No change. I could still smell his scent on my skin. When I licked my dry lips, I tasted him. He remained stable and unconscious. On the chief's orders, and to prevent my arrest for manslaughter, I kept him that way.

Kao was clinging to life, his broad chest rising and falling in slow repetitions. If an antidote or treatment was not found in the next few hours, he would die, too.

Through the night, I walked my rounds. Studied charts. Ran more data. Found nothing. Cursed at the console. Walked rounds. Held Kao's hand. Kicked inanimate objects. Went back to studying charts. It seemed endless.

Ecla exchanged places with me. I slept a few hours, jerking awake to the sounds of angry shouts. Outside the FreeClinic, the still-growing crowd was getting nasty. We could hear them plainly through a security monitor Ecla had switched on. A suggestion that all infected colonists be systematically exterminated actually got applause.

I deactivated the monitor. The patients didn't need to listen to their neighbors spewing that kind of waste.

The nurse brought me a meal that I picked at while she quietly reviewed individual case histories. Everything tasted like plasfood. We were halfway through the stack of charts when Dr. Rogan and a group of colonists burst through the corridor entrance, just outside Isolation.

"There she is!" Rogan said, pointing through the sealed panel at me.

I swallowed what I was chewing and got to my feet. "Ecla," I said, smiling at the wrathful mob. "Signal Security. Now."

The mob started to approach the clear divider, when Security forces came in from the opposite direction, brandishing weapons. The colonists turned on them, and the two groups began exchanging ugly threats. I went to the display and increased the audio level so I could be heard.

"Dr. Rogan, what a surprise." My voice echoed over the commotion. "How nice to see you and your . . . friends."

"She's Terran," Rogan ignored me as he incited the mob. "They're zealots, xenophobes! She was sent here to kill us all!"

"Rational as ever, too." I gazed at the faces creating a wall of rage behind the Security officers and addressed them. "I wasn't sent here to kill anyone. We're attempting to contain the contagion until we can find a vaccine."

"Lies, all lies!" Rogan said, polyps whirring madly. "She wants to wipe out every non-Terran on this planet!" The mob made a rumbling sound.

I lied. I wanted Rogan dead. Now. I kept the smile pasted on my lips. "This your idea of gratitude?" I asked him. "Or didn't you tell your friends here that I saved your life?"

"You tried to kill me!"

I made a deliberate survey. "You look pretty healthy to me. Why are you doing this, Rogan? Is it because you're half-Terran? Afraid someone might question your loyalties?"

"We want justice!" Rogan said, and the crowd echoed an uneasy agreement. Guess they didn't know Rogan had Terran blood.

I addressed the crowd. "The only thing between you and the contagion is this barrier." I tapped the containment wall with my fingers, and everyone went quiet. "If it is breached, everyone in the room will be infected." I put my hand on the barrier release. The click of the mechanism was like a gunshot in the stillness. "Of course, if you really want me . . ."

Fear worked wonders. The mob broke up and most fled. Rogan began to rave, darting through the frantic, retreating mass, tugging at limbs.

"Don't walk away! She's bluffing! She—"

"That's enough, Dr. Rogan."

Dr. Mayer and Dr. Dloh appeared, followed by a fresh contingent of Security forces. My boss faced what was left of Rogan's followers. "Are you people volunteering to assist Dr. Grey Veil?"

That cleared the last of them out. Dr. Dloh shambled over to Dr. Rogan, who viewed the total defection with sputtering incredulity.

"Phorap," the huge arachnid said, lifting an appendage. "You are zcheduled for a zhift in Trauma."

"I'm not leaving until that bitch—"

"Now."

Rogan sneered. "Dloh, you can't—"

Dr. Dloh spat a thin, semitransparent stream of fluid from his U-shaped orifice at Rogan. The substance hardened the second it encircled his body. Rogan struggled and yelled, but after a minute, he was completely gagged and immobilized. Dloh lifted him like a neatly wrapped package.

"I'll juzt take him back to work. Dr. Mayer, Dr. Grey Veil."

"Thanks." It was too bad Dloh was such an evolved creature. I would have been happy to watch my colleague make Phorap Rogan his next meal.

Dr. Mayer directed the Security forces to take positions inside and out of the facility, then gave me an update. The bad news came first.

"Transport has advised at least fifty more cases of pneumonic infection have been identified. Most working positions with high passenger contact."

That meant the contagion could no longer be contained. Anyone who had shuttled in would have been contaminated. The new arrivals, infected by the transport workers, would go on to spread the disease to the general population.

The colonists who had shuttled out—

"How many got offplanet?"

"According to estimates, over thirty. All still spacebound."

Thank God for that much. "Are they being instructed to return to the planet?"

"No," The chief replied. "None are well enough to pilot their vessels. Their ships are being towed back into orbit to be held until the Quadrant decides what to do with them."

"Not well enough?"

"All passengers are reported to be in critical condition. The contagion seems to work more quickly in space."

"Damned bug doesn't like leaving home," I said without thinking, and then my head snapped up. "Hold on." I remembered an embarrassing moment I had endured with a tiny life-form during my first weeks on K-2.

"What?"

"This may sound crazy, but . . . the pathogen itself could be sentient."

"You're right." The chief smiled sourly. "That's crazy."

"If Karas touched something—ingested a plant, perhaps—"

"It would show up on the toxicology series."

"Maybe not." I rubbed my hand over my eyes. "Our scanners may read it as digested food. Many of the colonists are vegetarians."

"Plants are not sentient."

"Some life-forms evolved from plants," I said. "Ecla's people were once rooted, flowering stationaries. Karas was collecting plant samples when he became infected."

"Sentient plant life?" Mayer scowled at me as he enunciated each word. "Even after consumption, it would show up as an organic. We would have seen the same in case after case."

"Not if it's an unclassified anaerobic microorganism."

His sharp eyes rolled. "You're inventing this theory out of desperation!"

"There's one person who can prove it." I nodded at the unconscious form of Duncan Reever.

"You're wasting your time."

Ecla hovered close by, looking bewildered.

"Only one way to find out. Nurse, prepare to revive the chief linguist."

We brought Reever back to consciousness. The chief warned me to guard against another seizure, and I monitored the electrical activity in his brain closely. There were still some small, random fluctuations, but this time he emerged coherent.

"Doctor." His eyes fluttered for a moment. "There is . . . something . . ."

"Reever, listen to me. I need your help. The pathogen may be a sentient life-form. I need you to try to establish that. Can you use your telepathic abilities?"

His head moved. A nod. "They are present."

"They?" I swiveled around from my monitor. His face was rigid. "You mean the contagion."

"The Core is present."

"Dr. Grey Veil," I heard Mayer say.

I ignored him. "You're calling them the Core?"

"That is how they refer to themselves."

He was already in contact. "Reever, where is the Core?"

"Inside me."

Mayer's voice grated over the audio. "Dr. Grey Veil, sedate him."

I did a quick brain scan. There was only a small increase of activity, but it was having a definite affect on Reever. His heart rate doubled, while his eyes began to rotate back under fluttering lids. Damn, not now. I grabbed a syrinpress, but tried to ask him one more question.

"Reever, why—"

"Sedate that man at once!" Mayer's voice thundered.

In frustration I administered the sedative and watched my only hope of a cure disappear as Reever slipped back into unconsciousness. I strode over to the containment barrier in high outrage.

"What are you doing?" I demanded to know.

"He is delirious," Mayer said. "You're not going to use that man's life to prove a ridiculous, unsubstantiated conjecture!"

"I was right there. He was in no danger."

"He was ready to seize!"

"I wouldn't have let him!" I shouted back.

Ecla touched my arm, and looked at Mayer. Her brow ridges undulated nervously as she spoke. "This cannot be resolved now. Pilot Torin is going into multiple systemic failure. Dr. mu Cheft is in a coma. Some of the other patients need to be placed on respirators."

Mayer turned away from the panel. "Attend to your patients, Doctor, and keep the chief linguist sedated."

Ecla and I hurried to Kao's bed. He was slipping away fast now, and my scanner indicated death was imminent.

"No." Tears blinded me.

Ecla began whispering a Psyoran prayer as we removed the intubation tube. My hands shook as I stroked his strong, beautiful face. If only I could give him my strength, my life force, my—

A daring idea formed.

"Kao," I said to him. "I'm going to try something. If this is good-bye, know"—my throat convulsed—"know that I love you. Honor you. Walk within beauty forever." I took an empty syrinpress, placed it against my arm, and filled it with my own blood.

"He's Jorenian," Ecla said. "Terran blood—"

"I know, Ecla." I administered the infusion to his jugular vessel. "I have to try anyway. It might help if"—I faltered as I watched his vital signs continue to fade— "some of my antibodies . . ." I buried my face in my hands. "Oh, God, no."

Ecla made a soft sound. "It was an act of love to try."

He stopped breathing. Kao was dead. I leaned down to kiss him good-bye. His lips were cool and firm and lifeless beneath mine. My tears mingled between our mouths. "I'm sor—"

A thick stream of fluid bubbled from his lips, and I jerked my head back. His body shuddered and twisted beneath my hands.

"Suction, stat!"

I took a probe and opened his mouth wider. The fluid spilled over his cheeks and chin without cessation. Clear amber in color, but not bile. Not from his stomach, either. His chest rose and fell as his lungs pumped out the liquid in a macabre imitation of respiration. Ecla handed me the suction tube, and I began to evacuate his airways.

As I worked, I glanced at the fluid all over my hands,

his neck and face. It appeared identical to the substance found on the exterior tissue of Karas's lungs. It had to be the same stuff.

Once Kao's pathways and lungs were clear, I sealed my mouth over his and began respirating him with my own breath. A moment later he coughed and inhaled on his own.

"I can't understand it," Ecla said as she scanned him. "He's—he's stabilizing, Doctor."

I sat back, wiping traces of the yellow fluid from my mouth, watched him breathe. The white within white eyes opened to slits, his large hand twitched, shifted toward me.

I smiled at the nurse's incredulous gasp and held out my arm. "Take another blood specimen, Ecla." I'd have done it myself, but I was shaking too much.

"Dr. Mayer—"

"Space Dr. Mayer." I thrust my arm toward her emphatically. "Take the sample."

"What are you going to do with it?" she asked. "You can't hope to immunize every patient. You don't have enough blood for that in your whole body!"

"I'm going to *analyze* it, Ecla. I don't have enough blood to inoculate everyone in the colony, but I'll bet I can synthesize whatever is *in* my blood that kills this pathogen."

That was when a Security officer signaled us. "Attention, Isolation Ward. Prepare your patients for transport."

"What?" I got to my feet and ran to the panel, jamming my fist against it. "We can't move them now!"

"You'll have to," I was told. "Council's orders."

Too little time, too much bureaucracy. The combination was contributing as much to an epidemic as the bug was.

I didn't report to Dr. Mayer and tell him my blood had apparently killed the contagion. I needed to analyze it first, isolate the base for a vaccine. Then I would tell him.

I didn't need the chief to point out I'd been desperate and foolhardy, either. I knew what I had done was dangerous, and could cost me my medical license. I could live with that.

So did Kao. In spite of the fact that he was dangerously weakened from the contagion, his condition remained stable, and there were no signs of relapse. If I hadn't been so tired, I would have done one of Rogan's little victory dances.

The immediate problem was, I couldn't analyze anything. We had to pack up and move the ward. I had Ecla send the blood sample over to the lab, tagged only with "Terran specimen," and ordered every test I could think of. Until I could set up my lab at the remote site, that was all I could do.

Transporting thirty-seven patients, the medical equipment they needed, and the contents of my lab took an entire shift. It couldn't be helped, no matter how I silently raged against the time lost. The Council ordered, we relocated.

Security escorted us to an enormous, empty storage facility situated on the far outer perimeter of Main Transport. When our contingent arrived, there were more than two hundred new cases waiting for me. Dr. Crhm and Dr. Dloh were already on-site, scuttling between the rows of cots as they triaged patients.

My first thought upon arriving was that if Trauma was chaos, this was comprehensive insanity.

The colonists who were still ambulatory were everywhere, colliding with members of the medical teams. They shouted, fought, wept, begged for help. Efforts to calm them down were futile. No one reproached them. I felt like screaming myself.

At last, exasperated by all the commotion, I told the orderlies to start restraining the more violent patients. I sent Ecla to set up a Triage station, and coordinate the nurses. I took a moment to stop by Kao's cot and check on him.

He was resting, but opened his eyes the moment I touched his wrist. "Healer."

"Hi, handsome." I smiled down at him. His pulse was steady and regular. "How are you feeling?"

"Much improved." His eyes scanned my face, then moved to the chaos around us. "You are in need of help." Suddenly he was pushing himself up, trying to get out of the cot.

"Whoa." I planted a hand in the middle of his chest and pushed. Normally this would have been like trying to shove over a starshuttle, but Kao was still very weak. Almost at once, he went back down. "Hold on. You're in no condition to do anything but lay there and look good."

He frowned. "I am warrior-trained. It is a matter of honor."

I did, too. "Listen here, pal. I'm medically trained. It's a matter of *relapse*." I performed a quick scan. "Now, if you're a good boy, I'll let you get up and take a walk later." The readings were almost normal. I wanted to weep with relief.

"You are a tyrant," he said with a dark look.

"And you nearly died on me, sweetheart," I said, and scowled right back at him. "So shut up and stay put."

A reluctant smile tugged at his lips. "Very well." He took my hand and raised it for a kiss. "Never let it be said that I dishonored the wishes of my Chosen."

"Keep up that attitude, and we'll get along just fine," I said with a tired smile. Out of the corner of my eye, I saw something strange. A group of dark-robed beings was moving slowly through the aisles between beds several yards away from us. Then I realized who they were, and my smile flattened. "Excuse me, Kao. I have to take care of something."

I made my way toward the group. Like hungry buzzards, the six Bartermen were going from patient to patient. A pause, a quiet exchange, then they moved on. I blocked their path and crossed my arms. My foot was tapping. Yes, I was upset.

"Are you infected?" I demanded without preliminaries.

"Bartermen are not infected." One slid back a hood to regard me with ferocious dislike behind a containment suit mask.

"Unbelievable." I recoiled slightly. "Is there anything you ghouls won't do for barter?"

"Bartermen do not define methods."

"Why are you bothering my patients? Don't you have any common decency?"

"Bartermen have trade opportunities." The repugnant creature gazed at the rows of beds with what could only be described as greedy glee. "Bartermen take them."

"Yeah? Well, you can take yourselves out of here. At once."

"Bartermen are not leaving."

I was prepared for that, and signaled to a member of the Security team. "Last chance." I nodded to the officer, who lifted his weapon and took aim at the center of the group.

"Bartermen do not—"

"Shut up." I turned my back on them, knowing it was an insult, wishing I could give the order to shoot. "Get these leeches out of my facility."

The group drew back, and hissed something at me that my TI didn't pick up. I looked over my shoulder.

The speaker stepped forward and pointed a finger at me. "You need trade," he said. "Bartermen will remember. No trade for you."

I pressed a hand to my heart and mimed cardiac arrest. "I'm devastated."

The Security officer made a curt gesture with his weapon. The hood was pulled back up, and the Barterman rejoined his group.

"Not yet," the Barterman said. From the dark pit of his robe, his eyes gleamed. "But soon." They left, a security guard right behind them.

The Bartermen and that evil prediction were quickly forgotten as I got back to the present crisis. There wasn't going to be time to synthesize a vaccine from my blood, not here. Like Dloh and Crhm, I found myself trotting between cots, scanning and intubating as fast as I could.

"Doctor, I need you over here—" a nurse called, struggling with a patient who was violently heaving against her hands. At the same time, Dr. Dloh scuttled by and asked me to assist him with a difficult ventilation.

I took care of the nurse first.

Dloh was pulling a sheet up over his patient when I reached his side. I held back his appendage for a moment and recognized the patient's pain-racked features. Akamm, the expert whump-ball con artist, white now with death.

"Oh, no."

"The ezophageal flap was obztructed, I could not induct the tube," Dloh said, and then coughed. "Dr. Grey Veil—thiz iz out of control."

"I'm sorry." I touched the boy's cooling cheek, then covered his face myself. "Damn it. We have to do something!"

"What iz the alternative?" Dloh made a hopeless sound. "We can try to keep them comfortable until the end comez. But"—he coughed once more, the force shaking all of his appendages—"I can't watch them all die."

Neither could I. The research I needed to do on my own blood would take too long. I'd have to forgo the hope of a vaccine for now and try something more direct.

"Listen, my friend, there may be an alternative." I described the events and circumstances that led me to believe the pathogen was sentient. Dloh seemed skeptical, but kept listening. "I've got to revive Reever again. He's the only one who can tell us what to do."

"The chief gave orderz to keep him zedated."

I fixed my gaze on him. "Tell me you have a better idea."

Dloh thought it over and then made a defeated gesture. "If you attempted zuch a prozedure . . . I am zure to be occupied and unable to obzerve . . ."

"Thanks, Doctor." I gazed around until I had located Reever's cot. "Ecla," I called to the nurse, who hurried over. In a lowered tone I said, "Prepare to revive Chief Linguist Reever."

Reever seemed to come out of the sedation more slowly this time. I was careful to keep a syrinpress within reach. At last he focused, and his lips moved, but no sound came out.

"Reever," I bent close. "We're in trouble. Can you establish a connection with the Core?"

Ecla monitored his vitals on her scanner. "Not good," she advised me. "Another few minutes at the most."

"Duncan!" I said, and his hands suddenly seized mine. This time he did not enter my mind.

I entered his.

I was in a tunnel of wind and light and blazing, relentless pain. Reever drew me in, his consciousness just ahead, out of reach. *Reever, help me!*

Not enough time. I could barely make out his thought patterns. *Must return . . . dwellings.*

What are you talking about?

Return the Core . . . Cherijo . . . hurry . . .

Distantly, far beyond our link, something went wrong. I heard Ecla shouting, felt the syrinpress wrenched from my hand. The link broke abruptly.

I saw the nurse sedating Reever in mid-seizure. Apparently she'd knocked me away from him, as I found myself on the floor, sitting on my abused buttocks. The Psyoran turned to me after she'd finished restraining the chief linguist's writhing body.

"Mind telling me—" I felt something dripping from the front of my tunic and looked down. "What the hell?" Amber fluid soaked my tunic, covering my chest, abdomen, and thighs.

"He tried to push you away before he went into seizure. That came out of his cranial orifices. It moved like it was—it looked like"—Ecla faltered, her expression one of horror—"like it was trying to get into your mouth."

I had no time to be disgusted. Besides, it wasn't doing anything now but staining my clothes.

"Take a sample for analysis." I stripped off my tunic and handed it to her. My thin undershirt was soaked as well. "I have to clean up, and talk to the chief."

We lost another thirteen patients. A temporary display console was put together and connected to the colonial database. At last I was able to signal the FreeClinic. Hooray for portable technology. Dr. Mayer responded within moments.

"We'll lose more of them," I said after giving him the statistics. "There's only one option left."

The chief's face appeared haggard. "What do you suggest?"

"Treat this pathogen as a sentient."

He chuckled bitterly. "You really *are* deranged."

"Hear me out. As an intelligent life-form, wouldn't the anaerobe regard being trapped in Karas's lungs as a threat to itself?"

"There is no anaerobic microorganism capable of intellectual reasoning."

"That we know of," I said. "Reever called the pathogen *the Core*."

"He called something the Core," Mayer said. "It proves nothing."

Proof. What was unique to the pathogen that would prove its sentience? Why were they killing the host? What were they thinking?

"If you were imprisoned in an alien environment, you'd try to free yourself," I said. "The symptoms of the contagion may be a counterattack."

"An effort to kill the host body?"

"The pneumonia it induces does in the end." I ignored his raised brows.

"You still can't explain why the contagion doesn't show up on our scanners."

An image of Karas's lungs sprang to mind. The missing tissue. Not destroyed—replaced?

"What if it could mimic the tissue it inhabited? By replacing native cells, simulating their structure and chemical signature, it would remain undetectable."

"Preposterous!"

"It's the only reason to explain why it doesn't read on the scanners, why biodecon doesn't destroy it. It becomes part of the body. A defense mechanism, like protective coloration."

"This is absolute nonsense." Mayer looked ready to strangle me. "Listen to what you're saying!"

I'd gone this far. "The pneumonia they induce could also be the only possible means they have of escaping—by killing our bodies."

"And transmission?"

"We know it can't be airborne. Saliva, or perhap"—I glanced over at Kao, who was now sleeping—"sexual transmission."

"Since none of the original cases experienced such intimate contact with each other—"

"Smaller amounts of fluid could still prove a viable transmission vehicle for a single-celled organism," I said. "Involuntary discharges they could access and control." I made the last connection. "Coughing. Sneezing."

Cold symptoms.

"You'll have to analyze a fresh sample of sputum to prove your theory," Mayer said. I didn't bother to tell him the pathogen could probably imitate sputum and anything else contained in a life-form. "None of this warrants putting Reever at risk for another seizure. Don't try to revive him."

"I won't. I already have."

"I see." Mayer's voice dropped a dozen degrees. "Is he still alive?"

"Yes. He began to seize, and we sedated him. Apparently the anaerobe has migrated to his brain."

"What did he tell you?"

"That the Core must be returned to their dwelling."

"More episodal gibberish."

"No. It was Reever. He's trying to communicate." I just didn't mention it was by linking our minds together. I'd pushed the chief far enough.

"You want to base treatment on a ridiculous theory and the delirious utterings of a patient in mid-seizure."

"I'd welcome an alternative theory," I said with exaggerated congeniality. "Got one?"

"A vaccine."

I recalled the blood sample. "We're working on that, too." I explained about the tests I'd ordered, skipping the part about it being my blood or that I'd injected a dying patient with it. I claimed it was from a Terran who had been exposed to the contagion but not contracted it as of yet.

Mayer considered this for a moment. "I'll do the analysis personally," he said at last. His eyes glared. "I should remove you from duty for reviving Chief Linguist Reever."

"I'm sorry I ignored your orders." No, I wasn't.

"Keep that man sedated or you will be held responsible for his death. Do you understand me?"

I nodded, and terminated the connection. When I turned around, I saw Dr. Dloh being carried off to a cot.

I got up and walked toward the front of the building. Just outside the entrance, an unending line of patients waited to be admitted. One of the nurses advised me that case count now stood at over four hundred, and Security was preparing a second storage facility for the overflow.

If this didn't work, we were all dead.

CHAPTER FIFTEEN

Epidemic

Paradise turned into Purgatory.

Kevarzangia Two's lush splendor appeared to dwindle as I watched. Perhaps it was the exhaustion. Or maybe I just couldn't see the beauty anymore. My eyes were filled with the faces of my patients. So many of them—twisting in pain, gasping for life, motionless in death.

The epidemic smashed through the colony, and hundreds of cases swelled to thousands. Most of those infected came flooding into the temporary facility, desperate to be cured. My job was to examine them, make them comfortable, try to keep them alive as long as possible.

I did my job. They still died.

There was no reprieve from K2V1, no cessation of the work that had to be done. Every hour's demands strained our capacity to deal with the overwhelming numbers. There was a thin edge between disaster and destruction, and we were teetering on it.

The intubation equipment ran out first.

"I need more ventilators," I demanded during one exchange with MedAdmin. "Patients are dying."

"You have everything in current inventory."

I didn't want to talk about stock levels. "Get more."

"Have you consulted with the Bartermen?"

I winced. "The request would be better coming from someone else."

"We'll do the best we can. I can't promise you—"

"No." I turned from the screen. "Don't promise me anything."

Familiar faces jumped out of the endless blur of bodies. Patients I had treated in the FreeClinic, neighbors, staff members. I didn't know what to say to them. I lied anyway. Some begged me to help them. Others seemed to know I couldn't save them and turned away from me.

I passed my scanner over a patient, checked and cleared airways, made a chart notation. On to the next. I did it over and over, a hundred times, a thousand. I looked into their eyes. I held their trembling hands, claws, tendrils. I listened to their prayers. I watched them die.

I checked on Kao whenever I had a spare moment, which wasn't often. He remained very weak, unable to do more than sit up for short periods. I worried the pathogen might be retaking lost ground, and God only knew what my Terran blood was doing to his internal systems. At last I drew a sample of his blood and sent it over to the FreeClinic for analysis.

"Doc?"

My gritty eyes lifted from the dead Chandral female I was tagging for removal.

Kyle Springfield stood across the cot from me. The aggressive, insolent Terran teenager was gone. In his place was someone much older and wearier.

"Hey, Kyle." I looked at the dead woman I was crouched next to. Imagined Kyle's face on her body. "Be with you in just a minute."

"Doc, please." He reached for my arm, touched me. "Can you help my dad?" He pointed across the rows of cots. "He's in trouble."

"All right." I got to my feet and let him lead me.

Harold Springfield was on a respirator, and a woman with Kyle's eyes sat holding his limp hand. She barely glanced at us, her face blank with the too-familiar shock and bewilderment. I'd seen that same expression on hundreds of faces in the past days.

"He's not breathing right," Kyle said, pointing to the ventilator's panel. "He started shaking, real bad, and then—and then—" The scan was complete before he finished speaking. He saw my face, and his shoulders sagged. "My dad's dead, isn't he?"

I disconnected the equipment, and Kyle's father stopped imitating life. "I'm sorry." I put my arm around his thin shoulders. The boy coughed a few times, and stared down at his father. The woman never moved or reacted at all. "That your mom?"

"Yeah."

"Why don't you take her over there?" I indicated a section with some empty cots. "See if you can get her to rest. I'll see to your dad."

Kyle went to his mother, and carefully pried her fingers from the cold hand she was clutching. "Mom. It's okay. Come on, Mom. Let's go. The Doc"—he glanced up at me, and his helpless fear had become a curiously adult compassion—"the Doc will take care of Dad now."

I watched him guide her away, then stared down at the dead man. "He's a great kid, Harold," I said. "You should have kept your promise and taken him back to Terra." I closed his eyes with my fingers, pulled the sheet up over his face, and tagged him.

Sometime later, one of the orderlies told me that all of the FreeClinic physicians, including Dr. Mayer and Dr. Crhm, were now infected with the contagion. I was evidently the only one still healthy. Knowing this, I was still startled to pass by a cot and see Phorap Rogan, fighting to breathe.

He had survived the contagion once. Why would he succumb to it a second time?

When I thought things couldn't get worse, they did. The pathogen seemed to be mutating again. Symptoms progressed more rapidly, and respiratory failure occurred within hours instead of days. Particularly vulnerable were the children of the colonists, whose smaller bodies were virtually defenseless. We lost dozens of them every hour.

Drones were programmed to assist us in removing the bodies of the dead. Security kept healthier members of the colony away. The death toll climbed as rapidly as the infection rate did.

I crossed Dr. Mayer's path on my endless rounds. He and a nurse were intubating Lisette Dubois. Tough, curt, beautiful Lisette. I sat down on the edge of the cot and picked up his scanner. The café owners's vitals were better than they should have been. She was still fighting.

"One of your patients?" the chief asked me.

I adjusted her pillow, tidied her long curls with careful fingers. "A friend."

"I see." He turned his face away, coughing heavily.

I scanned him and found second-stage symptoms.

"According to my last readings," he told me after he'd dismissed the nurse, "I will remain useful for several hours before I reach respiratory failure."

"You should be resting."

He looked insulted by the suggestion. "I completed the analysis on the Terran blood sample you sent me. Also the sample from the Jorenian whose condition you reported as improved."

"If you could have synthesized a vaccine, we wouldn't be standing here," I said. "Sorry I wasted your time."

"Other than some aberrant cellular aspects, I found nothing that would explain why Torin, a Jorenian, responded to an inoculation of human blood." I took a sharp breath, and he gave me an ironic smile. "I found traces of Terran platelets in Torin's sample. You injected him with your own blood, didn't you?"

I hesitated, then nodded.

"The polypeptides in the Terran sample were far outside the standard deviation range. Evidently they were genetically designed or enhanced." Mayer's eyes shifted to some distant point. "Joe finally crossed the line and experimented on a live human being, did he?"

"Yes." I wasn't going to explain. The chief wasn't stupid. "What are you going to do?"

"I recorded the results of my analysis." He handed me a sealed disc, which I slipped in my tunic pocket. "I recommend you destroy it. It's proof that you and Torin are apparently immune to the contagion."

Good advice. I could imagine the reaction of the dying colonists if they learned my blood created an immunity to the contagion. My life wouldn't be worth Terran spit.

The chief still wasn't looking at me. "You and the Jorenian will live, long enough to see the Quadrant's destruction of this colony, Doctor."

I went very still. "What?"

"If the contagion threatens to exterminate the majority of the population, the planet itself will be sterilized from outer space. PQSGO standard procedure." Mayer swallowed against a cough. "Observation drones are in place and send hourly updates to the cruisers above. The mortality rate should reach the appropriate level by the end of the week."

"Cascade inoculants," I groped for a possible answer. "We'll synthesize my whole blood chemistry."

"Incompatible with most of our diverse population's physiologies. You're fortunate you didn't kill the Jorenian." Now he glared at me. "Don't push your luck."

"You're right, my blood won't help us," I said. There was only one option left. "But Duncan Reever can. Let me revive him one more time."

"Your last two attempts failed," Mayer said. "He can't survive another severe episode. You'll kill him."

"If we don't do something, the Quadrant's sterilization plan will assure no one survives," I said. "It's worth the risk."

A Security officer stepped between us and took my arm. "Doctor, the Council members require your attendance."

Dr. Mayer made a sound that faintly echoed my stunned disbelief.

"Tell them I'm busy!" I said, then stared at the

weapon being pointed at my chest. "For God's sake, man, I'm one of the only physicians left standing!"

The Security officer's jaded eyes met mine. "The Council members were specific, Dr. Grey Veil. I have my orders."

"Go," Mayer said. "There's nothing you can do here."

I hated it when the chief was right.

Without further discussion, I was marched off to a waiting transport. Since the Isolation ward had been moved from the FreeClinic, I had been confined to the temporary facility. The bright suns' light hurt my eyes, but I stared anyway.

The colony resembled a war zone in the midst of a bloody campaign. Small groups of colonists gathered in tight clusters around the damaged buildings, others leading wild attacks against the threadbare Security forces. Fires burned, smoke clouded the air, and the debris of what had been a civilized community littered the ground.

The glidecar I was riding in was attacked several times along the route to the Council's chambers. Stones, metal components, and other projectiles clattered against the reinforced panels. One screaming humanoid threw itself on the engine shroud, bouncing off to land in a crumpled, writhing ball.

The Security officer shoved a palm-sized weapon in my hand. "Here. You'll need this."

"I heal people," I said, and dropped it on the seat beside me. "I don't kill them."

"With that attitude, you won't live long enough to heal anyone."

When I entered the Council chamber, I heard the familiar hum of bioelectrical static. Two portable containment generators were emitting a sterile field around the Council members themselves.

Well, that was *one* way to keep from getting the bug.

The Council itself had been reduced by two. Z-cdewnyhy was missing, along with another who had presided during my last appearance. Dsoo, the Lankhi humanoid, had assumed the place of Council chief and rose when he saw me. The Ataderician began belching and gesturing wildly. The third Council member covered its face. I didn't know I had that kind of affect on people.

"Thank you for coming, Dr. Grey Veil," the Lankhi said.

"I didn't have a choice," I replied. "Where are the other Council members?"

"One of our Council was not well enough to report for this session. Council Chief Z-cdew-nyhy was taken to the Isolation facility several hours ago." Dsoo's tone was strained. "I was just notified by his mate of his expiration."

"I'm sorry." This better not be the only reason I was there, I thought, or I'd make a few more vacancies on the Council.

"Dr. Grey Veil, the Council has convened to determine what measures, if any, can be taken to relieve the suffering of our colonists. We have received reports of inadequate medical personnel, equipment shortages, and the escalating mortality rate. You have been summoned to act as consult."

"Here's an idea," I said, my lips fighting a snarl. "Let me go back to my patients."

"We were thinking of more *definitive* measures."

I almost said, "Define definitive," and then realized how stupid that sounded. "What measures?"

"Measures that require both compassion and resolve be shown toward those infected. To relieve unnecessary suffering, of course. Simply a method of humanitary . . . assistance." When I didn't react, Dsoo muttered a single word. "Euthanasia."

Euthanasia? I hadn't heard that term used since my history courses at Medtech. "You mean to propose voluntary suicides?"

"The term voluntary need not apply."

I stood there with my mouth open for a few seconds. "So what you're telling me, Council member, is you want to *execute* the infected colonists," I said. "For humanitarian reasons. To keep them from suffering. Have I got this right?"

"Yes."

"This wouldn't be an attempt to prevent the contagion from spreading, would it?" I asked. "In addition to the humanitarian aspect, that is?"

The Council members displayed shock and horror when they heard this. They were terrible actors. Jenner did it better whenever I proposed he go on a diet. I had to look at my footgear or start screaming.

At last Dsoo said, "Doctor, Allied forces will soon begin surface sterilization." He looked unhappy. I supposed he wanted me to fake some horror, too, then go along with the whole plan.

I looked at each one of them before I answered. "Council members, your suggestion, well thought out as it may be, makes me sick. I'm going to try very hard to forget I ever heard it. Excuse me, I have patients to see to." I stomped off and got as far as the chamber entrance. Dsoo's voice followed me.

"You cannot save them, Doctor."

"Not if I stay here listening to a bunch of cowards snivel and try to save their own miserable hides," I said, and keyed open the panel. I heard one of the Security officers behind me arm his weapon. I paused, then said, "Hasn't there been enough death already for you people?" Without looking back, I walked out.

No one shot me. Outside the chamber, I exhaled a shaky breath of relief, then ran.

I had to steal an empty transport, then almost drove into a mob advancing on the Administrative Buildings. I steered frantically to avoid them, cursing as I saw a handful turn and chase after me. One of them threw a club that shattered the passenger view panel, and I was pelted with broken plas fragments. I rammed the controls to full speed.

Through the dense smoke billowing from a burning glidebus, I saw someone running parallel to the glidecar path. The woman was being pursued by another group of rioters. My eyes widened as I recognized her. I looked ahead, and saw an armed Security team coming at her from the opposite direction. She'd be caught between them. I braked to a coasting stop and flung open the passenger door.

"Ana!" I shouted. She stumbled and peered at me incredulously. "Come on! Hurry!"

She ducked to avoid a volley of pulse fire and ran for the transport. I grabbed her arm and pulled her in before I shoved the accelerator to maximum. We sped off. When I could look away from the front viewer, I saw she was shaking badly. There was a nasty cut on her cheek, and blood splotched the front of her tunic.

"Cherijo," she tried to smile, but her lips were trembling, too. "Thank God you came along when you did."

"Are you hurt?" She shook her head. "What happened?"

"Someone accused the Admin staff of trying to infect healthy colonists, or some insane nonsense like that. Security couldn't keep them out." She pushed at the tangled blond hair hanging in her eyes. "You look like I feel."

"I feel worse." I drove out to the colonial boundary line, hoping the less-used path would be deserted. It was, and I slowed down. "I have to go back to the Isolation facility. Is there a safe place I can take you first?"

"I was headed to the facility myself when we were attacked. Dr. Mayer signaled me, told me about Duncan. I thought I might be able to help. What's his condition?"

I related the circumstances of my unsuccessful attempts to revive Reever and use him to communicate with the pathogen.

"Your theory is radical, to say the least." Ana coughed, went very still, then laughed unsteadily. "Silly, I was beginning to think I wouldn't get sick."

"Oh, Ana." I felt sick myself. "Maybe this thing with Reever will work. Try not to be afraid."

"I'm not, not really. After Elars died, my life didn't

seem very important. I didn't give up, but I did come to terms with death." She gazed out at the remnants of the colony, tears streaming down her face.

"Then, why are you crying?"

"I was one of the first transfers here on K-2. We had so many plans for this world. So many dreams. All gone, destroyed now."

"Don't give up. Not yet."

We arrived back at the Isolation Facility, where the waiting cases had nearly doubled. There must have been close to a thousand colonists waiting for treatment. Some were still ambulatory, but most were sitting or lying on the ground. All were in some form of respiratory distress.

Ana faced the reality of the epidemic now without expression. While I treated her laceration, the color slowly leeched from her skin. By the time I was finished, her face was almost as white as the dressing I put on her cheek.

"Hey." I took her hand in mine, gave it a reassuring squeeze. "They're still alive. There's still hope."

Her voice reflected the strain. "Take me to Duncan, please."

She accompanied me through the makeshift hospital, back to where the comatose or dying were segregated. Each moan or cough seemed to make her cringe, and I noticed she kept her eyes carefully averted from the faces of the suffering. I put my arm around her. For an empath, I thought, this must be hell.

We found Reever still under sedation. I left her with him long enough to check on Kao and assure his condition wasn't deteriorating.

"A nurse told me you were summoned by the Council," Kao said after I finished my scan. The readings reflected no sign of the contagion, but there was a slight drop in his vital signs. Maybe he'd just woken up. "What did they want with you?"

I was tempted to tell him about the whole debacle, but there had been too many weapons pointed at me today. Kao would be furious and Jorenian enough to try to hunt down the responsible parties. Plus I had to get back to Ana and Reever. "Nothing important. The usual bureaucratic nonsense." With one hand I brushed the thick black hair away from his eyes. "I'll be back to see you later. Get some rest."

When I returned to Reever's cot, I found Ana kneeling beside him, her hands pressed to the sides of his face.

"Physical contact helps Duncan to communicate," she said. I didn't tell her I already knew that from personal experience. She concentrated for a moment, then shook her head. "There's something wrong. I can't reach him."

"It's no use." I touched her shoulder. "We'll have to revive him, Ana."

She looked down at her hands on Reever's face, then back up at me. Something vital flared into her gaze. "Wait. I have an idea. Give me your hand." She joined it to Reever's and placed hers on top of both. "He won't respond to me, but I think I can act as a conduit for you. Duncan discussed it with me once, a technique used to assist a nonverbal species. You may be able to reach him through me."

"He's sedated," I said as I shook my head. "It's not possible."

"If we do this while he's unconscious, will it prevent another seizure?" I nodded. "Duncan has . . . unusual abilities."

"Ana, he's on continuous sedation. Whatever abilities he has are fast asleep."

"We have to try."

"All right." It was a last-ditch effort, but at least it was one that wouldn't kill him. Another seizure *would*. "Tell me what to do."

Her hand tightened over mine and Reever's. "Call to him in your mind, Joey. Call to him as you would a lover." I closed my eyes, thinking of Kao. "No," she said. "Call to *Duncan*."

I tried. It was difficult to shut out the sounds of the

dying around me. I thought of the few times Reever had touched me, linked with me, and tried to summon that same sensation.

Reever. Come to me, Reever, I'm waiting. We need you. I need you.

Something slowly seeped into me, coalesced, became a presence. A semblance of Duncan Reever masked it, but I knew it wasn't him.

"Something else," I said. Ana made an encouraging sound, and I tried to intensify the connection by concentrating. "Not Reever."

I was plunged into a liquid, moving darkness. All around me, I felt not one presence, but a multitude. Hundreds, thousands, even millions.

Who are you?

We are the Core. We are the Core.

Distinct, emotionless, unified. They reached into my mind and solidified the link between us. I saw. I understood. The Core had infiltrated Reever's mind. Controlled it. The seizures came when he had resisted them.

Pain crashed over me as a million voices screamed. *You! Murderer!* I fought to keep from sliding into darkness, staggered by the psychic blast. At a very great distance, I heard Ana's voice.

"Cherijo. End the link. Let go of him."

"No, Ana," I heard myself say. "Wait. Wait." I was in contact with them. I had to make them understand.

No—I'm a healer—I want to help—I need your help.

Return us return us return us return us return us return us.

How? I mentally shouted over the shrieked demands. *How can I return you—I don't understand—help me to return you where?*

The dwellings return us to the dwellings.

What are the dwellings?

Existence in the green world home.

Show me the dwellings, I pleaded. The strain of communicating with them was sapping my energy, I couldn't keep this up much longer. *Show me. I don't understand.*

Like a light, I was flooded with the memory of the first time Reever linked with me. I stood in the grove where Alun Karas aspirated the sap from the gnorra trees.

More images came. Alun reporting to the exam room, covered in purple leaves.

The Engineering site, ringed by more gnorra trees.

Ecla telling me about her community service allotment—working in the groves. I saw her sneezing as she pruned the trees.

The orderly who had sneezed at the crash site had been standing next to the trees.

The trees.

"Cherijo!"

I saw it now. The Core weren't a plantlike life-form; they *lived* in one. Like fish in a sea, they lived in the weightless environment of liquid resin. The sap from the gnorra trees.

Here? I pictured one of the trees in my mind.

The voices roared in my head. *The dwellings return us the dwellings there there . . .*

I couldn't breathe. Something was enveloping me, smothering me. I let go of Reever's hand, staggered back, falling. I blacked out as the voices died, the images shriveled.

I woke up flat on my back, staring at the roof of the temporary facility.

"Cherijo. Hold still," Ana said. I choked, rolled to my side, and spat out a mouthful of fluid. When she helped me to sit up, I saw I was coated with a thick layer of amber fluid. It soaked me, from my hair to my footgear.

"It came from the patients." Ana answered my unspoken question. "Everyone around us began having violent expulsions. All at the same time. It flew out of their orifices toward us, but it never touched me. It just kept pouring over you."

She tore away a piece of her tunic and reached out to clean off my face. Reever unexpectedly appeared beside her, and caught her wrist. She gave a small shriek.

"Don't wipe it off," he told her.

I looked from Reever to Ana. "How?" Before either one of them could answer me, I blacked out again.

The next time I regained consciousness, Duncan Reever stood over me, Ana beside him. I frowned. He had no right to look so damn healthy.

"Cherijo." The administrator smiled her relief.

I looked around, and saw I was back at the FreeClinic, suspended in a lukewarm solution filling one of the fluid tanks used to treat aquatics. I was also stark naked.

"Don't move," Reever said.

"I'm not exactly in the mood for a swim," I said. "Would one of you mind telling me what's happened?"

"The contagion has stopped spreading since your contact with the Core. No new cases." Ana sighed. "The epidemic is over."

The Core. I recalled everything now. "Not for long. I've got to get out of here." I felt disoriented, my limbs rubbery. "Give me a hand, Duncan."

"Try not to disturb the fluid," he said as he leaned over. I saw how he averted his eyes as he reached for me. It was a little late for him to be worried about my modesty.

"Try not to drop me."

Reever carefully lifted me out. Once I was standing, Ana helped me dry off while Reever sealed the tank.

Puzzled, I asked, "What are you doing that for?"

"To preserve the Core that are still alive. The tank will have to be transported and drained in the groves."

"I'd love to hear an explanation of that, but it has to wait." I shivered and looked around me. "I need clothes, and then I need to talk to whatever is left of Colonial Security."

"We've already contacted them. They've combined forces with the Militia and are waiting for you outside."

Ana found a spare orderly's tunic, and I pulled it on. My damp hair clinging to me, I strode out of the treatment room. Reever and Ana followed. The men and women waiting outside looked tired, filthy, and at the end of their reserves.

"I'm Dr. Grey Veil," I said, facing the assembly. I was doing my imitation of Joseph Grey Veil, and that got me their full attention. I bet none of them noticed I was short, wet, or barefoot. "I've established contact with the pathogen. It's not a disease. It's made up of microscopic sentient life-forms who are native to this planet."

Reactions ranged from disbelief to outrage.

"There isn't time to debate this. We have to work fast, and I need your help." I told myself that rumbling sound they were making was unified agreement. "They call themselves *the Core*, they live in the resin of the gnorra trees, and they'd like to go home. We're going to help them."

"We are?" a voice asked.

"The only way we can do this is to move the infected patients to the Botanical Project. We'll place them in close proximity to the trees. The Core will do the rest."

"Transporting them will be a nightmare," someone else said.

"This isn't going to work," a third voice joined in. "We're wasting our time!"

I glared in that direction. "If we don't return the Core, everyone will die. Got it? We removed them from their habitat, we're going to put them back."

"What are you talking about? We didn't take them out of those trees!" another shouted.

"We did when we breathed them into our lungs," I told them. "What the Core has been trying to do is get back out."

"You're saying all we have to do is dump the sick ones under these trees, and they'll get better?" a reasonable voice asked. "Sounds crazy, Doc."

"It's the only way," I said. "Are you going to help or not?"

The officers took a few minutes to discuss the proposal among themselves. Voices raised in anger. Some pushed their way through the group and walked out. The bulk of the force, however, remained. One of the Militia commanders stepped forward.

"We can arrange to slow-glide some shuttles over to the groves. The problem is what to do about the rioters."

"Make an announcement that infected patients are being transported," Ana said. "That should clear the path."

"Better tell them we've found a cure, and they can get it at the Botanical Project," I said. "Make sure you keep enough of your people at the site to prevent any more violence. I'll coordinate from the Isolation facility." I gazed around the room. "We can do this. Let's go."

I left Ana behind and made my way toward the waiting transport outside the clinic. Reever silently shadowed me.

I came to a halt and turned on him. "Is the Core still with you?"

"No." He shook his head and came to a stop beside me. "They evacuated my body after your link with them was terminated."

So he had no excuse for acting like a jerk now. "Congratulations. Get away from me." I paused. "Wait a minute. Why did you put me in that immersion tank?"

"The Core exist in a fluid environment. They can survive for short periods when removed from it, even simulate solid forms, but eventually they die. Oxygen is toxic to them, and they are particularly vulnerable to changes in ambient pressure."

Now I saw the final connection. "That's why you didn't want me to move. Why they induced pneumonic symptoms in the lungs of each colonist. Not to escape, but to stop them from breathing. To keep from being squashed."

"Yes. Cherijo—"

I saw how he was looking at me, and I wasn't going to do this. Not here, not now. "Ana will need help with the transmission."

"I—" Reever hesitated. I kept my hands clenched but

at my sides. "I will see you later," he said, and turned back.

Not if I see you first, I thought, and took the transport back to the Isolation facility.

Once we had the shuttles hovering over the glide path, I escorted the first group of patients to the gnorra groves. We had to carry most of them to the trees, and lay them in litters on the ground.

I saw a face I recognized, and crouched down next to Lisette Dubois. My scanner read only negligible vital signs. She should have died when they'd taken her off the respirator. Knowing Lisette, I wasn't surprised to find her alive. The woman's determination was scary. I picked up her limp hand.

Nothing happened.

"No, come on, you bad-tempered witch," I told her. "Stop giving me a hard time and do it!"

Lisette's lips moved. Was she trying to say something? Her fingers twitched, contracted, then clamped down on mine.

"Lisette?" I patted her cheek. "Lisette? Can you hear me?"

She took a wheezing breath, letting it burst back out in a violent cough. I rolled her on to her side.

Clear, amber fluid streamed from her nose and mouth.

All around us at the same time, patients began to convulse. Seconds later every one of them was coughing, sneezing, or vomiting up the Core fluid. Other patients, incapable of such functions, exuded the resinous substance from whatever open membranes they possessed.

"Get the patients in recovery position, like this!" I shouted, pointing to Lisette.

Security trotted around, rolling patients on their sides. The yellow ooze expelled from their bodies collected in pools and sank into the ground.

"The roots," someone said in awe. "They must be using them to get back in the trees."

Lisette's eyes opened. She looked up at me, and frowned.

"Why . . . am I . . . laying here?" Her voice was raspy, her throat swollen from the esophageal tube. "This is . . . how . . . you treat . . . your patients?"

I laughed. Kissed her on the forehead. Laughed again. It worked.

Every patient I scanned was improving. People were delirious, crying, clutching at each other. Others simply sat, dazed at the near-instantaneous remission.

Kao Torin was transported with the others, and I went to him as soon as he arrived. Unlike the other patients, he experienced no expulsions. It should have reassured me, but I didn't like his color.

"Hey." I knelt beside him in the dirt. Tired white eyes focused on mine. "Don't you want to join the party and throw up?"

"Cherijo." A big hand groped for mine. "No, I am merely weary. It is good to feel the suns on my face again."

Maybe that was why he was so pale. I squeezed his hand. "I'm going to have you moved to Recovery. Work on your tan."

We repeated the process over and over. More patients were brought. More yellow stuff came out of them. More of the Core returned to their trees. I stayed on-site, just in case something went wrong. I'd be damned if I was going to go through all this and find out it didn't work. A number of patients were weakened from tissue damage wrought by the Core, but no one died.

I loved it when I was right.

The healthy, Core-free patients were sent to a new Recovery facility that had once been the Botanical Research Building. The FreeClinic doctors were among the first of the patients brought to the groves, and were able to provide follow-up treatment for subsequent patients purged of the Core.

Dr. Dloh caught me before he left the groves. I never thought getting hugged by a big spider would feel like *that*.

I set up a team of orderlies to continue processing and

went to help out at the Recovery site. It was there I watched with the other doctors as Ana Hansen made the colony-wide transmission and detailed our work.

"Attention all inhabitants. We have discovered a cure for the infection. We have discovered a *cure*. Please attend to this message. It is imperative that you follow these instructions."

Dr. Mayer walked up to me and stood in silence as we listened to the rest of the transmission. Then he turned to me. I didn't know why I'd ever thought his eyes were cold.

"Good work, Doctor." That was all he said before he went back to the patients.

It was enough.

It should have been simple to restore order after that. It wasn't.

Hundreds of colonists remained in weakened condition. Tissue damage was the most common complaint. When the Core simulated tissue, it left holes. We spent long hours performing surgery on the worst cases, and setting up the least serious for therapeutic or pharmaceutical treatments.

Now that they were no longer in danger of dying, the patients went back to being patients. Which meant they complained, argued, and generally gave the medical staff a hard time.

Rioters unconvinced by the promise of a cure had to be rounded up by Security and Militia forces. Several refused to submit to the cure voluntarily, and had to be forcibly taken to the groves.

Administrators worked triple shifts, like the medical staff, and the Council was replaced by new members who had endured and survived the contagion.

The dead were counted, and the number announced with solemn gravity: 7,380. Less than ten percent of the population, someone said, then wisely shut up. I took a moment between patients and washed my face in cold water. No one commented about the redness of my eyes.

A week into recovery, I found myself being escorted from the Recovery facility by two bulky orderlies. They claimed Dr. Mayer had ordered me to take a day off. I told them not to be idiots, there was too much to do. I could continue to take rest periods at the FreeClinic between shifts, as I had been.

They, naturally, didn't listen to me.

Alunthri and Jenner had remained isolated from the turmoil, but I knew the Chakacat had been monitoring events over the display. It was relieved to see me, and offered to prepare a meal.

"I can't eat now," I said as I collapsed. "Maybe later . . ."

I woke up a rotation and a half later. When I moved, it felt like someone had beaten me with a large, blunt object while I'd slept. My soiled clothes were clinging to me. I smelled worse than I looked. Even my mouth tasted foul.

I sat up and saw the Chakacat was sleeping in its room, curled up with Jenner. The door panel chimed, and I answered it without moving from the bed.

"Who is it?"

"A moment of your time, Dr. Grey Veil."

Reever got in only because I didn't have enough ambition to get up and key the panel lock. "Cherijo."

"Reever." I made myself get off the sleeping platform, and closed the door to Alunthri's room so we wouldn't disturb it. "I was just going to get cleaned up."

Given the fact he'd seen me naked twice now, it seemed ridiculous to be modest with him. He hadn't just seen me naked, he'd touched me, carried me, even had sex with me. I was a physician, I reminded myself. Above this sort of silly embarrassment anyway.

"Turn your back," I said. To my relief, he swiveled away, and I began stripping off my filthy clothes.

"How are you feeling?" he asked.

Ridiculous. Embarrassed. Even with his back to me.

"Fine." I stepped into my cleanser unit and went to work. The plas enclosure was opaque with humidity by

the time I'd finished. I opened the panel to reach for a
towel and found Reever standing there, holding it out.
He looked at me—all of me—as I snatched it away and
glowered at him.

"Do you mind?"

"No," he said, and turned his back to me again.

I dried the excess moisture from my skin and shrugged
into a light robe, then vigorously cleaned my face and
teeth. After that, I sat down on my sofa, the biggest and
softest furnishing besides my bed.

Reever waited, still not looking at me.

"Okay, I'm dressed. Let's get it over with."

He swung around. "I would like to apologize. For
what happened between us in the Isolation room."

"Apology accepted." I closed my eyes and leaned
back. "Now, please leave."

"I had no control over the Core." Reever sat next to
me. I sensed the scarred hand reaching toward me, and
my eyes opened.

"If you want to keep those fingers," I said, "get them
away from me."

"You will not resolve this."

"Resolve? What's to resolve? It's over. Anything
else?"

"Joey."

I grabbed his tunic then, grabbed it with tight fists.
One jerk brought that handsome, inhuman countenance
close to mine.

"The only person who ever loved me gave me that
name," I told him, teeth bared. "Don't use it again,
Reever. Ever." I let him go. "Let's go back to the apology, I liked that better. Why apologize for something
that wasn't your fault?"

"I hurt you."

"Not really. Try again."

"I was forced to infect you by the Core's control."

"Really? Is that what you thought you were doing?
By the way, I'm immune to the Core."

"They did not know your enhanced immunities would

destroy them. I was to maximize the transmission, or kill you." His eyes changed color, the blue darkened. "I would not cooperate."

"Maximize the transmission? Was that why you licked my wound? What was the next phase? Spit some of that yellow stuff down my throat?"

"Yes."

"I'm glad I missed that. So you raped me instead. Tried to infect me in a more civilized fashion. How magnanimous of you."

"I didn't rape you. I tried to help you."

My fingers dug sharply into my palms, leaving dents. "I didn't need your brand of help, Reever."

"I had no alternative. They would have killed you."

"I don't know if a near-rape is canceled out by a death threat. I'll have to think about it."

His eyes were so dark I couldn't discern the pupil anymore. "It *was* more than the Core attacking you, Cherijo. I wanted to do those things to you. You wanted me to do them."

"Wrong."

"You wanted me," he said.

"It's been nice chatting with you, Reever. Get out."

With that inhuman abruptness, he rose. His scarred hands grabbed my arms, pulled me to my feet.

"When I was a child, my parents left me on a world where native behavior was strictly governed by ritual disciplines. I was there for weeks."

"Really." I considered the places where I could kick him that would inflict the maximum amount of pain. There were a lot of them. Decisions, decisions. "You can let go of me anytime now, Reever."

He displayed the back of one hand. "You wondered about this, why I never had the scars removed. My parents told me to observe the inhabitants, who had agreed to give me instruction. During my first ritual, I was placed in a chamber with ample provisions, and my trainers. When I became hungry and reached for food, they used a blade on the back of my hand to discourage me."

My blood chilled. I felt my eyes widening.

"When I was thirsty, they did the same. I was not permitted to eat or drink. The discipline lasted five rotations."

"Oh, God," I said, the words hurting my throat. The scars seemed to burn into my flesh. "How old were you?"

"Six. I learned quickly. Their own progeny often lost many digits." A corner of his mouth lifted in a parody of a smile. "When my parents returned, they were very excited. I had undergone a ritual that had never been documented before. They wanted all the details for their database."

"How could they? How could—" I halted, confused. "Reever, I don't understand why you're telling me all this."

"I think of the ritual often now," he said.

"Why?" All of this was making me feel very ill at ease. "Get the scars removed, Reever, and forget about it."

He just shook his head, let go of me, and left.

I watched him slide the door panel closed behind him. Only then did I feel something wet on my cheek, and wiped it away with the smooth, unscarred back of my hand.

PART FOUR:

Resolution

CHAPTER SIXTEEN

That Which Recovers

After the epidemic, a temporary detainment center was constructed for the first time in colonial history. The Council didn't give it a name. I couldn't blame them.

Colonists who had gravely violated the Charter during the crisis were kept there, awaiting trial. Others, like one radical group who attempted to burn a grove of gnorra trees afterward, were also incarcerated.

"Epidermal singeing," Ecla said as a Security officer brought in one of the extremists, an Yturi, to my exam room. The soot-covered Yturi was insistently vocal, enough to make me toy with the idea of gagging certain patients prior to treatment.

"We have to burn them all down, don't you see?" it hissed as I probed its normally oily outer derma. Flakes of what had been hair and skin drifted like black dandruff to the floor. "They will exterminate us unless we do it first!"

"The Core are not interested in leaving their gnorra trees," I said as I carefully removed the charred ash over its skin.

"They are a pestilence!"

"They were here first," I said in a reasonable tone. "And intend to coexist peacefully with us."

The Yturi gave me an unpleasant smile. "Not if my friends can find enough thermal pruners."

The Bartermen Association was busier than ever. Cruisers were still enforcing planetary quarantine until the Pmoc Quadrant Council was assured no possible spread of contagion might occur. Everything in short supply was on the prime list of Bartermen appropriations.

"They offered me a new glidecar for all our containment suits," one orderly said to me.

Another shrugged. "I gave them mine. Not like we're going to need it now."

Three of our better ventilators disappeared outright, and I demanded Security post guards around Trauma. I was told to file a complaint. When I tried to do that, I was informed that I must have documented proof that the Bartermen were stealing our equipment.

"Documented proof? You're telling me that unless I have photoscans of the little weasels helping themselves to FreeClinic property, you can't do anything about this?"

The Security officer was sympathetic, but adamant. No matter how grateful everyone was to me, the Bartermen were for the moment the sole source of supply on K-2. No one wanted to risk offending them for fear of the Association declaring a trade strike.

The Militia shut down most of the common areas and declared a curfew on the younger portion of the population. The kids were getting into more than the usual mischief. It didn't help that most of the culprits had been orphaned by the epidemic.

That wasn't the only bad news.

"In order to assure our colony is free of the contagion, all colonists will be tested for Core life-forms," K-Cipok read the directive to me.

"Tested?" I actually stopped working, I was so surprised. "Why do they want us to do that? No one is getting sick anymore."

The nurse's hooves shuffled. "I guess they're not going to take your word for that, Doctor."

Dr. Mayer later confirmed the same.

"Are they kidding?" I asked him. "Test nearly seventy thousand colonists? We can't handle the post-bug cases we have already!"

The chief was worried, too. There was no test in existence that could rule out the presence of the Core, who were virtually undetectable. He was convinced PQSGO wasn't going to take our word for it, either.

Fortunately, the Botanical Research Department finally found a way to tag the elusive life-form through specialized thermogenetic analysis. Biodecon equipment could be adjusted to perform the test, which gave us the means to end the quarantine.

Recovery remained a slow process. Our shifts stretched to impossible hours. I often performed more than thirty separate minor surgeries during one rotation.

More issues emerged. Many of the recovering colonists were frantic to leave K-2, and I couldn't blame them. One group stole a shuttle, which instigated a tense standoff with the cruisers in orbit. Everyone was extremely unhappy. Administration had to conduct hurried negotiations with the colonists, while Security had to calm down trigger-happy Quadrant enforcers before the shuttle came within firing range. Somehow they got the shuttle to return. No one was injured, but it had been close.

Others had more specific agendas. Dr. Rogan, who unfortunately survived the epidemic, amassed a contingent that petitioned to have Drs. Mayer, Dloh, and myself removed from duty.

I'd give Rogan credit. He was a jerk, but at least he was a dedicated, *consistent* jerk.

The Council delayed ruling on the petition until after the quarantine was lifted. It didn't make me feel better. I knew Rogan's machinations only too well, and those who lost loved ones to the epidemic were still looking for a scapegoat. There was also the matter of my less than tactful conduct the last time I went before the Council. Had I really called them sniveling cowards? Maybe no one would check the data records.

I was tired. I could drown out the complaints of patients, work myself into a stupor, pretend to look omnipotent when my feet were killing me. It was my last encounter with Duncan Reever that still bothered me. At the oddest moments I recalled the sensation of his hands on my hair, or the way he'd looked at me before walking out of my quarters. Guilt plagued me as much as the memories. Kao was still recovering from the contagion, and there I was, constantly thinking about Reever.

Guilt became panic when Kao's condition began to mysteriously retrogress. I ordered tests, snapped at nurses, even had an argument with mu Cheft, who was in charge of the case. Why wasn't he doing this, why had he done that? I made such an ass out of myself that eventually the 'Zangian had an orderly to haul me out of there.

It was Dr. Crhm who finally isolated the cause behind the Jorenian's decline. When I received its findings, I sat down and stared sightlessly at the data pad for nearly a quarter hour.

"Kao."

I dropped the report and hurried off to the wards. When I arrived at his bedside, he smiled up at me.

"Healer Grey Veil," his lyrical voice was thin. He frowned when he saw my eyes. "What has happened?" When I searched for the words, his hand crept over mine. "Tell me, Cherijo."

I broke down Dr. Crhm's report to terms he could understand. Not that it took a genius to figure out what was happening. My blood had killed the Core and cured him of the contagion. Now it was working on Kao's own tissues, infiltrating them like a poison on a cellular level. Several internal systems were already compromised.

"I would have died, had you not given of yourself to me," he said. That unshakable Jorenian tranquillity only made me feel worse. Illness had drained his skin of its brilliant color, and his white eyes were deeply sunken. "That I am still alive I must see as a gift from you."

I squeezed his hand. Some gift. "We've sent a transmission to the Varallan Quadrant. Someone on your homeworld will advise us what to do." I kept my grip firm so that he wouldn't feel me shaking. "You know we don't have much on Jorenian physiology in our database. I'm sure your people can help us reverse this effect."

"And if they do not, my heart?" he said, already slipping away. "Will you . . . forgive . . . yourself . . . ?"

"No." I put his hand down and turned away from his unconscious form. "No, Kao, I don't think I'll be able to do that."

When I returned to Trauma, I found yet another summons from the Council waiting for me. It was too much. T'Nliqinara snorted rapidly as I told her what to transmit back to the Council chambers in response.

"Doctor, that sort of language is a direct violation of the Charter," my charge nurse said, then gave her version of a wicked grin. "I'll relay your message personally."

Halfway through that shift a Security team entered the exam room, carrying weapons. I looked up from the child I was treating. All the guns were pointed at me.

"Put those down. You're scaring the kid."

"We have orders—"

I sighed. "I know." I sent the child out and regarded the team. "Do you have any idea how many patients are waiting out there in Assessment?"

The officer in charge shrugged. "You received a summons, Dr. Grey Veil. We're only assuring you respond to it."

"Oh, just go ahead and shoot me now!" I said.

They didn't have to. They were bigger and stronger than me. I did manage to signal the MedAdmin office before I was half dragged from the facility.

"Tell Dr. Mayer I've been forcibly removed from the

clinic. The Council sent a whole team this time. Oh, and I'll need representation. *Again.*"

The new Council was up and running, at full bureaucratic throttle. When the Security detachment dumped me in their chambers, I was ignored. Apparently the five new members couldn't decide what portion of the Charter prohibited the use of native materials to repair housing units. A real riveting debate. I was just starting to nod off when a human voice called my name.

"Dr. Grey Veil." The chief Council member was Terran, oddly enough. He was a middle-aged man who wore the dark green jumper I'd seen on researchers at the Botanical Project. "John Douglas," he introduced himself. The balance of Council members included three other humanoids and one native 'Zangian. "We would like to begin by extending to you our personal thanks for your past and ongoing endeavors through this crisis."

"You're welcome," I said. "Can I go now?"

"A serious charge has been filed with the Council, one that pertains to your status as a practicing medical physician."

Rogan? I thought uneasily. Then I saw the chief linguist enter the chamber, carrying with him, of all things, a container of golden gnorra resin.

"Ah, here is Chief Linguist Reever, who has filed the charge."

Reever had filed a charge *against* me?

The chief linguist placed the container carefully on a table and addressed the board. "Council members." He inclined his head, then glanced at me. "Doctor. I am here to interpret on the behalf of the life-forms known as the Core."

No one looked surprised but me.

"What?" I pushed my chair back and stood up to face Reever. "What does the Core have to do with this?"

"We will proceed," John Douglas said, and motioned for both of us to sit down. "First the Council will affirm their individual commitment to treating this case without bias. Given the nature of the recent epidemic, it is vital that such statements be recorded prior to presentation of evidence and rebuttal.''

That meant I had to sit there for another hour. Listen to each Council member tell me how grateful they were for my work during the epidemic. And how despite said gratitude, if I was found guilty, they'd throw the book at me.

I didn't know what was worse—listening to the bureaucrats or knowing the chief linguist was trying to get me barred from practicing medicine. Or why I felt hurt by the knowledge that Reever would do such a thing.

Negilst, Ana Hansen's assistant, entered the chamber and hurried to my side. "Administrator Hansen is with the Quadrant Inspection Team," I was told in a whisper. "I was sent to assist you until she can join us."

"Great." I motioned for the dark-skinned humanoid to sit beside me. "Make yourself comfortable. This sounds like it's going to take forever."

Douglas gave a moving speech, Negilst commented when he was finished. Uh-huh. I would have clapped, but I was busy trying not to fall into a boredom-induced coma.

"Although Dr. Grey Veil may not remember," Douglas said, "I was among the first of the cases brought to the groves. I saw what she did for our people. She saved me from dying of the contagion, and saved our colony from planetary sterilization."

All this gratitude made me want to squirm. I didn't want accolades, I wanted to go back to work.

"However, no one individual's actions can provide any type of immunity from the Charter, and a valid charge has been filed."

At this rate I was going to nod off again. "What exactly is the charge, Council Chief?"

Douglas consulted his data pad. "You are charged with causing the deliberate eradication of Core life-forms. The Core occupied this planet long before the colony was settled. As recognized sentients, they have the same rights under the Charter as any colonist."

So much for gratitude from the bug. Maybe I should have let that Yturi know where he could find some more thermal pruners.

"What did you do to the Core?" Negilst whispered next to my ear, and I shrugged.

"Got them back in their damn trees, far as I know."

Douglas frowned at my lowered but still audible tone as he turned to address Reever. "Chief Linguist, you may begin."

Reever stood and carefully inserted his fingertips into the opening of the container. A thin layer of the resin ran up his arm and into his ear.

"Are you nuts?" I shouted, and jumped to my feet, knocking over my chair. I had to stop him. Negilst grabbed my arm.

"No," it told me. "He's acting as a translator."

"We represent the Core," Reever said, while his eyes rotated up into his head. Ana's assistant picked up my chair and forced me to sit down.

"Present your evidence," Douglas said.

Reever's body trembled as his link with the Core intensified. I swallowed against the fear rising in my throat, but never took my eyes from him. If he showed even one sign of seizure, I'd *definitely* exterminate every Core life-form I could get my hands on.

"The one who discovered us, the one who ingested us, passed us to this one. She was unlike the others. We were unable to infiltrate the cells. We attempted to communicate and were ignored."

"I ignored them?" I shot up again, and this time I shook off Negilst's grasp. "Do you know how many rotations I spent just trying to *identify* them?" Douglas motioned to the Security guards, and they made me sit back down with a nudge from their rifles.

Reever went on. "Her biological response exterminated our kind. All within her body were destroyed. She is a threat to our continued existence."

"See? My biological response didn't ignore them," I said, then my eyes widened. "They're talking about—"

I grabbed Negilst. "Go get Ana. I don't care if you have to tell QIT to jump in the nearest body of water. Get her over here, now!"

Reever ended the link, and the fluid left his body to ooze back into the container. I imagined dumping the Core into a waste receptacle. No, not horrible enough. I know, I thought. I'd slosh that resinous glop over the GravBoard track, and see how the kids liked Core lubrication under their rollers.

The chief linguist sat down, his face grey with fatigue, and I saw his eyes return to normal. He gazed over at me without reaction. Douglas and the other Council members conferred for a short period of time, then addressed me directly.

"Dr. Grey Veil, you may now respond."

I stood up, wishing I had taken a few more political classes as a student.

"I'm accused of murder by the Core, a species that no one knew existed until I established contact with them, through Linguist Reever. I'm not guilty. A physician is required to take an oath to do no harm to any patient. Once identified, the Core life-forms were as much my patients as the living organisms they infected. I didn't exterminate them. I helped them go home."

I gazed at each Council member before I continued.

"The Core charge that my biological response killed them. That's true. I was never infected, despite constant exposure. However, if I'm to be held accountable for my immune system, then the Core should be, too."

"Clarify, please," Douglas said.

I stared at Reever. "The Core deliberately infiltrated, destroyed, and replaced tissue in order to secret themselves from detection. They induced pneumonic symptoms to fortify their positions and provide escape routes from their hosts' bodies." I smiled sourly. "That biological response killed over seven thousand colonists. Sound familiar?"

Ana appeared with Negilst just as I was taking my seat. She immediately addressed the Council. "I have been monitoring this hearing and only wish to add that the PQSGO will support all of Dr. Grey Veil's actions—voluntary and otherwise—during the time of the epidemic."

That seemed to shake up the Council members, who took another interval to discreetly confer. Ana glanced at Reever before she leaned close. "Sorry I'm late. They're ready to lift the quarantine, and the adminwork is a nightmare."

"Tell me one thing," I said. "How did Reever get involved in this?"

"Duncan was summoned to the Botanical Project by the Core themselves yesterday. He had no choice but to act as their representative."

"He had no choice. Of course. That explains everything."

Ana nudged me. "Joey, I can sense what you're thinking, and you're wrong. He's only doing his job."

"His job reeks."

The Council completed their discussion, and all five rose.

"We find the charge of extermination of the Core life-forms to be substantiated, but in doing so find the Core also guilty of the same against the victims of the epidemic. Both charges can be enforced under the Charter."

"What does that mean?" I asked.

"It means," Reever said as he touched the surface of the resin once more, "that if you are found guilty, so are they. I will relay this to the Core."

After a short silence, the Core spoke through Reever again. "We will withdraw the charge against Dr. Grey Veil, if she does the same." Reever's voice shook badly. "We request Dr. Grey Veil be prohibited from any future contact with our dwellings."

"Right," I scowled. "I'm heartbroken. As if I wanted to poke around the damn dirt or those ugly purple—

Ana clapped her hand over my mouth. "She agrees."

"Charges are dismissed. Dr. Grey Veil." Douglas smiled at me. "You are free to go."

I hurried over to Reever to examine him. "Notify medevac and have them send a unit. Now." I eased him back down in his chair and leaned closer. "Don't say another word, or I swear I'll sedate you."

I beckoned to one of the Security team, and shoved the container of resin in his arms. "Get this glop away from me, before I end up with another set of homicide charges."

Dhreen was hovering outside of Trauma hours later, when I finally dragged myself off duty. I had every intention of going home and sleeping for a week. I barely managed a wave when I saw him. He was still using limb supports to walk while his broken legs healed.

"Dhreen." I tried to smile, but my facial muscles wouldn't cooperate. I was *that* tired. "What are you doing here? You should still be confined to a bed. Wait—" I held up a hand, imitating a gesture he'd made to me in a tavern, a long time ago. "Don't tell me. I'll probably have to testify against you."

The Oenrallian tried to look wounded. "Just came to see my favorite Terran. Who happens to be too conscientious for her own good."

"Who happens to know you too well," I said. "I'm headed for home. Can you walk with me to my glidecar? I need to keep moving or I'll drop where I stand."

"I know the problem." Dhreen shifted the supports under his arms awkwardly. "Right behind you, Doc."

I managed to snare a space for myself close to the entrance to Trauma earlier, so we didn't have far to go. Dhreen seemed nervous, and started to say something several times, only to break off.

"Here, sit down." I opened the passenger's panel for him, and gave him the once-over. He seemed to be healing satisfactorily. "If you want to come home with me, you can watch me sleep for ten or twelve hours," I of-

fered wryly as I went around the vehicle and slid behind
the controls. The orange head shook as he hiccuped.

"No, but thanks. I just wanted to tell you I've gotten
a position on one of the Quadrant's long-range freight-
ers. As soon as I heal, I'll ship out."

"That's good news, right?"

He nodded. "Now that the *Bestshot* is gone, I've got
to have steady work. I was lucky the Quadrant needed
a pilot who's jaunted the territories."

"You don't want me to clear you to go now, I hope,"
I warned, topping it with a severe frown. "Those bones
need to heal, or you'll end up with permanent
impairment."

"No, actually . . ." Dhreen turned yellow, which in his
species indicated a rush of blood to the epidermis.

"Dhreen. You're blushing."

"Doc . . . you saved my life . . . you've been a good
friend . . . see, when I heard the Council was trying to
get rid of you . . . well, I thought . . . I mean, maybe . . .
you know, I have cohab rights on the freighter, and . . ."

He was *proposing* to me. "You want me to go with
you?"

"We don't have to bond for life," he said to reassure
me. His amber eyes rolled. "I'm not good at this sort of
thing. I just thought . . . I wanted to—"

I reached up and kissed his thin cheek. "You're a
lovely friend. I'm very flattered, but"—I looked through
the glidecar's shield back at the facility—"my work is
here."

He looked even more yellow than before. "Are you
sure?" His spatulate fingers brushed my arm gently.
"We've always coexisted well. Shared some mirth." The
clear amber eyes narrowed. "I don't like leaving you
here. Not with the way things are."

I rested my head against the steering controls. Dhreen
shifted his broken legs uneasily. "You know, I'm almost
tempted." I was more tired than I thought. Tired of the
Council, the slow recovery after the epidemic, the politics, everything.

"I'd take care of you, Doc."

Dhreen grinned, and I knew life with him would never be dull. It would also mean running away from my problems. Running away from my past, my father, and now K-2. For a moment I was really tempted.

"Thank you, Dhreen, but I have to say no."

He didn't stop smiling. "Let me know if you change your mind."

"You'll be on K-2 for a few more days," I said, "so we don't have to say good-bye right now."

"No." He climbed back out of the glidecar, then ducked his head down to add, "Just remember, the freighter's route can take a dozen cycles to complete. I won't be back for a long time."

"I'll be here."

I was barely able to drive the glidecar over to the housing unit and drag myself to my quarters. Tears were running down my face, and I didn't know why. All through the epidemic I had been like a rock. Now I wept over silly things, like Reever's scars and Dhreen leaving. What was wrong with me?

Alunthri and Jenner were startled when I stumbled in and flung myself on the bed. They were also kind enough to let me cry myself to sleep.

My shifts gradually shortened, with help from our new medical students, former orderlies who were undergoing formal training. The chief himself initiated the program after PQSGO made it plain that no medical professional in their right mind would transfer to K-2. No matter how well recovery was proceeding, the stigma of the epidemic clung.

The medical students would take years to educate, but they provided valuable manpower in the interim. We were still swamped by a plethora of post-epidemic ailments. During each shift, four students worked on minor cases, supervised by a nurse. That freed up the physicians to deal with the more serious emergencies.

Duncan Reever's case was handled by Dr. Mayer. I

personally avoided further contact with him. The idea was for him to recover, and I was still furious. He was discharged a day after I admitted him for exposure to the Core.

Kao Torin's condition deteriorated further. His distant homeworld, Joren, eventually transmitted the necessary medical updates for our database, and it confirmed my worst fear. No one reported me for smashing the console screen.

I went to see Dr. Crhm, trying to find some small hope. It reviewed the latest pathological data on Kao with me.

"The transfusion of Terran blood acted as an antibody at first, and restricted itself to attacking the Core lifeforms. Once it had removed the immediate threat, it infiltrated the immune system, then the systemic tissues." It ducked its hard-shelled head, not catching my reaction as it continued. "Now the foreign blood has reactivated its cytotoxic properties and is destroying native cells. Tissue, bone, and fluid."

"It's killing him the same way it did the Core." My blood, eating away at Kao's internal organs.

"Yes, Dr. Grey Veil. Would you be able to obtain another sample of plasma from the original donor?"

Kao's chart reflected merely that he received an experimental transfusion of Terran blood. Only Ecla and Dr. Mayer knew it had come from me. Now I would have to lie again. "The donor was killed during the epidemic." I couldn't say from the contagion. "A glidecar collision. The body was completely destroyed."

"A pity. It would have been fascinating to conduct a proper study. I have never reviewed a hematological profile such as this. The cells are absolutely ferocious."

Bile was burning at the back of my throat. "How long do you estimate the patient has before complete systemic failure?"

"Three, perhaps four rotations."

I left Crhm's lab, stopped long enough to throw up in private, then went to Kao's ward. I sat with him for a while as he slept, holding his hand. The white eyes eventually opened.

"You look fatigued, my Chosen."

I was. Oh, God, I was. "Kao, I have to"—I choked on the words, hesitated, tried again—"I have to tell you some bad news. The latest tests—" How did I tell him my blood was killing him? "—They don't look good."

"How long do I have?"

I was startled, then I understood. The tranquillity, the acceptance. Jorenians were much more intimately aware of their bodies than Terrans. He already knew. "Not long. A few days."

Kao nodded. "That is enough time. You must do it now, Cherijo."

I didn't want to face what he was asking, and shook my head wildly. "I will keep working on a treatment— I can—I might—" I faltered as he gazed steadily at me.

"Send the message to Joren and tell them my time is upon me." He had discussed it with me in detail days before. "Those of my HouseClan within range will come for my last rites."

"I don't want you to die," I whispered. His big hand curled tightly around mine.

"You will like my HouseClan, Healer," he said, and smiled. "My ClanBrother Xonea has been eager to meet you."

"Space your ClanBrother!" I became irrational. "Kao. Don't give up. Fight it. Fight it for me."

"Don't cry, honored Chosen . . ." He lapsed back into unconsciousness.

Dr. Dloh was on ward duty and stood observing at a respectful distance. When I knew Kao wouldn't wake again soon, I rose and looked at him. He handed me the chart he was holding. "The latezt rezultz from the lab."

I glanced at the levels, which only reiterated what Crhm had told me earlier. Systemic failure was imminent. Suddenly I watched the chart fly across the ward and ricochet off the opposite wall.

"Doctor—" Dloh reached out a tentative appendage.

"Excuse me, Dr. Dloh." I walked off the ward before I started taking it apart, piece by piece.

I had to do something besides take care of the injured and repair the damage wrought by the Core. Something physical. Smashing the hell out of something was very soothing. I'd try that.

When I strode out of the facility's back entrance, I saw Duncan Reever. I swerved in order to put some distance between us, but he only trailed behind me. I crossed a hundred meters, glanced back. Still there. I needed to pound something into dust. Despite my rage, a small part of me didn't want it to be him.

"Get away from me, Reever."

He kept silent, but didn't go away. I walked into a narrow, boxed-in alley between some Transport buildings. I was trapping myself with him. Maybe it was for the best. He was a good-sized male. I might not hurt him. Much.

"Cherijo, stop."

I'd reached the end of the passage and faced a solid wall of plasbrick. No one but Reever was within sight. That was fine with me. The fury within me punched through my self-control and poured out.

"No!" I screamed at the wall. I whirled on Reever, my fists clenched as I jammed them against my temples. "I can't stop it! I can't!"

"No, you can't." His gaze held a glimmer of pity.

That was the last straw. I launched myself at him. Reever, who would never leave me alone. Reever, who had repeatedly forced himself upon my mind and made me share his. Reever, who had taken me, pleasured me, used me.

I wanted *him* to die.

He was strong, but I was unstoppable. With one vicious blow I knocked him off his feet, then threw myself on top of him. My fists struck him, over and over. Knuckles slammed into flesh. Bones jarred and grated. God, it felt good. Pain streaked up my arm. Breath burned in my lungs. Blood roared in my head.

We linked.

Reever's mind flooded over me like a wave. His thoughts slammed into mine, until I was caught between him and the violent despair that had me spinning out of control.

Cherijo, stop.

No! I will not! Let me go!

Cherijo. Stop fighting me. Let me help you.

I never wanted you. Never wanted this. Get out, just get out of me!

Let me help you.

Inside my head, Reever enveloped me. The churning tide of my emotions was thrust back, held at bay while new images appeared.

I saw the epidemic, its aftermath. Alun Karas's simple, comical accident. The horrible impotence as thousands died before my eyes. Then I was in the groves. I watched as golden fluid sank into the soil, and the dying recovered. *The colony lives. The Core lives. Your gift to them.*

Reever. I was inside Reever now. He was being controlled by the Core. Through his eyes I watched myself, being forced to submit, then to respond. I felt what Reever felt. Desperation. Terror. Humiliation. Unwilling pleasure. Guilt. It stunned me. Behind his eyes now, I knew his agony.

I wasn't the only one who had been violated in that Isolation room.

Back at the temporary facility. Ana and I holding his hand. Contacting the Core. Learning how to stop the epidemic. Ridding his body of the alien control. *I live. Your gift to me.*

I saw Kao Torin, dying on the ward where I had left him. Then further back in time, to the moment just before I had injected him with my blood. He had died. I'd brought him back to life. *Kao Torin lives. He has the time to bid farewell to those he honors. To you. Your gift to him.*

I can't bear it. Oh, God, Duncan, I can't. I can't.

I found myself on my knees, Reever holding on to me

tightly, my throat raw from screaming. The link between us was gone. I couldn't speak. He said nothing.

After I'd regained enough strength and steadiness to stand, he helped me to my feet. His face was bruised, the front of his tunic was torn. Blood ran from his nose and mouth in thin scarlet streams.

"Duncan." I reached out to touch his face, then snatched my hand back. "Oh, no, what have I done?"

"I will recover." He wiped the blood from his face with the back of his sleeve. "Be at peace, Cherijo. Be at peace with yourself." He released me, turned, and walked down the alley.

"Duncan," I said, and he paused for a moment. "I'm . . . I'm sorry." He nodded, and then disappeared.

I sat down on the ground and looked at the abrasions on my knuckles. I had never harmed another living being in my life. I'd just beaten the hell out of one who was only trying to help me. The anger was gone. I understood now. That only made it worse.

CHAPTER SEVENTEEN

Unexpected Allies

A week later it was announced that the Allied League of Worlds would conduct a full investigation of the epidemic on Kevarzangia Two. That was roughly equivalent to God announcing he would inspect the number of fleas on a single Terran canine.

Pmoc Quadrant's Inspection Team, along with the orbiting cruisers, left K-2 abruptly. Maintenance crews worked triple shifts. Everyone was speculating about the League's interest in what was surely Quadrant jurisdiction when League cruisers arrived and went into orbit. All fifteen of them.

I was the first summoned to be *interviewed*, if you could call it that. Interrogation by Security's Norash had been aggravating. This was more like an inquisition.

Record drones were everywhere as I was escorted into the special conference area. Squads of armed Allied forces lined the perimeters, passages, and entrances throughout the building. None of them smiled. A rare piece of hardware, one of the new 3-Dimaiyzers, was capturing the proceedings onto indestructible crystal discs for future generations.

This was considerable ado for an epidemic that was already over and done with.

"Identity presentation," a drone said.

"Grey Veil, Cherijo, Terran, medical physician."

One of the investigators glanced up and pointed to the only empty chair. "Sit down, Doctor."

Nobody looked at me. Highlights of my practice on the homeworld and personal history were cited by a drone. Fingers worked busily over touchpads. Someone coughed, but it was a normal, dry sound. I was asked to confirm the validity of these facts.

"Before I respond, may I inquire"—noticing that got everyone's attention—"am I being charged with something?"

"*We* make the inquiries here, Dr. Grey Veil," one replied. "Please confine yourself to responses only."

And they did. What followed was an exact, meticulous grilling. I was asked to provide only affirmative or negative responses. Yes or no. Nothing more.

"Dr. Grey Veil, did you treat Alun Karas immediately after he was infected by the Core pathogen?" I confirmed. Several chart notes I'd made during Karas's initial examination were read. "These are your observations?" I confirmed again.

I was given other charts from the Engineering Group. Watched a replay from a Security vid that showed me climbing around the site with Geef Skrople, checking the workers.

"Yes, I was there."

"Yes, those are my scan results."

"Yes, I examined those colonists."

A series of displays showed the results of the analysis Dr. Mayer had performed on my own blood sample. How the hell did they get that? I had what I'd thought was the *only* copy. I requested counsel, they refused. I didn't need representation, I was told, because I was not being indicted.

That didn't make me feel better.

"Do you recognize this, Dr. Grey Veil?" I inspected the anonymous tag on the empty specimen vial I was handed. "Is this identical to the sample Dr. Mayer tested? The same blood used to inoculate Pilot Torin during the epidemic?"

Yes, yes, yes.

They never asked whose blood it was. Incredibly I was asked instead to confirm my shift hours, which rotations I'd worked at the facility, the number of times I'd pulled more than one shift. Were they thinking about putting me on per-hour compensation? I wondered. After that, they started asking me about off-duty time.

"When Pilot Torin arrived on planet from his last escort assignment, did you meet him at Docking Station Sixteen?"

My spine stiffened. This was getting into very personal territory. I nodded.

"Did you then accompany Pilot Torin to his housing quarters?"

"I don't see how—"

"Answer the question."

My hands clenched. "Yes."

"After you entered Pilot Torin's quarters, did you engage in sexual intercourse with him?"

I checked. Yes, they were serious. "That's none of your damn business!" I said.

"Answer the question."

"I'm not going to—"

"Answer the question."

I folded my arms over my knotted stomach. "I refuse."

Two of the panel members conferred for a moment.

"Very well." The questioning veered away from Kao and on to other incidents. The whump-ball game with poor Akamm. The assault by Rogan. The Hsktskt quints.

I had to corroborate the events of every single cycle I had spent on K-2 since the *Bestshot* landed. The only other time I refused to answer again was when I was asked about having relations with Duncan Reever in the Isolation chamber.

"Why are you so interested in my sex life?"

No one answered me.

I was dismissed after ten hours of interview, and ordered to return to the conference area the following day. I was less than enraptured at the prospect. A Security officer drove me to my housing unit. He refused to speak to me or respond to any questions.

I wasn't afraid. I was terrified. Also confused, suspicious, and outraged. Something enormous was looming just ahead, I sensed. But what?

Outside my quarters, a familiar figure hovered. I was surprised; I'd never seen one of them alone before. I walked past the Barterman, but he forced his way into my rooms before I could get the door panel closed.

"Get out."

"Colonist Grey Veil, you will barter?"

"Leave." I was already at the display and signalling HQ Administration.

"Barter for safe passage off K-2?"

I delayed the signal for a moment. "Safe passage?"

The hood was pushed back from the square skull. The Barterman's features were contorted by some weird expression of victory. Or maybe he was feeling flatulent. I couldn't be sure.

"Barter for entirety of possessions. Offer is safe passage to neighboring world in immediate system."

"Why would the Bartermen be offering me safe passage?" I inquired. "Out of the goodness of your hearts?"

"Bartermen do not have hearts."

"No kidding." Get the little troll out of my quarters, that was what I needed to do. The offer it made—"You know something you're not telling me, don't you?"

I received a smug leer. "Bartermen know much."

"Why would I desire safe passage off this planet, Barterman?"

"Avoid League detainment."

"They're just questioning me because of the epidemic," I said, and eyed the Barterman. "Aren't they?"

"Barter?"

"Answer me!"

The Barterman said nothing.

"I refuse," I said, then turned back to the console. "HQ Administration, I have an intruder in my quarters—" I looked back, and the Barterman had disappeared. I shook my head. "Oh, never mind."

A Security officer appeared the next morning to escort me. The questioning continued. The chart for every case I had treated was now brought forward, my notes reviewed. They were meticulous. I wanted to scream. Good thing my voice failed to a husky rasp from uttering my responses, or I would have. I was "allowed" a "brief period of rest" before the panel started hammering me again. A whole fifteen minutes. Their benevolence was touching.

I endured four consecutive days of this nonsense before the panel at last informed me I was through. I didn't know what to do with myself. I laughed. I stopped laughing. I demanded again to know why I had been questioned so precisely.

All I got was, "Dr. Grey Veil. You are dismissed."

I went straight to HQ Administration. I was Terran, I knew my rights. When I arrived at Ana Hansen's office, I was turned away by her assistant.

"Administrator Hansen is currently in interview," I was told, but Negilst's eyes were frightened.

All I could do was wait. Not long, either. When I reported to the FreeClinic, I was detained by yet another Security officer and ordered to report to a League starshuttle the next morning.

"What for?" I asked, and I was handed a disc.

I took it back into an exam room and pulled up the data. After a quick scan I was speechless. The Barterman had been right after all. I removed the disc and strode to the MedAdmin section.

Dr. Mayer was reviewing charts when I opened his door without knocking and tossed the disc onto his desk.

"I'm being deported. Taken back to Terra," I said, while he put down a chart to pick up the disc. "Courtesy of the League."

"That's not possible."

"Read the disc."

While Dr. Mayer examined the order of detainment and deportation, I paced the narrow confines of his office. It was a closet. I was surprised he wasn't a raving claustrophobic.

"There is no explanation listed. They can't force you to return to Terra, unless you are a criminal."

"I am."

"Explain."

"Joseph Grey Veil's experimentation," I said, "and his precious Genetic Exclusivity Act. My existence violates Section nine, paragraphs two through four, I believe. Someone knows about me."

"I see." Mayer removed the disc, and his strong fingers snapped it into four pieces. I stopped pacing. "We will not, of course, allow your parent to do this."

"What does he have to do with this? He wouldn't report me. That would be like telling on himself."

"Now that his field research has concluded, he wants you back."

That looming sense of revelation was here now. "Field research?" I said.

"Cherijo, sit down." I dropped into the chair before his desk, and braced myself. He was calling me Cherijo, it must be pretty bad. "I've been performing my own investigation of your transfer, from the moment you arrived. Yesterday I discovered the real reason why your application was approved. Your father is responsible for you transferring to K-2."

"Hardly. He didn't even know about my transfer until after I arrived here."

"On the contrary, he did." Mayer sat back in his chair and folded his hands, then hesitated.

"*Tell* me," I said.

"Before you filed your application, he contracted with PQSGO to have you transferred here to K-2. You have been kept under constant remote drone observation since you arrived. Security vids, audio monitoring, the lot. He probably tapped into your terminal use as well. All sanctioned by the League."

That explained how they had knowledge of everything I had done from the moment I'd set foot on K-2. Some remote drones could be as small as Terran roaches. I would have never seen them.

Dr. Mayer went on. "Yesterday I was contacted by one of my more influential friends in the League. He warned me not to become involved in the matter. I demanded the facts. This is what I was told."

There could be only one reason. "It's all been part of his experiment, hasn't it? That cold-blooded son of a bitch." I gripped the sides of my chair with tight hands. "He sent me the anonymous package with all the evidence about his experiment."

"No doubt it was part of his plan. He chose K-2 as a viable site for the experiment to continue. Your life here has been just another series of tests to confirm his theories."

"How his perfect physician would perform under stressful conditions in an alien environment," I said. "Who else is involved?"

"No one here on the colony, I believe. Your parent would not have wanted to risk discovery. Even when he was a student, Joe was intensely guarded about his experiments."

"And now he wants this experiment back."

"Yes, I'm afraid he does."

"I've never done anything he hadn't planned for me to do, have I?" I stared at my hands, at the bruises and cuts from my fight with Reever. "So much for my magnificent get away."

"You couldn't have known."

"He had it all plotted. Hell, he probably forecasted my reactions. Ran statistical analysis of the probability of every variable."

"He didn't predict the epidemic."

I rubbed a hand over the back of my neck. "He must

have figured some type of exotic bug would take a shot at my immune system."

"Joe is an exceptional scientist," Mayer said, but not with admiration. "He remains a poor excuse for a human being."

I thought of the direct communications from Terra, the act he had put on, the mental anguish I'd suffered. All for nothing. "Yeah, well, *Joe* can go to hell."

"There's undoubtably a large section reserved for his exclusive occupation." Mayer gazed steadily at me. "What will you do?"

I stared at the broken disc between us. "What can I do?"

"Put a stop to this. Petition the Council with an emergency request and have yourself declared a sentient being."

I was dumbfounded. "I'm not considered sentient?"

Mayer smiled bitterly. "No, my dear. You are a clone. Created, modified, trained, and being observed during an extended experiment. You are not classified as human or sentient. You are Joseph Grey Veil's property."

Dr. Mayer accompanied me to HQ Administration to demand an emergency hearing before the Council. I never knew the chief could drive like that. On the way over he signaled Assessment from his glidecar and told the charge nurse to round up everyone who worked regular shifts with me and send along whoever could be spared.

"Cheering section?" I asked.

"Character attestants," he said. "They can cheer after we win a favorable ruling."

The clerk who examined our hastily prepared petition frowned. His six eyes looked at both of us as though questioning our sanity.

"She's sentient, isn't she?" The clerk yawned and dropped the disc on his desk. He was a bherKot and slipping into a pre-nocturnal state of relaxation, his colors fluctuating slowly. "Humans are classified—"

"She's not human," Mayer said. "File the petition."

"The Council is finished with the day's—"

I grabbed the disc and looked around me. "I don't have time for this. Where are they?"

The bherKot managed to get to his feet and grumbled as he snatched the disc back and led us down a side corridor.

"They aren't going to like this," he said as he signaled the entrance panel. The chief shouldered past him and stepped up to the audiocom.

"This is William Mayer. You must hear this petition at once. Lives are at stake." I lifted an eyebrow, and my boss shrugged. "Lives *could* be lost," he added in a mutter that wouldn't transmit. "Especially if I lose one-sixth of my physician staff."

"Nice touch."

The Council granted us access, and we marched in.

"Drs. Grey Veil and Mayer, welcome." Council Chief Douglas seemed bemused. "How may we assist you?" Dr. Mayer offered the petition disc and gave a brief description of its contents. Douglas's smile faded rapidly. "If Dr. Grey Veil is not human," he said, then cleared his throat. "Er—exactly *what* is she?"

"As a being genetically enhanced during embryonic development," Dr. Mayer said, "she is currently unclassified under the standard system."

"Why have you brought this matter before the Council?" one of the other members wanted to know. "What does it matter whether she is classified today?"

I answered that one. "If you don't recognize me as a sentient being, I will be forcibly removed from this planet tomorrow."

"Deported? For what reason?"

That was when one of the Allied investigators strode into the room.

"The Allied League of Worlds wishes to present an emergency petition," he said as he approached Douglas.

Behind him, a detachment of armed guards spread out to surround me and Dr. Mayer. "Detainment and deportation of a non-sentient to its owner and planet of origin."

Gee, wonder who he was talking about?

"I assume you refer to Dr. Grey Veil?" Douglas inquired as he took the disc with the second petition.

"The petition identifies the non-sentient by that designation, yes."

"Excuse me." Douglas and the other Council members observed me with little interest. Had I already lost the respect of other sentients? "We were here first."

"My petition negates the one being presented by Dr. William Mayer." The Allied investigator was smug. For him it was already decided.

Douglas may have been Council chief but he was also Terran. I was the embodiment of everything human beings feared: a mutant experiment, artificially conceived, scientifically enhanced. I was surprised the man didn't immediately award the Allied rep his petition.

That was when the home team arrived.

The chamber door panel slid open again, and a line of medical staffers filed in behind the guards around me and Dr. Mayer. I saw Ecla, Dr. Dloh, Dr. mu Cheft, T'Nliqinara, and even Dr. Crhm from Pathology. Nurses and orderlies who had worked with me during the epidemic. Former patients. Security officers involved in transporting patients to the groves. Finally there was no more room in the chamber, and a line began to back up and out the door.

I smiled at the Allied rep. See? Even the non-sentient hunk of property has friends. Lots of them.

Nurse Ecla stepped forward and made a particularly cutting gesture. I didn't know she knew that sort of language. "We are here to speak on Dr. Grey Veil's behalf."

Dr. Dloh managed to work his way over to come within a foot of where Dr. Mayer and I stood, and leaned forward to catch my attention. "Dr. Grey Veil, I muzt warn you, Dr. Rogan inzizted on appearing. He iz here."

I rolled my eyes, but winked at the big arachnid. "Don't worry, Doctor. I think we have the bad guys outnumbered."

"My zpinneretz are full," he replied with a buzzing chuckle. "Enough to cocoon the entire Counzil, if nezezzary."

The Council conferred quickly, and adjourned to a larger auditorium where everyone could be better accommodated. In other words, they panicked and sent us all to a bigger room so they could have space to make a hasty exit if necessary. The Allied rep looked confused. I was unsettled. The chief was actually *smiling*.

"What are you so happy about?" I demanded.

Mayer nodded toward Douglas. "He's stalling." When I looked directly at the Council chief, I thought I saw compassion in his eyes. A friend, after all?

We were escorted by armed guard to the new conference site. Medical staff, former patients, and other colonists continued to arrive. When they filled the auditorium and still kept crowding in, someone on the Council finally spoke up.

"See here, the entire colony can't appear on behalf of Dr. Grey Veil!"

"Why not?" someone called back. "She saved our lives!"

A rumbling agreement swept through the auditorium. The Allied investigator stopped looking confused and started looking worried.

Very worried.

After the auditorium was filled to capacity, the Council announced that it would hold subsequent hearings for those still waiting to present evidence and would now address the two petitions individually.

"In order of presentation?" Dr. Mayer asked, and Council Chief Douglas agreed.

That meant the petition to have me deported could not be heard until the matter of my sentience was decided. Bravo, Council Chief Douglas. I wasn't in the clear yet, however. I kept remembering how many times Ana Hansen had petitioned to have the Chakacats declared sentient.

There was a set of League standards used to determine sentience, well-known by all species. I had to prove I met them. The League had to show I didn't. My challengers went first, simply because there were only two of them.

Dr. Phorap Rogan rushed to have his say. He claimed to know I had been "preprogrammed" by my maker to perform "adequately" in the role of medical physician. Only sophisticated training had allowed me to ape my "betters."

"She has created difficulties between sentient physicians at the facility from the first day." Rogan ended his speech with a disgusting smirk. "Obviously an effort to deflect notice of her limitations."

I felt like deflecting something off his polyp-rich head.

The Allied investigator also had his chance, and was mercifully briefer, but no less derogatory. "Dr. Joseph Grey Veil has provided positive evidence to the Allied League of Worlds as proof of this life-form's non-sentient status. It is his hope that the enhancements she enjoys can one day be used to augment the lives of sentient beings everywhere."

What about my life?

The Council called for a short intermission in order to decide how to proceed. Everyone began talking, speculating on the outcome of the petition. I noticed a number of tall, silent beings moving discreetly throughout the crowded auditorium. At the same time, some of the medical staffers were quietly slipping out to make room for them. All of those who came in were wearing helmets.

"Who are they?" I asked Dr. Mayer after I nodded toward one towering figure dressed in a pilot's flight suit. Another pilot, as big and powerful-looking as the others, came right into my direct eye line.

He lifted a gloved hand and raised his visor, and his white within white eyes crinkled from a hidden smile. Then he tapped weapon-shaped bulges on his sides and legs. He dropped the visor almost at once, but I knew who had come.

Kao's version of the Calvary. HouseClan Torin.

Now I began to count the helmeted figures, and when I got to fifty I caught my breath. They now outnumbered Allied forces three to one. So many of them could only be here for one reason. Especially carrying concealed weapons.

Paul Dalton's voice came back to me. "Jorenian HouseClans are notorious for pursuing their adversaries, and those of their kin, to the end of the galaxy."

Kao must have sent them to insure I would not be taken against my will from the planet. I grinned. Rogan, not to mention the Bartermen, were going to be *so* disappointed.

Douglas called for attention and acknowledged that it was time to present evidence on my behalf. The number of presentations the Council could allow in order to responsibly rule on my petition was limited, since the deportation order was in effect for the next day. It was decided that I should choose three supporters to speak for me.

I didn't hesitate, asking that Dr. Mayer, Nurse Ecla, and Chief Linguist Reever speak on my behalf. I realized my mistake when Reever did not respond when called.

"The chief linguist is not present. You must choose another."

"I would speak for Dr. Grey Veil," a familiar voice called out, and I saw Alunthri moving through the crowded auditorium.

"A non-sentient can't present evidence!" Rogan said.

Douglas held up his hand. "There is no precedent," he said. The Terran looked at the Chakacat and sighed. "However, we proceed into such new areas with every moment that passes, it seems."

A brief conference between the Council members decided the issue. My friend and fellow unrecognized sentient, Alunthri, would be allowed to speak on my behalf.

Dr. Mayer went first. As he stood and began to address the Council, I couldn't help wondering where Duncan Reever was.

The chief described my struggle to adapt to an alien and sometimes hostile environment. He went on to praise my commitment to my patients and extended efforts to educate myself. He admired my skills and determination. He didn't say I walked on water, but it was pretty close to the same thing. I recognized that smile he made at the end of his speech. It was the one that he reserved for fools, malcontents, and Phorap Rogan.

"Should you determine Cherijo Grey Veil to be non-sentient, you defame all medical professionals on this world. Dr. Grey Veil embodies everything it means to be an outstanding doctor and sentient being."

Nurse Ecla talked about the humorous incidents, the mistakes and the way I had learned from them. She used her remarkable non-verbal gestures to spread laughter throughout the assembly.

Toward the end she grew serious. "I'm told non-sentient life forms do not have the ability to understand the meaning of death. During the epidemic, Dr. Grey Veil was often required to treat approximately one hundred patients per hour, to facilitate the most efficient care. I recall one of the many times she did not meet this quota. I saw her holding a dead child in her arms. She was praying to her God for that lost little soul." Ecla moved her limbs, and the air itself seemed to weep. "Council members, Dr. Grey Veil is not less than we sentient beings. She is an example to the rest of us."

The Chakacat came to my side, and regarded the Council with calm, unblinking eyes. It was the kind of gaze that made several squirm and look away.

"I have appeared before the Council many times," the Chakacat said. "Each time I was judged not to be sentient. Until now, it was simple for me to accept such

rulings. I had never known freedom." Alunthri bowed
its head. "When my last owner expired, I faced deportation and continued slavery. Dr. Grey Veil was kind
enough to declare herself my owner in order to spare
me that ordeal."

"One non-sentient protects another," Rogan said. No
one looked at him, but the waves of hostility were apparent even to him. He had enough sense to shut up.

"I find it remarkable that Dr. Grey Veil, as a non-
sentient, identified the Core life-forms, took measures to
end the epidemic, and restored the Core to their natural
environment. A non-sentient aiding, and protecting, a
host of sentient beings." Alunthri cocked its head. "If
Dr. Grey Veil is declared non-sentient, then I request
any future petition made on behalf of my kind for the
same be withdrawn. The Chakacats do not want freedom
on such terms. It is beneath us." The big cat gazed at
me with deep affection. "I prefer slavery to hypocrisy."

It was over. The Council adjourned to confer on the
testimonies. The Allied forces remained in place, and it
was announced (rather nervously by the investigator)
that I would have to stay in the auditorium until the
Council reconvened.

The Jorenians were now over a hundred in number
and well positioned throughout the auditorium.

Dr. Mayer leaned close. "Your friend Torin has no
faith in our ruling Council."

I flashed him a grin. "Neither do I, to be frank. This
may get ugly, if the Jorenians choose to fight here. What
should I do?"

The chief looked grim. "Keep your head down and
get out as fast as possible."

I expected the Council to take their time, but they
filed back into the room after only a brief interval. Faced
with the overwhelming numbers present, they were no
doubt too anxious to deliberate at length. They'd seen
too many mob riots during the epidemic.

They requested a record drone list the standard requirements for sentience under Allied League precepts. As I listened, I noted the exact criteria I did not meet.

I had not been conceived, gestated, or delivered by natural or legally sanctioned methods.

I possessed enhancements deliberately bred by experimentation.

I had never been allowed to live freely.

There were other, greyer areas, but I had a sinking feeling as Douglas got to his feet once the record drone was through.

"We are all very grateful to Cherijo Grey Veil for her service to the community. We sympathize with supporters present—"

They were going to rule against me.

"—however, no matter what the majority prefers, there are legal standards by which we are all governed and must adhere to. In light of the evidence presented, the Council has no alternative but to deny this life-form sentient status."

The auditorium was dead silent. Mayer tensed beside me, and I saw the face of the Allied investigator glow with satisfaction. He stood, and began to present his petition to have me deported back to Terra.

That was when the Jorenians made their move, and pandemonium broke out. Throughout the auditorium, HouseClan Torin engaged the Allied forces, aided by some of the colonists. I saw Ecla knock down the Allied rep herself and sit on him. A helmeted figure appeared before me.

"Healer Grey Veil." The Jorenian pilot removed his headgear and made a quick bow. "Xonea Torin, to escort you to safety." He took my arm and began to guide me through the fray.

"Kao?" I asked, and he gave me a sad glance.

"My ClanBrother may still live. He waits for you on our vessel."

I couldn't ask when or how they had removed Kao from the inpatient ward. No time. We were running through the Administrative Building, and I had my hands full just trying to keep up with those long legs of his. Other helmeted Jorenians appeared to flank us. From the angry shouts behind us, I surmised the Allied forces had regrouped and were in pursuit. Xonea took double the strides I could manage, and before long he turned and picked me up with one arm.

"Allow me, Healer." He carried me to a glidecar in a long line of empty vehicles, placed me inside, and nimbly vaulted over it to take the driver's position. "Brace yourself, this will be quick."

K-2 blurred around us as he jammed the controls to maximum speed and pointed the glidecar toward the Transport area. The other Jorenians did the same, creating a wall of vehicles behind us. I held on to the restraint grips and looked back.

"We've got company," I said.

An ominous cluster of Security transports sped after us, weapons firing. Though the other Jorenians ran interference, some of the Allied pursuers got through. I cringed when our vehicle was rocked by the impact of pulse fire. Xonea grinned at me and steered a weaving pattern to avoid another hit.

"An interesting world, this Kevarzangia Two," he said. "Are you prepared to leave?"

"No," I said, and looked back. "But it doesn't appear that I have a choice."

"I will keep you safe, Healer." Xonea scanned the access paths and chose one that led to the shuttle docks. "There is our vessel."

The Jorenian ship was beyond huge. It must have overloaded the Transport Grid when it landed, taking up the space of ten starshuttles with its mass. Yet for all its enormous size, it was beautifully made, a towering sculpture of silvery amalgams and gleaming lights.

"The *Sunlace* awaits your company, Healer." Xonea helped me from the glidecar and looked behind us. The pursuing vehicles were approaching at high speed. "It seems I must carry you again. Your pardon." He picked me up in his arms and ran to the ship with me.

There was no entrance ramp in evidence, and I found out why when we were surrounded by a brilliant light. Grav-displacers. I felt our bodies being slowly lifted from the ground and pulled into a small, telescopic gap in one of the outer hull panels.

"P'narr knich retach foro," Xonea said, and I realized my TI was no longer functioning. The big Jorenian set me gently on my feet while I shook my head, bemused. At once he produced a short chain of flat-linked discs, which he attached around my neck. "Can you understand me now?"

I nodded, fingering the device. "What's this?"

"A vocollar—what we Jorenians use for inter-species communication."

"My insert should do that," I touched my ear, puzzled.

"The *Sunlace's* hull blocks transmission from the colonial database," Xonea said. "Come with me, this way."

We followed a central corridor into the heart of the *Sunlace*. The ship inside was as beautiful as its hull, elegantly appointed with HouseClan Torin's myriad aquamarine colors. Alunthri would have loved it.

Complicated-looking equipment was recessed into the structure supports so that large Jorenians could move about freely. As small as I was, I felt like I was being swallowed up by all the space.

"Can I see Kao?" I asked Xonea, and he nodded.

"We go to him now."

The Jorenian guided me through the spiraling corridor, then turned. I followed him through a door panel into what had to be a medical bay. Gleaming equipment surrounded a bed where I saw the motionless form of Kao Torin. He was being scanned by a tall Jorenian woman.

I practically ran over Xonea to get to him. "Kao?" I took his cool hand between mine and held it tightly. "Kao, I'm here."

The exhausted white eyes opened, and I thought for a moment he smiled. Then his eyes closed once more.

"Kao, your HouseClan rescued me," I told him.

"They were wonderful. Xonea brought me here to you. I don't know how to thank . . . Kao?" His hand went limp. No, not now! I gazed blindly at the attending Jorenian. She shook her head. "Kao?" My voice broke. "Kao, please?"

Xonea came and put his hand over mine and Kao's. "He hears you, Healer. In eternity, he hears you."

I closed my eyes, and lowered my cheek to rest against Kao's unmoving chest.

CHAPTER EIGHTEEN

Last Rights

After Kao died, the Jorenians cared for me as one of their own. Xonea called one of the women to assist me when I left the Medical Bay. Probably because I couldn't function on my own. She held my arm and guided me through a long, twisting passage to a room she said would be my quarters.

"Healer, may I be of some service to you?" she asked. I shook my head. "Would you prefer to be alone?"

I was alone. Completely, horribly alone. "Yes. Thank you." I sat on the sleeping platform and watched her depart through a numb haze. I had no idea what she looked like, I thought absently. I'd never once glanced at her face. Didn't have to. She looked like Kao. They all did. I never wanted to look at another Jorenian again, for the rest of my life, and I was on a ship teeming with them.

Why couldn't I feel anything?

When Maggie had died, I'd been devastated. I remembered feeling a peculiar kind of rage, one that sprang from my need to defeat illness and death as a physician. I'd gotten mad at Maggie, too. How could she have left me like that?

Now there was no rage. I was responsible for the life

that had been lost. I'd brought death to him. With my own blood, I had killed Kao Torin.

For a time I was frozen, immobile. A statue of Cherijo Grey Veil carved from ice.

Tears came later, when I was startled by the sound of a raw wail tearing from my throat. My burning eyes filled. I heard sobbing, felt racking shudders. Fists beat against the mattress, hair loosened, tangled. It didn't touch me. I was simply an observer, watching a pathetic tantrum of grief.

At last I slipped into a quiet stupor. I stared at the soft-swirled pattern on the deck above me, trying to make sense of it. Kao was dead, and I had killed him. The brilliant surgeon. The daughter of Joseph Grey Veil. I was more like my father than I wanted to be.

I must have fallen asleep at some point. Someone must have looked in on me, for I woke up hours later under a soft, woven cover. My eyes felt swollen, my hair was a matted, hopeless snarl. I was a disaster, and I didn't care. The dried tracks of tears streaked my face. I could taste their bitter salt on my bitten lips.

Enough of this, an inner voice said.

Pushing my weary body off the platform, I went to the room's main terminal on slightly unsteady legs and checked the display. No messages, but I didn't expect any. I requested a current ship's status, and was informed the *Sunlace* was on standby flight status, whatever that meant.

When I looked out the room's viewport, I saw we were in orbit above K-2. The planet, in all its green splendor, looked as beautiful as the first time I'd viewed it from Dhreen's ship. It had scared me then—a strange, alien world. Now it was simply a planet. What I cared about I had been forced to leave behind. All my colleagues and friends. Alunthri and Jenner. Even Reever. No, I wouldn't think about Duncan Reever. It seemed obscene now that Kao was gone.

A signal came from the door panel, and I answered it dully.

"Healer? I bring a friend."

I opened the panel and Xonea came in carrying, of all things, my cat.

"Jenner!" I said, and my disgruntled pet leapt into my arms, meowing plaintively. I ran my hands over him. He was real. He didn't even bother to torment me as usual. The silvery head snuggled against me, and a thick, heavy thrumming sound poured from his throat. He was purring, for God's sake. Jenner hardly ever purred!

"This small one was impatient to see you," Xonea said. "My HouseClan managed to retrieve him before we left the planet."

"I don't suppose you were able to retrieve anything else from my quarters?"

The big Jorenian appeared concerned. "Forgive me, no, but we can arrange—"

I shook my head. "That, Xonea, was a sad attempt at a joke. I've left nothing behind that could not be replaced," I said, and hugged my cat gratefully.

"Even us?"

Dhreen limped into the room, followed by Alunthri.

I blinked several times, sure it was an illusion. "Dhreen? Alunthri?" I rushed over to them, to touch them, to make sure they were real, too. "How?"

Dhreen balanced himself on his supports as he made a slow, complete turn. I finally noticed he was wearing the same type of uniform as Xonea and the other Jorenians.

"You're looking at the newest addition to the crew of the *Sunlace*." He hiccuped at my expression. "Don't look so surprised. I'm a terrific pilot."

"Yes, I know you are." I gazed at the Chakacat and sobered abruptly. "I'm so sorry I left you behind."

"I know you would have helped me if you could." Alunthri tried to put me at ease. "That is why I signaled the Jorenians and asked if I could join you."

I turned to Xonea. "How can I thank you? What you've done for me—there just aren't words to describe how grateful I am."

"You can help us send my ClanBrother Kao on his final journey." Xonea's smile faltered as he read my expression. "Healer, I did not mean to bring you pain, only joy."

"I'm sorry. I wasn't—I—" I turned quickly to the viewer and stared out at the blackness. The stars only blurred a little. "I'd be honored to help you."

"In four rotations, we will send Kao into the embrace of the stars. Until then, walk within beauty." The Jorenian made a lovely gesture, bowed, and left me with Dhreen and the cats.

"She's a big lady, this *Sunlace*." Dhreen whistled under his breath. "It takes more than a day to walk all twenty-eight levels." He described his impromptu introduction to Kao's HouseClan when he'd arrived to rescue me from the Allied forces. He was only mildly annoyed that he had been preempted by the Jorenians. "I asked if they needed a spare pilot on board." He grinned and rubbed his almost-ears. "Lucky for me they did. Have you seen the women?"

I suppressed a smile while he hiccuped. Jenner jumped down and began to explore. "Be careful who you try to romance, Dhreen. These people bond for life." The Oenrallian stopped in mid-hiccup and paled.

Alunthri chose that moment to diplomatically interrupt.

"Cherijo, I should tell you what has occurred since your departure. The Jorenians have been kind enough to allow me to monitor Colonial transmissions from the ship." The Chakacat described the outraged response of the colony to the Council's decision. Apparently the entire population was in uproar again. Allied forces had discovered most of their vehicles vandalized, their shuttles inoperable.

Just when the maintenance crews had cleaned everything up for the League, too. What a tragedy. "How did the League forces feel about my rescue?"

"Surface forces fired on the *Sunlace* as it launched. From what Xonea told me, there was only minimal damage to the stardrive. The League subsequently demanded the Jorenians turn you over to them. Xonea responded that as there were no non-sentient beings presently aboard the *Sunlace*, he could not comply."

Clever Xonea. "That won't stop them."

Dhreen confirmed the League cruisers were now shadowing the Jorenian ship, but Kao's HouseClan was apparently not concerned about a confrontation. Once repairs to the stardrive were completed, the Torins fully intended to leave Pmoc Quadrant space, and take me along with them.

"How are they going to do that, with fifteen League ships out there waiting to stop them?"

"Xonea referred to something called multidimensional flightshields," Alunthri said.

"What's that?"

Dhreen supplied the explanation. "It's a form of space travel not used by the League, popular in other, distant systems. The *Sunlace* jaunts light speed the same way League ships do, but they can enter other dimensions as well." The Oenrallian pretended to yawn, but I saw the excited gleam in his eyes. "I wouldn't be too worried about the League pursuing us. You're free, Doc."

The hour was late, and both my friends showed increasing signs of weariness. I learned both Dhreen and Alunthri were happily situated in comfortable quarters close by, made an excuse about being tired, and waved them both out the door.

Nothing was farther from the truth. I wasn't tired, I wanted time alone. Well, alone with my cat. Jenner and I spent a long time cuddling. When he settled down for an extended nap, I decided to take a walk around the big ship and get a good look at my new home. Thank some of these people, too.

Anything to keep from thinking about Kao.

I expected to see only Jorenians on board, and was surprised to pass several other alien species during my rambling. Humanoids, for the most part, and none that I recognized. Kao had explained his world was a distant one. Perhaps the crew were all from the Varallan Quadrant.

I ran into Xonea almost literally as he came rapidly around a corner I was turning into at the same time. He looked happy to see me, if a little surprised. I explained I was restless and had wanted to take a walk.

"Then, I shall escort you," he said, and I didn't have the heart to refuse him. He checked in with his duty station via a corridor console, then conducted a thorough tour of one small section of the giant vessel.

"It would take days to see everything that encompasses the *Sunlace*," he said as he showed me a large department devoted to charting the many systems and dimensions the ship traveled through. "But there is one more you may find particularly interesting."

The Medical Bay was equivalent in size to K-2's FreeClinic. There I was introduced to the Senior Healer, the oldest Jorenian I'd encountered so far. Her name was Tonetka Torin, and related herself to Kao as his ClanMother's sister.

"My ClanNephew spoke of you with great warmth, Healer."

"I'm flattered to hear that." My reluctance to talk about Kao must have shown, for that was all she said about him. Tonetka spent the following half hour going over parts of their general operation. Finally, the Senior Healer surveyed me with her sharp eyes. "You look rather fragile. Xonea should take you back to your quarters."

"No, please." I gazed at a chart display with naked longing. The older woman burst into laughter and handed it to me.

"Come, Healer." She shooed Xonea out. "Leave her here, she needs work."

I made rounds with the Senior Healer and reviewed each patient's case history. Like most doctors, we found we didn't agree on every point of testing, diagnosis, or treatment. Still, I liked her. She didn't hand me a lot of ego along with her opinion.

Once we had seen all of the thirteen cases presently in the ward for treatment, the Jorenian left one of the nurses in charge and took me to her office for tea.

Jorenian teas were floral, and tasted the way a flower smells. Tonetka described some of the long journeys the *Sunlace* had made during her tenure. As she spoke, she fingered a lock of her hair, its rich ebony sheen reflecting a deep purple cast. An indicator of her advanced age, I was surprised to learn.

"I should have retired to the homeworld a dozen revolutions ago, but it is hard to give up the life. My mate and I are lucky that we have always shared the same love of travel, but I am no longer young enough to continue." Her white eyes narrowed as she considered me thoughtfully. "The *Sunlace* will need a new Senior Healer after we return to our homeworld."

I smiled. "You must have a dozen residents waiting for that position."

"None as qualified as you are."

"I find that hard to believe." I was startled. "I've yet to complete one revolution here on K-2 as a Trauma position. A very junior position, I assure you."

"Modesty is not something most Healers have in large quantity," Tonetka said. "Neither should you. On your homeworld, I am told, you were a seasoned practitioner. That, combined with your FreeClinic experience, far exceeds the capabilities of my residents. Including your unique genetic enhancements—"

"For which I'm being persecuted," I said. "Think about that for a minute, Senior Healer. Just how would the *Sunlace*'s crew feel about me taking over, someone declared to be nothing more than a sophisticated test animal?"

Tonetka thumped her tea server on her desk in disgust. "Here, Healer Grey Veil, you are one of us. My nephew Chose you. That makes you part of this HouseClan, whether you wish it or not."

Maggie couldn't have done better. I apologized.

Tonetka waved her hand impatiently. "Enough of

that. You have an opportunity to use your skills, Healer. For people who will protect and honor you. Not like those on that planet, who used your abilities to serve their purposes and turned their backs on you when it was convenient."

"I feel as though I'm running away," I said. "Hiding from the truth."

"Whose version of what truth? On that planet down there you are seen as a beast of burden, automated machinery. Here you are honored as the woman Chosen by a Torin. Here you do not have to fear or pretend. You can thrive."

Tonetka took me from her office on a short walk to another section, where I saw dozens of Jorenian children playing in a modified chamber. They romped in an artificial environment that simulated the natural landscapes of their homeworld. Lots of kids, having a great time. Tonetka tapped on the clear viewer.

"There are some reasons to consider my proposal. More than thirty percent of those on board are children." She smiled as she watched them. "They need strong protectors. You could be one of those who watch over them."

"It would be a challenge," I said, peering in. "Seeing as most of them are taller than me."

Tonetka laughed.

I stood and watched the children after Tonetka returned to the Medical Bay. So many eager, happy faces. It didn't matter that they weren't Terran. That their eyes were white and their skins were blue. If Kao had lived, our offspring would have looked something like these. Just a bit shorter.

I made my way back to my quarters. It was good to have a reason to go on, I thought. Even if it was for the children I would never have.

I requested and was given official permission to work in the Medical Bay alongside Healer Tonetka. The Senior Healer never brought up the subject of my serving as her replacement during those rotations. We did, however, discover we worked well together. We shared concerns, ideas, even a few moments of humor when we argued over treatments. Tonetka liked a friendly fight. So did I.

The League made repeated requests to board the Jorenian ship in order to search for an "unrecognized" nonsentient life-form. The Jorenians politely continued to turn down their requests.

Xonea and Dhreen were inseparable friends now, and each day the pair arrived at my quarters during my off hours to "liberate" me. Usually for a game of whumpball, which I invariably lost to one or the other. We also shared several meal intervals, during which the two pilots tried to top each other's outrageous adventure stories.

Alunthri had been to visit me as well. It was becoming very involved in its new study of Jorenian art forms. According to it, they were mostly utilitarian objects, created from woven grasses and used for ceremonial gatherings. Alunthri gave me a morning bread basket, with a weave that showed a complex, lovely pattern of bird shapes.

I explored more of the ship, and quickly discovered that the Jorenian crew members were very open and friendly. They also seemed to have an inordinate amount of interest in me personally. I constantly got stopped while walking down the main corridor, and invited to join them for some activity or another. The console in my quarters always had a minimum of a dozen signals to be returned. If I dined in the galley, I never sat alone for very long.

I couldn't get used to my sudden popularity. At first I suspected Xonea or Tonetka had put their HouseClan up to it. After the first rotation, I saw it was simply their natural behavior. The Torins were just as gregarious with each other. I didn't know quite how to handle it, either. My life had always been so wrapped up in work that I hadn't had time for a social life. Now it didn't look like I could avoid one.

Jenner, who was as popular with the crew as I was, had the run of the corridors, spoiled and adored by hundreds. He always turned up at my quarters at the end of the day, however, to be fed and attended to by his most devoted admirer. He slept with me as well, and when the nightmares woke me up, soothed me back to sleep.

I received many, many personal messages from the colonists on K-2, among them, carefully worded recordings from Dr. Mayer and Charge Nurse Ecla. Xonea showed me that when both were played simultaneously, a coded third message was revealed.

"See thus?" He pointed to the terminal and eradicated every third word or syllable. "As we arranged with your friends. Watch now."

Ecla and Dr. Mayer's messages blended together to reveal: *Mercenary incentive offer being discussed between JGV and League. Do not attempt to return or leave ship. Have your belongings, will forward.*

"What's this about mercenaries?"

"They think to contract them to pursue you."

Anger gave a particularly spine-tingling cast to Jorenian features. No wonder they hardly ever got mad. Anyone could have easily imagined the man crossing the galaxy to hunt down his enemies. I was scared just looking at him.

"Maybe they'll change their minds," I said.

"Let the League send hired thugs to challenge the *Sunlace*. They will learn how HouseClan Torin deals with those who threaten our own." Xonea separated the discs and handed them to me. "I must speak with you about tomorrow's ceremony."

I gripped the discs tightly. "To honor Kao."

He smiled. "To honor you both." He held up a third disc. "We have always celebrated life in death, Healer. Please view this today; it will help you to understand the ritual. Your presence will grace our House."

Later I reviewed the disc in my quarters. For Kao's sake, I made myself study the ceremony carefully.

Jorenians believed death was the beginning of another journey. A return to an original, primordial life, when the physical body was discarded. They believed the soul "embraced the stars" after death. In symbolic commemoration, Kao's remains would be ejected from the ship and sent directly into the heart of one of K-2's twin suns.

Select members of the HouseClan participated in the actual ritual. HouseClan Brothers and Sisters prepared the body and the receptacle in a traditional manner. The bondmate—or in my case, the Chosen—offered a blessing for the soul's journey. At last someone called the Speaker delivered the last message from the deceased.

I wondered about that part. Kao had not confided any final message to me. I thought of Dhreen. Had he received Kao's last wishes, while they were both on the ward?

One of the Jorenian residents I worked with, a young woman with a depressingly cheerful manner, delivered what she called the "journey robe" to my quarters. It was a lovely, flowing river of iridescent cerulean material that seemed almost too fragile to handle. She showed me how to wear it and even talked me into unbraiding my hair.

"Kao would want you to appear as he saw you in his heart."

I didn't sleep that night. I didn't want to give the ritual blessing. Kao had died because of what I had given him. I wasn't his mate. I was his killer.

That thought haunted me, up until the moment the ceremony began. The Torins assembled in a special area reserved for such rituals. I'd met some of the crew, but to see them gathered together like this made my eyes sting. So many of the males resembled Kao. It was as if he was reincarnated, over and over.

HouseClan Torin dressed in their family colors, robes of a thousand shades of blue and green. With their black hair and sapphire skins, they reminded me of a twilight sky over a Terran sea.

I was brought to a dias on which the special receptacle was prepared for launching. Kao's coffin was sleek and dark. A towering circle of Kao's brothers and sisters, Xonea among them, surrounded me. They began to weave an intricate dance around the dias as they bound the outer panels with strand after strand of silvery threads.

I stared at the pattern, saw more wings taking shape. I lifted my hand, touched the now-fading mark on my throat. I had to let him go now. Had to.

The rest of the Jorenians chanted a low, continuous series of prayers. Their melodic voices harmonized into a throbbing, rejoiceful song. It tore at me to hear them. No one wept. They were really happy about this, I thought. Happy for Kao, whom I had killed.

At last his siblings were finished, the receptacle adorned with an intricate web of glittering light. One by one the voices died away. Silence enveloped the dias. Together Xonea and his brothers and sisters bowed to me, then stepped down to join the others looking up at me.

Now I stood alone. The woman he Chose. His executioner. How could I be both? How could I even stand here and do this? I recalled the ancient words from the disc Xonea had given me. HouseClan Torin had honored Kao's body. It was up to me to honor his soul. And here I was, ready to fall to pieces.

Stop thinking about yourself and honor *Kao*, you twit, I thought viciously. *You* can fall to pieces *after* the ceremony.

That anger made my voice steady and strong. "From your Chosen, your heart, can only come what is bright and beautiful and honorable." I looked at the rapt faces around me. Felt their unity as a family. Not one glimmer of anger, hatred, or even mild dislike in their expressions. Only happiness.

I went on. "You and I will never lose each other. We

have blended our souls. Kao Torin, I send you into the embrace of the first life. I send you with joy, smiles, and my honor forever. The new path awaits you."

Yes, and I had sent him along that path very effectively. But if I hadn't, the pathogen would have. There was no other way I could have kept him alive. Kao would have been dead long before we discovered the truth about the Core.

It wasn't fair. Tears streaked down my cheeks and nose as I placed my hand upon the receptacle. That wasn't in the ceremony, but I didn't care. I would carry the burden of Kao Torin's death with me for the rest of my life, but for now, I had to come to terms with it. If not for myself, for him.

In a voice now thick with pain, I spoke the last words of the ritual. "Blessed be your journey, Kao Torin. Your House rejoices. Your Chosen will follow."

Xonea helped me down from the dias, and the receptacle was lowered into a discharge shaft. One interior wall retracted to reveal a huge view screen, and I watched with the rest of HouseClan Torin as Kao's body was ejected from the *Sunlace*. The sleek shape dwindled as it sped away, pulled by the magnetic fields of the twin suns. Embraced by the stars. It was gone. I covered my face with my hands.

Kao was gone.

I heard the voice of the Speaker, who closed the ceremony with Kao's own last words. My hands fell from my eyes. No. I stared, and still could not believe what I was seeing.

Duncan Reever stood there, dressed completely in black.

"I speak for the son of this House, Kao Torin. His words were given to me, to be brought to those he honored. I bring them with joy."

Xonea's hand touched my arm. I flinched, then stepped away from him. Reever? Kao had spoken his last wishes to Duncan Reever?

Heat rose up my neck, flooded my face. He didn't

wear one of the vocollar devices, I noted. He apparently didn't have to. He probably spoke flawless Jorenian, along with ten million other dialects. I didn't even know how to say "I honor you" in Kao's own language.

"I would be with you for journeys ahead, my family. That is not my path. Go forward, remember I am in your hearts. Know our House lives in each of you. Walk within beauty." Reever turned slightly until our eyes met. "Honored Chosen."

I bit my tongue sharply. The outraged shriek never left my lips.

"How you have struggled for me. Endured as I have endured. I must leave you. You, who have been all things to me, friend, companion, and Chosen."

How dare Reever look at me like that? I could have killed him.

"Do not grieve for me, my Chosen. I honor you above all. A path exists into eternity where we will be reunited. We will travel together again. Never forget that." His eyes flickered. "I dwell within you."

The shock of seeing Reever combined with my over-wrought emotions, and I swayed. Xonea pulled me into the curve of his arm. I didn't fight the support.

Reever faced the assembly once more. "I charge the HouseClan Torin with my last request: protect and honor the one I Chose. Only death prevented our bond. I give her into your keeping. Honor her as you have honored me. Farewell and safe journey. I embrace the stars."

The ceremony was over. The family divided, some to return to their duties, others to celebrate in smaller groups. Xonea led me away from the chamber and escorted me to my quarters. I went along without protest.

Outside the door panel, Xonea bowed. "You have honored our HouseClan, Healer." He made a gesture that encompassed his heart and head. "HouseClan Torin would honor you. If you will accept, our House is yours."

I knew what he was offering. And I wanted it. "I accept, with gratitude." I made the traditional answer.

He smiled with delight, bowed, and touched his brow to the back of my hand. "ClanSister Cherijo. Welcome to our House."

I had been declared non-sentient, rescued, watched my lover die, been reunited with friends, offered a new life, celebrated my lover's death, heard his last words.

Now I had been adopted.

Xonea was quick to spread the word to the rest of the crew. They in turn did their best to make me feel part of the extended Jorenian family at once. I was addressed as "Healer Cherijo Torin," or "ClanSister," or "Clan-Cousin" and so on, depending on who spoke to me. I compensated by answering to pretty much anything called in my general direction.

Xonea had given me more than a new last name. I was considered as much a member of the HouseClan as if I had been born to it. That made the honor of the HouseClan, and its preservation, my responsibility. I wasn't sure I deserved any of it, but I wanted to be a part of these people. Judging from his last words, it was what Kao had wanted, too.

The day after seeing Duncan Reever at the ceremony, I asked Xonea about him and how he came to be Kao's Speaker. I couldn't help myself. I learned Reever had been with Kao while I'd appeared that last time before the Council. Kao had sent specifically for Reever, given him his last words. Reever had even assisted HouseClan Torin in removing Kao from the FreeClinic ward and transporting him to the *Sunlace*. He had been on board as long as I had. I felt slightly ashamed of myself. I'd believed Reever had abandoned me, and the whole time he had been honoring Kao's last request.

Negotiations between League forces and the Jorenians were beginning to break down. Insult was added to the strain when a group of mercenaries tried to storm the ship by force.

Tonetka casually mentioned it during rounds, and I stared at her, completely aghast.

"Five of them tried to ram through the portside docking couplings," she said, and chuckled. "They quickly discovered what happens when a League vessel encounters Jorenian alloys."

The captain of the *Sunlace* was generous enough to rescue the would-be intruders before their small ship imploded. Pnor Torin's generosity only went so far, however. The mercenaries were sent back to K-2, with a warning that any further attacks would be taken much more seriously.

More cruisers joined those currently surrounding K-2 and the *Sunlace*. Once repairs to the stardrive were completed, Captain Pnor decided it was time to leave orbit before someone started firing. The order to prepare for dimensional transition was signaled throughout the ship.

I was in the Medical Section with Tonetka when the word came. We prepped the patients and secured ourselves in the launch pods provided for that area. The Senior Healer patted my hand as I snapped on my restraint harness.

"The jump between this dimension and the next is jarring, especially the first time. Do not fight it, relax and allow yourself to be passive."

I hadn't enjoyed knowing that on the *Bestshot* my cellular structure was being altered. Now that my cells were about to be altered *and* thrown into another dimension, well, I was more than a little tense.

Relax, don't fight it, I thought. Be passive. Right.

The *Sunlace*'s powerful stardrive throbbed into life, and for a moment I thought I felt the impact of something smashing into the outer hull just beyond Medical. What was—

Reality twisted.

Colors and shapes ran together in a confusing blur. My body was being sucked in, folded and tangled by the whirling blend. Tonetka's advice rang in my ear. I tried not to resist the effect. Something was wrong, I thought.

I was being wrenched apart, my flesh stretching, nerves screaming. Tonetka had never said anything about pain. I blacked out for what seemed like eternity.

Reality righted itself. Tonetka was speaking to me, saying my name, over and over.

"How long did that take?" I said as Tonetka released me from my harness. I collapsed into her arms, and she exclaimed something my vocollar wouldn't translate. Jorenians didn't use expletives often, but when they did, there was little parallel in any language.

"Hold on to me." She lifted me in her arms like a child. "Look at me, Cherijo. Keep your eyes open. Good."

Tonetka placed me on an exam table. I was barely aware of the scanner she passed over me. Vaguely I heard her barking out orders. Someone must be hurt. She only sounded like that when—

A crushing weight descended on my chest. I was paralyzed, unable to breathe. My eyes felt as though they would burst from my skull. My ears were filled with millions of bees. I opened my mouth to scream, but there was no air. No air at all. Then my heart stopped beating.

"By the Mother," Tonetka said. "She's—"

I blacked out once more. The pain dimmed. I opened my eyes a century later, to a tangled procession of images. Wide white eyes. Scanner grids. Blue hands. Optic lights.

A syrinpress nuzzled my throat. Must be serious, I thought. My mind felt groggy, drugged. Direct jugular . . . injection . . . for what? I fought to clear the haze from my head. Discovered the pain that was waiting behind it.

Gravity crashed down and squeezed the breath from my lungs. Not again, I wanted to whimper, but I couldn't get a breath. My heart slammed against the stony cage of my ribs. Voices jabbered around me in a disconnected frenzy.

"Nerve cells firing—"

"—toxic level—"

"Get the one who—"

"—er, she's arrest—"

My heart stopped beating again. I was going to die. I was ready. The pain was so vast, so unmanageable that I couldn't grasp it anymore. Time to embrace some stars. That was a nice way to think about it. Would Kao really be waiting there for me?

Beyond the pain something else moved into competition for my attention. I glimpsed a glittering light, and thinking it was Kao, I tried to move through the pain toward it.

Come to me.

It was warm and kind, that voice. It wanted me. I certainly wanted to get to it. I considered the layers of pain almost clinically now. Such a large, looming wall of torment. I had no more time for that sort of thing. Some unfamiliar part of my mind told me I could move *between* the pain. I found the path easily.

The light grew dazzling, and I was flooded with a serenity I hadn't felt since I'd made love with Kao. Only he could have come for me, given me this blessed relief. I opened my arms to the light. *Here I am. Over here.*

Cherijo. At last.

The pain was behind me, wasn't it? Why was I feeling it now? Slowly I recognized the light, the voice, the one who called to me. I was wrong, it wasn't Kao. Kao was dead.

It was Reever.

The whole thing was really absurd, in a macabre sense. On one side, unbearable pain, extended suffering, and death. Opposite that was Reever, linked with my mind, coaxing me from that unpleasant but necessary release.

Fought too long. My thoughts were lackluster, comical. *Can't decide which is worse.*

Come to me, Cherijo, Reever demanded harshly. A moment later, with more persuasion, *Come back to me.*

You won't ever leave me alone, will you? I thought, feeling sorry for myself. *I can't get away from you. Not even to die. You're always in my head.*

Reever made a rough sound that made no sense. *You can't die like this,* he told me. He was coming to me now, forcing himself further into my thoughts.

Oh, yes I can. I drew back.

He halted. *I will not let you go alone.*

I won't let you come with me, I told him wearily. *I don't want you to die, Duncan.*

Then, come to me, Cherijo. Just come to me.

I didn't trust him. I didn't even like him. He was a reminder of what I had lost, and what I would never have. Yet still I went to him, and lost myself in that strange white light.

At last I opened eyes that felt glued together, and found myself flat on my back in the critical-care berth. My body was hooked up to every piece of equipment known to Jorenian Healers.

Above me Tonetka's eyes crinkled with pleasure. "Greetings to the living."

"Tonetka—Healer Torin," I swallowed against the horrible rasp of my voice and tried again. "Give me my chart."

The Jorenian woman shook her head. "Once you have stopped trying to frighten the rest of the journeys I possess out of me, I might let you have a glance at it." Her hands moved over my head and chest as she scanned me. I tried to get up and assess the damage for myself. The best I could do was a weak twitch. "Be still."

"What happened?"

The Senior Healer was muttering to herself. "No residual brain damage, and thank the Mother, minimal damage to the mitral valve."

"Do I want to *know* what happened?"

"Probably not, but I suspect you'll give me no peace until I tell you. You died twice on my table, Healer Torin." Tonetka made it sound like a personal insult. "I will thank you not to try that a third time."

"Cause?"

"A brain episode I still can't fathom, which began in the middle of flight transition. I barely got you out of the harness before you went into shock. Once I'd stabilized you—I *thought* I had stabilized you, I should say—you suffered massive cardiac arrest. Twice. Every God of Luck in existence has smiled upon you since then."

"There is no such thing as a God of Luck," I managed to say before I fell into a healing sleep. As I entered the darkness again, I thought I felt a gentle hand touch my face, then the cool drops of someone's tears.

CHAPTER NINETEEN

Begin Again

Kao had never told me that Jorenians were overly protective. I found out the hard way.

I spent a week flat on my back. When I tried to get up, Tonetka made threats. A few times she actually began to strap me in restraints.

"If you embrace the stars while I'm treating you, the HouseClan may stuff *me* in your receptacle," the Senior Healer said. "Now, rest."

"Give me my chart, and I'll read it while I rest." Said chart was being kept far out of my reach.

"Healers make the worst patients," she said, sidestepping my request. Again.

In the meantime, Tonetka ran every test she could think of on me. I suspected she made up a few of her own, too. I was probed and scraped and prodded to the point of screaming hysterics.

"That's enough!" I said after a week of the same routine. "I won't have any blood left soon!"

The Senior Healer made a peculiar sound with her lips that was the least musical of Jorenian expressions. I laughed in spite of myself.

"Who is in charge of your case, Cherijo?" She checked the scanner she'd passed over me, nodded to herself, then frowned at me. "Don't argue with your Healer."

"I may do more than argue if you don't let me out of here soon," I said.

The only bright point was the fact that I had scores of visitors. During my convalescence, I think nearly every member of HouseClan Torin tried to personally visit me. At last the Senior Healer ordered everyone on board to stay out of her department unless they needed treatment. She backed it up with a threat to put me in suspension sleep until we reached Joren.

"Out—out—out," she said when she found Dhreen and Xonea at my bedside—again. "By the Mother, you'd think she was ready to be bound and praised."

"I'm ready now," I said, impatient with my confinement and needing a good fight.

"Not anymore," Tonetka said, "but do not tempt me."

Dhreen started to make a comment about how quickly I was infecting the Jorenians with my particular language idioms. He decided to leave rather quickly when the Senior Healer picked up a syrinpress and waved it under his nose.

Xonea chuckled and managed to beg a moment alone with me before Tonetka threw him out, as well. She granted it with a grudging look and muttered something about containment fields as she left us for her office.

"How are you, Cherijo?"

I shrugged and sat back against the head support. "As well as can be expected. Bored, mostly. I need something to do." I eyed him. "Why?"

He put his large hand over mine. "Need you ask?" He gazed over his shoulder and leaned close. "Your company is missed. Dhreen would win every credit I possess."

"Stop playing whump-ball with him."

"It keeps my thoughts occupied." He smiled slowly. "We all miss you, Healer."

"Hey, when I get out of here, I'll be after your credits, too."

Xonea laughed, and squeezed my hand. "I accept your challenge." Then, with a more sober air, he touched my cheek. "Grow strong, ClanSister." He left me just as the Senior Healer approached to chase him out, too.

As she took my vital readings, Tonetka looked after Xonea thoughtfully. Then I got the same speculative look.

"What?" I thought she saw something wrong on the scanner. "Don't tell me I'm going to be stuck here any longer."

"I plan to release you within the hour," she said. I whooped with glee. "I await the peace and quiet with great anticipation. As well as the absence of certain pilots I have stumbled over several times a day."

"Xonea and Dhreen are just trying to cheer me up."

"Dhreen, yes, but Xonea—" Her shrewd eyes met mine. "He honors you greatly."

"Right." I snorted. "He just wants to clobber me at the whump-ball tables."

"Perhaps." Tonetka put down her scanner. "Now, I want to talk to you about your test results."

She had been keeping most of them from me. I steadied myself. "Tell me the bad news first."

She smiled. "It is not bad."

I didn't trust her. She was being too nice. "There's cardiac damage, isn't there? Have I developed arrhythmia?" I sat up and folded my arms over my chest. "Go ahead, tell me. I can take it."

"My initial scans indicated some significant ischemic damage. Mitral insufficiency was probable, along with arrhythmia."

It wasn't bad, I thought. It was terrible. Oxygen deprivation had affected my heart's cells. Had killed them. "So I need a transplant."

"Cherijo, the last scans I performed were vastly improved. Ischemic damage is negligible." At my gasp, she patted my shoulder. "The first series of scans may have been inaccurate. Or perhaps the ischemic cells are healing."

"Healing?" I made a scoffing sound. "Not possible in Terrans. Your scanner must have fused."

"It is difficult to say." Tonetka handed me her scanner. "Check for yourself."

I read the data quickly. "This can't be right. Not after two consecutive myocardial infarctions. There's hardly *anything* registering."

"It may be explained by the unusual measures the League took in their attempt to retrieve you from the *Sunlace*."

This was news. I frowned. "What are you talking about?"

"Your violent reaction to transition was caused by the League. Before Captain Pnor transitioned, cruisers began to attack the ship. We believe they tried to isolate you with one of their containment devices during transition. The physical stress triggered the episodes of heart and brain dysfunction. It was fortunate they did not succeed. The disruption of the flightshield would have caused the stardrive to implode."

They'd tried to take me off the ship? And kill everyone on board the *Sunlace* in the process? "Why didn't anybody tell me about this?" I demanded.

"You have been ill," Tonetka said, then leveled a direct gaze at me. "Now, tell me, why would the League sacrifice a valuable treaty with Joren and exterminate every member of this crew merely to remove you from this vessel?"

"I don't know." I had some ideas, but I wasn't going to tell Tonetka.

"There is more. Reports have come to us of a massive recovery operation initiated by the League. They will undoubtably try to pursue us, if they can ever locate the ship again."

I stared at my hands, which by now were white-knuckled. "They'll never stop hunting me."

"You will need to plan your path accordingly, my colleague." She sat down on the side of my berth. "Cherijo, I have spoken to you about my retirement. If you desire the position, I will recommend to Pnor that he appoint you as Senior Healer."

I lifted my face to watch hers. "Do you really think I can handle the job?"

Tonetka was equally grave. "You will bring honor to it."

That was a sterling endorsement, in Jorenian terms. I couldn't go back to Terra or K-2. The *Sunlace* had provided sanctuary for me, and now offered continued freedom and purpose.

"I accept the position," I said, and watched the big grin spread across her face. She turned and announced it to the entire staff, who within moments were crowding around and congratulating me, too.

I thought that was the end of it. I got dressed, bid everyone farewell, and went to see my cat. Dhreen kidnapped me practically the moment I walked in my quarters. He informed me Jenner had been staying with Alunthri, and that I had to come with him at once.

"Where are you taking me?" I demanded with a laugh as the Oenrallian hauled me down to the central corridor.

"Be patient, Doc. Here we are." He stopped at one of the environomes that were located throughout the ship. The self-contained modules' dimensional imagers could be programmed to simulate virtually any environment in the ship's vast database. Tonetka had told me they were used primarily for recreational and training purposes.

Dhreen's spoon-shaped fingers tapped the controls, then he pulled me through the opening door panel. A flying bundle of silver fur jumped into my arms.

"Jenner." I buried my face in his fur, and chuckled as his rough tongue rasped against my cheek. "I missed you, too." Then I looked up. "Oh, Dhreen. It's beautiful."

I was touched to see the imagers had been programmed to create a formal European garden I had once described to Alunthri. New friends and old were waiting to welcome me as the new Senior Healer.

"In training," I said as Jenner and I were swept off. Gentle hands delivered us to Xonea, who was waiting by an elaborately scrolled gazebo. A huge buffet had been arranged inside. Alunthri waited there, too. The Chakacat accepted my thanks for caring for my pet, as well as the exquisite program design.

"Did His Majesty behave himself while I was in Medical?" I asked, smiling indulgently as my cat left me to give a plate of Jorenian fish his exclusive attention.

"He was most distressed over your illness," the Chakacat said with a pained look of remembrance.

"Don't tell me. I can imagine what he did to your furnishings." I gazed around at the lovely gardens. "This is so amazing, Alunthri. How did you do it?"

"The dimensional imagers are quite advanced," it said as it selected a vegetarian variety of canapé from the buffet. "I was intrigued to see if my calculations would produce such a result. Jorenian technology is very precise."

I enjoyed the party immensely. The food was imaginative and plentiful, Jenner ate until he was nearly gorged, and Dhreen told his funniest stories. The Torins were particularly effusive with their praise for the beautiful landscape, and a group of programmers got into a technical discussion with the Chakacat. By the end of our meal, Alunthri had become the center of attention. Which was fine with me.

I left the gazebo and drifted through the gathering, exchanging pleasantries, enjoying the company. It was a nice change from being stuck in Medical for days. I scanned the surroundings to look for Reever—not that I wanted him there—and my eyes met a familiar gaze.

Xonea was smiling at me. In that moment he looked so much like Kao it almost broke my heart. Some of what I felt showed, for he came to my side and took my arm.

"Walk with me, Healer." He led me a small distance

from the party, where we halted beneath a lattice of thick vines heavily laden with brilliant flowers. "You were thinking of my ClanBrother just now, were you not?"

I was not going to cry. Not at my own party. "Xonea . . ."

"I understand," he said, and regarded the blooms above us. "The path has been difficult for you, has it not?" I didn't answer. I was too busy blinking hard. "Healer, my ClanBrother and I were very close. I would have you be the ClanSister he would have given me, in Choice, in bond."

"Yes, well, Kao's dead." I scuffed the toe of my footgear against the simulated grass beneath us. "I'll just have to be your adopted sister."

"We are HouseClan." He released my hand and plucked a rose from a vine above us, handing it to me. "You are Torin now, bound to us all. Yet you keep yourself apart." I gave him a perplexed look. His brows drew together. "You had no ClanSiblings in your life before?"

"You mean, brothers and sisters? Back on Terra?" He nodded. "No. I was an only child." Thank God, I added silently.

"I would be your ClanBrother, Healer." He made a beautiful gesture with both hands. "In heart as well as name."

I regarded him suspiciously. "If I say yes, do I have to put on a robe and stand up in front of the whole crew again?"

He threw back his head and laughed. "No, I promise you, no more robes."

That was a relief. "Then, what do I have to do?"

"Allow me to share your path and your burdens, when you have need." Serious once more, he handed me another rose. "Honor me with the same."

"Okay. I'll try." I'd never had a big brother before. Kao would have liked this. He had spoken of Xonea with such affection. The pain swelled, suddenly beyond my control. My voice broke about the same time that I crushed the two roses in my hands. "Oh, Xonea. I miss him. I miss him so much."

"I know, Cherijo." He pulled me into a gentle embrace, and pressed my head against his chest. "I do as well."

I tried to return to duty the next day, but Tonetka chased me out of Medical with a threat to put me in a berth if I showed my face again for the next three rotations. On the way back to my quarters, I nearly walked into Duncan Reever.

He was thinner. He didn't look as if he'd been sleeping well, either. I stepped back, and opened my mouth to say something inconsequential. Nothing came out.

"Dr. Grey Veil." He studied me as one would an uninteresting leukocyte. "You have recovered from your illness."

Yes, I thought to myself. That I had. I moved around him without responding. Of course, Reever followed after me.

"I thought you went back to K-2," I said as he caught up and walked beside me.

"It was not in my best interests to do so."

"Why not?"

"The Allied forces were not pleased to discover I could board the *Sunlace* when they were barred from it."

I gave a short laugh. "I bet they weren't."

"There was some discussion of the exact placement of my loyalties."

I stopped for a moment. "Exactly where *are* your loyalties, Reever?"

"As I have none, the question is rhetorical."

Of course he had no loyalties. I was being hunted down by the League, he was just on board because it was the prudent thing to do, and if I didn't walk away I was going to start yelling at him.

"You are upset."

"Yes, I am."

"What will you do?"

I stopped in front of an available environome. "Try not to wreck this equipment permanently."

"I will accompany with you," he said. I wondered if I had hallucinated the link with him during my illness. He was the old Duncan Reever once again. Passionate as an exterior hull panel. Possessing as much warmth.

I activated the entrance console and selected a preprogrammed file. Jorenian technology had advanced beyond what I knew as familiar, and I really didn't want to wreck the equipment with my fumbling. I should have expected to be dazzled. Still, I was startled to find that in natural habitat re-creation, Kao's people once more exceeded the League. By light-years.

Within the chamber was an unspoiled vista of an alien world. Dominating the scene was the remarkable re-creation of a purple sea rushing up to lap gently against deep amber sands.

"Where is this place?" I asked out loud.

"Environome file designated HouseClan Torin Marine Province, Joren, Varallan Quadrant," a drone automatically answered. "Please select desired amplifications."

"No amplifications desired," I told the drone, and walked into the sea territory of Kao's homeworld.

I could smell the sweet tang of the water, feel the cool, soft air against my skin. The crackle of the spiny, feather-leafed plants fringing the shoreline blended with a melodic hum emanating from clusters of enormous scarlet flowers. I trailed my fingers over the velvety petals of a tiny, star-shaped plant that grew in staggered levels. I closed my eyes for a moment. The sea even sounded like those back on Terra. Rushing, ebbing, eternal.

That last thought snapped me out of the pleasant trance. I didn't want to think about eternity. I wanted to stop thinking altogether for a while. I strode down the sand.

"You have agreed to take over as Senior Healer," Reever said just behind me.

I nearly jumped out of my skin, whirled around, then forced myself to calm down. I'd forgotten I had company. "What?"

"I said, you have—"

"Never mind, I heard you. Yes. That's the plan." I knew I was being unpleasantly curt. I wasn't going to apologize to someone who invented the technique.

"You won't return to Kevarzangia Two."

"No, and I've had my fill of interrogations, Reever."

"There is something I must discuss with you." He put a hand on my arm. "It will not take a great deal of time."

"Good." I shook off the hand. "What is it?"

Duncan Reever's eyes went from my face to the horizon, and back again. His face didn't show what he was thinking, but his hands clenched. Whatever it was, it was important to him. I owed him a great deal, I acknowledged grudgingly, in Kao's memory. I could try to be patient and a little less hostile.

"Duncan, just *tell* me." Okay, I'd have to work on patience.

"The Jorenians have offered me passage to the Varallan Quadrant in exchange for my services. I wanted to know if that is not acceptable to you."

"You want me to tell you to get off the ship?"

"Is that what you want?"

I hated it when he answered a question with a question. "I don't think it's any of my business."

"My presence causes you discomfort."

I shrugged. "I'll learn to live with it."

"Will you?"

"What do you want from me, Reever? My blessing?" His expression never changed. Not that there was much of one to start with. "Fine. Stay on the damn ship. It doesn't matter to me!"

"*I* don't matter to you."

"No—" I let out a pent-up breath. "No, of course not. All I'm saying is what you choose to do with your life is your decision. I won't interfere. I have no right to interfere."

"And if I gave you that right?"

"Gave me—what are you talking about?"

"Link with me."

Oh, no, not that again. I whirled away and started back down the shore. A few steps away from him, I felt the power of his mind reaching out to me. I started to run.

"Cherijo." He was following me again, shouting after me. "Stop! Please!"

It felt wonderful. I thought I could run forever. Run away from Reever. From the League. From everything and everyone. Just lose myself in the sea. I barely registered the shock of the cool water when the first wave splashed against my legs.

Reever's ability to link with me evidently had no limit on distance. From across the environome I felt him initiate the connection. *Cherijo. Don't run from me. Wait. Listen.*

Go away, Reever. And don't paralyze me. I'll drown.

I dove under the water, and began to swim with rapid strokes out from the shore. At a distance I heard running steps approaching, and the splash Reever's body made when he hit the water.

You are possibly the most intractable female I have ever encountered, he thought as he swam toward me.

Get out of my brain.

You must allow me this.

He was an excellent swimmer, far better than I was. He caught me in his arms without a great deal of effort. I didn't fight him. We floated together in the dark water of an alien world, our minds sifting into each other.

I can't go, Reever told me as the blinding light of his thoughts swept over me. *I have tried. I want—*

An image of the one time we had sex immediately came to me. I felt him harden against my body as he shared the memory. I was faintly disgusted to feel my own senses stir to life.

You aren't doing that to me again, pal.

Reever didn't have an alien life-form controlling him now. He released me at once. *No, Cherijo. I won't force myself on you again.*

I thought of Kao, of what my father had done to me. I thought of how little I really knew about Duncan Reever.

The link broke like a line snapping in half.

I was oddly shaken by his sudden withdrawal. He put an arm around me and guided me back to the sand. When our feet touched bottom, we both stumbled together, soaking wet, to drop onto the golden beach.

Reever didn't touch me again. "I apologize."

"Don't, Reever. I think I'm actually getting used to it."

The chief linguist pushed himself onto his feet. He stood over me, his fair hair streaming to his shoulders. For a moment he looked like something out of a dream.

"Doctor." He inclined his head, and trudged away and out of the environome. I stayed on the sands, my arm flung over my face, and listened to the sea rushing up, trying to touch me.

Captain Pnor had made a point to visit me in the Medical Bay during my convalescence. Since I knew he was one of the busiest Torins on board the *Sunlace*, it was a definite compliment. He was about the same age as Tonetka, and had an acrid wit that reminded me of William Mayer.

When I returned to my quarters, I was even more surprised to see him there in the hallway, as if he had all the time in the universe to spend waiting for me. I invited him in, and left him to change into dry clothes. He amused himself playing a game of dangle-the-ribbon with Jenner.

"You seem completely recovered from your illness, Healer," Pnor rose and examined me with a practiced eye upon my return. "What did you think of environome seven?"

"It was incredible." I briefly described the program.

"I have my home in that province. The sea has always fascinated me. It is the reason I've spent most of my journey out here, exploring the stars." The captain smiled, then added, "They are both vast, powerful, full of mystery."

"I was surprised at how much your world reminded me of Terra, where my people originate." I went on to praise the ship's technology for a few moments while I prepared two servers of the Jorenian iced fruit beverage I had grown fond of.

"You're not here to talk about the environome technology, I gather," I said at last as I handed him his drink. "Is there a problem?"

Polite but practical, he made a fluid gesture and got directly to the real reason for his visit. "I must inform you that our government has decided to sever all relations with the League, effective immediately."

"All relations?" My server slipped from my fingers, and I had to make an awkward grab for it. That was a lot worse than a broken treaty.

"I, too, found it startling news, but it is done. Jorenians throughout League systems have been recalled."

"What will this mean for your people?"

He smiled wearily. "A great deal of change." He saw the strain I felt, and added, "You must not in any way consider yourself personally responsible for the rift."

I made a short, bitter sound. "I'm the reason it occurred, aren't I?"

"The events, Healer, not you, forced this decision. My people have very strong traditions. We do not adjust our beliefs to suit the greed of an already avaricious alliance."

"But to sever all relations simply because they tried to deport me against my will—"

"The League has done more than insult a Chosen of our House. They have discarded the remnants of what honor they once possessed."

I didn't know what to say.

"I must tell you what it will mean. Jorenian ships will be hunted, detained, and searched. Your life will be at risk if you remain a member of our crew." He frowned. "I can find another non-League world, if you wish, and put you off the ship."

"No." I shook my head. "I'd rather be with HouseClan Torin."

"Senior Healer Tonetka has been most emphatic to appoint you as her successor." Pnor gave me a wry glance. Emphatic was apparently putting it mildly. "Fortunately for me, I am in complete agreement."

"Then, this is where I belong, Captain."

He smiled, delighted, and stood. "As Commander of this vessel, I formally accept and welcome you as a member of the crew. Thank you, Healer." He made a gesture of relief. "My crew will also be gratified to know they will not have to stage a mutiny. I believe that was the plan, in the event I *attempted* to put you off on a non-League world."

We laughed together at that, then Captain Pnor bid me farewell and departed. Tired from my swim, Reever's latest link, and now this newest twist to my situation, I took a sleep interval.

I dreamed of Maggie.

We were back on Terra. Maggie was walking beside me as we made a haphazard tour of taverns and dock suppliers who offered everything from counterfeit credit profiles to illegal synnarcotics.

This is odd, I thought in a fuzzy, half-aware lethargy. Maggie would have never taken me near these places when she was alive.

"You're not paying attention." Maggie took my arm in hers.

"Oh." I breathed in the scent of exhaust, sweat, and a curious musky perfume. "Sorry. What were you saying?"

"You've got to begin again."

"Uh-hum." I was fascinated by the sight of two drones who had been refurbished with an odd selection of accessories. Finally I realized they were soliciting the crowd for sex partners, and laughter bubbled out of me. "God, look at that. Sexdrones. I've never actually seen one of them before."

"You don't seem too worried about it," Maggie said with an acrid smile. She was just as abrasive as she had been when she was alive. "Well, start worrying, kid."

"Why?" I was serene as I skirted a pair of dockworkers slashing at each other with short, bloody daggers. "This is just a dream, right?"

"No, baby girl, this is a subliminal memory I planted in your mind when you listened to my 'if-I'm-dead' disc."

I swiveled my head around, emerging from my euphoric haze at last. "You didn't."

"I sure did."

I came to a stop. "Maggie! How could you?"

"It's for the best, sweetie. What I'm about to say was already on the disc, you just forgot what you heard. Now you're remembering. I set it to trigger a few weeks after the first time your heart stops."

"Why would it depend on that?"

"Because after that you would know you're not human."

"I am." I stuck out my lower lip like a child. "I'm as human as you are."

Maggie sighed, and pulled me into a tavern she once worked in. She yelled at the tending drone to bring us bitterale and pushed me into a chair.

"Damn, you're stubborn. Stop arguing with me." Maggie waved away the drone and thrust a plas server of bitterale into my hand. "Drink."

"I hate syntoxicants," I said.

"Drink it or I'll pour it down your throat myself."

I took a sip and made a face. Maggie swigged half the contents of hers with a few gulps and wiped her mouth with the back of her hand.

"I know I'll hate being dead." She sighed wistfully. "Nothing to drink and nowhere to go."

"This dream is ridiculous," I said to myself. "I've got to wake up."

"Not until you recall and accept what I stored in that smart-ass brain of yours. Got it?"

Had I ever said I'd loved this woman? I must have been out of my mind. To keep from snapping back, I took another sip of the revolting bitterale she'd pressed on me. It didn't taste any better.

"Your father discovered he could not repeat the process once he had created you. It's important for you to know that. You are the tenth and only one who was viable. What he doesn't know is why."

I looked up and understood at last. "You," I said. "You're the reason why I succeeded and the others failed. You did something."

Maggie smiled slowly, nodding as she finished her drink.

"You're not just an ex-waitress hired companion, are you?" I asked.

"Bingo."

"You said you had access to my father's experiment. Did he tell you to send the package to me?"

"I always said you were a bright kid."

I slammed down the server. "Why? Why did you set me up for him?"

"It suited me to go along with his next stage in the experiment."

"Suited you," I said in disbelief. "My God, Maggie, I had just buried you! Do you know what it was like losing you? Finding out what he had done to me?"

"I know."

"You and Dad both played me like a game. I've never mattered to either of you."

"That's not true." Maggie shook her head. "I was dying, Joey. I didn't have enough time to finish the work I started."

"What work?"

"You'll understand everything, in time."

"Tell me now."

"Listen to me. Store it in memory for future reference. You are not human. Joseph Grey Veil may believe he's created you, but he didn't. Not entirely. You must never allow yourself to fall under his influence again." She said some other things that barely registered on my consciousness. "When the time comes, you will remember. That's all now. Time to wake up."

I resisted the sudden urge to break from the dream and instead reached across the table and grabbed her hands.

"Maggie," I said. "Who are you?"

She began to change in front of my eyes. The tough-lined face softened, her hair darkened, and her skin tone glowed. It was like looking into a distorted mirror. "Someone you loved. Someone you trusted. Someone like you, Joey."

I woke up with the covers knotted in my fists, my body as taut as a lasutured seam. Maggie's last words still rang in my head.

"Someone like you."

Why did it sound like a prayer—and a curse?

CHAPTER TWENTY

Calls from Home

I discovered it would be months before we reached Joren. Our journey would also take us through territory the crew of the *Sunlace* had never explored. During a shared meal interval, Xonea and Dhreen both talked about the convoluted route and the equally involved reasons for following it.

"We transition through different dimensions, then resurface in conventional space. Some areas we have traveled before, but others—" Xonea made a quick gesture. "It will be an opportunity to survey uncharted systems."

"Okay." I considered this as I chewed, then swallowed and asked, "But wouldn't it be safer to get out of League space and transition ourselves straight to Joren as fast as we can?"

"Our technology has some limits," Xonea said. "It is not possible for the ship to remain in transition indefinitely."

Dhreen was more blunt. "The captain isn't going to take any chances by traveling the usual routes, either." He ignored Xonea's warning frown. "He knows the mercenaries will set up surveillance posts in those systems."

"So we have to fly around half the damn universe just to dodge the League?" I asked, exasperated.

"Pilot Dhreen exaggerates, Healer," Xonea said to me.

"Pilot Torin doesn't know the League like I do," Dhreen said.

"You are *alarming* her, Dhreen."

"It's better than *handing her a lot of waste*, Xonea."

Both men by now were on their feet and glaring at each other. I sighed, put down my fork, got up, and stepped between them.

"Okay, boys, settle down, or I'll have to send you to your quarters to cool off." I looked from Dhreen to Xonea. "I'm not kidding."

"Sure, Doc." The Oenrallian gave in first and smiled down at me. He eyed the Jorenian warily. "She merits the facts, Xonea."

"You are correct, of course, Dhreen." The Jorenian's big frame relaxed, and he gave me a rueful glance. "Your pardon, Healer."

"Can we just drop the subject?" I said. "My food is getting cold."

After a grueling round of transition testing, I was in no mood to referee a fight. The tests were necessary, Tonetka insisted, to assure I could tolerate interdimensional shielding without the negative effects of my first experience. Necessary or not, it didn't make the hours I spent in the simulator go any faster.

The next day Captain Pnor confirmed I'd passed the testing with flying colors. League forces *had* inflicted the damage by their attempt to isolate me in the midst of transition.

"Now that you know you are physically capable of serving on board," Tonetka said with satisfaction some time later when I reported for my shift, "it is time to begin your training."

"Training?"

She made a sweeping gesture. "Medical Bay management is but a portion of the duties assigned to the Senior Healer. We have much to do."

I was surprised to learn that Tonetka not only supervised the inpatient and outpatient cases, but had a myriad of obligations to other departments. She was even required to go on most of the diplomatic visits to worlds the *Sunlace* would encounter during the journey.

"How else can you assess what needs we have that can be served by other species' knowledge and resources?" the Senior Healer said when I objected to sojourn training. "Or decide what we can provide to them of the same?"

"I just don't see myself as an emissary for Joren," I said, uneasy. "I've never set foot on your world. I don't look like you—"

"By the Mother, you spent too many years on that pathless ball of intolerance you call a homeworld!" the Jorenian said. "Open your mind, Healer, and forget outer physical dimensions and pigmentations!"

The Jorenians were an intrepid bunch, that was for sure. I wasn't afraid of the work or the position, but a new sense of caution had evolved in me. So I studied hard at being a diplomat and supervisor as well as a Healer.

Tonetka sacrificed a lot of her time for my education, too. To compensate, I often reported for duty early to help the Senior Healer catch up on her own work.

"So many signals from the Joren." Tonetka pretended to be irritated as she sorted through the latest relays from the ship's communications one morning. "My bondmate, my ClanSisters, even my mentor. It will take me a week to review and respond to all of these."

I glanced at the list. "Why are they sending direct relays to the ship? Is something wrong?"

Tonetka tried not to look pleased. "They have conspired to make this my last journey," she said, then laughed softly as she accessed one of the signals. "For example, my mate states here he cannot survive another revolution. He says I must be present to insure his last rites are performed properly."

"Is he that old?"

Tonetka snorted. "He is my junior by a dozen revolutions. I should be in such fine physical condition. Why do they worry over one soon to be embraced, like me?"

"I think I know why they're so insistent." I smiled. "What will I do without you once we reach Joren?"

Her expression grew stern. "Exactly what I am training you to do, Healer."

"I can handle that," I said. "Now we have patients we need to argue about. Ready to do rounds?"

We had fallen into a comfortable routine of spending the early hours with patients. Training continued after that each day. This morning was no different, except that one of the patients was a pre-surgical case, and his condition was deteriorating rapidly.

Jorenians had a complex metabolism that was especially resilient, and overall were an extremely healthy species. The main problems we had with them were injuries, or in a rare case like Hado Torin, effects of long-term space travel. Forty revolutions of dimensional transitioning had caused extensive vascular damage. Hado's heart was particularly weak.

"Good morning, Hado," I greeted the middle-aged navigator.

"Healer Cherijo, Healer Tonetka," he said, giving us both his endearing grin. I performed the routine scans, while Tonetka observed. "All is well?"

I handed the Senior Healer my scanner before I answered him. "To be honest, Hado, your condition isn't getting better." I exchanged a glance with Tonetka, who nodded slightly. "We'll need to perform the surgery soon." I reviewed the specifics of the operation. When I was through, Hado requested a moment alone with Tonetka.

I left the old friends together to continue rounds. The Senior Healer caught up with me a few minutes later, her face etched with worry.

"He's almost convinced it is useless to operate," she said. "He tried to persuade me to let him embrace the stars."

"You told him to jump in a lake, I hope."

She nodded. "I want to prep him now. I don't like the way his pressures are vacillating, or this sudden desire to make the final journey."

We alerted the surgical staff, and prepared for the procedure. By the time Tonetka and I were scrubbed and in our gear, the team had Hado in a coolant cradle, prepped and ready. The cradle maintained body temperature at the level needed to keep Hado from bleeding to death during surgery.

One of the residents in training made the initial lasincision, while I monitored Hado's vitals and put the vascular regenerators on line. The painstaking work of repairing over fifty separate compromised vessels could now begin.

Minutes after the Senior Healer and I began simultaneously operating, Hado's pressures began to fall.

"Increase oxygen flow, and begin saturating the blood," Tonetka said. "Cherijo." I looked at her from the edge of my mask. "Take the damage to the heart."

I nodded. I worked up to the triangular organ and began to assess.

"Left center aortic juncture is compromised in three different places. Severe coarctation. We'll have to replace or bypass." I already knew what my colleague was going to say. Replacement was out of the question. We simply didn't have time, and Hado would not survive long enough for another operation.

"Bypass," Tonetka said.

"Wait a minute." I found four more aortic junctions equally insufficient. "Can't. He's got nothing left to compensate." I indicated the area to Tonetka.

"That's it, then." Tonetka squeezed her eyes shut for a moment, then stepped back from the table. "We'll close him up now. Request Hado's Speaker attend—"

"Hold on." My mind was racing as I studied the open chest cavity. "The superior mesenteric artery." I reached down and traced its path with a probe. "Here. There's eighteen millimeters in this I can safely remove."

"Even if we further reduce body temperature, we'll

still have to stop his heart and clamp off the artery," Tonetka said. "How long to remove the section you need?"

I was fast, and she knew it. "Thirty seconds."

"By the Mother, don't drop the lascalpel," she said.

The team immediately prepared Hado for the open-heart procedure. While Tonetka and I waited, we continued with the lesser repairs.

"His signs aren't good," one resident said when they were done. "Are you prepared to begin, Healer?"

I took up the lascalpel. "Ready."

The Senior Healer stopped Hado's heart. I removed the arterial section in exactly twenty-four seconds. While Tonetka repaired the extraction site, I put the replacement on a tray to one side and began operating on Hado's heart.

"Pressures falling. Red range."

That meant I had to work even faster. My hands flew as I removed the damaged section and prepped the site for the replacement. Hado's monitor started to bleat slowly.

"Cherijo," Tonetka said. "One minute."

Without replying, I positioned the replacement section and began to suture it into place. That was when the ship was rocked suddenly by a sudden, terrifying explosion. Hado's body shook from the vibrations, and the bloody surface of my glove slid against the lascalpel.

"I don't need this right now," I said.

"Mother of All Houses!" Tonetka marched over to the suite panel and slammed her fist against it. "Captain Pnor! We are trying to perform cardiac surgery down here!"

"*Sunlace* under attack," someone said. "Prepare for weapon fire."

"Prepare my ass," I said, grumbling under my mask. I continued to make the tiny, tightly packed lasutures to hold the replacement tissue in place. Another series of explosions rocked the ship, and this time one of the assistants bent over Hado and held the body motionless with her own weight as I swore at length.

"Time!" I said, and was told less than twenty seconds remained. "Resuscitate now."

"You're not finished—"

"Do it!" I said. "I can finish with the heart functioning." I wanted to see if the replacement artery would hold against the powerful cardiac contractions anyway. Hado's heart was restarted, and spurting greenish fluid leaked from two areas. I swiftly closed the gaps. Operating on an organ while it was beating was a lot like trying to dance ballet in ankle-deep sand.

"Check your juncture site." Tonetka leaned over, and examined my work. "Good. Let's close him up now, quickly."

"I'll do it." I could work faster than the residents or Tonetka, and had Hado's chest closed in another fifteen seconds. I took a moment to breathe and then glared at the suite panel. "We'd better be under attack by someone important. Like the Hsktskt."

"I agree." The Senior Healer motioned to the assistants. "Move him into post-op."

I stayed with Hado, although there were no more vibrations indicating a battle continued. I had a tension headache the size of the *Sunlace*, and wondered if the drastic measures I had taken would keep this man alive.

Tonetka stormed off to vent her frustrations in person, only to return a short time later looking more worried than outraged. She checked Hado's chart and nodded over his vitals. "He's doing as well as we can hope for now."

"Who tried to blow up the ship?"

"A mercenary ship attacked us. One of the larger deep-space trackers. They managed to launch a displacer volley before Tactical Operations could return fire."

"League?"

Tonetka nodded. "The attack ship was destroyed, but Captain Pnor intends to transition the ship as quickly as possible. Someone might be following the first tracker."

"We can't relocate with Hado in his condition," I said. "He'll arrest, and everything we've done will have been for nothing."

"We have no choice."

We had just enough time to put Hado into suspension sleep before we prepared for the transition. I refused to leave him for a moment, and had a harness rigged beside his berth.

"If we come out and he goes into cardiac failure, don't revive him," Tonetka told me. "Keep him in suspension and initiate low-grade electristim."

I agreed, and strapped in for the jump to interdimensional flight. The Senior Healer harnessed herself in a pod across the section from us, and closed her eyes. Maybe she was praying. I was.

The *Sunlace* transitioned. I kept my eyes on the data monitors as Hado and my body were thrown into the state of dimensional flux. His pressure rose alarmingly, and I thought I saw him open his eyes.

An eternity of seconds passed, and then we snapped back into normal space. I kept thinking about how often this might happen with me on board the ship. How many patients would have to risk their lives to have me as the Senior Healer?

Hado survived—barely. His body went into immediate shock, but Tonetka's advice worked.

The emergencies began to arrive from the ship sections bombarded by the displacer beams. Some broken bones, and a few minor lacerations. One serious head wound I attended to immediately. By the end of our shift, we had admitted a dozen new cases.

I wouldn't leave Hado, nor would Tonetka. We stayed through the night, spelling each other as we monitored his condition. By the next morning he had improved enough for us to move him out of suspension. When at last he opened his eyes, I grinned with relief.

"Navigator Torin," I said. "You made my first surgical

procedure on board the *Sunlace* a real thrill. And Jorenian medical history while you were at it."

"Glad to be of service, Healer," was his weak reply.

After we'd finished our scans on Hado, the Senior Healer kicked me out of Medical.

"Go to your quarters," Tonetka said, and shook her head when I began to argue. "Immediately, Healer. I still run this Bay, supervise the cases, and schedule shifts."

"You've had less sleep than I have."

"I require less than you do. Go."

"You're a bully," I told her as I stretched.

"All Healers are. Go now, and Cherijo—" She smiled as she looked down at the sleeping navigator. "Thank you."

I trudged out of the Medical Bay. By the time I got to my quarters, I was ready to admit Tonetka was right. I needed the sleep. Jenner was out prowling the corridors, so I was alone when Reever came to see me several hours later.

At first I didn't want to let him in. I was still groggy from my interrupted sleep interval. "Go away, Reever. I'm too tired to deal with you."

"I must speak with you now."

"This had better be good." I opened the door. "What?"

He brushed past me. "Captain Pnor asked me to view the transmission," he said, and sat down on the edge of my sofa. Resigned, I walked over and dropped into the chair opposite him. He leaned forward. "You will not return, of course."

Transmission? What transmission? "Are you asking me, or telling me?"

"Cherijo." He obviously wasn't in the mood to spar, either, from the way he got up and started pacing.

"I'm not going anywhere." I barely smothered a yawn. "Um . . . what's this about a transmission?"

"The League often resorts to unethical tactics, but this goes far beyond that." Reever hadn't heard me. He was that agitated. "He must be unbalanced. The crew naturally reacted with outrage over the bounty. They are determined to protect you. Even if it means sacrificing the ship."

"That's nice," I said. Sacrifice the ship my foot. Who was unbalanced? And what was this stuff about a bounty? Maybe I should just go back to bed and stay there until we reached Joren. "I'll be sure and thank the crew."

He stopped and actually glared at me. "Your humor is inappropriate, Cherijo. His threats are a serious matter."

Whose threats? "Reever. Listen to me for a minute, will you? I don't *know* what you're talking about. I haven't *seen* any transmission from Captain Pnor."

"You haven't." He appeared bemused.

"Look, I'm tired. I'll deal with this later. Anything else?"

He switched gears as abruptly as I did. "We will be reaching a populated system within a few weeks," Reever told me. "The Captain has scheduled a sojourn to one of the more developed planets. I requested to be withdrawn from the mission, but he indicated my services would be vital."

He was losing me again. "Why skip the sojourn?" I rested my chin on my hand and fought to keep my eyelids open. "Don't you want to go?"

"Not if it would make you uncomfortable."

"I thought we covered this already," I said. His unblinking stare goaded me into anger. "What do you want from me, Reever? A note for the captain? Do whatever you want." I got up and went to the mirrored unit where I kept my grooming supplies. A glance confirmed it. I was a mess. "Is that it?"

"I can think of several other topics of interest."

"Don't get sarcastic with me. I just woke up, I'm not responsible for my actions." I picked up my brush, peered at my reflection, then went to work. "Damn."

There was a huge knot at the nape of my neck. Reever took the brush out of my hand. "Hey, what are you—"

"Let me do it." He carefully untangled the snarl, then worked the brush through my hair. The gentle strokes lulled me out of my irritation. I watched his reflection. He appeared totally absorbed in the task.

"Reever?" His eyes met mine in the mirror. "Why are you doing this?" I didn't mean the hairbrushing.

He understood me. "Don't you know?"

"No, and forget I ever asked," I said, then turned and took the brush out of his hand. Wondered how effective it would be as a weapon. "As for the sojourn, you don't have to ask my permission every time we're scheduled to work together. Like I said, I'll handle it."

"I want more than your tolerance." He touched my hair, running his hand over the smoothness.

Yeah, I could just imagine what he wanted. "Don't push your luck." His fingers tightened for a fraction of a second. I had to get him out of here, I thought, before he said or did anything else. Or I *would* hit him. "Thanks for dropping by. You know the way out."

I watched his hand fall away. "This is not finished, Cherijo." Without another word, he left.

No, I suspected it wasn't. To avoid dwelling on that, I got up and went to my console. A signal from Operations was indeed waiting for me.

A serious-looking Jorenian appeared on the screen. "Healer Cherijo Torin, Ndo, ship's operational officer. We have a transmission from the Allied League intended for you."

"When did it come in?"

"The signal was received shortly after the skirmish with Allied forces mercenary ship. I will relay it to you now."

"Thank you, Ndo."

I went to my food unit and dialed up a server of hot herbal tea. It was pretty obvious I wasn't going back to sleep anytime soon. From Reever's reaction, the League's message was bound to be entertaining. I returned to the console, punched up the transmission and sat down to watch the show.

My father's face appeared on the screen. Behind him, uniformed officers were walking back and forth. League officers. At the estate?

"This is Dr. Joseph Grey Veil, signaling from the L.T.F. *Perpetua*, Pmoc Quadrant."

I nearly dropped my server in my lap. "What are *you* doing on a troop freighter?" I asked out loud.

He couldn't respond, the signal was prerecorded. Despite that, I still expected him to tell me to shut up. Maybe it was the way he was glaring at me through the screen.

"This message is for the non-sentient designated Dr. Cherijo Grey Veil," he said. Well, he was still sticking by his story that I was his lab specimen. "It is imperative that you return to Kevarzangia Two and surrender to League forces immediately."

"Sure." I lifted my server and toasted his image. "Just let me finish my tea."

"If you are unable to return to Kevarzangia Two, you may surrender to the authorities on any Allied League world. Transport will be arranged."

"A pickup service?" I said. "That's convenient."

"Your oath as a physician directs you to do no harm. By ignoring the deportment order, you are violating the oath you swore to uphold."

"Am I?" I took a sip from my steaming server, enjoying my pretend conversation now. "How so?"

"Your presence on board the Jorenian ship puts every member of the crew at risk."

"They don't seem to be worried about it." All right, I'd thought the same thing. So what? I was his clone. It was to be expected that we'd fire the same brain cell on occasion.

"In exchange for your voluntary surrender, the League will allow you to resume your former position on the planet Kevarzangia Two. I have agreed to continue my clinical trials there."

My Father? On K-2? It was such a delightfully pro-voking thought. Rogan could be his research assistant.

"Additionally, I will allow you unlimited access to my complete research database. This will clarify and resolve issues that will otherwise taint your existence."

"Taint my existence," I said. "I'm confused now. Wasn't that what *you* did?"

"If you do not surrender, you will be pursued. The Allied League of Worlds has offered a generous bounty for your delivery to Terra." He named a sum that made my eyes widen.

"That much?" I put down my tea and got to my feet. No wonder the crew was upset. "You must have called in a lot of favors to get the League to agree to that," I said out loud as I found my robe and pulled it on. "Or did you take out a mortgage on the estate?"

"Cherijo, you are my property."

"Really?" I turned around and smiled at Joseph Grey Veil's stern image. He'd forgotten that I was encoded with some of that unyielding determination, too. "I don't think so."

"Think on this." He said it as if he'd heard every word I'd uttered. "If you choose not to surrender, the League will take whatever measures are necessary to capture you."

Here come the threats, I thought. "They have to find me first," I told the display.

"The League's resources are virtually unlimited. They have allies and treaties in a thousand different systems. They will track you down."

"You hope."

"Any planet that gives you sanctuary will be invaded. Any ship you travel on will be targeted. Anyone who helps you will be considered an accomplice and elimi-nated. You will be hunted down like an animal until you are apprehended." He paused, giving me a moment for that to sink in.

It sank in. Reever was right, this was no laughing matter.

I could see worlds being occupied and terrorized by the League. Ships exploding in the midst of battle. People being systematically exterminated. My father would stop at nothing to get his hands on me.

"No," I said. I reached for my server of tea, and saw that my fingers were trembling. I snatched them back, and glanced up at the display. He was smiling at me, his dark eyes glittering with a strange, terrifying anticipation. What had Reever said? *He must be unbalanced.*

"They will bring you back to me."

You must never allow yourself to fall under his influence again. An unexpected surge of renewed confidence burned through me. Maggie was right. I hadn't come this far by giving in to fear or Joseph Grey Veil's threats. I wasn't going to start now. Maggie hadn't raised a coward, and this fight was just beginning.

"Enjoy your freedom while you can, Cherijo."

Before his image faded from the display, it shattered. There was an immensely satisfying explosion of sound. The saturated console sparked and sizzled, then went dead. Wisps of smoke rose from the shorted internal components. Shards of vid screen and server littered the top of the unit and the floor around it like plas confetti.

No big deal. Consoles could be replaced. I had plenty of servers. I'd just make more tea.

The exciting story of
Dr. Cherijo Grey Veil continues
in *Beyond Varallan*.
Available now from Roc.